I0582193

In Dracula's Shadow

Megan E. Vaughn

FSF Publications
Copyright © 2025 by Megan Vaughn

Cover art and design by Scott P. "Doc" Vaughn

e-Book ISBN: 978-1-950532-05-6
Print ISBN: 978-1-950532-04-9

Manufactured in the United States of America.

FIRST Edition
First US Printing: 2025

www.fivesmilingfish.com

This one is for my parents who nurtured my spooky childhood obsessions
and my brother who gave me a complete synopsis of the film Bram Stoker's Dracula when I was too young to watch it.

And to readers like you.

We judge ourselves by what we feel capable of doing,
while others judge us by what we have already done.
Henry Wadsworth Longfellow

If you live to be a hundred, I want to live to be a
hundred minus one day so I never have to live without
you.
A.A. Milne

I have never met a vampire personally, but I don't
know what might happen tomorrow.
Bela Lugosi

Prologue:
"One of Those-Two-Pages-to-a-Day-with-Sunday-Squeezed-in-a-Corner Diaries
A Note from the Heroine to Teen Girls Everywhere:

I know we have all mooned over that brooding vampire novel, wishing for our dark prince who is just a misunderstood beastie. Hell, deep down we want Angel, Dracula (preferably the Gerard Butler Dracula, no matter how bad that movie was), or that sparkly guy to rescue us from a mixture of boring school days and other supernatural monsters. I'm looking at you werewolves! And when we find them, they will promise us eternal love and not to suck the blood of our family or friends. Well, my fellow angst-ridden dreamers, it is all a crock!

Sincerely,
Mina Harker

The pen left the paper and the author's father looked down upon the words. "Lee, I don't think Mina Harker would've used the word crock. . . or know who Gerard Butler is."

His daughter crumpled the notebook paper and told him disdainfully, "You don't like it, don't give me homework on a weekend."

Chapter 1: "Deep Awful Silence"

Lee loved long train rides. She always managed to sit at one of the molded plastic tables close to the window with her bag in the seat beside her. Despite screaming children and swearing teens, she curled up with her new copy of *Dracula*. Her parents sat across the divide. Her father busied himself with a book of logic puzzles he had bought from the train station shop. Meanwhile, her mom organized official-looking documents into an accordion file.

To break the silence, her mum glanced up and sighed. "I knew you'd like that book. Did Harker find the brides yet?"

Lee shifted her position and buried her nose deeper into the pages of the cheap paperback.

With another deep breath, her mother grumbled, "You are just going to ignore us for the next four months?"

"She's been talking to me," Lee's dad defended, but a sharp look from his wife drew his attention back to the book of puzzles. In an attempt to apologize, he addressed their daughter. "You'll like Whitby, Lee. It's right up your alley. They have goth festivals more than once a year and lots of the pubs and hangouts cater to a certain clientele you might enjoy."

"I don't have an alley, Dad, and wearing black does

not make me goth," Lee argued without setting down the book. "I don't see why I had to leave Harrow in the middle of the term."

"And this time two years ago you couldn't understand why we had to leave Maryland," her mom pointed out.

Lee attempted to scrunch further against the seat, as if she could hide in the corner. Her short purple hair spread across the window until she felt the cool glass on the back of her head.

"I thought you were going to be grown up about this," her mother muttered.

"The manner in which I behave has very little bearing upon age, as proof by you and Dad. Besides, if you want me to prove I'm a grownup then why don't you let me stay on my own in Harr—"

"You cannot live in London alone, Lee. You're only sixteen," her father put in. He then murmured, "I'm nearly forty and I wouldn't live alone in London."

"Besides Chelsea will be up next week. The two of you can decorate your new room together. No painting the walls black this time. Lease agreement won't allow it," her mother added.

With an agitated sigh, Lee slammed her book down on the table. "This isn't going to be like that flat in Manchester where I couldn't hang curtains from the ceiling because it was against the fire code, is it?"

"Did you bring those curtains? Good, I like those," was the only response.

Lee rested her head again, staring out as the city landscape changed to frost-covered hills. Echoing through the windowpanes she could hear the angry words of a man a few rows behind them. Sitting up, Lee focused on the growls.

Her parents gave her a silent expression of worry as

the swears and taunts reached their ears. Mr. McDaniels and his daughter slid out of their seats at the same moment as the voice announced to the whole of the train car, "Go back from where you came from, you Paki!"

As they stood, they could see a man swaying to the movements of the train as he towered over a person in the seat across from him. The edge of a tense shoulder showed the small stature of the victim.

Other passengers looked awkwardly out the window or stared in disgust yet did not speak or move. Mrs. McDaniels stood up as well and nodded that it was time for her husband and daughter to go.

Lee's father moved through the train aisle closely behind her, his hands gripping the same tops of seats as hers for balance. She thought she would smell whiskey as she got closer, almost hoping that this hateful tirade was the result of too much liquor. The man was not very tall. He hunched his back a little, keeping his racial slurs pointed directly at the little figure sitting before him.

"You ragheads! You come into my country with your bombs and —" A spray of saliva rained from his lips at the beginning and end of the word "bombs".

Ignoring the man, Lee turned to the person sitting. A woman in her late teens or early twenties, stared down at the book in her lap in a desperate attempt to ignore the man. She wore a bright pink head scarf which matched the stylish tights under her blue skirt. As droplets of the man's spit landed upon the page of her paperback novel, she looked ready to cry.

"There you are!" Lee exclaimed. She spoke directly to the young woman as her father created a barrier between his daughter and the angry man. "We thought you were in the next car."

A wide-eyed stare met with Lee's smiling eyes. "Oh?"

was all the young woman could muster.

Mr. McDaniels added, "We saved you a seat." He glanced briefly at the angry man with a charming grin. "Excuse me," he stated as he purposely backed into the man, causing him to trip backward into his chair. Lee also backed-up toward her dad in order to give the girl room to slip out in front of them. Mrs. McDaniels stood in the aisle and directed the young woman into the window seat where Lee had previously been sitting.

The angry man shouted a few final curse words in their direction as Lee's dad walked between her and the somewhat stunned man. Once Lee was sitting beside the young woman and his wife was back in her own seat, he continued walking in search of a railway employee.

It took a moment for the young woman to collect herself before speaking. "Thank you."

"Nothing to thank," said Mrs. McDaniels. "Where are you getting off? Do you want us to exit the train with you?"

"York," she answered meekly. "Going to see my brother."

"Good! We have to stop in York. I'm Lee." The teenager moved her things across the table in order to give the new member of their party some room.

"Deena. Are you reading *Dracula*? That's funny. I'm reading *The Vampyre*."

"What's that?"

The table chatted until the train pulled into the City of York. By that time, the angry man had vanished into a different car after Lee's father had train security speak to him. Nothing was done to punish his harassment, but at least he was not on the platform as they left the train.

The small family shrugged on their purses and briefcases. They struggled to pull their overstuffed suitcases. Deena, who only had an overnight case, helped with some of Mrs. McDaniels's luggage. The many platforms of the York station stretched out in front of Lee like the crowded scene of a Christmas shopping ad.

Deena pointed at a dark-haired young man waving just beyond the platform ticket gate. He held up a cup with her name scribbled on it. "That's my brother. Oh! And he bought me coffee." She turned back to them and said thank you once again. She held up her phone and added, "Lee, if you text me your address in Whitby, I can send you *The Vampyre* once I'm done with it."

"That would be great!" With numbers exchanged, Denna left. As she vanished into the crowd with her brother, Lee surrendered once again to the bad mood she'd been directing at her parents.

Instinctively, Lee's parents searched for the board announcing trains and platforms. "Scarborough. . . Scarborough…" her mother muttered.

"There it is! Scarborough, platform 6," her father announced. "Oh, bollocks. Running late." He surveyed the many bridges running over the tracks connecting the various platforms. With a shrug he added, "At least we don't have to cross the stairs." He slipped a ten-pound note into his daughter's hand. "Why don't you pick us a few snacks from the shop? If they have those flapjacks I like get me two."

Her mom made a seat out of her largest suitcase. "And flat water for me." Lee turned toward the little newspaper stand, but her mom added, "And no chocolate. We're going to eat supper when we get into Whitby."

As Lee rolled her eyes, her dad suggested, "If you want food, Lee, you can buy crisps."

She trudged to the shop, her boots sluggishly moving along the pavement. She proceeded to gather up three water bottles, two flapjacks as well as several candy bars and chocolate cream eggs.

A man already standing at the counter glanced over at her purchase through his thick sunglasses. He couldn't have been more than five years older than her, but his perfect posture surprised her for someone so young. He carried himself like one of her parents' university colleagues. He wore a light-colored jacket, too thin to keep out the cold. He chuckled at Lee.

"May I help you?" She handed the money to the store clerk while glowering at the stranger.

"Like chocolate?" he asked with another laugh. His southern English accent flowed with perfect eloquence, like the actors in a Jane Austin movie.

"I'm sorry, I'm not inclined to answer idiotic questions," she told him curtly, collecting the snacks back into her arms.

He quickly sobered, but a slant in his shoulders suggested a certain amount of continued amusement. "I'm sorry. I was rude. For all I know, you could be feeding a family of four with all that chocolate. May I help you carry any of that?"

Lee headed out of the shop, suppressing a smile of her own as he followed. The young man was far from her type, yet the way his hair fell across his forehead and his blue button-up shirt clung to his chest made him nice to look at. "No, I can handle it. And just to clarify, I happen to be having a chocolate rebellion."

"I'm sorry, I think I heard you wrong."

"If you heard the words rebellion and chocolate put together in a label-like manner, then you heard correctly."

"And are you going to explain?"

Lee stopped moving to face the man, staring up into

his dark glasses with a sigh. "Are you going to say please?"

His teeth shined at her as his face broke into a smile. "Please, kind and gracious lady, would you tell me, what is a chocolate rebellion?"

"It is a way to annoy my mother beyond reason. You see, she doesn't believe in eating chocolate before a meal. She says nothing spoils your appetite for healthy food more than the good, old-fashioned cocoa bean. At the moment, I am not pleased with my mother, so in true teen angst fashion, I will do all I can to bother her." Lee nodded her head as she finished her sentence. "Understand?"

"Crystal clearly." He touched the side of his glasses to make certain they sat firmly on his nose. The young man then stuck out his hand in a friendly manner. "Aubrey Ruthven."

Lee stared skeptically at the hand, considering whether it was worth it to shift the candy in her arms to offer her own hand to him. Instead, she simply replied, "Lee McDaniels."

"Lee? Is that the shorter version of another name?"

"Aubrey, is that feminine version of another name?"

She expected him to roll his eyes or insult her in turn. His shoes held a brief fascination from him as he answered, "Old fashioned family name." When he lifted his head, he was careful to keep his sunglasses in place with one hand.

She glanced upward to avoid his face for a moment, looking at the tin roof of the train station. "Can I ask, what's with the glasses? There isn't any sunlight in this country as it is."

"Obviously, you've not lived in Britain long enough yet to be used to our unique weather."

"Actually, my dad's from a town near Canterbury. I was born here. I spent most of my summer vacations here." Lee often flaunted her American accent, however, she disliked it when people assumed she was an ignorant tourist.

Aubrey crossed his arms across his chest and whistled. "Canterbury? What are you doing so far north?"

"My mom. She's an archaeology professor and got offered a position on a big medieval abbey dig in some insignificant fishing village. I wanted to stay where we were. She was working on one of the abbeys in London, but it lost funding—" Lee's lips slammed shut. She could feel a ramble forming at the edge of her mouth, willing the long-winded tale of her academic parents to spill forth.

"You must be on your way to Whitby." His smile had not wavered at her explanation. Aubrey reached out and straightened one candy bar threatening to spill over her elbow.

She gave him a grateful smile with her eyes. "You ever been there?"

"Not for a very long time. But trust me, it's not insignificant. In fact, that village is one of the prettiest places in the United Kingdom." Aubrey stopped to release an envious sigh. "It really has been too long since I was there last."

"Well, in that case, you'll just have to come visit me." Lee tried to stop herself from speaking, but the wider his smile grew, the more words spit from her mouth, "Come to Whitby! Save me from the smell of fish and pier-side taffy vendors."

His smile practically overtook his face, the corners of his mouth disappearing behind the bottom rims of his sunglasses. "I just might take you up on that offer."

"I really should be getting these snacks to my parents," Lee quickly said, realizing with horror that he was serious. In an attempt to hide her embarrassment, added, "See you later, Shades" and made a run for it.

As the minutes ticked by without a sign of a train, Lee watched Aubrey Ruthven disappear into the crowd. Excitement bubbled within her stomach. She barely heard her mom's speech about buying chocolate or her dad asking where the change from the shop purchase had wound up. Lee rationalized that this young man would never actually come to Whitby. Even if he did, he would not be able to find her easily. She learned from experience how difficult it was to locate people renting a home.

Still, Lee watched for him amongst the rushing people. An elderly woman struggled with her suitcase over each step leading to the bridge built over the train tracks. Aubrey jogged up to her, grinning politely and taking the burden from her gnarled hands. He carried the luggage across the walkway and down the other staircase, then set it at the lady's platform for her. She beamed at him, shaking his hand and praising his kindness.

Aubrey then vanished once more, like a comic book superhero off to find other good deeds. With him gone, the train station grew very dull. Lee studied the pigeons fighting for half of a fallen bagel, the porter running frantically up and down the platforms, the changing billboard announcing the latest television programs. None of these could keep her brain occupied for long.

Their train came into sight, slowing as it neared the covered platform. A scream called out across the station. Four policemen rushed to the side of the old woman with the heavy suitcase who lay unconscious on the concrete.

As Lee tried to determine what had happened, the train rolled into the platform, blocking her view.

Chapter 2: "Turn of the Tide"

Since primary school, Mal followed Ian. Ian made Mal feel normal. And Ian did not control or bully Mal. Never once did he threaten to end their friendship if Mal chose to do something different. Ian did not even consider himself a leader. As far as he was concerned, Mal simply had all the same interests and hobbies which he did. It was Mal's family he found a little strange.

Ian convinced Mal to go out for football with him. Not only did Mal make the team, but he turned out to be the fastest midfielder the coach had ever seen. Therefore, it was Ian who was the most shocked when, after years of playing, Mal quit.

"Family stuff." Mal used those words a great deal. The words held the ability to fill him with regret and leave a bitter taste, yet he continued to use them. The truth hid in those words.

Mal realized that, for the first time, Ian did not accept the excuse. He chased Mal down for about a hundred yards, barking an insistence for a proper answer. At last, Mal cut off the broken record of "why" with a swing of his left fist. The punch created a wide threat, fully missing his friend's jaw. Ian ducked backward on instinct. Mal jogged away without another word.

Mal normally didn't slam doors. Instead, he preferred the festering angst of silent anger. The day he quit the team was different. His parents owned a tourist shop on Church Street, a cobbled shopping lane lined with shoe stores and bakeries. They lived in a flat over the shop which could be reached either by a set of steep metal stairs at the back of the building or through the stockroom of the shop.

He chose to storm through the shop, ignoring his twin sister who sat behind the cash register, reading a magazine. A single customer browsed, paying no attention to the stomping teenager. He took the steps up to their home two at a time, flung the door open, and proceeded to crash it shut again.

His father jumped up from his recliner. "Malachi, you look like the devil himself is after you. He's not, is he?" The man's creased face grew excited.

"No!" Mal snapped.

His mother emerged from a nook of their living room where the computer sat. "Mal? What's happened? Why are you yelling?"

"I quit the team," he grumbled, calming down at the sight of his mother's stern eyes.

"Excellent!" his father proclaimed. "Get the book!"

"Abelard," his mother hissed. Using the edge of the oversized black stone upon her finger, she smacked her husband upside the back of his head. Looking to her son, pity melted her face. "Mal, I know you didn't want to, but you knew when you joined the team that this was going to have to happen."

"You should be excited," his father added. "You're finally old enough to learn all the ins and outs of the family business. Your sister's not complaining."

"Nothing upsets Miranda, Dad." Mal slid into a chair. "And she isn't giving up anything. She still has her friends and all their girly activities."

15

"You still have your friends," Abelard replied with confusion.

"It's not the same thing..." Mal felt his body tense and his mind grow tried. "Look, forget it. I'm going to take a walk."

"Good idea," his mother cooed. She hugged him around his shoulders. "I do understand, really. I had to give up quite a bit when I married your father, but everything worked out. You just can't have it all, Mal."

Malachi decided against slamming the door once more as he exited. His sister glanced his way as he came down the stairs. "That was quick. What happened? You fight with Dad?"

Mal tightened his jacket around his body. "I'm going up to the church."

"You did fight with Dad! Hold on a minute!" She snatched up her coat and ushered the single customer from the shop. "I'm sorry, sir, but family business. We need to close for an hour."

He looked her directly in the eye, offering a disgusted expression as his heavy boots carried him outside. He silently observed the twins leaving the shop, sneering as Miranda hung a "Be back in 20 minutes" sign on the door. She glared back at him, then chased her brother up the street.

Mal attempted to walk ahead of her. He kept his chin pointed in his intended direction.

"So, did you finally bring up the Uni thing?" she asked as she stuffed her hands into her pockets, mimicking her brother's angry swagger.

"No. I quit the football team."

"Oh. Sorry." The pair passed one of their neighbors, a friendly doctor from India, on the street. She smiled at the teens. Miranda waved at the woman before lowering her voice. "So... when are you going to tell them about university?"

Mal squinted upward. He could see St. Mary's Church high on the hill overlooking the little town. The church was a part of his heritage, a part of the family identity. "I don't think I can. Why bother? You know Dad keeps pushing that family journal on me like it's a gospel. He'll never let me go."

"University of Hull! You can go to the Scarborough campus and come home on the weekends. It's better than nothing!"

"All that work just to have a degree I can never use. Face it, Miri, we're stuck here."

"Here isn't so bad, you know." Miranda breathed in and out, as if to swallow a piece of their surroundings. "Besides, no matter where you go, the family trade is going to find you. We don't—"

Mal halted. Faint buzzing occupied his ears. He took a deep breath to relieve the pressure in his chest and whispered, "Hold on. Where did that man go?"

"The man from the shop? I don't know. He was behind us, wasn't he?" The girl listened acutely, counting the number of people she saw walking and comparing them to the number of footfalls she heard. "I don't remember hearing him go."

"Damn." Mal kept his hands wrapped up in his jacket, but swiftly turned a corner onto a small street. Miranda followed with less obvious panic.

"Do you have anything?" Her fingers encircled an object within her coat pocket.

"I left it all in my football bag."

"You idiot," Miranda sighed.

As she shook her head at her brother, the man from the shop followed them around the corner. His steel-toed work boots hit the cobblestones hard, yet they made no sound. "Pardon me, but I meant to ask you back in the shop. Do either of you know which way it is to Hadley's Fish Restaurant?"

Malachi rolled his eyes. "Fish, huh. I thought your sort preferred red meat?"

At first, the customer looked ready to object to the statement. His confusion became a scowl. "Oh, sod it." The man instantly leapt forward, his mouth wide to reveal a pair of sharpened teeth. He'd shot at least four feet into the air on little more than a slight push from his feet. Arms stretched, the man came at Mal as his tongue waggled hungrily around his lips.

Mal squared his shoulders, his hands braced in front of his chest defensively. The snarling man changed his focus to Miranda, landing briefly in order to push off the cobblestones and a second inhuman bound.

Neither showed trepidation, the muscle memory guiding both without fear or panic. However, where Miranda's eyes shown with delight, Mal went through each motion without reaction.

Miranda spread her feet into a fighting stance. A miniature plastic bottle came from her pocket. She tossed the contents into the attacker's eyes as soon as he was upon them.

Clear droplets sizzled as they struck skin. The man screamed, curling up into a ball in the middle of the road. As the monster held his face in his hands, Mal struck strong blows with his foot at the man's stomach each time the opportunity arose. Miranda stepped over their attacker's pain-wracked body and took a rosary from her pocket.

"See what I mean," Miranda told her brother while she bound the man's hands with the beads.

Mal grimaced. "You better get Dad." He sighed heavily as he hovered over the howling fallen man. "He's not going to be happy I was unarmed."

"I know," she teased. "You'd think a vampire hunter's son would remember to at least carry around some holy water."

Diary of Thea Tepes
Whitby June 14th, 1932

Last night, they came. They came through the town, the sounds they made gnawed at my ears and made me wish I could take a nice cold plunge in the sea. They have invaded Whitby, every populated haunt, pub, and even the cinema. I have nowhere to hide and I pray that the truth of my background is not discovered. I admit it. I'm afraid. I'm more afraid than I was when that bat nearly murdered John Blaine the night we went dancing. I'm more afraid than when the last storm drove everyone into hiding and made them all so difficult to protect. Tonight, I would give anything to be back there, in those moments. Even the Nos are not sure what to do. Whitby has been overrun with an abundance of morbid cinema-obsessed tourists. Damn you, Bela Lugosi, and damn your stupid movie.

Chapter 3: "Dangerous to Him"

Lee's family had to catch a bus in Scarborough to complete the last leg of the journey. Her parents were frugal people who always chose what they considered to be the least costly way to travel, even if it was the most inconvenient.

Snow scattered across the flat moors stretching alongside the bus. The reality of the ashen moors disappointed Lee. She expected the romantic imagery painted by the Bronte sisters of this gothic wasteland. The previous summer, Lee had read *Jane Eyre*, *Wuthering Heights*, and *Agnes Grey* one right after the other. Every now and again a few sheep or a farm could be spotted, but most of the trip consisted of broken fences and the last remnants of dead heather.

The bus rounded near the gulf. The sea captured what little sunlight peaked through the gray and dazzled the travelers with the sparkle of winter waves. After a short pause in a place called Robin Hood's Bay, another of the towns within the area full of cute houses and friendly knick-knack shops, Lee heard someone yawn. She realized the yawn belonged to her when her lips parted involuntarily a second time. She felt her eyelids slipping.

Then, the great stone shell of a medieval abbey appeared on a hill in the distance. The water shimmered behind it and the clouds passed over the ruin, casting shadows and turning the windows into the eyes of a skull. Lee managed to wake herself up again just as the bus entered the tiny town.

Whitby existed as it did in Bram Stoker's time and long before. The buildings were small, crammed against one another in odd directions. The tiled roofs created a striking contrast against the blue-gray sky. Even though she had expected the green rolling hills and bustling seaside life Stoker had laid out in his novel, she reminded herself that it was March. The tourist town stayed brown and frost covered, eagerly awaiting the spring.

The sun nearly finished setting by the time a taxi delivered the family to their new home. The place the McDaniels family had rented had two bedrooms and a study. Relief filled Lee that her parents' academic papers and stacks of books wouldn't be taking up room around the house this time. In their London flat, her dad used to keep copies of *The House of Seven Gables* in the kitchen pantry. Both he and her mom had a tendency to get so wrapped up in their work they'd forget essentials like buying food. If Lee complained, her dad would proudly quote Henry Wadsworth Longfellow. "And all the sweet serenity of books!"

Lee could hear her mother and father fighting over space in the study as she went to find her room. Just as she heard her mom insist, "You don't need that many shelves for your Emily Dickinson resources. I mean, you read one depressed poem, you've read them all." Lee shut her door just as her father released a pained, insulted gasp.

Despite being cramped, the bedroom's furniture had been arranged to create the illusion of a wide area. She felt more like she'd entered a dorm room unlike their previous rental which had been set up like a cheery catalog photo. The bare mattress atop the metal frame and box spring were shoved against one wall. Facing the bed was a cheap wooden desk just big enough for Lee's laptop. A wardrobe set beside the entrance meant she would need to close her door each time she needed to retrieve her clothes. Lonely hangers awaited her inside, anxious for a purpose. Periwinkle blue curtains hung over the only window.

"Those have got to go," Lee commented, thinking about the amount of light the thin fabric would allow come daytime. To Lee, curtains should be like club bouncers: thick, imposing, and doing all they can to keep things out.

The first thing Lee did was dig out a stuffed toy from her backpack. The rag doll had black felt hair which started far back on its pale forehead. It wore an early nineteenth century vest, high waist trousers, and little black boots. A tiny white cravat rested at the plush throat and on its fingerless hand sat a lopsided miniature stuffed raven.

Lee set the Edgar Allen Poe doll down on the desk. "What do you think, Eddie? Are we having fun yet?"

The black embroidered eyes simply stared back at her. Lee knew the childishness of talking to dolls and simply smiled at her own habits. Her aunt had made her Eddie for baby Lee. It was meant as a joke, way of poking fun at the old fashioned, literary name her parents had given her. Yet since Lee had been old enough to talk, she confided in this Poe doll. He knew her every secret, tear, and joy. And, like only the greatest of confidants, he never told anyone.

At first, Lee thought of unpacking. Violently pulling around the zippers and flipping open her suitcases and she left them in that position, her possessions hanging out over the edges. She flung herself on the mattress, realizing that she had no bedding. Maybe she wouldn't say anything and see how long it would take her parents to realize her suffering. She pulled out her mobile phone and texted the name Chelsea. "Here & bored!"

Chelsea instantly text back. "Alrdy?"

"Yes! BORED," Lee's text insisted. She followed up with an emoji of a skull followed by a knife and a yellow face throwing up.

She could almost imagine Chelsea sighing as she text back. "Go out and do something!"

"Can't! I'm rebelling!"

"Rebel outside." A second text from Chelsea appeared a second later. "Find stuff to do so I won't be bored when I visit you."

Lee pulled herself off the mattress and grumbled, "Fine. Eddie, unpack while I'm gone."

The doll responded with another blank stare.

Lee did not acknowledge her parents as she left the house, even as her mother called out, "Where are you off to? Lee, it's almost seven o'clock and we were about to order take away!"

Mostly she just didn't want to admit to her mom's correct statements; the chocolate had spoiled her appetite. She quickened her pace, allowing the front door to swing closed with a satisfying crash.

Lee imagined how Bram Stoker would have felt passing the poky alleyways with their menacing shadows as the street grew darker and she walked out of the rows of houses, following the smell of sea air to where the town split due to the river. Two cliffs sat at either side of the water, menacing giants guarding the town from the sea beyond. The bridge connecting the two sides contained a light amount of foot traffic as people shuffled home from work.

She wandered. She stayed along the major roads and followed a crowd only a little older than her on their way to dinner. They led her over the bridge where she paused, straining to see the cliff face in the dying light. Sand gathered along the edge of the precipice. The landscape made Lee forget London for a shining, hope-filled moment.

Her father was going to love forcing her to imagine Dracula's ship, the Demeter, crashing there. The novel painted a frightening yet impressive sight with the dead captain lashed to the wheel. It really was the perfect setting for such a gruesome story. Of course, anything would be better than when he made her learn all about whaling as a side lesson to Moby Dick.

Her phone buzzed, the light shining through her pocket. Removing the device, she read a text from her mother. "Pizza is here. Saving you some. Don't get lost."

Lee rolled her eyes. She could not help but be grateful that her mom did not insist she come back to the house. Imaginary rebellion seemed a moot point as a breeze filled her lungs with salty air. Reluctantly, she text back, "Thanks."

Malachi closed up the souvenir shop for the night. Someday, the boxy building with the three-bedroom flat above would be his or Miranda's. Most likely, it would be thrust upon him along with all the upkeep. The same went for the family name. The son, that was him, expected to make certain the name of Tepes lived on.

His sister called him the "breeding stock" since their heritage did not require her to have children. He never understood how she made jokes. The same fate trapped her. The thought forced him to twist the key in the lock in a swift, angry motion. He listened for the creak and the sharp click but felt no relief.

Mal's earliest memories did not involve vampires. In fact, his furthest and haziest memory was of the park near his grandmother's house in Edinburgh. He and Miranda fed the ducks old bread all afternoon while their grandma took pictures. As an amateur photographer, her grandkids were her favorite subject.

When she called them to come along for supper, the ducks tried to follow them home. Three-year-old Mal begged to keep a duck. But his grandma explained how unfair separating a family would be. Mal loved being with his grandmother at that park, safe and quiet. He and Miranda blended with the other children there.

Three years later, brother and sister returned for another weekend with Grandma. As his sister came down a slide, a vampire waited on the bottom for her like a parent with outstretched arms. Grandma Tepes, a vampire hunter's wife for almost her entire adult life, moved swifter than her years normally allowed. Instantly, she lunged at the vampire. Her actions were so seamless; she pushed the monster behind a van in the carpark without a single parent or other child seeing. There, she destroyed him as easily as squishing a cockroach.

When she returned to the slide to check on her grandchildren, she found six-year-old Mal crying. "It's all over, Malachi," she told him soothingly. "No reason to be scared."

Little Mal rubbed the back of his eyes and whimpered, "I was not scared."

"Then what's the matter?" She reached out to touch his back, but the boy stepped away.

"They found us here," he stated, the tears coming again.

"Oh, darling." His grandmother's breath caught in her throat. "Come here." He allowed himself to be gathered into her lap as she pulled herself onto a bench. She rocked him a little and told him with a mixture of sadness and acceptance, "They'll always find you. It's who you are."

That was the moment when Malachi realized that he could never choose to be a doctor or a firefighter or even a shoe salesman. His family blood picked out a career for him. When Mal was six years old, he realized that he never owned his future.

As his reverie ended, Miranda walked up to him. He flipped the door sign from "We're open" sign to "Sorry, closed". A cheap ice cream cone dribbled her hand. "Still sulking?"

Mal just grunted.

"You look stupid when you sulk, you know," she curtly stated. "If you keep that face, you'll never get married and have kids."

"Good." Mal dropped the shop keys into his pocket. "You going up yet?"

"I'm not going inside yet. I don't want Dad to know I got ice cream and didn't bring him any," she explained. She paused, glancing down at the half-eaten vanilla atop the sugar cone. "I didn't bring you any either. Sorry."

Mal pulled on the door handle as a security check. He shrugged at both his sister and the shop. "Didn't want any anyway."

"Ug, you're so boring when you're depressed," Miranda whined. "Come off it. You knew when you joined the football team that you'd have to quit someday. Besides, chasing after those blood-sucking scavengers is much better exercise."

Mal noticed a girl their age walking along the street. He harshly motioned for his sister to hush. Miranda turned and eyed the girl in her heavy combat boots and purple hair.

"I like that skirt," Mira awed.

"Great. Go ask her where she got it and leave me alone." His voice went up an octave with fake hopefulness.

Miranda stuck her tongue out at him. "I bet she's more fun than you are." Jumping up on tiptoe as if that would help carry her voice, she shouted, "Hey! I like your skirt."

Lee paused, glancing around to see who the stranger shouted at. Realizing no one else stood outside besides herself, the yelling girl, and the young man wearing a pout, she answered with a confused mumble. "Um...thanks?"

"What?" Miranda bellowed back.

"I said thanks," Lee replied again with more volume and annoyance.

Miranda jogged toward her, much to Lee's horror. Why was this perky brunette in the designer knock-off pumps galloping her way?

Miranda stopped short of Lee, respecting personal boundaries despite pushing a conversation upon the girl. "American or Canadian? Tourist or resident?" she asked.

It took Lee a moment to register the conversation beginning. "Me? Half-American. Resident? No. Captive." She watched Miranda's face sober. Dark eyes scanned Lee for wounds or signs of a struggle.

Her brief inspection finished, Miranda's eyebrows shot to the top of her forehead and her lips broke into a smile. "You're kidding."

Lee nodded, feeling a little superior to this young ditz.

Miranda went on, not caring what sort of an impression she made. "How long have you been in Whitby?"

"Just got off the bus. Look, I have to get back home and unpack—" Lee attempted to sidestep Miranda.

Without missing a beat, Miranda followed. "Where are you living? Are you lost?"

"Nope. As soon as I get back across the bridge I know exactly where I'm going," Lee swiftly replied.

"Do you need help finding the bridge?" Miranda asked in an irritatingly helpful manner.

She avoided eye contact and tried to speed up her steps. "Nope."

Miranda sighed, her expression turning to something close to serious. "Look, I'm bored out of my mind tonight and my knob-head of a brother over there is being a pain. Can I please walk with you?"

Something about the honesty of the statement and the humor of Miranda's words caused the new girl to mutter, "Fine." She glanced over at Mal loitering in front of the shop, watching them with bewilderment. Obviously, he had not expected his sister to actually run after the strange purple-haired girl. "He looks like a knob-head. No offense."

With a laugh and a shake of her long hair, the female twin introduced herself. "I'm Miranda Tepes. The knob-head is Malachi."

"Lee McDaniels," the second girl said, choking up the information like vomit. She wasn't entirely sure if she wanted to be friends with this chatty, trendy Whitby native. They reached the end of the street and Lee realized that the brother also followed at a slow pace without purpose. Yet he tailed them like a private investigator who thinks he has stealth.

"Leia? That's pretty."

"No. It's Lee. It's short for Annabel Lee."

"Like the poem?"

Lee sighed. "Yes, like the poem. My parents met at a rally to save Poe's house in Baltimore."

"That's really cool. The only thing our dad is really into is dusty family antiques. We live above the shop there, so if you ever need anything just come on by." Miranda pretended to be unaware of her brother lurking under the eaves of a nearby house when they turned a corner.

"Okay." The word stayed flat and left no promise of a visit.

The bridge came into view and Lee allowed relief to wash over her. She would be rid of the pair in another minute. She blurted out as she pretended to glance at the time on her mobile phone. "It's really late. I better run home. I appreciated the company." Despite the lie being obvious, Lee carelessly waved and sprinted across the bridge.

Mal caught up with his sister at the edge of the bridge while Lee vanished into the rows of houses. "You scared her off, you psycho," Miranda scolded.

"You're the one walking around town with an obvious supporter of *them*," he cautioned. "Did you see the way she was dressed?"

"You are an intolerant bastard. Just cause she wears thick eyeliner and dyes her hair does not mean she's a Nos supporter," Miranda responded after making a tsk sound.

"I bet she reads Sylvia Plath and cuts herself," Mal added.

Miranda let out a disgusted "bleh".

Mal wondered if the sound was another criticism of his prejudice or the realization that she'd dropped ice cream on her shoes while walking.

Instead, Miranda said, "Whatever. I'm going to walk a little way and double-check that she gets home okay. Are you coming?"

Without answering, Mal followed. They tracked Lee down several streets. The girl changed directions four times before Miranda whispered, "Is she lost?"

"No. She knows we're behind her," Mal hissed back as they waited in a doorway for Lee to pick her next route. "I'm telling you, Nos supporter."

"And I'm telling you, stop judging her before we know for sure." Miranda watched Lee choose to go right. The sound of heavy boots pounding against the pavement resounded through the close-set buildings.

"She's running for it," Mal stated, breaking into a sprint in order to catch up. They began to cross a road without a check for traffic. He and Miranda skidded as a bus unexpectedly passed between them and the girl. Lee escaped.

The two stood for a moment, as if Lee would suddenly reappear. The bus arrived without ceremony. Mal watched it carefully, a strange feeling creeping over him. Normally, when danger neared his ears would almost ring and for a brief second and the oxygen would leave the room. He understood it compared to being on an airplane as it descended from 20,000 feet. The feeling he had as the bus stopped intensified. His stomach turned over and his legs felt like they would seize if he tried to move.

Miranda grabbed him. "What's wrong?"

"I feel sick."

"Then let's go home." As his sister pulled him away,

Mal watched the people pile off the bus. None of them appeared out of the ordinary. Then again, none of them ever looked unusual until it was too late. Whoever or whatever was on the bus, Mal would worry about it later. If he was lucky, he would never have to deal with it at all.

The twins left the city center, crossing the bridge back to their side of town. They missed the final passenger descending from the steep bus steps. A tall young man stepped off. He nodded his head at the driver. He breathed in deeply and removed his sunglasses. His eyes shone like polished gold. Another man emerged from the shadows to greet the newcomer.

"Aubrey Ruthven. I didn't believe you when you said you were on your way," the second man said to the man from the bus. The second man gave a quick glance to a pair of teenage girls crossing the road, shaking his golden-red curls at them. He then grinned, a wicked toothy grin revealing a pair of sharp fangs. "It's an honor to have you here."

Aubrey stowed his sunglasses in the inside pocket of his jacket and sighed. "We can skip the pleasantries, Jonas."

An expression of obvious annoyance crossed Jonas's countenance. "It's been a long time since you were here last. I assume you need to be brought up to speed."

"Just because I was prohibited from setting foot within Whitby does not mean that I didn't keep up with the latest news," Aubrey stated. He surveyed the town with a slight grimace. "Not exactly how I remember it."

He noticed a modern glass building to his left. The blue sign on the door read "Tourism Center".

"Damn," he muttered thinking of what sort of merchandise the little shop sold. Probably pictures of Bram Stoker and plastic fangs. Stepping away from the bus stop, walking confidently across the pavement as if he owned the town, Aubrey called over his shoulder, "Excuse me, Jonas, but I have some long overdue business."

Jonas, his face scrunched up with insult, could not help asking one last question, "You have to tell me, how you had the curse broken? How were you able to come back?"

Aubrey turned to give Jonas a secretive smirk. "You reminded me, there's a new friend that I need to thank."

Testament of Morsus Atum
1504

Am I growing old in spirit? I do not know how long I can keep moving. Still, I must keep them from finding it. The blood I carry in me and pass down to my son continues to course through their lifeless bodies. They sense the power of what I carry. I can never stop. I have killed so many of them, including the body of what had once been my beloved nephew. Perhaps now his soul will rest. Despite my efforts, despite the countless numbers I take from their armies, they still hunt me. They will always find me.

Chapter 4: "Noble Ruin"

Lee spent her first day in Whitby continuing to resist unpacking. She checked her e-mail and surfed the web for good prices on train tickets back to London.

Around three-thirty, her dad poked his head into her room. "Can't stay in here all day, Lee."

"Can too."

"Why don't you go to the ruin where your mum is working? I haven't been there since I was a boy, but I remember it being really cool." Mr. McDaniels tried to tempt her by holding out the "oo" sound on cool.

Another ruin. Another abbey full of historically significant rocks. "I'd rather not. I have more crucial activities to fill my weary hours."

"Lee." Her father's voice turned stern.

"Dad." Her tone mimicked his.

"Now, Lee." He tossed her coat at her and left the room to return to his work.

She sighed as she pulled on the worn wool garment. She sighed louder as she passed the study door. She released a long, dramatic breath as she opened the front door. Her dad's response was to yell after her, "Have fun."

Somehow, up close the hill overlooking Whitby proved more strenuous than it seemed from the bridge. A set of one hundred and ninety-nine stairs wrapped up and around one side of the cliff, giving somewhat easier access to an old church and the famous abbey. She huffed a little, counting each slippery stair. The numbers came through her lips as petite clouds.

Lee passed the church and cemetery first. The building fulfilled requirements for the word quaint, smaller than most of the other churches she'd visited "in the name of historical research". It lay nestled amongst a metal fence and stone markers depicting several centuries of families laid to rest.

Yet another setting used in *Dracula*. Lee circled the graveyard, trying to picture where Bram Stoker had intended Mina to find her nearly drained friend Lucy after scaring off an attacker. Lee was surprised by the lack of actual Dracula appearances within the book. He had been the cause of everything, and he barely existed on the page.

Leaving the churchyard, Lee followed a road up to a driveway of what remained of a Georgian mansion. At one time, she was sure the beige building had been the luxurious home of some barrister or general. Now, it served as the museum for the famous Whitby Abbey ruins. Signs took her to a side door, and she entered a large modern room sectioned off by display cases. Posters under plexiglass in the middle of the room told the story of the town and abbey.

Mrs. McDaniels stood at the ticket table with a map of the area spread out in front of herself and the woman working the desk. Her petite form managed to stand out in the way she carried herself; shoulders down, eyes forward, constantly on a mission.

"You see, what my team really wants to do is check on this area down here, just past the cemetery. I know it was excavated recently but what we're hoping is that if we dig a little deeper it'll give us insight into the early monastery," Lee's mother passionately explained.

The woman at the desk nodded her head, obviously not listening. In contrast to Mrs. McDaniels, she was round and older with a gold bumblebee pinned to her cardigan. She looked relieved when Lee interrupted.

"Hey, Mom. How's digs?" the daughter started with, her hands stuffed in her coat pockets, still trying to recover from the cold outside.

"Hi honey," her mom greeted as she rolled up the map. The full focus of her eyes fell on the teen girl. "Get bored at home?"

"Dad thought I needed to get out," Lee grumbled.

"Well, great," Mrs. McDaniels exclaimed, ignoring her daughter's attitude. She introduced her to the bumblebee pin woman with pride, then wrapped an arm around Lee's shoulders. "Let me show you what we're doing."

Lee welcomed the warmth of the single limb draped across her shoulders. Over the years, she'd beat her mom in height by only an inch or two, yet somehow the woman always managed to embrace her daughter in this way.

She led her daughter though a modern glass door and back into the chilled air. "You should have brought a scarf," Mrs. McDaniels commented, pulling her own jacket tighter around herself.

"I'm fine," Lee lied yet missed the heat from her mother's arm as it drew away.

People in comfortable, easy-to-clean clothes milled around the hillside, their forms slight and insignificant beside the impressive ruin. Lee watched them move along the ground as if avoiding broken glass, despite the fact that the usual preparations for a dig had not even begun yet.

Lee noticed a familiar face amongst the grad students

and historians. "Hey, Val," she called.

A man in his late twenties waved at her. Val, her mother's assistant, had a crooked grin. It gave him a ghoulish expression which Lee enjoyed speculating about. Under his nice-guy demeanor beat the heart of an obvious fiend. However, Val never realized his potential for villainy and continued to be a nice guy despite Lee's attempt to provoke a villain within him.

Val met her part way. "General Lee!" He lifted her off the ground as best he could and swung her like a little sister. "You're just in time. We're surveying the work of the last archaeological team that was here."

"Oh goody," Lee groaned. "Why don't you just start digging?"

"Ground is still frozen. First month is just going to be researching what is already known," her mom explained.

Val added through his thick Welsh accent, "But you bet, come late spring I'll be the first one out here with a shovel! Gonna help me?"

"You just keep dreaming," Lee sneered as she adjusted her weight before she started to sink in the mud. "Why can't you guys just ever once pick someplace warm and...yeck!" She paused to inspect the brown caking the bottom of her shoe. "And dry!"

"Not enough of an adventure for me, love," he replied. "You know that." He wrapped one arm around the girl's shoulders just as her mom had done. "Tour?"

"Do you really need to shed any light on the subject? It's an abbey. Or more to the point, a few walls and some bases of columns," Lee countered as he moved her toward the ruins. "Let me guess, Catholics worshiped here, and guilt-ridden residents of medieval Whitby came here to buy indulgences."

Val rolled his eyes. "I think you might like some of

this story. It's about a strong, independent woman."

"In the Middle Ages? Let me guess, someone burned her at the stake," Lee groaned. Despite her manner, she really was impressed by the towering stone built up around her. At one time, the abbey must have been magnificent with elaborate windows and detailed carvings. Now, what remained were disembodied walls reaching up into points where a roof had once housed centuries of parishioners. Empty arches acted as the only indicators of doors and windows. Every brick fit together masterfully, standing up against time and refusing to be pulled down by history.

"Not this time, Lee. She was actually respected for her leadership." He released her as the pair of them walked further into the ruins. They stood at the center of what was once the nave. Tired pilgrims no doubt trekked that hill in order to stand exactly where Lee's boots left a waffle pattern in the ground.

Lee sighed, pivoting on her heels as the grass bunched up into her shoe's tread. She tried to imagine the column that would have lined the nave, leading up to the altar. "Okay, Val. I'm listening."

Val went to sit on one of the short, round stone tables that had once been a lofty column. His arms rested on his knees and his fingers weaved in and out of one another as he started the story. "Her name was Hilda, or Hild depending on which book you read, and she ran this entire monastery back in 650 BC."

Lee sat beside him. "This is a saint story, isn't it?"

"It's a co-ed saint story. This abbess actually was in charge of both nuns and monks. You remember what I told you before about that time? Britain was not really unified. Everyone was kind of mucking about and they all wanted to be in charge. Christianity in this part of the world was still fairly new so there were a lot of religious problems going on."

"I remember. After the first of the Roman and the Saxon conquests, but before the Normans," Lee recited. "Why did everyone invade England? It couldn't have been for the weather."

"Probably for the fish and chips," Val joked then continued his tale. "Well, Hild's father was an Anglo-Saxon nobleman, related to the King of Northumbria, and her mother was Celtic. According to the story, Hild's father was poisoned in the midst of a family political struggle and Hild eventually had to become a part of the royal society in this part of England."

"She must not have enjoyed it if she became a nun," Lee commented. "From one form of torture to another, I guess."

"Be a cynic if you must, but she was a powerful woman. The king who put her in this position was part of a campaign to unite Britain under the idea of Christianity. Remember, back then—"

"England was separated into kingdoms. I know, Val. It's not like Mum doesn't give me these talks around the table every evening." Lee noticed Val's expression sink. She sighed and gave in to his history lesson. "Okay. Hild is set up by a king and—"

"King Oswy," Val cut in with renewed vigor.

"Right. King Ozzie. And she becomes the abbess of this big building here." Lee pointed at the ruin, twisting her wrist with a flourish like the assistant on a game show. "What happens next?"

Val took a trowel from his pocket. Despite the fact that the tool was useless during a British winter, he kept it with him. He pointed with the gardening utensil and explained, "Actually, this wasn't here yet." Picking himself up, he walked Lee around what was once the choir of the cathedral.

Lee had been dragged through old churches, minsters, and abbeys her entire life. She hated to admit it, but she was pretty good at figuring out which part of the ruins were what. People would have most likely entered at the west end through heavy doors. The central aisle of the church, known as the nave, would have led through the building, perhaps pausing at the center to stare at the high ceiling.

The north and south transepts jutted from either side of the abbey, the north transepts still intact with several walls and windows. Worn angel faces studied her. From the air, the transepts made a church look like a cross. From within, the windows would have been full of magnificent colored glass and probably had benches or relics on display. At the east end of the long ruin was what would have been called the choir, or as her mom liked to call it, an apse, where sermons echoed once upon a time. An altar could have stood with as much awe-inspiring splendor as the church could afford, and usually, Catholic churches could afford a lot of splendor.

Val drew her attention to stones barely excavated between the remains of columns. "This was built either directly over or near the church she was in charge of. We know that even these parts here are from after Hild's time. Who knows what her abbey really looked like, but I'd imagine something like that priory in Cambridgeshire. Isleham."

Lee remembered it: a rectangle with a triangle roof and few windows. Rather bleak and boring on the outside.

"I'm sure it was pretty big though. They held a religious council here during Hild's time, the Synod of

Whitby in 664. All of this architecture came long after she was gone." He set his trowel against a full column and clapped his hands together eagerly. "Back to my story! Hild lived here with monks and nuns. At least five of the monks under her went on to become famous."

"Did they actually listen to her when they were here though?"

"Of course. She was in charge. She wanted a unified Britain, so she was a beacon of political hope. And she taught her successor to be just like her, who happened to be Oswy's daughter."

"Kelly Oswy?" Lee teased.

"Aelfled was her name, smart ass. When she became abbess in 657, she continued the ideas of having a common religion and having the kingdoms work together instead of against each other. She kept the relics of a famous king at the time, King Edwin, safe from siege. These were amazing women, Lee."

Lee slumped atop a broken column. "Oh yes, amazing. Wanting everyone to think the same and be the same religion. Brilliant."

"Britain was in trouble. You had invaders coming to constantly take advantage of the fact that many of the kingdoms had no protection from their neighbors. These were women who were involved in politics—"

"When did they build the abbey?"

"What?"

Lee stood up straight and pointed at the apse wall, its empty window staring at her dumbly. "When did all of this start?"

"Oh." The topic obviously interested Val less than his tale of the two abbesses. "After William the Conqueror and the Battle of Hastings. In the 1070s, a knight named Reinfrid turned the original abbey into a Benedictine order. They had a bunch of pirate attacks and lost a patron here or there, so they started building all of this toward the end of the eleventh century." He sat beside her with a loud exhalation.

"Let me guess, Henry VIII struck a few hundred years later and shut the whole thing down? That's how all these British Catholic church stories end."

"In 1539," Val confirmed with a nod. "The land ended up in the hands of a rich family, the Cholmleys, and started to become. . ." He set a hand against the column beneath him, lovingly stroking the stone.

"A ruin," she answered.

He moved his hand to Lee's shoulder. "I know what you'd enjoy. Come on." They walked along the nave and out toward the north. The cliff lay out before them, the wind pulled at Lee's hair and clothes. The sound of the waves drew her from the abbey.

Val kept her grounded with a, "Come over here."

Lying on the uneven ground was a line of stone slabs. One or two had Anglo-Saxon headstones, marking the unnamed body of someone long gone.

"Tombstones!" Val declared as if he had shown her a box of kittens.

"Whose are they?"

"We don't know for certain, but some of them date incredibly far back. And this—" He set his hand atop one, leaning over it as if he'd known the person beneath the ground. "We think this was Abbess Aelfled's."

Lee shook against the still chill when he said the name. The chill had not existed before, the wind had not changed, yet somehow as she stared at the woman's final resting place, she had a sense of impropriety, a feeling Lee rarely had. She dropped her gaze.

The roar of the wind stifled. Lee settled herself

carefully onto the ground as vertigo swept her senses. A charge rushed through her fingers. She turned her eyes upon the tombstone once again. Suddenly, she hated the story of the two abbesses, as if the long-dead women were somehow to blame for her sudden nausea.

"You okay?"

She nodded, unable to express what she truly felt.

"Val, have you educated my daughter sufficiently?" Mrs. McDaniels inquired as she came out from the ruin.

He smiled and nudged Lee on the arm. "You like it. Right, General?"

"Sure," she answered with as much of a good-natured tone as she could muster. Slowly, she picked herself back up, feeling normal once again. Patches of damp seeped through her jeans. "What sort of stuff are you even looking for? This place has been picked over a dozen times already, hasn't it?" She motioned to the frosted ground and the scattered topography equipment measuring the slant of the hill.

"Anything we can." Mrs. McDaniels brought her daughter back within the ruin where the wind could not bite as harshly.

At the end of what used to be the nave, a table set on two hobby horses was laid out with a cotton cloth. Atop the cloth lay all the things Lee had grown accustomed to seeing, broken clay pieces, bone combs, and shattered bronze which her mother loved to speculate about. Also, alongside the medieval brick-a-brac were what her mother would call "modern artifacts". An eighteenth-century buckle laid next to a sixteenth-century bit of leather. Things left by people who walked the grounds after Henry VIII had forced the closure of the abbey.

"I liked the things you found in London better."

"We didn't find these. The previous team did. And,

darling, that was a medieval plague pit in London," her mom corrected as if she had forgotten. "Most of what we found were bones."

Lee confessed, "Yeah, but they all had stories, you know. And the forensics man came in to help with the ages and genders. That was pretty cool." She couldn't help getting tired of her mom basically marveling over things dead people had thrown out. As she continued to study the objects on the cloth, something caught her interest. "Is that a key?"

"Yes." Her mom pulled on a cotton glove from within her pocket, then carefully held the metal object closer for her daughter's inspection. "We haven't determined the date yet. Possibly fifteenth or sixteenth century." She tilted the key in her fingers. "I bet it was pretty once."

The top was rounded with a design straight from an English storybook, with grooves for what were once probably precious stones.

"What do you think it opened?"

"Not sure. It's a small key, so most likely a chest or a reliquary or a cabinet of some kind."

Val stepped over, grabbing Lee by the shoulders and swaying her playfully back and forth by her shoulders. In his best Boris Karloff voice, he said, "Or maybe it's the key to the cage where they locked up the Whitby Beast every night. Muwahahaha!"

"Val, don't you have work to do?" Mrs. McDaniels suggested as Lee rolled her eyes at the man's teasing.

"I happen to be finished with my work. What's holding you up on yours?" He waved at Lee as he smugly sauntered away.

Mrs. McDaniels mimicked her daughter's reaction. "He is just lucky he was top of his class." She set the key back on the tabletop. The two started back toward the visitor's center as she scoffed. "Going through all of the records from the dig crew before us is not easy."

"He should just be glad you're not making him do it," Lee added. "What are we doing for supper, anyway? That walk back down the steps is going to leave me starving."

As they re-entered the building, Mrs. McDaniels checked the time on her cell phone. "I need to finish some forms so I can file them first thing tomorrow."

"Oh, the wonders of bureaucracy," Lee dryly replied. She walked a couple of steps behind her mother with her hands stuffed back into the pockets of her black coat.

Mrs. McDaniels rummaged through her own pockets, finally producing a piece of paper and a ten-pound note. "I promised your father I'd bring home fish tonight, but I really need to get this done. Lee, do you mind? I have the order written down right here." The piece of paper was forced into her daughter's hand. "And come straight home afterward. Love you!" Mrs. McDaniels escaped behind the ticket desk with the bumblebee pin woman. She buried her nose in a heavy binder before Lee could protest.

Chapter 5: "Phantom Shapes"

The closest chip shop involved a four-street trek in darkness slipping over the town. Lee carried the list of her parents' requests on the back of a lesson plan of her dad's. On one side was an outline of how to start an essay on Nathaniel Hawthorne's *House of Seven Gables*, while the other side read "3 Cod, 3 chips, 3 sodas, 1 kebab." The kebab was for Mr. McDaniels.

Lee frowned at the words "explore the theme of hope by comparing Phoebe and Hepzibah". He was already setting up his online class for the summer, all of which he mapped out on paper before plugging it into the computer. Mr. McDaniels didn't trust technology — he preferred hard copies. However, his wife hated having stacks of paperwork strewn around the house. After his lessons existed safely on the computer, a USB drive, and a backup hard drive, the original written copies became scrap paper.

As she turned a corner onto a street with few lights, Lee spotted the chip shop like a beacon in the darkness. The cobalt blue electric sign called to her from the other end of the road and Lee could read the block letters, "Al's Fish and Chips". Stuffing her list into her pocket, she strode toward her destination with a relieved sigh.

Lee may have spent her life surrounding herself with the strange and creepy, but she concluded that Whitby at night was not her idea of a good time. In London, people always crowded the streets, any time, day or night. Police patrolled and lights stayed on. Parts of Whitby at night existed as an unsettling stillness. Her mother told her this was normal in small towns and no doubt it was a completely different story during the tourist season.

She could smell the grease of the battered fish when a woman stepped out in front of Lee. Not an extraordinary woman, just the stereotypical senior citizen wearing a turquoise wool coat and orthopedic shoes. And yet, Lee froze.

Lee's brain clicked, knowing that she recognized the woman. The woman who'd collapsed at the train station.

The woman stumbled. Her steps were sluggish as if weights had been attached to her feet. "I'm hungry," the withered voice whimpered.

"I'm sorry?" Lee asked with trepidation, looking longingly at the chip shop.

"I'm so hungry," the woman repeated.

Lee pointed to her destination. "They sell food. And I believe I saw a Co-Op a couple of streets back."

"So. . . hungreeeeeee." The words passed the wrinkled mouth with slow, pronounced syllables.

Lee swallowed hard. Her heart sped up and she tried to think of a way around the woman, talking to distract both herself and the human roadblock.

"I know that hunger can be trying, but you mustn't allow it to bring your spirit down. I mean, we can't have everything in life, right? I do wish you luck though. Have a good night." She faked to the right then sidestepped to the left, hoping this would give her a getaway opportunity.

The old woman cut her off with sudden composure and stealth. Lee extended her hand with the cash out as far as she could. "Okay, fine! Take it! Go buy yourself something to eat!"

The flabby arms wrapped around the teen with surprising strength. The old woman embraced Lee, overwhelmed with the smell of denture cream and Vaseline. Stale breath stirred the short hairs on the back of Lee's neck.

Lee's mind reeled. What was happening? Was this old woman about to whisper sweet nothings in her ear? Lee shuddered as she heard the word "hungry" whispered against her hair. Flat teeth gnawed futilely at the girl's shoulder.

"Gross! Get off me!" Lee rotated her arms and stomped wildly.

Two more shadows emerged from around the corner. She became convinced of an old people gang, retirees with their golf pants hiked up to their mid-waist and thick glasses magnifying their eyes. They probably stalked the streets in search of fiber they could steal.

Instead, two shadows, the siblings Lee had met the night before, stepped into the light. The boy had a duffle flung over one shoulder and sheathed Samurai sword on his back while his sister wore all black with a headband keeping her long hair out of her face.

Miranda crinkled her nose at the scene. "This is new," she commented.

Mal reached into the sack for a small silver object on a long chain. He held it out in front of him. A Star of David dangled before the old woman's red nose. She released Lee with a snarl and backed away. A pair of dentures remained stabbed into the girl's jacket.

Lee scrambled away to stand by the twins. Panic pushed her heart into her throat. "What in the name of hell is going on?"

Miranda smiled at her as if nothing strange were happening. "Oh. It's you again. Lee, right?" She pointed at the pair of teeth stuck to Lee's shoulder. "That's. . . not right."

Lee just repeated "what the hell" as she saw Mal and the old woman circle one another.

"Lee," Miranda told her calmly, "I suggest you run."

Spreading her feet out a little to take a resolved stance, Lee replied sternly, "Not until someone explains."

The old woman bared new teeth at Mal, sharp fangs protruding from her upper gums. Lee gaped for a moment as the vein-covered legs in saggy nylons gained speed, heading toward her once again. Mal jumped in the way, knocking the old woman down with his heavy sack.

"Run now," Miranda commanded. Lee obeyed this time, escaping around the corner as quickly as her heavy army boots would allow. The dentures released her. The bottom jaw broke free first and fake teeth scattered across the road.

Lee peered around the edge of a house. Brick dust dug into her cheek as she tried to blend into the wall. She tried to make out what still occurring on the street, however, the blue neon of the shop in the distance blurred the three figures.

Rummaging through the bag, Mal retrieved a plastic bag of uncooked rice. Just as the old woman began to pick herself up, he dumped the rice out in front of her. Instantly, she crouched back on the ground, beginning to count each individual grain. She collected them in her hand. Every time a grain slipped through her fingers, she would drop them all and start over.

"New Nos," Miranda critically said, shaking her head.

The old woman hissed at the comment but did not stop her counting.

Mal tossed his sister a wooden stick with a pointed end. He then unsheathed his sword. With the woman still distracted by the grains of rice, Miranda slammed the stake into the old woman's arched back, piercing through the wool, polyester, skin, and sinew until the point reached the un-beating heart. A shrill, fire alarm noise projected from the old woman.

As she rolled on the ground trying to get the stake out of her back, her fingers and legs twitched with agony. Blood dribbled at the corner of her mouth, and she choked on bile rising up her throat.

Mal raised the blade over her as she flailed, waiting for the jerky moments to slow before slicing through the old woman's neck. As the head fell from the body, everything stopped moving. The screaming faded and the body instantly decayed into ash, leaving a perfect dust outline of a person on the street.

Mal kicked at the remains. Turning, he noticed the broken dentures and almost laughed. "Her teeth fell out. Seriously?"

"It's just like a Bugs Bunny cartoon!" Miranda giggled happily.

Her brother sobered, thinking how this woman may have been someone's mother or grandmother. Maybe she used to bake shortbread and watch her neighbor's dogs when they went out of town. All of that had been taken from her. "Why would anyone turn a little old lady into a Nos? That's as rare as seeing children of their kind."

"She was sure determined to catch Lee too," Miranda noted as she flung the fallen sack onto her back.

Mal sheathed his blade and glanced around. "Which way did goth girl go?"

Lee escaped the rest of the way around the corner, wishing her boots did not echo against the hard pavement. Her eyes could not make out their actions, but the words "goth girl" echoed against the building. She checked behind her only once then kept her eyes on the escape ahead of her. Her mind questioned about the two teens she had left behind and yet, suddenly, the need for answers had become less important.

From the dim streetlights, a yellow haze hung over the world. The light shimmered against a pair of circles in the distance. A young man, early twenties, stepped out from a doorway. "Lee," a voice called out to her with friendly eagerness.

Lee's feet slid against the street. "What are you doing?" her brain yelled at her. "Flee! Run! Don't stop for strangers in doorways!"

Still, she panted and waited for the face from the doorway to come into her sight. It was the man from the York train station. He wore a black button-up shirt and tight jeans, looking like he had been out at a club and forgotten his coat. The sunglasses still rested on the bridge of his nose, protecting his eyes from the night sky.

Aubrey Ruthven approached Lee slowly. "Don't run off. It's just me. I don't bite." He smiled. His teeth were perfect; straight and proportionate like the caps struggling actors spend all of their rent on in hopes of looking more attractive.

She halted, staring him down. "It's you! You're here," she marveled, still out of breath from the chase, wondering how long it would be before the twins followed.

"You asked me to come," he answered, holding out his hands as if to present himself before an audience, "I have come to keep you entertained, however, you seem fairly busy at the moment." He glanced back in the direction that she had run from with curiosity.

Lee pointed at the corner. "This woman. . . She. . . I—" Lee's hand dropped to her side, and she realized, "I'm stuttering."

"Yes," Aubrey laughed with admiration. "You are."

Lee concluded, "I'm not exactly sure what just happened, and I doubt you will believe me." She reached up to smooth out her hair. Even though she had just seen a little old woman burst into dust, it was no reason not to regain enough composure to flirt. A thought wiggled within her, something important that she was forgetting. "Why are you really in Whitby?"

He looked hurt. "You don't believe I would come just to see you?"

Her shoulders rose and fell, her jacket slipping. "You know stalking is illegal."

"It's not stalking," he countered. "It's adoration."

"I doubt a policeman would agree with you." Lee almost blushed. She readjusted her coat and felt the bruise on her shoulder. Her panic and wonder came back in a flash. "Do you remember that woman you helped up the stairs at the train station?"

Aubrey seemed disturbed by this sudden change in topic. His mouth turned to a thin line. "Woman?" He tapped his index finger on the side of the thick plastic sunglass frames. "I think I do. Are you talking about the one who I carried luggage for?"

Lee nodded.

"You were watching me," he mused, his smile returning.

Lee scoffed at this comment, about to make a mean comeback, but focused her mind on the old woman with the biting habit. "I'm being frank. It's a little odd that I see both you and her here at the same time. She collapsed at the station after you helped her and now, she is here.

Was here."

Aubrey wrapped the tips of his fingers over one side of his glasses. He looked ready to remove them. Instead, he tapped them once again and straightened his stance. "I want to thank you for inviting me to come see you."

"What?" Her question came out upon a short inhale, as if she had gasped it. The thoughts of the old woman began to slip away once more.

"You seem flustered. Shall we begin again? Hello, I am Aubrey Ruthven."

"You!" another voice cried out. The twins appeared, taking a stance between Lee and Aubrey. Mal unsheathed his sword and a drop of blood descended from the blade. He held it up defensively, his knuckles white around the hilt. "You aren't supposed to be here."

"And yet, here I stand," Aubrey jeered. He turned to Lee and sighed. "I apologize, but I have to be going. I'll see you again." His shielded eyes fell back to Mal and Miranda as he added in a dark tone, "Soon."

He walked away at an easy pace. Lee watched him go, feeling cheated that the only person she really wanted around in that dull town had been chased away by the weirdo twins.

Mal refused to blink as he also watched him go. His brow creased casting a shadow over his eyes. "This is not good."

"Who was that, Mal?" his sister asked.

"Mira, we have to go home, right now." He snapped the words and took the sack from his sister. Miranda lingered for a minute as her brother started to jog in the direction of home. He glanced back at her and repeated, "Now."

She shrugged. "Okay. Come on, Lee."

Mal instantly stopped. "We can't bring her with us."

Lee placed her hands on her hips. "Do you really think I'm going to let you guys out of my sight after what just happened? I demand answers."

"You didn't care a minute ago when you were talking to that—"

"I am in a state of trauma. I cannot be held accountable for my actions or lack of logic at this time."

Mal's face crimsoned and his sister jumped in. "We can't leave her on her own. You know that."

"Then I'll wipe her. Hold her still." He started toward Lee with his left hand outstretched.

Mira slapped his hand away. Her voice lowered so only he could hear her. "No. You're bad at that. And if she knows something about that guy who freaked you out, wouldn't it make more sense to keep her mind intact."

With an irritated sigh which slowly turned into a growl, Mal gave in. "Fine." He figured his dad could come up with a much better lie than he ever could. Most of his friends attributed fighting in the streets to gangs and drunks. Of course, none of them saw him and Miranda stop an attack before. Blaming drugs and society would not be enough of a lie for Lee.

Miranda and Mal's dad met them at the bridge. He wore a long, leather duster which had been the standard uniform of their family for over a century. He clapped his hands together to keep them warm. "Any kills?" he asked, and then noticed Lee. "I mean—"

"She knows Aubrey Ruthven," Mal spewed out, nudging Lee toward his father.

Lee glared at Mal for pushing her. She turned her gaze slowly to their dad. His hair was thin, and his face was a little saggy, but the Victorian coat hid a well-toned body.

Mr. Tepes eyed her carefully, "How do you figure that, Mal?"

"Because he's here and she was talking to him," Malachi explained. "We just saw him, and he looked exactly like that portrait."

"Portrait? From the Philippa Tepes diary?" Miranda put in, suddenly wishing she had studied more of the family history.

"But he's no longer welcome in Whitby. He can't enter the town," Mr. Tepes insisted.

"Then you better tell him that, because he's here!" Mal barked, irritated that his father doubted him.

Lee rubbed at her jacket's shoulder where the dentures had been. The fake teeth had managed to work a hole through the thick fabric, exposing her skin to the chill. "I have an idea! How about if we tell the one who was bitten by a Golden Girl what the hell is going on!" Her words ended in a screech.

"She was bitten?" Mr. Tepes asked with interest.

"I'm standing right here," Lee whined. "And yes! It was horrific and nauseating and now I demand an explanation!"

"And you didn't want to be bit?" he clarified.

"That is the most imbecilic question I have ever heard in my entire life! And I've heard some truly idiotic things — my father teaches university, after all!"

Miranda, Mal, and their dad gazed at the exasperated Lee.

She quickly added, "No, I did not want to be bit!"

"Then you aren't a supporter?" Mr. Tepes queried, obviously not caring about the young woman's distress.

"A supporter of what?" Her body soaked in each question, allowing them to sap her energy.

Mira set a hand on her dad's arm. "She won't turn.

The teeth weren't real." At her own words, the girl smirked. "I'll tell you later."

"She was talking to Aubrey Ruthven like she knew him." All eyes fell again to Mal whose own stare coldly judged Lee.

Miranda remorsefully nodded in agreement. "He seemed happy to see her, Dad."

Rubbing his clean-shaven chin, Abelard Tepes thought over the situation. "First thing is first. We can't panic, but we can't have that thing here either. How did he even get in?" At last, he turned to Lee. "How do you know Aubrey Ruthven?"

Lee glanced at Miranda who avoided her gaze then back at their father. "I don't know him. I just met him yesterday at the train station in York. Why?"

"What did you talk about?"

Lee felt like she was on trial. She watched her tone as if a jury would choose to hang her if she yelled again. "Nothing," she answered quietly. Her tone was far from meek however she stayed guarded. She sensed that they faulted her for whatever they were in an uproar over. "I told him I was moving to Whitby."

Abelard Tepes positioned himself against the bridge railing. "He knew that was where you were going?"

"Yes."

"And did he ask you to invite him to Whitby? Did he ask to visit your home or something along those lines?"

Lee's rebellious streak kicked in once again, suddenly not caring if the Munster family thought she had committed some kind of crime. Her voice steady and almost proud, she told them, "He didn't ask me to invite him anyplace? I invited him because I wanted him to visit. What's wrong with that?"

Abelard's hand went to his forehead to press against

a forming migraine. "You wanted him here. You let him in." His voice was a sick moan.

"I don't understand what is going on, but I assure you that I will not allow this exploitation to continue!" Lee pushed away from the family. "I am going home!"

Mal grumbled, "You wanted to come."

Miranda ran after her. "Lee, wait." She jolted after the new girl, apologetically calling, "I know you don't know what you did wrong, but if you let us walk you home, I'll explain everything." Lee doubled her pace but was somehow stopped by Miranda calling out one last, "Lee, please."

She looked at the brunette who wanted so much to be her friend and to give her the benefit of trust. Miranda's eyes were wide as she caught up with Lee. "I'm sorry," she said again, "but we aren't used to having to explain things to people. Most of the time people rationalize things the way they want to."

"Rationalize what things? What happened tonight? What did I do that was so wrong?" Lee ranted, pacing back and forth. "What is wrong with Aubrey Ruthven? He's my friend." She said the words without thinking yet she realized what she meant by them. She barely knew this young man, yet she felt a connection to him. She liked the ease with which he spoke to her and how comfortable she felt in his presence. If he wasn't truly her friend then she most definitely wanted him to be.

Miranda sighed. She set a hand on Lee's arm as if they were a pair of caring sisters. "Oh, Lee," she started as if she were about to announce the coming of the apocalypse. "Aubrey Ruthven is a vampire."

Journal of Markus Tepes
1879

I may have made a grave error last night while in the company of an acting troop. Perhaps Prudence is correct; my mouth does get bigger when I consume what she calls 'the demon liquor'. I do hope my chatter will be taken as drunken ravings, otherwise, if my wife finds out what I have done, I will gladly forfeit my life to the Nosferatu. They will give me a kinder death compared with any punishment she will devise. I just wish that Abraham man had not asked me so many questions.

Chapter 6: "Creatures of the Night"

No one slept. After proclaiming the madness of Mal and Miranda, she'd been left unceremoniously at her home. Aubrey Ruthven couldn't possibly be a vampire. She'd seen him in the daytime. He wasn't pale and didn't have pointed teeth. Instead of arguing, the twins told her to sleep. They abandoned her at her door.

"Lee, where's the food?" were the first words out of her father's mouth.

Staring at her empty hands, Lee muttered, "Someone tried to mug me. I ran. I must've dropped the food." The lie slipped out unconvincingly, sliding into the blurred space in front of her.

Still, her parents instantly wanted details and fussed over her like she had been on the brink of death. Hands scanned the sides of her face and patted her arms for injury. Lee managed to stay still as they grazed the places where her skin had made contact with the street. Eyes stared directly into her own as if trauma left a mark.

"You are not going outside by yourself anymore," Mrs. McDaniels proclaimed. "I would have expected this in London, but here?"

Her parents continued worrying aloud when she escaped to her room. Stepping out of her clothes, she felt the scrapes and bruises upon her shoulder more sharply. Each time Lee closed her eyes, she smelled the denture cream of the old woman. Even when she pulled on a t-shirt to sleep in and kept the cotton under her nose for several minutes, the detergent's clean scent could not clear her nostrils. She hugged Eddie and lay on her side, staring out the window until the sun came up.

Meanwhile, Miranda spent the night thinking. Every half an hour or so she would hop out of bed, trek down the hallway, and knock lightly on her brother's door. Her questions mostly involved the background of the man Lee seemed to know.

Each time she asked, Mal tossed an article of dirty clothing or a pillow at her. "Go read the archives if you can't remember," he grumbled.

Around sunrise, she was back. "Mal? You awake?"

He opened the door with an annoyed grimace. "I never fell back asleep from the last time you woke me."

His room reflected a dull representation of himself. No movie posters or artwork hung on the walls. His bookshelves were overrun with occult readings given to him by his father. The computer desk appeared to be the only part of the bedroom that was truly his. He cluttered the surface around his keyboard and screen with photos of his friends, small toy surprises from chocolate eggs or cereal boxes, articles about his favorite sports teams, ticket stubs from his favorite films, and other tiny remnants of the normal life he wanted.

Miranda curled up into his computer chair. "I don't think Lee is a threat and I think we should be nice to her."

Mal sighed and rubbed his eyes. "Yeah? Well, I think she's a pain in the ass. I don't want to talk about this anymore, Mira." He hovered at the open door, hoping she'd take the hint and leave.

His twin stood up with a whimper. "What are we going to do about tomorrow?"

"It is tomorrow, Miranda."

"Okay, what are we going to do when we go back outside in a few hours and Lee wants more answers?"

Mal leaned against the bare wall of his room, wishing he could hang one of the Lord of the Rings posters he had stashed under his bed. "You're the one who wanted to bring her to meet Dad. I wanted to wipe her."

"You haven't wiped anyone's memory in a year and the last time it barely worked. I bet you can't even do it anymore. Dad said it's a rare gift."

"Don't turn this on me. I still say bringing her to Dad is all your fault."

"Yes. But that's when I thought she might be hurt or a supporter." Her brother gave her a sideways glance. "You win. The thought did cross my mind, but I didn't think Dad would take such an interest in her."

"Dad said we need to know what she knows. Aubrey Ruthven likes her, that's obvious. We need to keep an eye on her."

"Okay. So, we tell her the truth at least about how dangerous—"

"Everything." He rubbed at his face and shook to make certain he was fully awake.

"Wait. *Everything* everything? We've never done that before, Mal. Is Dad okay with this?"

"It's sort of his idea. Or at least that's how we're going to spin it to him when we tell him. He said to find out what she knows. How else can we without filling her in on the why?"

Mira's eyes gleamed with excitement. "We are finally going to have someone to talk to."

"Don't get too attached. You know Dad will just want me to wipe her memory when this is all over."

"Shut up. You won't be able to wipe her memory and I

will get a new friend. This will be wonderful."

Mal muttered sarcastically, "So wonderful." He flopped face-first back into bed, attempting to suffocate himself on the duvet.

Lee finally slipped into an unsettling dreamworld sometime after six a.m. Her mother entered around noon, gently shaking her daughter's shoulder and setting a mug of coffee on the computer desk.

"There are two kids waiting for you in the kitchen," Mrs. McDaniels explained. "Miranda and Malachi? Seem nice. They said they scared off the mugger for you. You didn't tell me you made friends."

Lee groaned in response and turned her pillow sideways, attempting to burrow her face into the case.

Her mom thought nothing of this sluggish behavior. "I'm going to the dig site if you need me. Your father is at the library. Something about needing a copy of Hawthorne's biography," Mrs. McDaniels explained. She shook the mattress after Lee did not respond. "Get up. Join the world. Go talk to your friends."

"They aren't my friends," Lee grumbled, wishing she could chuck her pillow at her mother's cheerful disposition.

"Either way, don't keep them waiting. Love you." And Mrs. McDaniels vanished before Lee could lift her head.

The effort to move her worn body on the walk from her bedroom to the kitchen proved to be a struggle. Mal and Miranda sat at the metal folding table, sipping tea her mother had made for them. Lee didn't care that her pajamas bunched around her or that her hair stuck straight up. She didn't even care about the dried drool at the corner of her mouth. All her energy went into glaring at the twins.

"Why are you here?" she groggily asked, hovering in the entrance to the kitchen in case of a quick getaway.

Miranda smiled at her. Mal spoke up first which surprised Lee. "We came to explain."

"Go get dressed," Miranda softly requested. "It's easier if we show you."

Lee scoffed at them. "Nothing you show me will convince me that Aubrey Ruthven is a vampire. Seriously, are you guys just trying to pick on me because of the way I dress?" She paused in order to make her voice sound deep and dopey, "Let's tease the goth girl. I bet she's gullible."

Mal had been staring into his tea, but his head rose at her impression of them. With sullen eyes, his tight lips parted with a long exhale. "This isn't a joke."

"I don't believe in vampires or ghosts or evil beasties."

"You don't have to believe us. We just need you to come with us and listen." Lee studied Mal more closely. He appeared to be serious, far too serious for his age. The worried lines her father had earned from years of bad bosses and annoying students already existed at the corners of Mal's eyes.

With a frown, Lee left them in the kitchen. As she showered, her brain kept yelling at her not to trust them. She should just stick to her room until Chelsea came. Yet, as the water slid down her back and smoothed her hair, Mal's expression niggled at her curiosity. She took her time getting dressed, hoping that the brother and sister would be gone. Gone meant none of this was Lee's problem.

After the application of eyeliner and a comb removed any tangles from the purple tresses, Lee rejoined the twins in the kitchen. Pulling on her jacket, she asked,

"Where are we going, exactly?"

Miranda smiled again, another silent offer of friendship. "Up the hill, to the church."

The three teenagers filed out of Lee's flat one by one, pausing so she could lock the door. Outside, Whitby was filled with the laughter of children and the gossip between neighbors. The dark and frightening events of the night before did not exist in this average little place.

Lee inspected the twins better in the daylight. Miranda Tepes was a slim beauty atop a pair of long legs. She wore the same skirt and tights as her classmates, yet her fur-lined winter coat revealed a certain sense of style. Her dark hair had been lightened, frosted, and ironed until it framed her face in straight tresses.

Malachi Tepes held himself with a confidence unusual for a teenager. His hair, dark and soft, was kept short and easy to manage. His spindly frame brought her mind to the words of Washington Irving when he described Ichabod Crane as ". . . some scarecrow eloped from a cornfield".

Mal played with the hood of his sister's jacket, tugging her along with determination. Miranda swatted him away. She smiled at Lee and whispered something to Mal. He responded with a swift shake of his head.

"What?" Lee insisted.

Mal instantly stared ahead of him, returning to his serious demeanor. Miranda did not shy away from Lee. Instead, she walked shoulder to shoulder with their new acquaintance as if they were old friends. "I was saying that I can see why Aubrey Ruthven picked you. You have a very unusual beauty. Nos like him always collect beauty."

Lee's first response was to insist on Aubrey Ruthven's innocence once again, but her attention was drawn back to Mal's stern gaze. "You don't agree?"

He shrugged. "I think Aubrey Ruthven is the sort of Nos who wouldn't worry about looks as long as he gets what he wants." The words seemed to sting Mal who spoke them with a tentative wince.

"You don't think I'm pretty then?" Lee asked, half-teasing, half-insulted, "Dost my form and face not please thine eye?" If she was to be dragged about, Lee was determined to get some chances to mess with the pair.

Mal continued to watch where he walked, leading their way through downtown Whitby.

"Hey!" Lee added, "I'm waiting."

Taking the shortest of glances in her direction, Mal rattled off under his breath, "Youreprettyeyeguess."

"What was that?"

"He said you're pretty...he guesses," Miranda translated giving her brother a dark look, "He's bad with compliments, but at least you got him to answer."

Mal changed the subject. "What has Aubrey Ruthven told you when you've talked to him? Did anything strange happen when he was around?"

Lee huffed, "You aren't seriously still trying to convince me that he's a vampire, are you?"

"Just answer the question. Please."

As they entered the open air away from the tall houses, Lee debated what to tell them. She didn't want this crazy family attacking the only potential friend she had. "I've never seen him bite anyone, if that's what you mean."

Mal pointed to the bridge, indicating that they were crossing. "He's not that kind of Nos."

Miranda skipped a little, ready to tell a story. "There are two kinds of Nos. The first—"

"Nos? As in Nosferatu?" Lee snorted, "I'm sorry, but

that's utterly moronic."

"Why?" Miranda squeaked, "You try saying the Latin all the time."

"You English and your shortened words; veg, telly, mash, adverts, loo . . . I don't even know what 'loo' is short for. You people are so lazy."

Mal, walking alongside Lee, raised an eyebrow in protest. "Being called lazy by an American. How will I ever think of a comeback for that one?"

Miranda steered herself through the traffic on the bridge and walked between her brother and Lee. "Stop fighting," she insisted, then slapped her brother on the shoulder. "We're not going to find out anything if you keep insulting her." Then, she turned on Lee, "And you. At least hear us out."

This earned another roll of the eyes from Lee, yet the young woman stayed quiet as they continued across the bridge and toward the one hundred and ninety-nine steps up the hill.

The silence by both pleased Miranda who continued as if the interruption never occurred. "Like I said, two kinds. There's the blood vampires that you hear about in all the movies. We call them Sanguis Nos. They can't come out in daylight, hate garlic, and are kinda obsessive-compulsive. Leave beads or sticks in their path and they have to count it. I have no idea why."

Mal explained, "It goes back to the vampires of ancient Sumer. The Ekimmu were spirits who did not get proper funeral rites or were killed without their bodies ever being found. They moved on the wind and consumed lives and human energy like demons by planting ideas that caused people to kill either themselves or each other. You could ward them off with something to distract them like—"

"Those aren't really vampires," Lee argued curtly.

"No." Mal frowned at her as if finding her attitude distasteful. "A lot of people believe they gave way to vampires, for the idea of something solid to find a way to feed off human lives. The Strigori, the Shtriga, the Succubae, and Incubi —Egypt, Greece, Rome. Everyone shares stories about things that hide in the shadows and feast on blood and human energy."

Lee leaned forward, unable to hide her curiosity. "Human energy?"

"That's the second kind of Nos," Mira explained. "They are the Percutio Nos, similar to Incubus and Succubus and the like. They feed off human emotion and basically, what makes you . . . you. They are more powerful and rarer. They can be out in the daylight; they can sire a Nos just by feeding—"

Mal cut her off this time. "They only sire bloodsuckers. Soul stealers are amongst the oldest. No one knows how they came to be."

"How do blood suckers sire new vampires? Don't they just have to feed on a person as well?" Lee asked.

Mal picked up a blade of grass from the hill beside them and started to absent-mindedly tear at it. "No. Bram Stoker got that part right. First, they feed on you. Then, you feed on them. When you're bled dry and your heart stops, that's when you rise again as one of them."

"That sounds unpleasant."

The three paused at the top of the hill. Tourists and locals passed them, unaware of the unusual conversation. "And why do you guys know all this? Are you some kind of vampire slayers?" Lee scoffed at her own words.

"Yes." Mal was deadpan. He hovered before Lee. "It's in our blood."

With an unblinking glare, she told him with complete

frankness, "Don't look at me like you're trying to prove that you are some awe-inspiring badass. It isn't very flattering to a young man." Mal's expression did not change as Lee caught up with Miranda.

"Ever heard of Prince Vlad III, also known as Vlad the Impaler?" Miranda asked.

"Yes. Ruler of Romania; fought the Turks; brutally killed hundreds of people," Lee stated.

"In Romania, he's considered a great hero!" Miranda insisted with a little insulted gasp.

With a sigh, Mal told Lee, "He was both. He was the hero and the monster. He did do great things for his country, but he also loved blood and war. When he was alive, vampires had nearly died out. Supposedly, it's because of him that they are still around today. Ever heard of the Order of the Dragon?"

"Like the Order of Dracul? It's supposedly where Bram Stoker got Dracula's name from," Lee clarified. "My dad and mom gave me a whole history lesson on it when they bought me the book."

"Same thing. In his time, Vlad used his position in the Order to track down some of the last remaining Nos in his area of the world and had himself turned into a soul stealer. The legends don't say how he managed this. There's no record of how to change someone into that kind. We always assumed they were just so ancient that they just always existed."

They entered the cemetery, passing by a group of visitors huddled together against the sea winds. The quaint Elizabethan church was less inviting to Lee than it had been the day before. The black clock within the tower stared back upon her with the harsh criticism of a parent. *Why are you with these crazy people? Didn't your mother teach you better?* The wind sang to her as it darted between the centuries of stones.

Lee watched the way the twins moved so respectfully around each weathered stone. She spent a good part of her life in graveyards, first through her mother's digs and second through her ghost-hunting society. The thought of hundreds of years of decaying bones beneath her feet never bothered her nor did the thoughts of the names on the tombs make her melancholic. Life was what it was and when it was done all those bodies had to go someplace. Graveyards were more of a fascinating mystery than a reminder of mortality to her.

However, as Malachi and Miranda stepped along the footpath, leaving as little trace of their existence over the resting place of the dead as they could manage, Lee felt a wave of guilt for her previous graveyard antics.

"One of our ancestors, who was a Nos hunter that was turned, once wrote that while she was dying of the lack of blood, she tried to fight the urge to be a Nos. She said it literally felt like a part of your soul or mind was locked away, screaming and yelling to stay human, even if it meant dying as a human." Mira leaned against a tombstone. "In the end, the demon always wins."

"Not in Dracula," Lee corrected. "Mina fights it. She insists that everyone stay away from her and tries to lock herself away. She won't even let her husband kiss her—"

"That's a book, silly," Mira countered with a giggle.

Mal thoughtfully added, "There's some old legend that says some soul stealers tried to fight what they are. They set up a hidden community and lived like humans, taking the energy from one sacrifice a season to sustain them, a willing victim sent by a neighboring village. They usually took the old or the already dying, although that seems hard to believe. Old and dying people don't have strong energies."

"And the stronger the energy the better the meal?" Lee put in.

"Yep."

"I don't remember that one," Miranda whined.

"I read it in that fifteenth-century grimoire," Mal clarified.

"That big heavy thing! No wonder I haven't read it," Miranda said, "Anyway, blood feeders are destroyed by a stake through the heart and removing their heads. They are also the most prominent and common."

"A little like the common cockroach," Mal added with disgust.

"No commentary from the peanut gallery," Miranda chided before going on, "Like we said, we honestly don't know what creates the second kind, the soul stealers like Aubrey Ruthven. According to our cousins on the continent, there is probably less than a hundred of that kind left in the world."

Lee thought back on the way Aubrey Ruthven had helped the little old woman at the train station. His help caused the woman to collapse. She showed up in Whitby at the same time as Ruthven and attacked. She quickly re-evaluated her logic. "Vampires aren't real. That's what this comes down to."

"You saw us destroy that woman last night. She turned to dust," Mira insisted.

"I don't know what I saw. I do know that there are no such things as vampires and therefore Aubrey Ruthven cannot possibly be one. He doesn't even have fangs. I saw him smile." She almost blushed remembering his smile. Lee rolled her eyes, "You cannot possibly understand the inner depths of my mind if you expect me to fathom such implausible tales."

Mira looked at her brother quizzically. "Do you notice

that she has a funny way of talking, sometimes?"

Mal's annoyance swiftly returned. "Why would he need fangs? He doesn't need to bite. He hypnotizes and sucks out essences like cider through a straw. No bite marks required. No marks at all if he chooses to keep you alive. If he drains you near death or kills you, that's when people can finally see the damage. Yellowing skin. Hives. The sort of thing people mistake for an epidemic." He moved directly in front of Lee, realizing that she was attempting to ignore him. "You have no idea how many abilities Ruthven has. He can be out, day or night. He never needs rest. Blood feeders have to sleep in the daytime. He can't be affected by crosses or any other symbols. You can at least use symbols of faith to keep blood feeders at a distance."

"I assume you are both Jewish." Lee pointed at the six-pointed star glittering against Mira's dusky skin.

"Our mum is. She has faith in this symbol and we have faith in her."

"What about your dad?"

Pushing his chin into his chest, Mal muttered, "Our dad isn't religious. He has faith in relics based on tradition more than actual belief. If it worked for his grandfather then it better as Hell work for the rest of us."

For a moment, Lee saw it. She saw the rebellious teenager struggling to break free from within Malachi. Instead of allowing sympathy to soak within her judgment, she took a decided step between the twins and a tombstone. Her gaze darkening, Lee pointed at the hole in her jacket shoulder created the night before. "I'm still not particularly thrilled with any of this. You wanted to show me something. Something that would make me believe in all of this. Where is it?"

Miranda took a deep breath and checked the time on

her mobile phone. She then checked the clock on the tower. Looking upon her brother, he gritted his teeth and glanced at his own wristwatch. At last, she said, "You'll see soon enough."

Chapter 7: "Effects Persons of a Sensitive Nature"

The number of people wandering around the cemetery thinned as the sky thickened with clouds. Mal and Mira exchanged glances. They led Lee to the backside of the church where no prying eyes could see the trio's actions.

A cluster of worn tombstones nestled along the edge of the churchyard. Mira pointed at one, the surname having aged away, but the first name was still barely legible.

"Thea. . . something? Died in 1941? One of your relatives?" Lee crossed her arms and leaned against another stone, growing tired of the history lessons.

"Yes." Mira looked up at the clouds rolling in and double-checked for any other nearby souls. "Since we are Nos hunters, we get a few powers of our own."

Lee laughed outright. "Oh, please tell me that you brought me up here because you are both going to turn into bats and fly off the cliff."

Mal removed his coat and laid it over Thea's grave. "Our abilities are more like defense tools. They only work when we are in immediate danger."

"Or when we are on this cliff. We think it's being close to so much family that does it. This was the only way we could show you without a Nos attacking."

With both eyes closed in frustration, Lee grumbled,

"Please, if you're going to talk about vampires, then just call them vampires."

The female Tepes twin tapped Lee on the shoulder. "Me first. Are you watching?"

The twin walked casually to the side of the church. She leaned backward in order to slip off her shoes. She surveyed the church as her tights soaked up the mud. St. Mary's Church had crenelated parapets running along the tops of the walls like a fortified castle. Long glass windows provided daylight to the church visitors within. At one end of the structure was an extension of the church where two sides of the roof met in the traditional triangle shape. The area had fewer windows which kept them even more sheltered from nosy onlookers.

Miranda bent her knees a tiny amount, just enough to force the edges of her skirt a little higher than her knees. When she straightened, her toes dug into the earth, and she propelled herself up to the roof of the church in one graceful bound. With the agility of a monkey atop a tree, she climbed up the brown shingles until she touched the ridgepole at the top of the triangle. Her shining eyes only glanced down upon the ground once in order to give Lee's astonished stare a playful wink.

Mal gave her a quick hand signal to come down. Silently, she slid back to the edge of the roof and leapt. Her feet returned to the ground without a single slip in mud or thud to her landing.

Regaining her composure, Lee stammered, "O— okay. So, you can jump unusually high. That's not really a superpower. I think you'd be a shoo-in for an Olympic team though."

Retrieving her shoes, but not putting them on, Mira walked to her brother and nudged him. "Your turn."

Her brother reluctantly walked toward Lee who took

a step back.

"What are you going to do?"

"Mira got most of the agility and strength. I got the abilities that are a little harder to show." Mal took her hand.

Yanking her digits away, she barked at him, "You should never grab a person. It's rude."

Sneering at her, his palm hovered in the air in front of her. Lee looked to the abbey ruins behind him. Her mom was close by. If something bad happened, she could scream. Even if the worst were to happen, Mrs. McDaniels knew how to use a wide range of medieval weapons. Lee's death would be avenged.

Grinding her teeth, Lee set her palm within his. His eyes shut and his fingers gently encased hers. She squirmed and wondered if her skin turned clammy or sweaty or both. A little jolt passed from him to her and the world melted. She faced an alleyway at night where Miranda and Malachi fought a man in steel-toed work boots. Seconds of the brawl filled her brain and she almost felt as if she were there, save for one detail, muted sounds. Each muffled grunt and punch made her feel a million miles away from a scene occurring directly in front of her.

Mal released her hand and studied her face as her mind returned to the present. He was unconcerned with her reactions, just ready to get his explanation over with.

"I see things," he stated quickly. "Mostly the recent past. It's hard to see things from years ago. But it's how I sense them."

"You sense vampires through memories?"

Setting an arm around Lee's shoulders, Mira added, "Nos carry the past they try to bury with them everywhere they go. He can sometimes see visions of their weaknesses."

The human girl roughly shook Miranda off her. Her head swam. Her palm ached. She wanted to scrub away the vampire hunter boy's touch. She wanted to scrub her brain from the violation it felt.

She turned away from both of them and started to walk away swiftly. She could hear them calling, but she had no response. She had no words. She had no reality.

Lee left the footpath as she walked, not watching where she went. It was not until a massive Celtic-style cross blocked her way did she at last pause.

The large stone cross lorded over Lee. She tried to focus on the symbols and words carved into the rocks, but they danced mockingly. Blackness crowded at the edges of her eyes as she lost balance. Cross, church, graves, twins, and grass buzzed by her face in a blur. Her legs gave out directly before her eyes shut.

Lee saw first the incoming storm clouds being pushed by a bullying wind. As her eyes focused, her fingers grazed the sharp blades of the frozen lawn. The back of her head stung. Hands grasped her shoulders, slowly bringing her to a sitting position.

"What happened?" a voice she assumed to be her own grunted.

"Do you get vertigo from the altitude?" Mal asked.

She looked over her shoulder and noticed that he was the one holding her up. Shaking him off, she leaned forward until her aching head landed in her hands.

"Show me your eyes," Mira insisted, the flashlight from her mobile phone seeking signs of a concussion.

"That was weird," Lee grumbled. She'd grown up around unsteady parapets and medieval spiral staircases. Never in her life had heights ever affected her. "I'm probably in shock. I probably need pills. Lots of pills to calm my mind and keep me sane."

"Time to go," Mal announced with the authority of a father ending a picnic.

Mira pouted. "Let her sit a minute."

"No. No, I'm fine. I want to go." Lee rose to her feet. She expected to be groggy or for some residual dizziness to hamper her movements. Her head was clear. Each muscle listened to her commands without complaint. She could almost forget that she had fallen at all. "I suppose you two are coming with me?"

"You suppose right." Mira's voice was sweet concern, a sound Lee found familiar only to her parents and her closest friends. The sound stilled Lee's heart. She did not try to flee from the twins again.

The way down the steps, although not nearly as daunting as the climb, was stained with a slow drizzle. The slick surface objected to being walked upon. People ahead of them slid a little almost as a warning to others.

Mira walked first. "Oh, I forgot the third kind of Nos!" The wind carried her words backward to Lee and Mal.

"Those don't exist any longer. That kind died out thousands of years ago." Mal looked ahead of him at Lee and said resolutely, "There are only two kinds of Nos."

"Too late, she said there's the third kind. What's the third kind?" Lee asked, as she stayed close to the side of the hill for support.

Miranda took to the slippery stairs like a goat to a mountain. She bounded down them happily, dancing on her way back to earth from Heaven. Her tights were soaked through, and her shoes dangled from her hand. "Like Mal said, we think the third kind is extinct. You only read about them in ancient texts. But they were a mix of the two kinds. They needed blood and life energy to survive. All they left of their victims was a gross human husk."

Lee noticed how Mal walked behind her. If she shifted her weight to the right or the left, he did the same. She stumbled once and he instantly caught her arm to hold her upright. She quickly shook him off. He never smiled at her or gave her a reassuring glance.

Mira raised her arms over her head and stretched up on her toes. "Some stories say they were gigantic, others say they took animal form most of the time."

"In other words, you really don't know anything about them."

"Pretty much."

They reached a landing, a resting place with a bench about halfway down the stairs. The rain began to beat in a heavy rhythm.

Lee took refuge upon the bench, resting her head in her hands. "Give me a moment to evaluate the facts. There are vampires. Aubrey Ruthven is a particularly nasty type of vampire. You are both vampire hunters with . . . special abilities. And you are telling me all of this because, why?" She lifted her head. Rain dripped down from her forehead. She did not bother to wipe away the droplets as they blurred her vision and froze her cheeks.

The twins stood before her. Mira seemed anxious. Her eyebrows furrowed into a worried crinkle and her throat tightened. Mal's face remained unreadable, staring back at Lee with no emotion in his eyes.

"We need your help." Mira rushed to the bench, sitting in the puddle that had collected upon the seat without a second thought. Her hand sought Lee's, trying to catch the cold fingers in a tender hold. "Ruthven shouldn't be here. He was banished a long time ago. He's powerful and smart and going to be difficult to trick."

Pulling away her fingers and tucking her hands into her lap, Lee concluded. "So, you want me to help you catch him?"

"He likes you."

Mal spoke up with a growl. "And you were the one who let him in. You invited him here."

"I didn't know! And what does it matter? He hasn't done anything to either of you, has he? Whatever he did was a long time ago, right? He might have changed."

"They don't change!" Mal insisted.

Lee jumped up and pushed against Mal's shoulder. "At the moment he's been kinder to me than either of you and I've barely spoken to him! You really haven't answered anything you know. I just have more queries now. My mind is all abuzz."

Miranda once again looked confused. Instead of questioning, she started to walk away stating, "You can handle this one, brother of mine."

Mal's lips trembled, as if he were trying not to laugh. "You always talk like this?"

"When I'm upset, I tend to exercise an extensive vocabulary, yes." Lee crossed her arms and barked, "Now, you've revealed this much, finish the story. Tell me the rest before I agree to abet to anything."

With a steady finger, Mal pointed back up the hill. "There's something buried up there. Something that draws the Nos to Whitby and it's the reason why one part of the Tepes family is always stuck here."

"There are more of you?" Lee sounded disgusted.

"Extend family all over the world. Even some with high political power. And we all come from the same family blood. Vlad Tepes blood."

"Vlad the Impaler?"

"Yes. When Vlad III died, there was a mysterious rise

in the number of Nos— vampires in his country. The legend is that when the vampires rose, they were led by an undead Prince Vlad, but his own son hunted him."

"You're suggesting that modern vampires and your family both came from Vlad the Impaler?"

"I am telling you what Miranda and I have been told our whole lives. In the fifteenth century, our ancestor, a man called Helsing Tepes, came to Whitby from Germany. Bram Stoker borrowed that from our family, along with several other things thanks to my big-mouthed great-great-grandfather, Markus Tepes. He told Stoker all kinds of stories after a few whiskeys that were twisted around, then put into *Dracula*." Suddenly, the young man's head fell. He had never been able to tell anyone so much about his family. He hated the look of disbelief in Lee's eyes. Mal walked away from her, grumbling, "We are a pretty messed up family."

To his amazement, Lee caught up with him. "That's what got you emotional? Alcoholics and crazy family stories are pretty normal."

"We aren't alcoholics. We hunt vampires."

"You think you hunt vampires. I have a great-uncle on my mom's side of the family who thinks he's the abolitionist John Brown. He's always setting fire to things in the name of freedom." Mal at last smiled at her comment. "Did he, Markus, get in trouble with the rest of the family?"

Mal nodded. "His wife and his son worried that Stoker or other authors would come to hear more stories, so they sent him away to live in Reykjavik."

"As in Iceland?"

"Yeah."

"Harsh."

She watched Mal look like he was about to smile

again, but he quickly quelled the urge. She asked, "Back on topic, what does Aubrey Ruthven have to do with any of this?"

He spoke as if reciting a bedtime story. "They were drawn here at the same time. Aubrey Ruthven and Helsing arrived almost on the same day. At the time, most Nos in Britain hung around the big cities. It felt strange to Helsing to want to go to a place so small and out of the way. His ship arrived early in the morning and carried with him something special to the family. Another ship with all the crew close to dead on it arrived in the afternoon. People passed it off as plague, but Helsing knew right away. After hiding the family object, he followed his instincts and searched for whatever made him want to come to Whitby. And he found Aubrey Ruthven here, in that churchyard."

"What was he doing?" Lee heard herself whisper the words and realized how anxious she was to hear about the man's alleged dark deeds.

"Digging. Helsing approached; Aubrey Ruthven attacked."

The drama dropped from Lee's voice. "Are you sure it wasn't the other way around? Aubrey Ruthven was digging, not killing anyone. What's wrong with that?"

"Just listen. My ancestor managed to throw Ruthven over the cliff and into the sea. Before Ruthven was able to climb back up, Helsing saw that what the Nos was after was the family object he himself had hidden." Mal waved a hand in the direction of the cemetery. "And he buried it again."

"You keep saying object. You don't have any idea what it is, do you?"

"It's written in Helsing's journal that it's better if we didn't know what was up here. Theory is that it's a relic of the Order of the Dracul. But ever since, Nos have come to this village in swarms. Even they don't know exactly why. They just know this is the place to be."

Lee felt her pulse race. "So, your ancestor banished Ruthven because he wanted some old relic."

"Our family didn't' banish him," Mal tried to say.

The girl continued to rant, ignoring him. "My mom keeps tons of relics around the house. Most of them are just dusty, you know."

Mal interrupted, "You've read Dracula?" She nodded, not pointing out that she wasn't finished yet. "You know how vampires can't come into a home unless they're invited? Once given, the invitation can never be taken away, not even by us. But someone not named in any of our family journals had that power. Someone managed to do that on the entire town of Whitby and Aubrey Ruthven could only come back he was if some idiot invited him."

"Are you calling me an idiot?" Lee stomped the rest of the way down the stairs.

"Well, you did let him back in!" Mal called after her.

Miranda, having overheard her brother's yell, instantly defended Lee. "It's not like she could've known, Mal. Give her a break."

The twins chased after Lee as Mal took his turn to rant. "Who invites complete strangers to visit them in other towns? I bet she goes on dates with blokes she meets on the internet too."

Lee stopped, planting her feet on the cobblestone street. She faced Mal, glared at him, and without thinking, slugged him directly in the nose. Her knuckles stung and she could hear him moaning in pain, yet she felt better. Miranda laughed so hard her stomach ached.

As he held his bleeding nose with one hand, Mal's

muffled voice amended, "Sorry, maybe I went too far."

Instantly, Lee's anger waned. "You what?"

"I didn't mean it," he stated calmly. "I'm just. . . you've never read the files on Aubrey Ruthven. He is not someone we ever wanted to have to deal with."

Lee pulled a tissue from her pocket and shoved it into Mal's free hand. "You're scared of him?" Lee realized. "It's some old legend. How do you know any of the stories are even true?"

"Why would our ancestors lie?" Miranda argued.

Mal pressed the tissue against his nose. As he tried to stop the red from gushing out his nostrils he commented, "Shit. That hurt." He then lowered the handkerchief for a moment, the blood splashed above his upper lip like a thin mustache. "If you had read some of the stuff I've read," he said wearily, "you'd be scared too."

Miranda only nodded in agreement, even though in truth she had not read a tenth of the books her brother had studied. Lee wrapped her arms around herself, feeling the softness of her coat against her fingertips.

"What do you want from me?" she asked quietly.

"Like we said, he likes you," Mal told her bluntly. The rain washed his face of the blood and his dark eyes sought hers.

Lee felt her cheeks turn red and she pretended to be interested in the slick road behind her so the twins would not see. He continued despite seeing the soft blush on the girl's face. "He'll want to keep you for himself. If we monitor you, we can stop him before he starts digging around."

Miranda grabbed her arm and Lee tensed. "You won't be in any danger. We will keep you safe. Start by coming to our house tonight."

Testimonial of Henrick Tepes, third child of Helsing and Molly Tepes
Written upon the twenty-ninth of January in the year of our Lord, Fifteen Hundred and Ninety

This shall be my first entry, where it should have been the words of my brother, Walter. I have already taken a great many lives of the unclean enemy which my family has sworn to defend the town from. I did not see until now how important chronicling our history was until today. Aubrey Ruthven returned to Whitby. My cousins in Glasgow warned me of his movements. I never thought such a monster would even dare to near the River Esk after his years of travel.

Upon his arrival, he took the lives of both my father and my brother. Is it a crime to confess that I wish for vengeance? God forgive me. Forgive my anger and the hate within me. Each night, I consider leaving. I think of abandoning my position here in Whitby, leaving the town defenseless so I may hunt that barbaric creature. I try to be humble and patient. I must have faith that his fate will bring him to the end he deserves. For now, I continue to guard that which my family died for.

Chapter 8: "For a Personal Reason"

Lee was told to arrive by six. Her parents were thrilled that she'd already been invited to supper at the home of children her own age. Her dad walked with her to the house, assuring himself that she would be safe.

Mr. McDaniels spoke to his daughter about his latest lesson plans about "Feathertop", a story about a sentient scarecrow, not caring that she was more preoccupied with her phone.

"Got invited to dinner by weird bro & sis tonight. Don't want to go," she texted to Chelsea.

The response lit up her screen instantly. "Then don't go – Is the bro hot?"

Lee wasn't sure what else to say. "I have to go. They're going to train me to be vampire bait. And no, he's not hot." Instead, she answered, "Call me later in case I need an out."

"Not if he's hot," Chelsea responded, and Lee wanted to toss her phone in the river.

"Lee McDaniels." Her name caught her off guard. Aubrey Ruthven, sunglasses securely resting upon the bridge of his nose, walked directly up to her and her dad.

Mr. McDaniels addressed Lee before he answered the stranger. "Is this one of your new friends?"

"Yes, but he's not who I'm hanging out with tonight." She gave Ruthven a dark, warning stare. Could he hypnotize her or her father? She wondered if she should scream out for the twins.

Ruthven's face fell at her expression. Still, he held his charm to the last. Mr. McDaniels accepted his strong handshake while giving his name. "Your daughter and I met the other day."

As he allowed himself to be impressed by this straightforward young man, Lee's father thought aloud. "Ruthven? That's a familiar-sounding name."

"Old family. One of the clans who started off as Norse invaders in Scotland, then helped the English in all of the wars. One of my ancestors actually served Robert the Bruce."

"Interesting. I can easily respect a man who knows his family tree. You should have a chat with my wife sometime. She is always anxious to brush up on her Robert the Bruce history."

Her feet shuffling in place, Lee tugged her dad's arm. "We've got to go."

"Sorry. Wasn't trying to make you late for anything." Ruthven grinned. A wave crashed within Lee's stomach.

"Whatever," she answered coldly. She instantly regretted it. She was supposed to trap him, to use his friendliness toward her. Yet the idea of him introducing himself to her dad made a protective surge block any plans.

Pulling her father away, she did not look back at Ruthven. She heard her dad say, "He seemed nice" then nothing else until they reached the Tepes's home and souvenir shop.

Backpack in hand, Lee started up the back stairs where she'd been instructed to go. Mr. McDaniels followed close behind. "You don't need to come up. I'm fine."

"I'd like to meet this family."

"I'm not ten years old anymore. My mobile is turned on. Their parents are home. I promise there will be no alcohol, drugs, sex, or human sacrifices. It's fine," she insisted.

The words drew deep lines at the edges of her dad's mouth. "Are you sure?"

"Yes!"

"Are you too old to give me a hug goodnight?"

She gave a quick look at the windows of the flat over the shop, wondering if anyone was watching. Both arms embraced her father while still keeping him at a distance. The so-called hug lasted a total of three seconds.

Sarcastically, he said, "These bonding moments are very special to me."

"Yeah. Yeah. Night, Dad."

"I wuv you, my Annabel Wee," he loudly announced in a baby voice.

She ran up the stairs in mortification. Her knuckles wrapped desperately upon the door. Miranda answered wearing jeans, a bright yellow jumper, and an excited countenance. She welcomed Lee in as if she'd been to visit a million times before. Mal watched from the edge of the room, not greeting Lee with anything more than a blink.

The little flat over the shop looked normal upon first appearance. The family room and tiny kitchen were adjacent to the door leading up from the souvenir store. Their father was watching television; their mother was setting the table. The whole house smelled like salmon and steamed vegetables.

Three bookshelves had been set against one wall. Lee breathed in the heavy musk from the dusty pages. As the twins moved into the kitchen to warn their mother of who had come to supper, Lee walked backward until she was close to the shelves. Some of the books were ancient, including what looked to her to be the old, scribed tomes of medieval monks. Most looked to be from the last two centuries, the thread from their binding beginning to peek out from the edges of the spine. A title caught her eye and she realized she was reading Latin.

"Livre Nosferatu," she muttered under her breath. The Vampire Book, she translated in her head from the small amount of Latin she knew thanks to her mother's profession. She looked at another book; "The Grimoire of Merlin". And another: "Lycanthropy Signs and Symbols". All occult books. Not a single piece of modern fiction or self-help book in the bunch.

Along the top of the shelves were a series of books with no titles on the spines. Each book seemed to get progressively modern, arranged from oldest to newest. Mal stepped over, investigating the way her neck strained to inspect the many mysterious volumes.

"Those are the family journals. Or at least some of them. A couple have been lost and a lot are passed through other branches of the family tree."

He waited for Lee to respond, but all the girl said was a sarcastic, "Neato."

"That's how I knew about Aubrey Ruthven," he whispered. With a curious expression, as if he could read doubt on her forehead, he added, "You want to borrow one and read it?"

Lee simply glared at him. She did not want to reveal her encounter only minutes earlier.

Miranda and their mother came from the kitchen and their father finally looked up from his show. "Tea time?" he asked, then finally noticed the guest. "Why on earth is she here? I thought you said you would sort this out?"

Mal knew the question was directed at him. Still, it was his mother who answered. "Abelard! She's company. Now you be polite." The woman smiled at Lee. "You can call me Karen. And do I call you Lee?"

"Yes." Their guest answered as she used the opportunity to move away from Mal.

"Is Lee short for something?"

"Yes," Lee repeated.

Not offended by the curt answer, Karen added, "Welcome to our home, Lee."

At first, Karen had little else to say while the family sat down to their meal. Abelard Tepes eyed Lee with utter contempt. "My children already explained the situation to you. Why are you here?"

"Dad!" Miranda sat between her father and their guest. "Can't you just be nice? She agreed to talk more about our plan and I thought the least we could do was give her food."

Karen raised her glass to this. "At the very least."

Lee could not help but like the twins' mom. The woman did not completely fit in with her husband and children. She was average-looking in every sense of the word. Average height and weight with no dark, Eastern features. Her skin was the average pallor of a native Britain, her hair was graying which she distracted attention from by sweeping what was left of the true blond along either side of her temples.

The only glaringly unusual object on her person was her wedding ring. A crude gold band supported a rough black stone. Lee assumed it was jet, the petrified wood turned black by the sea which Whitby had once been famous for. She could not help but speculate whether the ring held any powers of its own. Perhaps it was meant to safeguard this very human wife of the vampire hunter.

With a wrinkle of her nose, logic won out and Lee reminded herself that it was probably just a ring.

"What do your parents do for a living?" Karen asked while passing around a bowl of mashed potatoes.

The normalcy of the question caught Lee off guard. "My parents? Living? Do?" As the table stared at her, food falling from their mouths or off the ends of their forks, Lee caught herself. "Oh! My parents!" Regaining her senses, she answered quickly, then stuffed a spoonful of peas into her mouth.

Karen seemed to be the only person interested, leaning in a bit. Her family went back to shoveling food into their faces. "American literature?"

"This year he's teaching through online. He loves it, except for having to record lectures into video files. As long as he doesn't have to take attendance every day, he's pretty happy.

"But you're in Whitby for your mother's work?"

Abelard Tepes leaned across the table, nearly smashing his elbow upon his plate. "Let's get some things straightened out, young woman. You are aware that our children told you some very delicate information."

"Dad, she knows how to keep a secret," Mira whined before taking another bite of potatoes.

"Good!" He aimed a glare directly at Lee. "Even if you did tell, no one would believe you anyway."

A deep clang rang through the room as Lee dropped her fork upon her plate. She returned the man's expression. "I don't even really believe it. Why would I think anyone else would?"

Her words intrigued Abelard. "If you don't believe then why did you agree to help us with Aubrey Ruthven?"

"I didn't. I agreed to be open to the idea of helping."

Karen tossed a pea at her husband which struck him

upon the temple. "I would not blame you for saying no after the third degree this man is giving you."

Mal gave a wry laugh. "It's like we never have company over for dinner or something."

Ignoring his son and wife, Abelard leaned back in his chair still eyeing Lee. "Look, I just want to make things very clear. It may not have been your fault. Ruthven must think you are easy for him to manipulate or he wouldn't have chosen you. You're caught between. Therefore, you are either with us or you are with them. We want your help, but we don't need your help."

Their dinner guest flinched. Cumbersome tension drowned every noise in the room before she replied in a slow, clear voice, "No one manipulated me."

The telephone started to ring, a sound that caught Lee off guard since she had grown so accustomed to the digital trills of cell phones. Her family had never owned a landline. Mira hopped up from the table as if expecting the call. Her mother continued to talk to Lee, despite her daughter leaving the table and speaking loudly into the receiver in the other room.

"Hello? Marshall! A film? I can't tonight—"

As Mira's conversation continued, Lee attempted to keep her attention on Mrs. Tepes. The woman stubbornly picked back up the small talk where it had been interrupted. "Your mother's work must be exciting. They are always finding new information out at the ruins."

"Not as exciting as my mom likes to make me believe." Lee took another bite of her food, suddenly self-conscious of whether she chewed too loud.

"Maybe you just don't know how to pay attention to things," Mal grumbled as he pushed around his peas with his fork.

Lee's head shot up. "What was that?"

"Nothing."

"Mal," Karen Tepes warned as if telling him not to fight with his sister on a car trip.

Lee tilted her head at Mal from across the table. "Maybe I should go. I would not wish to overstay my welcome, despite the lovely meal and your graciousness to invite me. I'm sorry, Mrs. Tepes." She started to rise from the table after shoveling in a last mouthful.

She passed Mira as she took her plate to the kitchen. The girl covered the mouthpiece of the phone with her hand. "Where are you going?" she whispered.

"Home. I'm tired and I have unpacking still to do. I don't think this was a good idea." She set her dish in the sink and zipped back up the coat she'd failed to remove.

Mira frowned as she spoke to the phone again. "Hold on a mo, Marshall." She then shouted backward at the dining room, "Mum, don't you think Lee should be walked home? She's new in town and there's Nos out there."

Lee began to protest as did Abelard Tepes. Karen Tepes gave her husband another dirty expression and ushered Mal out the door after Lee.

The girl began to walk quickly away, hoping to lose Mal before she even reached the bridge. Instead of running to catch up with her, Mal simply trailed at a leisurely pace.

As they wound through the city streets, she finally paused to wait for him. "I can walk myself; you know."

He shrugged, continuing his steady pace beside her. She waited for him to say something, anything. He continued to stroll, looking at the closed-up shop windows and keeping his mouth closed tightly.

"This is ridiculous!" she exclaimed in frustration. "Go home and leave me alone!"

Mal slowed his steps, his head raising a little and paying attention to something over her head.

When he still did not leave or respond, she added, "Please."

"Don't move." He reached into his coat where he kept a weapon prepared.

She froze. "Is there something behind me?"

Making the slightest motion with his head, he pulled her arm until she moved beside him. Lee turned and faced the spot where she had been standing. Dangling just above, his feet hooked upon an awning, a man hid in the shadows. His eyes were closed tightly, and his chest did not rise or fall.

"He's upside down like a bat! They really do that?" she hissed to Mal.

He squeezed her arm to insist upon her silence. Retrieving a wooden stake from within his jacket, he waited until the Nos's nose began to twitch. The eyes popped open, spotting them instantly. The upside-down man let out a hiss and plunged toward them. Mal pushed Lee down and skillfully leapt in the air at the same time the vampire landed. As the man showed off his fangs, Mal jumped upon his back. With the vampire tackled, he dug the pointed end of the stake through the man's back. There was a strangled cry, followed by silence.

"Didn't bring my sword," Mal grumbled. "They don't turn to dust until you remove the head. Here, help me prop him up in the alley so he looks asleep. Then, I can come back later and clean up."

The vampire lay dead at her feet, drool and red leaking from his mouth and eyes. "Gross." Still, Lee helped him drag the vampire into a shadowy place and slump the shoulders into a sitting position.

Mal surveyed their work, wiped his hands on his

trousers, and motioned to the road ahead of them. "Shall we?"

Lee wanted to be cool and match his easy-going stance. Instead, she screamed, "What the hell?" She pulled at her clothes as if blood had touched her from the battle. "You can't just murder a guy in the dead of night then turn to someone and say 'shall we'. How insensitive are you? I mean, for one thing, he was asleep. Maybe he wasn't planning on attacking if you hadn't stopped and startled him. Second, you pushed me to the ground and I think I landed in something. Third…No! You know what? One and two should be enough."

Mal stared at her blankly. After a few stunned seconds, he justified, "He would have killed someone." She gave him a glare, then twisted her back in order to check the seat of her jeans. He nervously watched and added after a while. "Um. Sorry, I pushed you."

"You should be."

He pulled his stake from the corpse's back. "I am."

"Good."

"Fine." They stood for another minute, looking awkwardly around the street, and avoiding each other's eyes. At last, Mal broke the moment with, "You do still want me to leave you alone?"

Lee gaped. "What? No! Are suffering from a form of lunacy? A vampire just jumped off the side of a building upside down! I want you to finish taking me home, damn it."

"Okay. Let's go."

"Fine." She muttered the word as a reluctant surrender.

"Fine," he repeated, hesitating in order to walk a step behind her. The back of her jeans was covered in a rusty color. The Nos must have fed upon someone just before they got there. The thought struck Mal as odd. Nos didn't eat people whole. Where was the human body?

"Are you looking at my ass?" Lee accused.

"No!" he answered much too quickly.

Silence engulfed them as they finished the walk to Lee's home, going from awkward to tense. She wished he would leave her at her door, yet somehow, he followed her inside. Her parents left a note that they were having dinner with Val and his girlfriend. The interior of their rented house seemed eerie and emptier than usual.

Mal came with her to the kitchen. "You okay to be alone?"

"I'm not a child," she countered.

"Give me a break," Mal grumbled.

"What?"

"Nothing."

He started to wander through the house without invitation. He scanned the partially unpacked books, a mix of classic and modern literature. Almost all award winners and bestsellers. An occasional trash novel infiltrated the collection, still the academic persona dominated. His parents never kept novels in the house. He and Mira usually borrowed fiction from the library. Both preferred the fiction about everyday life, no fantasy or horror involved.

Somehow, he ended up at Lee's door. He pushed it open and Lee jumped in his way.

"What are you doing?"

"Sorry, I just—" Mal really had no excuse. He did not know what compelled him to go snooping. He missed the feeling of normalcy he got when visited Ian's home. Ian had not even bothered to text him since he quit the football team.

His face must have betrayed some of his frustration

and disappointment because suddenly Lee was releasing a sigh and opening her door. "You checking for evidence of my other vampire-related crimes?"

Mal said nothing as he entered her room. Boxes and suitcases still littered the corners. He hovered near her desk, not wanting to further invade her privacy and yet not able to pull himself back into the hallway.

Lee quickly scooped up stray pants and straightened the little messes she normally never cared about. When she moved a wrinkled top, an electric wave reader and a flashlight fell out. Without waiting for him to ask, she explained, "It's from my ghost-hunting kit. I was in a club in London."

"You mean this isn't your first time dealing with the paranormal?"

The skepticism in Mal's voice for some reason made Lee smirk. "We never found anything. The guy who started our group, Oscar was his name, he called us the Future Resident Apparition Union Detectives."

The young man paused, uncertain if he should point out what he was thinking. However, he could not keep the thought back. "You know that stands for Fraud, right."

"Yes, I know. You see that was my job. I was the scientist. Oscar wanted me to join so they would seem legit."

"That's right. You said you don't believe in ghosts."

She gathered the kit and brushed her short hair over her ear. "Indeed, I do not."

He coughed a short laugh and studied her desk, which she had already managed to clutter in the few days she'd been in the house. Mal picked up her beloved rag doll, turning it over in his hands. Lee snatched it away from him protectively. "You have an Edgar Allen Poe doll," he stated without much surprise.

"I do," she answered, turning her back to him as she set Eddie on the bed, "I'm impressed you knew who he is supposed to be."

"It's hard to miss that receding hairline," Mal pointed out. "Besides, he wrote one of my favorite poems."

"You read poetry?" Lee spun back around to face him with disbelief.

With a shrug, he explained, "Not really. But my mom used to read it to Miranda and me."

Crossing her arms over her chest, she challenged the boy with her nose high in the air. "Let me guess; 'The Raven', right."

"She used to read us that one, yes." Lee turned away from him once more, making a scoffing noise that translated to a "thought so". Mal added swiftly, "But it's not my favorite."

"Dare I ask what your favorite is?"

He squinted at her for a long minute, a minute that made her remember that she did not particularly like this guy who had insulted her, pushed her, and treated her like she had done something wrong by talking to a charming, handsome young man in a train station.

He shook his head at her. "Nope." He walked from the room, wandering back to the front door. "Lock this behind me and do not invite anyone in."

"I've seen *Lost Boys*, thank you." She crossed her arms over her chest and cleared her throat, determined not to tell him good night or goodbye.

He wandered down the steps with a little smile, his relaxed pace carrying him through the dimly lit streets of Whitby. He tried pushing it away. The usual curmudgeonly voice at the back of his mind reminded him that he was a vampire hunter and there was going to be hell to deal with when he got home. His father never did see any of his actions as logical. Still, he had to admit, having someone know was nice, even if she was a pain in the ass.

His mind turned to Ian, as he crossed the street and passed the best friend's house. He knew he should talk to him, give some kind of further explanation. Mal hovered in front of the stoop, wondering if he should ring the bell. He tried to imagine the conversation in his mind. It ended in Ian not ever speaking to him again.

Mal turned from the stoop only to run directly into Ian. "Hey man," he muttered quickly, hoping Ian would let him pass without any further conversation. He studied the street, wishing the streetlights were brighter so he actually had something to look at.

"Hey mate," Ian replied. He sounded casual, yet his shoulders tensed, and additional words hovered at the corner of his mouth like crumbs.

Mal waited another twenty seconds, allowing the moment to grow steadily more awkward and more hopeless. Finally, he sidestepped his oldest buddy. "So... Cheers mate."

He made it to the end of the street before Ian trailed after, stopping Mal with a request. "Hold up." Mal obeyed, standing with one foot pointed in the direction he wished to escape. "Sooooo," Ian started with, holding out the word.

"So?" Mal responded with caution.

"So, I just saw you going around with some punk girl. What's going on there?"

At first, Mal was grateful for the familiar sound of Ian taking the piss out on him. Oddly, he wished the rest of their football team was there to razz him as well. Then, what Ian had said sunk in. His stomach knotted, a feeling he could not pinpoint the reason for. "She's a new friend of Miranda's," Mal explained flatly. "And not worth the trouble of anything more."

Ian looked upwards, squinting into the little bit of moonlight peeking through the clouds. "Mira's friend, huh? I was thinking she was the reason you left football."

"Oh, come off it!" Mal groaned as he tried to step around his friend.

Ian blocked Mal's escape. "It's not the first time a guy's picked a girl over sports, I just wanted to let you know that when you're ready, there's still a place on the team for you. Remember, we have months before the official practice season starts."

"It's not because of a girl, Ian," Mal insisted, wanting to tell his friend the truth. Mal knew what would happen to Ian if he knew. He would either think Mal was mental or he'd be a target for Nos who would assume he was a new member of the hunter party. And his brain faltered for a proper lie, one that would not be a complete lie and not completely end his friendship.

"Then what's going on with you?" Ian wanted to know, placing a hand against his friend's shoulder as if threatening to shove him.

"I told you, family stuff," Mal told him. "My dad doesn't want me playing. He needs me to work in the shop more."

"What if I talk to him? Or you could sneak out? I bet Miranda and that creepy new friend of hers would watch the souvenir shop when you go to practice," Ian suggested, his voice growing excited as more solutions flowed into his mind. "We can figure this out."

"I told you, I can't!" Mal growled.

Ian conceded, obviously angry. "You know I get wanting to help your family, but why can't you do both."

A deep, aggravated sigh emanated from Mal, an

attempt to breathe all his frustrations out. "Just drop it," he said with a calmness wrangled by his tense shoulders and the tightness in his chest.

Without a word, Ian turned and left, purposely walking along the opposite side of the street from Mal. As he watched his friend leave, Mal thought about all the times he had needed to lie to Ian. There was the time he had to cancel a double date, another occasion where he was supposed to help Ian babysit his little brother, and the worst was when missed Ian's thirteenth birthday party.

He stuffed his hands into his trouser pockets and took his time going home in the hopes that by the time he reached the flat over the shop, all the vampires of the world would magically disappear.

Chapter 9: "How True the Old Proverbs Are"

The sun did not wake Lee nor did her parents come in to see how her night had been. When she finally rose, her mom and dad both worked in their respective places, Mrs. McDaniels at the ruins and Mr. McDaniels in his office.

Lee hung in the doorway for a long moment, waiting for him to finish rifling through papers.

"Is something wrong?" he asked as he barely glanced up from his organizing.

She rubbed her black trouser leg with the opposite foot. "Nah." She shrugged.

He looked up, remembering something from long ago, something from when she had still been his little girl. "What is it? Do you want an egg? We can discuss whatever it is over eggs."

"It's nothing, Dad. I'm just standing. Jeez." She marched off to the kitchen. She stayed in the other room for five minutes, pretending to rifle through the cabinets in search of breakfast. After giving up, she returned to her father's study. "Dad?"

"Yes, my darling girl?" Her father sat on the floor with stacks of papers and books in purposeful piles around him.

"When you were a kid did you even believe in . . . weird stuff?" She wanted to know almost mournfully.

Mr. McDaniels stood up straight, giving her his full attention. "Is this about your paranormal club? I'm sorry you're going to miss your ghost-hunting mates, but you always said they were illogical anyway."

"No. No, this isn't about that." Her eyes faltered, thinking again about the friends she had left behind. She physically shook them away, returning her brain to its original worry. "I mean like vampires and monster type of stuff."

He mulled over the idea while moving a folder from one pile to another. "Are you wondering where Stoker got the idea for Dracula? We talked about some of this already, remember? Order of the Dracul and all. Lee, stories can be born from some of the strangest sources. Did you know, when James Fennimore Cooper began to develop the idea for the Pathfinder and Last of the Mohicans—"

Frustrated, Lee crushed her fingers into a ball. "This isn't a literary question. I'm talking about believing in something, even though you know it couldn't possibly be true." She tried to think of an example he would relate to. Instead, she found herself giving vague scenarios. "You know, like when you see something for the first time, something you never thought could be real, and you just— You just don't know what to do after that. Like knowing that a new thing changes too many other things? Do you understand?"

The man released a grunt as he rose from the floor. "No, I don't think I do." He moved toward her with a concerned expression. "Lee, what is this actually about? Did something happen with that family who invited you over for dinner last night? Or is this about that about that Ruthven person we ran into on the street?" Waiting only a minute, he added in his most uncomfortable and uncertain parental tone, "You can tell me anything, even if you think I won't like it."

She mulled over the words. "Dad, I was attacked by vampires and now I feel like the whole world is upside down and out to get me. I don't know how to feel normal again." They summed everything up so well that she did not know how else to put it. Yet, when her jaw dropped, she told him, "It's just that Chelsea thought she saw something and she's all freaked out. I don't know what to tell her."

Mr. McDaniels rested his hand atop his daughter's head. "Oh, to be a teenager again. I don't envy you, I can say that much. Everything is so new and every day you feel as if your world could collapse after the littlest upset. Do you know what Washington Irving said once?"

"I'm sure he said a lot of things."

"One of the greatest and simplest tools for learning more and growing is doing more." He removed his hand, spun her around by her shoulders, and commanded in his strongest, most convincing voice, "Now, put on your coat and go for a walk!"

He pushed her gently back toward her bedroom. "A walk?" she called back as she wandered down the hall.

"Of course. Clear your head. See sights, hear sounds, and buy some taffy. Things will look better with some fresh air and then you can call Chelsea."

"Do you just want taffy?"

Her dad paused for several seconds, staring at her blankly as if she spoke Japanese as a first language. He pointed a stern hand at her at last and repeated with renewed vigor, "Go for a walk! And be careful!"

Lee did as she was told, after showering and dressing. The calm after so much storm upset her further. She waited for the other shoe to drop like a vampire would simply burst into her home for no reason. Still, as she mulled over the idea of going for a walk, she suddenly realized that she was outside.

The cold air brought her out of her thoughts, awakening her senses and making her more aware than she'd felt in days. The sun peeked through the clouds, playing against shop windows and off people's mobile phone screens. The lights reflected and danced on the sidewalk, leading Lee out to the boardwalk. Despite the cold, people moved at a steady pace as if the rhythm of the waves nearby dictated their steps.

When they lived in London, her parents would send her out in the same manner and she would be happy to go. She and Chelsea would hop on the underground or a bus and travel to corners of the city they'd never visited before. Within the heart of the city, they could people-watch the tourists and flirt with university students on holiday. A walk in Whitby did not offer the same sense of excitement.

She ended up near the statue of Captain Cook, the staunch-looking British sailor who stared off into the distance. The statue had been placed in an open area with a compass rose decorating the ground. She really had no interest in him or who he had been, yet for some reason, as she stopped at the base and read the name of his ship carved into the stone, she felt better.

"Resolution," she muttered to herself. "Funny."

She stayed at the statue for a long while. "There are no such things as vampires." She repeated the phrase to herself as she bought taffy for her dad. She thought it while she text Chelsea, confirming that her friend was coming for a visit that weekend. And she was still thinking about it when she saw a handsome young man wearing thick sunglasses waiting for her near the mouth of the river.

"Hello," he greeted with a gentlemanly smile, making Lee's heart flutter.

"There's no such thing as vampires," she replied. In the back of her mind, the old phrase taunted her, *"There are exceptions to every rule."*

Aubrey Ruthven's face fell. "I suppose the Bobbsey Twins told you some vague, despicable reason why I've been banished from Whitby," he said with a sneer. "Did they also tell you that I'm a fiend?"

Lee felt her lips part and words spill out. "They haven't told me many details. They didn't really make you out to be the horrible Bela Lugosi monster of old horror films." She studied him with curiosity. "You keep following me, don't you?"

He answered with complete seriousness. "I like you. I won't deny it."

Her eyes frowned, yet the rest of her face stayed matter-of-fact. "They told me there's something in Whitby that keeps them here. They said you want whatever it is." Lee pointed upward in the church hovering over them, the tower visible from the cliff's edge. "You know what's up there, don't you?"

"Not exactly," Aubrey explained. "A legend says that it would rid the world of our race."

"And you want to make sure you have control of it? Or is it that you want to die? Am I supposed to believe you are this noble monster trying to save the world from yourself?"

"I don't think it means death. Much of what I've translated suggests that we will become something else, something that will not need to feed off human life." He tilted his head up at the cliff. "It was one of my kind who first chanced it through the continent. His name was

Udolpho and he feared change so much that he spent his entire life in search of this object simply so he could destroy it. But the hunters were searching too. We are still drawn to it, to here, blood suckers and soul stealers alike. Even though we know the permanent Tepes family in residence creates great danger."

Realizing that they were surrounded by normal people routinely living out their lives, Lee lowered her voice. "Are you trying to manipulate me? Did you pick me because you thought I'd be easy to trick?"

He removed his glasses. Beneath, his eyes were closed tightly, and he rubbed his hand across them. "I'm sorry, Lee. I got you mixed into this. I saw an opportunity and I took it. I used you and it almost got you killed."

"The old woman. You sent her after me, didn't you."

Aubrey Ruthven motioned to a bench. He sat first. Lee deliberated before sitting as far to the opposite side of the seat as she could. "I turned her. That I confess. And I did send her to Whitby. When a new vampire is sired, they can be given a single command from their master. That command must be acted out or they are forever within the power of their master. The command I gave the woman was to follow you." He rubbed his hand along his thigh anxiously. "I should have been more specific and said look after you. She apparently thought I was giving her a snack."

"Why should I believe you?"

"I'm not here to convince you. I'm here to beg forgiveness. When I sent the old woman to watch you, I thought that would give me an opportunity to finish what I came here to do and still have a chance to run into you again." His hands continued to worry at the fabric of his jeans. "I didn't think about what the old woman would do when she had found you. I don't sire many vampires, you see." He paused, thinking Lee would have a comment. Her jaw clenched and continued. "I also did not take into account that the latest Tepes generation would be a pair of twins following you around. They must like you to keep you safe."

"Like you, they think they can use me for something." She leaned forward and dug her fingers into the bench on either side of her.

Ruthven also lowered his shoulders so his elbows rested upon his knees. His fingers wove in and out apprehensively. "And that's the other thing I want to apologize for. I've put you in the middle of something, haven't I? Lee, listen to me, but don't look at me if you're worried that I'm, as you so delicately put it, manipulating you. I am so sorry that I ruined things for you. You can't be ignorant to the monsters and the dangers of the dark. You probably feel like you can never be a normal girl again. I just wanted to know you." She heard the release of a deep breath. "If I can find a way to fix this, I will. I just need to do what I came here to do first."

She kept her eyes staring straight ahead. Lee did not watch the sea or the people as they passed. She just stared. The urge to spill her life's story to Ruthven did not come this time. She did not wish to flip her hair and giggle. Her mind wondered about his sincerity. The fretting sound of his rough hands rubbing coarse fabric was not the sort of uneasy noise she expected to hear from a smooth, debonair vampire.

"Damn it. You are good. You are very good." Lee gave him a merciful smile. "I had to hear the twins out. I guess I can extend to you the same courtesy."

The wrinkles in his brow melted and he flashed her the knee quivering grin. "That's more than I deserve."

"Yes. It is." Leaning against the bench back, she

proclaimed, "This is me listening."

From beneath his sunglasses, she realized he was studying her. "Where should I start?"

"Start with the thing you came here for. The mysterious mumbo-jumbo causing object is hidden somewhere on the cliff. I already know that it's why the vampire hunters are here. So, why do you want it?"

"The mysterious 'it' is, I believe, a crest, the family symbol of the vampire who sired me. Many vampires are drawn here, to it, without them even realizing."

"Mal and Miranda said they are drawn to it too," Lee spoke with hesitation, uncertain if she should reveal too much of what the twins had shared with her.

"It might be the same family bloodline."

"Tepes? You were sired by Vlad III's bloodline." The words were a statement that he did not dispute or confirm. "Is that why they banished you? It is because you were sired by Dracula?"

Aubrey Ruthven sighed, rubbing his eyes once more and forcing his glasses to momentarily lean against his forehead. When he removed his hand, the glasses slipped back into place, never giving Lee a chance to see his true eyes. "I did something. . . horrible. I mean, I *am* a monster, but this was my lowest moment."

She waited patiently for him to answer, all the while keeping on the lookout for passing strangers who might overhear their conversation. She coaxed him with a nudge of her fingers across the back of his knuckles. He responded with an uncertain expression.

"It's the one thing I must do in order to be free. I must find the crest and bring it to the one who sired me. In theory, all of my kind will be free." He removed an old locket from the inner pocket of his thin jacket. The object was heart-shaped with a metal frame and red stones along the top. Glass had been used in place of the usual gold doors so Lee could easily see the lock of brown hair within.

"This is a reminder," he started with three protective fingers curled at the edges of the locket, "of the last of my humanity I lost in trying to get that crest." He tucked the locket back out of sight. "I betrayed someone and, in turn, I think she betrayed me. She trusted me to be better than I am, but I was so desperate to fulfill my duty—"

"What did you do?"

"The last time I was here, it was still a time when people suspected, even believed in vampires. The generation of the Tepes family at the time was exceptionally skilled and revered. The people of Whitby never said it out loud, but they were secretly grateful they were there. However, the truth was that they were perfectly safe from my kind. The vampire hunters went on a killing spree, exterminating most of us. They went so far as to check every ship coming into harbor executing anyone who they even suspected of being a supporter."

Longing burned through the lenses of his glasses, seeing something in her that he wished for. She thought maybe he was remembering when he was alive and innocent to all of the darkness in the world. "I was obsessed. You are probably not familiar with that kind of want. When I think of the crest, my skin literally itches at the thought of not having it. And the Tepes family was in my way."

He trailed off, not certain if he truly wanted her to know. His hand ran down the side of her face, tracing her ear and playing with the purple hair at her temple. Lee froze, not sure if she should run or allow the action to continue. Her hand gently pulled his away and she exhaled heavily, attempting to stay patient. "What happened?"

His arms dropped and his face turned to a horrified frown. "I wanted revenge on the vampire hunters. One night, as their father and mother were exterminating my people, I crept into their home. They had seven children, six boys and a girl—"

Lee breathed lightly, wanting him to finish and dreading it at the same time.

"The girl escaped me and she took the smallest of her brothers with her. But the others— I made certain their parents would feel everything I did to them. My goal that night was not simply to kill, but to destroy. I left their bodies mangled and placed where their parents would have that image as the first thing to greet them at home." Aubrey Ruthven slumped against the bench and grumbled, "I had never done anything so awful or intimate."

Lee's pulse raced, not wanting to know the details, but still full of questions. She may have been curious about the morbid and dark, yet she drew the line at stories about murdered children. Her paranormal group once wanted to explore the former hometown of Mary Ann Cotton, the famous child slayer, and Lee could not handle it.

"But you're a vampire. Don't you kill to live? And in all of the great vampire stories they eat children. Are you trying to tell me you had never killed a child before that?"

Aubrey Ruthven stood, pacing with his perfect posture betraying his discomfort at telling his dark secret. "Never intentionally or when a child was healthy. Occasionally, I have fed on children who were near death, I admit to that, and I know that many of my blood-sucking cousins will feed on the young. This was different than eating. This was me mercilessly destroying lives just because I wanted something." His fist balled up and slapped against a wall nearby. Blood dripped from scratches as he retracted the hand. "I tried to justify it in my mind. I told myself that someday they would grow up and kill me. Then, the image of them, of their faces, haunted me. Their mother committed suicide. She threw herself from the East Cliff. Their father eventually went mad and was locked away. What I had done had even stunned him."

"Then who cast the spell that kept you from ever coming back?" Lee wanted to know, nearly forgetting that she was talking to a horrible creature.

His hand touched the place where the locket remained hidden between the fabric and his chest. "That's a story for another day."

Lee whistled. "Wow. That's—" A realization hit her and she stood to smack his arm. "Wait! If you did anything that horrible here, why did you even bother ever coming back?" She awaited an answer. She received an ashamed downcast of his head and an embarrassed shuffling of his feet. "You still want that thing! Even after what you did? This is not the proper way to display remorse for an evil deed."

"I am remorseful," he insisted. "And I still want the crest. You have to understand. The crest can create peace!"

Lee's chest swelled with annoyance, yet she couldn't bring herself to shoot him down as quickly as did the Tepes siblings. "Did Dracula tell you that?" Lee scoffed. "Peace with whom, may I ask? You kill humans to survive. I'm really doubtful that my race is going to be too accepting just because you wave around an ancient artifact." Lee rose from her own seat in an attempt to look braver than she felt.

Aubrey Ruthven took a step back, giving her distance to judge him or believe him as she needed. "Peace with the vampire hunters. There are plenty of ways for us to feed ourselves these days without being killers. And there are more humans than you would think willing to be a living drinking vessel to a vampire who needs blood."

"If that's true, then why did you kill the old woman at the train station in York?" Lee wanted to know, the thought of the vampire dentures still made her uneasy.

"An accident. Which proves why I need the help of the Tepes family. They could regulate us. Maybe set up ways for us to live without accidents like that one. They probably know more about Nos, as they call us, than we ourselves do."

She considered Mal and his reaction to such an idea. Or worse yet, Mal's father. He would chop off Ruthven's head before any words could be spoken.

"And if they won't help you? What then?"

"I can only hope that the crest will convince them." He eyed her and dared to move closer once again. "You don't have to believe me, but please, just think about what I'm saying. Life would be easier on all sides if no one had to attack another in the streets any longer. And Whitby is the perfect place to test ideas for reform. The one who sired me would not mind if I used the crest for this purpose before I deliver it, I'm sure of it."

Lee wanted to believe him, yet the entire plot sounded preposterous. Vampires weren't peaceful. She already knew that from first-hand experience. Ruthven did not seem evil either. People didn't call a lion evil when it fed on a gazelle. It was simply the circle of life. Then again, the Disney song never mentioned children of the night in their diagram.

She turned away from him, not ready to say anything else.

"Can I talk to you again tomorrow?" he asked after her.

"Why?"

"Because I like talking to you. Trust me, the older you get, and the worse society becomes, the more difficult it is to find intelligent conversation."

Lee continued to walk, saying more to herself than to him, "Do you expect me to just be so happy that you said that?"

"Time will tell. Until tomorrow."

She rolled her eyes at him and escaped down the road toward the shopping center.

Chapter 10: "Of Wolves and Poison and Blood"

There were a few days before Chelsea's arrival and the thought of her friend visiting created a sweet relief within Lee's mind. Her dad sent her out to pick up the necessary junk food required for company.

Lee had never been a big fan of crowded shopping centers, yet she could not deny that she enjoyed shopping. She liked not only the hunt and surprise new products could bring, but also the people watching. Men, women, and children displayed all the greatest examples of disappointment, elation, and desperation when they scoured stores for that perfect item. Through it all, her heart stopped whenever she saw a man wearing sunglasses; then delved into disappointment as she realized it was not Ruthven.

She noticed a group of kids her own age all gathered near a toy store. One of the boys, who seemed to be the very essence of immaturity and irresponsibility, had purchased a robot dog that did flips when you put in batteries. His friends were all telling him what a nerd he was while he attempted to convince them of the awesomeness of his new toy.

"Seriously, were you drunk?" Lee heard a familiar female voice inquire. She noticed Miranda standing amongst the group, laughing and blending in. A normal teen. Her head started to turn in Lee's direction and the girl spun on her heel.

Lee heard the soft-soled boots follow her along the pavement. She ducked into a shop, not caring what they sold. The plastic sack full of snacks banged against her side. Miranda caught up with her and flung herself into the building so quickly that she nearly plowed over Lee.

"Oh, sorry," Miranda stated as she realized who she had run into. "Hey, sorry Mal and my dad were knob-heads the other night. What are you up to?"

Taking a look around, Lee searched for an escape. She stood in an electronics shop, full of DVDs, Blu-rays, and video games. "Just looking for an old movie," she lied.

"Which one? I can help you look," Miranda volunteered as she began to paw at the shelves. Lifting up a '70s horror flick, she waved the image of a buxom blond screaming at a floating skull at Lee. "I have this film! Ever seen it? It's bad, but fun! If you haven't, you should come over and watch it tonight!"

"Don't you have school tomorrow?"

"Our parents have us skip a lot for family stuff. Don't you have school too?"

"I'm finishing the term through online schooling."

"Then it's perfect!"

Lee wanted to make a snarky comment and use a lame excuse to escape. However, Miranda was blameless. Her actions were not malicious or teasing. With a sigh, Lee responded, "This is probably a despicable question, but don't you have some friends you can be hanging out with?"

Miranda's smile did not falter. She bluntly stated, "Sure. I have quite a few friends actually. I guess I'd be considered popular. But half of them aren't really real friends and the others have been the sort of people that are great for pub crawls and nights out. I wouldn't bring any of them home though. Even if my home wasn't full of Nos stuff."

"Oh." Lee wished she could think of something more to say. She took the DVD from Miranda's hands and read the description on the back cover. The back of her mind poked at her, reminding her of the number of times she could never have anyone over because her mother didn't want Lee's friends to see the academic mess their home was in. Or the number of times they moved and she didn't even have time to make friends. A soft spot grew in Lee's heart for Miranda. Maybe the girl would be more open if she told her about Ruthven's want for peace. And the movie summary made Lee want to watch it. "What time do you want to hang out tonight?"

Miranda squealed slightly; a ditzy excited noise that made Lee regret her decision. "Nineteen hundred hours. Bring a sleeping bag if you want! You can stay over so long as you don't mind if my dad wakes us up in the middle of the night because he senses a Nos. That happens a lot."

"Seven it is," Lee replied, nervous at the idea of staying in that house overnight with Miranda's suspicious father, despondent brother, and, of course, bubbly Miranda herself.

"Great! I'll make popcorn! Microwave cooking is about all the cooking I know." Miranda giggled at her own joke. "What film are you looking for here?"

"I don't think they have it. It doesn't look like this place has a wide selection of black and white movies," Lee fibbed. "I should get going home and eat before I go to your house, so I'll see you in a bit." Miranda waved at her as Lee exited the shop.

As she turned a corner, Lee felt someone closely follow her. Halting her steps, she waited as Ruthven revealed himself. "Were you spying?"

He moved up alongside her, motioning that he wanted her to keep walking. She did her best to match his wide gait.

"I'm not the only one keeping an eye on you," he told her in a low whisper. "That woman has been watching you ever since the vampire hunter girl chased you down."

With as little turn of her head as she could manage, Lee glanced back to see a petite lady clinging to the shadow of a building. The woman was in her thirties, dyed black hair hung in over her gaunt features. She dressed in a velvet skirt and jacket which matched the fabric of the choker covering her throat.

"Is that a Nos supporter? She looks like a drug addict."

She felt a protective hand at the small of her back leading her through the crowd. "I've been trying to convince most of my friends in Whitby that you aren't a threat, but when you accept invitations to sleepovers at the home of vampire hunters—"

"I'm trying to help. You want to be able to talk to them, right? Mira will be your best chance."

"Yes, but are they willing to keep you safe when the bloodsuckers come after you in a blind rage? Lee, I didn't tell you any of this so you could get yourself killed." Realizing that the goth woman had started to chase after them, Ruthven stopped Lee. People pushed around them, not noticing how he focused on the thin shape barreling in their direction.

Ruthven leapt up into the air with complete grace and stealth. He drifted swiftly over the heads of the shoppers. Lee waited for someone to stop and take photos on their phone, or at the very least point. Instead, he landed directly in front of the spy, his boots hitting the sidewalk without a sound.

The woman held up her arms to him with the wrists pointed upward. "My lord?" she meekly offered.

Ruthven wrapped his hand into the folds of her jacket to keep her in place. She cowered, keeping her wrists between them. Lee could not hear the words he spoke, but she felt the growl of each syllable within her stomach. He then tossed the woman backward.

"Take us to who sent you!"

"Of course, my lord," she squeaked.

Ruthven walked back to Lee and wrapped a protective arm around her waist. "We are going to set a few things straight. But I need you to be brave and to trust me."

They moved in synchronization through the crowd a few feet behind the goth woman.

"She wanted you to kill her." Lee studied the unhealthy frame and unsteady movements of their guide.

"She wanted to sacrifice herself as punishment for getting caught. This is what I'm talking about, Lee. Being friends with those twins is dangerous."

"And they say the same thing about you."

The woman directed them to a building not far from where Lee and Mal had seen the vampire hanging upside down. The place looked deserted with boards and no trespassing signs covering the windows. The Nos supporter took them along an alley to the back and slipped easily through a half-open window. Ruthven followed, adjusting the window's height then helped Lee through. His arm resumed its place at her waist once they entered the dimly lit room.

Lee's eyes adjusted quickly to the dark as she tried not to trip over any stray furniture. They ended up in a center room where no windows or sunlight could find the occupants. The smell, a mix of body odor and copper, caught her senses first. Neon signs hung along each wall, being used to provide a soft, multicolored illumination to an otherwise black room. One person retrieved a clear, mylar bag of deep red from a mini-fridge at in a corner. People sat huddled together upon old sofas and on blankets against walls. Lee studied each person, realizing that some were vampires, with desperation and hunger in their eyes, and others were the supporters.

One woman upon a chair removed her fangs from within a blond man's upper chest. Wiping the crimson from the corner of her mouth as she moved toward the unexpected company, her food source moaned, "My lady, you are not finished. You need to keep up your strength."

The woman offered him a sweet smile. "Robby, your concern is very endearing, but this is more important." She crossed her arms over her hourglass figure. "Isn't it, Ruthven?"

"Sibella, I have not come for a fight—"

The eyes of the female blood sucker glistened. The red of a neon sign advertising body piercing reflected all of her pain and worry. "Ruthven, what have you done? I created this place for us to hide. And you showed her exactly where to find us. And if she can find us, so can the Tepes family." The calm turn of her head and steady cadence of her voice could not hide how she pleaded with Lee. "We are not killing or hurting anyone. Everyone here is a volunteer and we are able to supplement out diet with bagged blood. Do you understand that? We are not like some of the other groups. We just want to be left in peace!" Her cold hands grasped for the edge of Lee's top wildly. "I keep them safe. I keep them from killing. Why can't the hunters ever understand that?"

For once, the teenage girl had nothing to say. She

stared pitying at the anxious creature. Ruthven pushed Sibella gently away. "She is not here to report you. She's trying to help us. And in return, you must swear to me that you will not follow or harm her."

"How can you trust her? She is one of them—"

"Sibella!" Ruthven snapped his warning and the hysterical vampire calmed herself. The human she'd called Robby rushed to her side and led her back to the chair. He and the rest of the room gave Ruthven a collection of nasty expressions. Their looks did not faze Ruthven who addressed them with all the poise of a diplomat.

"You put yourselves at risk by mistrusting a girl. I need you to trust me and in order to do that, you must trust her."

"You've been gone for centuries. You don't know what it's like!" Another male vampire sitting on the floor accused. He cocooned himself in an old quilt as if it would guard him from Ruthven.

The matriarch leapt, a beautiful fluid motion that took a mere second to take her from her seat to pinning Ruthven against a wall. Lee felt his arms violently ripped away from her and the woosh of wind.

He reacted with a snarl, clawing all ten fingers at the wall behind him. "How dare you!"

"You will not harm us!" Her words were low, no hiss or monstrous sound, just a promise.

"You think I don't know what you've been through! I have been hunted across the globe. I was hunted before you were ever sired." As his speech ended, he jerked his shoulder forward, using the wall to fling her across the room. The faded wallpaper against his back chipped off as he pushed himself to the center of everyone.

The others, human and vampire, tensed, ready to

protect their mistress. She waved them off, silently insisting on a fair fight. Sibella's legs steadied. Creases along her eyes and mouth drew the story of her rage.

Without a thought, Lee ran to the middle with Ruthven. "Please don't! I'll leave! I'll never tell anyone, I swear!" Her heart banged away like the bass of a metal song and sweat trickled along her brow. Ruthven's hand came around her back and protectively pulled her against him.

At the movement, Sibella went instantly limp. She sat herself back down with a tired sigh. "You poor girl." She pinched the bridge of her nose and she repeated in a barely audible tone, "You poor foolish girl."

Lee wanted to ask why this elder of monsters pitied her but felt Ruthven's arm tighten along her waist.

"I need your word that that you will leave her be!" he demanded.

Sibella nodded her head weakly. "I do not see what choice we have."

Nothing more was said. Ruthven took Lee from the building and held her hand as they walked back out to the crowded streets. She squinted up at him, daylight burning her retinas. "Are you, like, a king or something? They treated you like a leader."

"It's because of who sired me. They give me reverence because I'm a servant to someone older and more powerful than them. Now, just because I asked them to leave you alone doesn't mean that there are not still groups of my kind that will kill a human on sight, especially a human who is hanging around vampire hunters. That in there—" He quirked his mouth at her with concern. "Are you alright?"

Lee slipped away from him. "What was that place?"

"The ones who do not want to kill or attack to feed

must live in hiding in this town."

"I feel bad for them. Do you think the crest would really help them?"

He gave her arm a friendly squeeze. "I think you could really help them."

She bumped her grocery sack playfully against his leg. "Can you walk me home? I need to mentally prepare for another evening in the Tepes home."

Chapter 11: "I wish I could fathom his mind"

Lee's parents were shocked when she announced that she was going to a sleepover. Her mother, sensing a new form of rebellion, asked with trepidation, "A sleepover where?"

Lee repeated that it was the same family she'd had dinner with, leaving out any reference to vampires. Her mom grew even more suspicious.

"This girl? Doesn't she have school tomorrow?"

"Her parents said it was okay." Not entirely true, but Lee assumed it would be by the time she arrived.

"And the parents are going to be home tonight?"

"Yes."

"And this twin brother, he's not going be. . . sleeping in the same room as you girls?"

"Mom!"

"It's a legitimate question."

"I'm leaving. I'm leaving now." Lee was not sure which was worse, staying home or going to the Tepes' house with the angered expression of Sibella still in her mind. Still, something pulled at her in her gut, telling her to go. She packed up her pajamas, toothbrush, and clothes for the following day in a messenger bag decorated with characters from Tim Burton films. She also rummaged through her wardrobe for anything she could use as a weapon. She settled on an old dowel that had broken off from a cupboard within the closet.

She kept the "stake" in her coat pocket as she exited and started for the "old town" area across the bridge. Her walk was full of purpose, her head high and her strides swift, hoping nothing would mistake her for an easy target. With so many vampires in the city, how did anyone go out at night? Why wasn't Miranda out patrolling like Buffy the Vampire Slayer? Maybe Abelard Tepes still held the main role as vampire hunter until his kids were older?

As she crossed the bridge, her eyes were drawn to St. Mary's Church on the hill. Her mind thought of both the twins' and Aubrey Ruthven's tales. Something was up there in the graveyard, something that could change it all. And the town went about its life with schools and shopping and catering to tourists, never knowing the number of them in danger by the war occurring.

She reached the shop without incident, going up the stairs at the back to knock on the door. She thought of staying for only a little while, then faking sick and leaving. But then she would have to explain herself to her parents. As Lee resigned herself to an evening of girly talks and vampire lore, Mrs. Tepes answered the door.

"Welcome back," she greeted with a grin.

"Thanks." Lee went awkwardly into the small home, all of the manners her parents had forced upon her running through her mind.

Karen Tepes bolted the door after. Miranda had been sitting in a large chair, watching the latest prime-time soap about teenagers in London dealing with sex, abuse, and other cheerful topics. Mal and Mr. Tepes were nowhere in sight.

"Oh good!" she exclaimed as she jumped up. "Come on." She had already popped a bowl of popcorn in preparation. She carried it with her and motioned eagerly for Lee to follow through a hallway.

The family portraits hung throughout the house were mostly musty paintings or old photos. Many of their ancestors glared at Lee from their sepia-tone prisons. A number of them were missing eyes and hands. Vampire hunting seemed to be just as dangerous as it sounded. Each portrait included a wife and family. Despite the idea of mortal peril and the short lifespan, each generation managed to marry and bear a son to carry the family name. Lee counted the children in each generation, trying to guess which poor group had been Ruthven's victims.

They paused at an open door and Miranda ducked into the room. It was a small bedroom without much in the way of décor. Her brother sat at a desk covered in thick, leather-bound tomes.

Mal wheeled himself closer to the table, concentrating intently on the ancient text as if cramming for an exam. His sister skipped into the room and leaned down beside him so her face was at the same level as his. "Boring," she mumbled. "The Witches Hammer was much more interesting."

"It's also rubbish and you know it," Mal grunted, burying his nose further into the book. He heard the squeak of a floorboard behind him and spun about. Lee stood just outside the doorframe scratching the back of her right ankle with the left end of her steel-toed boot. "Why is she here?" he added, not caring if the goth girl heard him.

Miranda hopped back from the table. "She's my friend and I invited her over. We're going to watch 70s slasher films and gorge ourselves on sugar. That way we can be keyed up and scream like banshees at the scary bits, like what normal girls do. Want to join in?"

"I don't really want to be a girl, but thanks."

"Ha. Ha."

"Horror movies? Don't we get enough of that around here? And what are Mum and Dad going to say when they see you brought her round again?" Mal was now pointing rudely at Lee who glowered at him.

Lee opened her mouth to defend herself, but his pointed index finger shook as he said, "This is family business; you don't get to talk." And the girl turned red as she held her breath.

"Mum said it was alright," Mira smugly declared.

"Alright?" Mal repeated with a cough. "Why don't we just have her over for Christmas as well? She can see how instead of tissue paper crowns, Dad stuffs the crackers with Japanese protective spells. You'll love it."

"I won't be here at Christmas," Lee put in, relieved to punctuate how short her stay in Whitby planned on being.

Miranda just smiled. "Really, Malachi? Is the problem that I am letting a friend into our little private world or is this because Mum never let Ian come over?"

The boy's ears tinted pink as his rude stare attempted to turn Lee to stone.

His sister's smile grew into a knowing smirk. "Or is it that I'm letting this particular person in?"

Instantly, Mal's scarlet face returned to his book. "Please yourselves," he growled.

Miranda skipped back to Lee, taking her bag without asking. "I do believe I won that fight. Come on. There's a telly in my room where he can't bother us."

Miranda's room smelled strongly of sage and roses. It was as equally tiny as her brother's room; still, she utilized the space well. She had a desk cluttered with notes from classmates, photos, and tiny stuffed animals.

Her computer tower was decorated with zany, multicolored stickers. The bed sat at the center of the room facing a television atop a chest of drawers. Her clothes were scattered, most likely from morning after morning of changing her mind halfway through dressing.

As they settled in, Lee had to confess that it was a cozy, bright room. She was not really a fan of bright, but it worked. The only features out of place were the many strange symbols carved into the wood around her window. Outside of the windowpane was a planter box full of the shriveled remains of long green leaves.

"Garlic," Mira explained when she noticed Lee's curiosity. "Frost killed it. I have to plant more in the spring."

"That stuff works?"

"It doesn't disintegrate Nos into dust or anything. It's more like it gives them hay fever or asthma. They try to avoid it at any cost, but it won't kill them even if they breathe it in."

Lee lay on the bed on her stomach with her feet kicked into the air. "You know, that word is really dumb. Can we just call them vampires?" Her heavy boots sat on the floor next to her messenger bag.

Miranda set up the DVD player, excitedly telling the story of the appliance. "Mum and Dad told me that if I brought my marks up last year, they would pay for my telly license. I don't think they actually thought I could do it, but—" She waved her hands in front of the TV like a magician attempting to pull a rabbit from a hat. "I showed them," she said with a laugh. Then she reached across the equipment and pressed play. "Lights, on or off?"

"I don't care either way," Lee confessed. She had watched enough horror movies that the amount of light didn't matter to her. Fictional beasties with long claws and psychos in hockey masks rarely upset her.

The lights shut off and the room was soaked in the blue and white of the copyright warning which played before the movie started. As Miranda settled on her stomach beside Lee and the opening credits of the movie rolled, Lee happened to think about Miranda's struggle with grades. "If you're going to be a vampire hunter, why is it so important that you do well in school?"

"Mum says there is never any excuse for being non-academic," Miranda repeated, her voice chiming like a recorded phone message.

The spooky music of the film began, leaving Miranda's words in an eerie haze. As the first victim of the killer was chased up the stairs when she should have run out the front door, Lee laughed. "Could academics have saved this girl?"

"Exactly," Miranda replied, "You can't hunt vampires if you're letting yourself get trapped upstairs and wearing a prom dress. Are proms really that big in America?"

Lee raised an eyebrow at Miranda. "I haven't lived in the states for a few years now. Besides, do I really look like someone who would keep track of high school social rituals?"

Rolling onto her side, Miranda scrutinized Lee jokingly. "You mean, you weren't the head cheerleader at your last school?" She giggled the last words, as if she could not tease with a straight face.

"Okay, smarty, if you could do something else with your life; be something else, what would you be?" Lee questioned curiously.

Laying herself flat on her stomach once again, Miranda made a "Huh" sound which was nearly drowned out by the shrieking actress on screen. "You mean if I wasn't a vampire hunter's daughter?"

"Yep."

"I never thought about it. I like my life, Lee. Really." She thought about pausing the film, but went on talking without rising from the bed or searching for the remote.

The movie continued to play. One of the actresses choked and scrambled as the killer sauntered toward her with an axe. His pace was steady, yet the running girl could not escape him. Miranda giggled at the silly girl's terrified movements.

As the fake blood splattered the actress's frilly prom dress, Miranda added, "I think I'd still want to be a vampire hunter, if I had the choice. It's what keeps my life exciting."

As Mira spoke, Lee's brain clicked to life. Mira was the normal-seeming one, keeping up the pretense so their lives did not draw attention. Mal wanted to be normal but could not pretend. Fitting in came naturally to his sister.

"Vampire hunter is not usually something they check for on career aptitude tests," Lee pointed out dully. "I mean, from the boring, ordinary, average job choices, what would you want to be?"

Rolling over onto her back, Miranda sighed. She reached her hands up over her head, watching the light from the TV cast shadows on the ceiling. "I like working in the shop. But I wouldn't want to sell souvenirs. Maybe accessories, like cute handbags and hats. Oh! And scarves. I could see myself selling scarves."

Lee nodded. She couldn't really relate. She'd grown up being encouraged to be a research assistant or a doctorate of some obscure topic or a museum curator. None of her dream jobs or family career paths included "cute handbags". In order to be supportive, Lee simply replied, "I like scarves. I have about a dozen at home. They're all black though."

"Doesn't that get boring?"

"No. They're different shades of black."

"It doesn't matter anyway. I was born this."

"Yes, but what if vampires were no longer a threat? You'd be out of a job."

Miranda rolled over onto her back as she laughed heartily. "Oh yes! I can see it now. Nos lining up with CVs in hand trying to find jobs that would make them good members of society."

"It was just a thought," the second girl muttered.

They continued to chat through the film, pausing at only the most ridiculous scenes in order to laugh at the fake blood or bad acting. When the film was over, Mira suggested they play a board game. Much to her own shock, Lee answered, "Why not."

As Mira set up the murder mystery board, Lee left to take the empty popcorn bowl into the kitchen. She heard the voices of Abelard and Karen Tepes and prepared herself for the awkward parent talk. Then, she caught her own name in their conversation. She hung just behind the doorway.

"Are you serious? You just came home and you want to argue about this sort of thing?" Karen said to her husband in a condescending tone. "This is why your blood pressure is high! Would you please just sit down for five minutes?"

"That girl should not be here, Karen. What were you thinking letting her stay the night?"

"I was thinking that our children need some friends—"

He interrupted, yet his voice sounded downcast, like

a pouting child. "They have friends."

"Not friends who know. Let her be their friend, not just the bait in your awful plan. You should have seen how excited Miranda was to have a friend stay over."

"How can we be certain that girl isn't a Nos supporter?"

"We've been over this! The kids had to save her from a Nos and she didn't complain. Sounds to me like a normal girl."

"She also let Aubrey Ruthven in! I know you can't fully understand but—"

His wife must have given a terrifying expression because he stopped short. Lee counted to three before Karen Tepes spoke, her voice tight with anger. "Understand? Understand!"

"Karen, I didn't—"

"No! Abelard, I may not have been born into this family, but I understand perfectly well what we all have to give up to keep the people of Whitby safe. When I married you, I agreed to be your partner in this, knowing we could never move away and that our children would have to follow in your footsteps. And I have been patient, helpful, and I've killed my share of Nos. Now, all I am asking of you is to butt out of our children's lives, at least in this case."

She started to march out of the kitchen, coming out so swiftly that Lee had no time to hide. She stood there, clutching the popcorn bowl like a lifesaver. Her eyes, two perfect owl orbs, stared at Karen Tepes as she exited. The woman did not seem particularly surprised. She took a deep breath in, exhaled, and then smiled at Lee. With an added wink, she pointed to the hallway and whispered, "I think it's time we all get some sleep, don't you."

Lee nodded numbly and rushed back into Miranda's

room like a frightened rabbit, closing the door behind her as quietly as she could manage in the creaky old building.

In the time since she'd left, Mira had changed into a matching pajama set decorated with mod flowers. "I thought you were putting that away," she asked as she claimed the Miss Scarlet token for herself.

Lee set the plastic vessel on the dresser beside the television. Without a thought, she said, "Your parents were talking. I didn't want to interrupt. Hand me the Mrs. White piece. Let's get this game started."

After one game, a knock came on the door. Mira rolled her eyes and whispered to Lee, "Mal. He must have gotten bored." Lee made a disgusted face back at her, causing the girl to laugh.

She hopped up, nearly standing on the hem of her own pajama trousers, and answered the door. Mal stood there in a pair of shorts and a ratty tee-shirt. His cropped hair managed to look disheveled and his eyes blinked at them sleepily. "Are you both going to be giggling all night?"

"I do not giggle," Lee protested. "I chortle."

"Rubbish," he grumbled with a yawn and forced his way into the room. "Well, as long as I'm up hand me Mr. Green and deal me in."

"Let you play with us? After the way you treated my guest?" Miranda scoffed and leaned out to meet her new friend's eyes. "What do you say, Lee? Should we let him?"

Mal's eyes studied the cardboard house layout on the floor and nudged the playing cards with his foot bashfully. She remembered their mother and her acceptance of having this strange girl with purple hair in her home. Her purpose was to give her kids someone to talk to. And maybe if they finally trusted her, she could get them to trust Ruthven.

With a deep, overdramatic sound, Lee passed her hand over the floor. "I suppose we can take pity on him—but only if he apologizes to me."

Mira clapped her hands in agreement and Mal looked ill. "Seriously?"

"Do you even have to ask?"

He shuffled his feet and looked distractedly around the room. "I'm sorry I didn't want you to come over tonight." The words were a long string of consonants strung together by the occasional grunting sound.

"Eh, it'll do," Lee conceded.

Mal sat down and the three began the game. The suspicions of who killed the victim in the game somehow turned into a lesson in vampires for their guest.

"All that rot about them having to travel with soil from their homeland or that they can't cross running water is such bull," Mal explained as he marked on his game card. "They just put it in their shoes and then they can go wherever they please."

Miranda added, "And I hate how easy they make staking look in films. It takes years of practice and a ton of upper body strength. Dad used to make us swim in the ocean using just our arms to build muscle."

Lee blushed at the thought of her flimsy wooden dowel hidden in her coat and the fact that she felt safer walking with it. "Why is it that the vampires aren't bleeding everyone around here dry? I mean, if there are as many as you say, why doesn't everyone know about it?"

Rolling the die so they nearly hit Lee in the knee, Mal took his turn explaining. "Nos supporters. Thanks to *Dracula*, Goths and lost teenagers show up in town for a little morbid entertainment and somehow end up as a part of the underworld. As long as they have that steady food supply of willing people, the attacks stay down to a minimum."

"Makes our lives a little easier," Mira added.

"Maybe they should start making pamphlets for schools to teach kids the danger of being a supporter. They could call it, 'So you want to be Vampire Chow'." No one laughed at Lee's joke. She thought of the sad scene within the abandoned building. "If they are willing to be food and if it keeps the vampires from killing people, what's wrong with it?"

"No more shop talk." Mal moved his pawn the correct number of spaces into the billiard room. "I want to guess. Mrs. White in the library with the rope."

Mira and Lee both shook their heads after studying their own cards. The answers revealed from the paper sleeve and Mal playfully stuck out his tongue from the corner of his mouth. "Hey, I was right."

Lee wrinkled her nose at him. "Is there any reason why you suspected my piece of being the murderer?"

"You have the look of a killer and you know it." Mal's tone had been teasing, then suddenly he sobered as if Lee truly did frighten him. He started to clean up the board.

"One more game?" Mira asked between yawns.

"Actually, I'm tired." Lee helped put away the game, realizing that normally when she hung out with friends, they had out a Ouija board or would be experimenting with new hair colors. For one night she had not been missing her old life. The change was nice. The thought of bringing up Ruthven's idea turned her stomach to a stormy sea and she bit her tongue.

Mira climbed up onto her bed and turned down the covers. Lee rose to hand Mal the game as he left the room. "Apologize to me one more time," she insisted as he started to leave without looking at her.

"What?"

"I said apologize."

His shoulders tensed and his eyes glazed over. "For what?"

"For thinking I am a killer." She crossed her arms over her chest.

"It's a game, Lee. Let it go."

"The more I think about the fact that you based your assumption upon my appearance, the angrier it makes me. Therefore—"

He tucked the long game box against his side and bowed, an unsteady and minor movement barely recognizable as a gentlemanly gesture. "I apologize."

"Good. Now go away."

He did.

February 5, 1940: From the Diary of Poppy Tepes

A few nights ago, the impossible occurred. A Nazi bomber came to destroy our coast, destroy the beautiful moors, and possibly cut off our means of leaving Whitby. Or maybe simply going to demolish the town itself. Either way, the plane came and crashed in a field. And of all the forces, natural or man-made, that could have saved us, it was a Nos.

I saw a soul stealer turn himself into green smoke and shoot into the air toward the plane. I do not know exactly what happened after that, but I can guess because the plane crashed right onto the Bannial Flatts farm. Can I actually allow myself to believe that a Nos saved the town of Whitby? Then again, it would be his town too.

I hate this thought. The thought that a Nos could do something noble gives me a headache. Then again, that pilot was killed. Enemy or not, he died in a violent way that might have been avoided. I just have to keep reminding myself, Nos are the only real monsters out there. All of the others are simply misguided men.

Chapter 12: "And Death Be All That We Can Rightly Depend On"

The three teenagers all awoke earlier than Mrs. Tepes had anticipated. She asked Lee how she had slept, as if the conversation the girl had overheard the night before never happened.

Mal wandered to the kitchen table looking worn and annoyed. "What's with you?" Mira asked him, pushing him on the shoulder. He leaned to one side, then bounced back to his straight posture.

"Weird dreams," he growled.

"About what?" his mother inquired as she set out various cereal boxes for everyone to choose from.

With a quick, guilty glance in the direction of their guest, he murmured, "Don't remember."

Lee left before noon that morning, telling them how her best friend was coming up from Harrow soon. "My mom threatened that if I didn't have at least half of the house unpacked before Chelsea got here, she'd make me work at her dig site for an entire weekend."

"I'd think that would be fun," Karen Tepes offered.

"Yeah, hours of digging in the dirt in order to sort through broken bits of dead people's stuff. Not the barrel of laughs Indiana Jones makes it look like."

"Do you want us to walk you home?" Mira asked, reaching for her coat. Mal seemed uncomfortable with the idea yet nodded in agreement.

"Nah. It's daytime. Nothing ghoulish waiting out there for me during the day, right?" Lee meant the words as a joke. In truth, she knew they were all thinking of Ruthven. She gauged the waters, waiting for someone to make a comment.

"I think you'll be fine," Abelard Tepes answered, stepping in from the hallway. He made an effort to smile at the girl in all black. "Either way, walk home safely."

"Thanks." The single word came out with little conviction, his words from the night before poking at her. Lee escaped out into the world, the gloom of the late winter skies giving her a sense of calm.

Once she exited, Mal pulled his sister down into the shop with the pretense of working. Miranda glared at him as they descended the stairs.

"You don't have to pull my arm out of the socket just to tell me something." She rotated her shoulder dramatically when she was behind the shop's counter.

Her brother glanced nervously up the stairs. "I had a dream about Lee. She was with Aubrey Ruthven."

"Doing what?"

"Just talking. I don't about what."

Mira's hand crashed down upon the counter. Somewhere within the thud, he could hear her swearing at the universe.

"It's not my fault that visions don't come with a volume dial." Her brother leaned his hands against the edge of the counter, pressing until he warmed the metal and glass beneath his palms. "Do think she's spying for him?"

Mira watched his knuckles strain as his fingers curled under. The skin across his hands grew taught until two painful, pale fists faced her own hands from across the surface. "He really scares you, doesn't he?"

"Dad gave me back family records to re-read. Ruthven hates our family."

"Duh. We hunt his kind. They all hate us."

"The journal wasn't specific. It just said that he blamed our family for something and took revenge. Our great-great-however many greats grandfather wrote it and I think he'd gone barmy by that point."

Several minutes of silence slipped away from them, minutes of stiff breaths and dark thoughts. Mal kept his gaze trained upon the backs of his hands, waiting for them to relax.

"I want to trust her," Mira at last concluded.

Mal released the counter. "Fine. Then let her prove herself. We need a plan."

"We have a plan. Destroy Ruthven."

"He's too strong and too old." Mal picked up a cheaply made Dracula doll from a shelf full of products popular with tourists. The toy fit perfectly within his palm. "Think we better not rely on Lee. I think we need to finally find whatever is buried on the cliff."

"Dad told us to never go looking for it. He said if we find it, the Nos will come after it too."

Mal stabbed his fingers against the cotton neck of the plush doll. "Nos are already after it. We need help. Maybe whatever is up there will help."

With her renewed sense of safety and a surprisingly good night's sleep, Lee shouldered her bag and readied to face a new day. She decided to walk near the edges of the cliffs and enjoy the sea air before she started home. The thought occurred to her rather suddenly. Despite her excitement about her friend visiting, she realized the last precious moments of quiet time would keep her sane.

Chelsea had a habit of making her crave a little time alone after a while.

She was starting to know her way around, finding even the narrowest of streets easy to maneuver. As she neared, the cliff face and the one hundred and ninety-nine steps leading to the church and abbey, she noticed a man seated on a bench. He waved at her; the clouds overhead reflected in his sunglasses.

At first, she thought to turn and walk away, thoughts of her failed mission the night before coming back to her. He appeared perfectly serene amongst the sharp wind and dismal settings. He turned his sunglasses in her direction and smiled. It was a true smile, the sort someone gives when they see a long-lost friend or are cheered up after a hard day. It was far from one of Miranda's overly optimistic, common smiles. This gave Lee new warmth.

He motioned to the empty part of the bench. The girl took the spot beside him, arranging her scarf to keep her from sitting on it. For a long while, the pair of them stayed quiet as old men and noisy children ascended the treacherous stone steps. The clouds above them remained gray, allowing for strips of white but no patches of blue. The wind kicked up the sea in the bay. Lee thrilled a little at the sight of it splashing against the edges of the touristy boardwalk.

Suddenly, he started to recite, his voice almost possessed by the poetry as if he could not stop himself. "And he had strayed into the Town,

And paced each alley up and down,
Where still, so narrow grew the way,
The very houses seemed to say,
Nodding to friends across the Street,
'One struggle more and we shall meet.'

And he had scaled that wondrous stair
That soars from earth to upper air,
Where rich and poor alike must climb,
And walk the treadmill for a time."

Lee glanced at him sideways, noticing the wistful smile playing just at the corners of his mouth. "Lofty timbers, the walls around are bare, echoing to our laughter as though the dead were there–" She realized how sarcastic she sounded. "Sorry. They say that in the Bela Lugosi *Dracula*. I thought we were doing a poetry thing and it seemed appropriate." She looked down at her shoes. "Or was that horribly offensive?"

He rubbed at his mouth, suppressing a smile. "No. No, that was alright. As long as you don't quote anything from a Hammer film at me, we're good."

Lee suppressed a frown. She liked cheesy Hammer horror films. She returned the conversation to his random poem. "What's yours from?" she asked.

Aubrey Ruthven looked as if he'd forgotten she was there. The smile faded and he explained, "Lewis Carroll."

"The Alice in Wonderland guy?" Her father had never been overly fond of reading her what he considered opium-induced nonsense. Most of what Lee knew of Lewis Carroll came from a day trip to Oxford she'd taken with Chelsea.

He nodded. "He wrote it about Whitby."

"Oh." Lee wished she could think of something witty to say. For some reason, this man had begun to make her tongue-tied. She wanted desperately to impress him, which was an altogether new feeling for her. Normally, she spent her time proving that she didn't care what people thought of her. She wanted to sit there with him as long as possible just talking, yet no words would come out.

He leaned forward to rest his elbows on his knees, at last speaking again. "And how did the night go?"

Lee gave him a sideways glance. "I didn't have a chance to really talk to them about you. They don't like the subject unless they bring it up." A part of her wanted to say that she had fun; that a part of her was starting to like the strange twins. She kept her face as stern as possible. "You're dangerous."

"You don't sound surprised."

"Should I be? I didn't think a man parading around on a dusky day in sunglasses was out to do good deeds." She turned to him and challenged, "Take them off."

He returned casually to his upright potion, never touching the dark shades. "You believe them, yet here you are."

"You told me yourself that you're dangerous. Besides, there are different kinds of dangerous." Lee saw one of his eyebrows rise from behind the left lens as he awaited further explanation. Suddenly self-conscious of the attention being given her, Lee cleared her throat and played with the tassels of her scarf before continuing. "When I was little, we spent summers in the Southwest part of the U.S., you know New Mexico, Texas—"

"Yes, I lived in Virginia for a time, then traveled westward. I know the United States pretty well," he put in.

"Virginia? How long of a time?"

"Virginia specifically? A few months, but I traveled all about after that."

Lee asked her next question with more force. "And when in time?"

"1855." It was obvious from his tone that he had no intention of lying to her, "Please, go on."

The date and place nagged a little at Lee, knowing

she'd heard the combination before. Pretending not to be shaken by this new evidence, Lee told him, "When I was little my mom was always telling me to go outside and play. I used to argue that it was dangerous with all the rattlesnakes and scorpions. Not to mention heatstroke. She used to tell me that it was the sort of danger I could avoid if I was smart."

"You don't think of me as a venomous danger?"

"That's not what I said. All I'm saying is that I'm going to be smart about this."

"Most would say that you sitting here would not be considered smart."

"Middle of the day. . . . I assume it's still daytime. Hard to tell with all these clouds. Lots of people around. And a very high wall that I can jump to my death from if you try to turn me into one of your undead legions. I think I'm good."

He rose with a chuckle. "Interesting way of looking at it. Still not smart. I would catch you from that fall before you hit the ground."

Lee felt a blush creep into her cheeks and she ducked her head. "Yeah..."

"I know the vampire hunters will object to what I have to say. You don't have to talk to them about the crest if you don't want to. It's not like any of us knows exactly where it is."

She kept her head down. "Tying to get rid of me?"

"I was thinking more about the position I put you in. I can't see how this won't end in a fight—"

"I think they trust me or are at least starting to. They might listen if I ask." Her eyes remained locked upon a single stone kicked into the path of travelers. "Or you could all just give it up. Leave the crest where it is and leave each other alone."

"Neither they nor I could do that. We all have our callings." He moved his head close to her. She realized how frightened she should be. The edge of his glasses scraped lightly near her temple and he muttered, "I know there are things I should give up on, but I just can't."

"Now that sounds dangerous," Lee tried to joke. When she lifted her head back up, he had left. "Figures," she muttered.

Chapter 13: "Poor Desdemona"

When Lee arrived home, she had an e-mail from Chelsea with a list of travel plans, confirming when her friend would be there. Lee answered with a two-word reply and hit send. Closing out the internet browser, she stared at her desktop wallpaper, the image of two headstones on either side of an angel. She'd taken the photograph in a cemetery the last time her parents had taken her to Scotland. The symmetry and stillness used to calm her instead of the irritation she now felt for the bowed head of the stone angel.

Lee twisted the chair from side to side, running her fingers over the keys without pressing down. Her mind kept screaming for her to click on the internet icon once more, while her heart fluttered a little with a wish to let it go.

As she kicked off the ground and let the chair spin in a perfect circle, she asked aloud, "What would you do, Eddie?" The doll remained silent, but she double-clicked for the internet and typed "Virginia 1855" into the search engine. Thousands of matches all reading "Virginia 1855: Yellow Fever Epidemic" came up.

Her hand quickly closed the laptop, trying not to allow the information to sink in. She leapt from her desk and dashed from the house, barely pausing to pull on her coat. She practically ran back to the steps, taking them as quickly as she could without slipping. She burst into the Whitby Abbey visitors' center, yelling to the ticket woman, "It's okay, I'm Lee McDaniels", hoping the woman remembered her from the previous day.

She nearly slipped in a patch of mud. Somewhere in the midst of her jog, it had started to rain lightly. She wished she had thought of bringing a hooded sweatshirt or an umbrella. Shielding her eyes from the drizzle, Lee spotted her mother and Val.

"I need some digging tools," she exclaimed as she barreled toward them, interrupting a conversation with a professor from a regional university.

Her mom stared at her blankly, allowing her mouth to fall slowly open.

Val scratched his head at her, his smile going from friendly to confused. "Lee, you don't dig—"

"I know! I just—" She faulted, momentarily at a loss for a decent lie. Her brain picked out one, whether it seemed believable or not, and went with it. "Miranda, that girl whose house I stayed at last night, is thinking of being an archaeologist. I was going to let her see some of the stuff you guys use. I can borrow one of your private sets. I don't need to show her any of the rented stuff."

"Why not just bring her here and show her everything up close?" Mrs. McDaniels asked suspiciously.

"She's at home sick today. I thought I could go by and show her before I get ready for Chelsea. Please. I'll be unbelievably careful and—"

"Alright, alright," Val cut her off with a laugh. "You can borrow some of mine." He retrieved a cloth tied with a leather cord from his backpack. Within were trowels, paint brushes, and other simplistic tools of the trade. Most archaeologists' kits where not as fancily wrapped, existing in water-resistant canvas or resting in toolboxes, but Val considered himself old school.

She sighed in relief. "Thanks, Val."

Her mother gauged her reaction and crossed her arms over her chest. "Lee, what is this really about?"

"Exactly what I said. I just want to show her—" She stopped short, taking a deep breath to relax her entire body. "Oh, come on, Mom. What are you worried I'm going to do with them? Dig up a grave?"

The sarcastic tone instantly put Mrs. McDaniels at ease. "Okay, okay. Sorry I asked. Just remember to get things ready for Chelsea. Don't spend too much time with your new friends."

"Right. Got it. Unpack, clean, raise the mainsail, secure the mizen line. Aye aye, Captain, everything will be ship shape." Giving her mother a mock salute, Lee clutched the tools to her breast and ran off back through the visitors' center. She slowed down her steps as she neared the church.

Being the middle of the afternoon on a Friday during the bitter end of winter, the church was fairly deserted. The doors had been locked, waiting to be opened again for evening prayers. Lee walked slowly in amongst the graves, not sure what to look for. Many of the names and dates had been worn away by the salty sea air. In Dracula, Bram Stoker had an old man point out to the characters Lucy and Mina that many of the graves were empty, meant to make the families of sailors and drowning victims feel at peace.

The idea made sense. She assumed it had to be true. Perhaps the crest that Aubrey Ruthven wanted so badly and the Tepes family feared so much was in an empty burial plot. A part of her wished for this, knowing what she was planning to do and fearful of dealing with a fine for disturbing centuries-old bones. She wandered to the area of the churchyard between where Mal and Miranda told her of their family history and where she had fainted. She looked out at the sea, the cliff on the opposite side of the town, and the many ships coming through. Most were not picturesque. They were industrial-looking cargo vessels and fishing rigs. In Stoker's day, she imagined it looked very much the same, simply replacing the motorized engines and propellers for billowing sheets.

She tried closing her eyes and walking through the cemetery until she got a feeling, something that would hint at the crest's specific whereabouts. Instead, she tripped on a short stone half buried in the soggy ground.

As she hopped up and down, holding her wounded ankle as though she were attempting a dance move, she realized she was being watched. A man in all black raised both eyebrows at her and smirked. He was older, in his last sixties, with a ring of white hair sparsely covering the back of his head. His clothing was business casual, trousers with a button-up shirt and blazer. Despite his outfit, she guessed he was an employee of the church. He carried a small lunch box in one hand.

She turned away and fixed her attention on the towering cross she'd noticed the previous day. Images had been carved into the stone, most notably a relief of a man with a lyre in his hands. An angel hovered just above him. The words around the carving read "Caedmon. To the glory of God and in memory of Caedmon the father of English sacred song fell asleep hard by 680."

"Nunc laudare debemus auctorem regni caelestis, potentiam creatoris, et consilium illius facta Patris gloriae." The man recited the Latin with complete ease. When she did not turn to face him, he translated anyway. "Now we must praise the author of the heavenly realm, the might of the creator, and his purpose, the work of the father of glory."

Lee glanced over her shoulder to squint at him then quickly continued to study the cross.

"Caedmon. He was England's first known poet and took care of the animals at the monastery back in St. Hild's day. Do you know of St. Hild?"

With a tightlipped nod, Lee attempted to hobble away from the man.

"Are you alright?"

"Yes. Thank you." Her ankle throbbed and her steps stopped. She lifted the injured foot and started to hop.

He good-naturedly smiled at her. "I think it would be better if you sat for a moment."

She sheepishly limped over to a seat and groaned. "I'm fine. It was just my—"

"Pride? You know, they say that should goeth before a fall," he finished for her.

"Actually, I was going to say sense of adventure, but pride works too." She rolled up the hem of her jeans and rolled down the top of her sock. There would be a bruise, but she would be able to walk evenly again before the night came. Her exposed skin prickled at the cold air.

"What sort of adventure are you looking for?" the man asked, coming toward her, yet keeping a respectable distance.

The query did not faze her. "The sort where everyone comes out okay in the end. The 'no casualties' sort, if that's a better way to look at it."

"A graveyard seems a strange place for that sort of an adventure." He eyed her clothes warily. "You aren't here for a photo shoot, are you? We don't allow gothic lounging and unwanted attention to the graves any longer."

Releasing a long sigh, Lee tested the weight on her ankle by setting her foot down in the grass. "No. I'm going. I promise."

He sat his weary body on an aboveground tomb across from her. "Anything I can help with?"

She leaned against the back of her bench, listening to the old wood creak. Her butt started to feel damp from the rain which must have pooled on the seat. "No. Thank you, but no. Not unless you know anything about secret town conspiracies and hidden family heirlooms."

"Are you referring to the Crest of Dracul?"

Lee almost fell off of her bench. "How do you– Are you one of– Huh?!"

He chuckled. "Generations of the Tepes family have been scouring this churchyard for hundreds of years and none of them ever think to speak more softly. We can hear them from in there." He pointed at the Tudor-era building. "What do you want with it though? You don't seem like a member of their family. Are you a vampire helper of some kind?"

The girl was floored. This guy knew everything. His smile at her broadened a little. He opened the lunch box as she stumbled over her answer. "No. I'm not a supporter, but I'm not sure if it's right to just kill them left and right without. . . I don't know. Some kind of trial or something."

"I see." He tore apart a sausage roll with his fingers and handed her half. "Don't tell anyone about this. I'm not supposed to be eating them, according to the doctor, but it is my belief that God knows we need to indulge every now and again. He knows my weaknesses and forgives me them, after all." He started to unpack a thermos, a box of cooked parsnips, and an extra cup.

"Thanks. Secret is safe with me," Lee told him as she

nibbled on the meat wrapped in pastry dough. "If you know about the vampires, why do you live here? Or, why don't you tell anyone?"

"There are dangers anywhere in the world. Besides, this is my home. I grew up here. We have the Tepes family for protection. As for the telling, who would believe me? They would cart me off to the looney bin before I could finish this." He held up his last bite of the meat to illustrate.

She finished her half and stared at the ground. People knew about the family, and Abelard, Karen, and their children had no idea. "Do others know?"

"I doubt it. But I come from an old Whitby family myself. My people have been here since before our ancestral tree can record." He held out the box of parsnips to her for her to take a few.

"And you know about the Order of the Dragon Crest? Mal and Miranda don't even know that it's a crest," she explained in awe.

"Again, old family. My great-great-grandfather had a brother who was turned into a demon; a vampire. My ancestor was a ship's captain who kept a log that people thought was lost. Truth was my family took it to hide the shame of having something so evil in the family. Or to keep people from thinking our ancestors were barmy. The log talks a little bit about the crest." He bit down into a parsnip after his speech and held out the box again to her.

Lee took another vegetable and asked, "Did it say what it does or where exactly it is?"

"My great-uncle didn't know. He told my great-grandfather that he refused to leave Whitby because he was part of a faction searching for it. We pass the story down in my family so we have the cautionary tale of never becoming one of them."

"What happened to the vampire brother?"

The man sighed and shook his head. "He was set adrift in a dingy which was also on fire, in order to save his soul."

"Okay, that's awful. I mean, seriously, I read Edgar Allen Poe and Stephen King and H.P. Lovecraft and I think that's terrible." She tried to amend her statement, realizing that these had been this man's family. His grandfather did what he thought was best. "I'm sorry. I know he was bad and a killer, but that's a horrible way to die."

He rested a hand on his knee and spread the little picnic on his lap. "Are you afraid of vampires?"

Lee looked down at the parsnip in her hand. "I don't know. I don't know how I feel. I'm still trying to get a handle on the fact that they exist."

He opened the thermos, pouring half of the contents into the lid and the other half into his cup. He handed her a lid-full of soup. "What you need is faith. What is your name?"

She wrapped her fingers around the lid, letting them tingle from the warmth. "Annabel Lee McDaniels. Lee." It seemed right to tell him her whole name.

"Do you believe in God, Annabel Lee?"

"Honestly, I'm not sure." She felt guilty about saying such a thing to a member of the church.

"If you are going to be involved in all of this, I suggest you find something that you believe in. Find something that makes you feel safe and gives you faith in the world. And never let that object leave your side." He sipped his soup. "Why do you want to find the crest?"

"I want to put it where neither of them will look. I don't want the vampire hunters or the vampires to use it against each other. Is that childish?"

"A wish for peace is never childish. Of course, you might have chosen an easier project." He finished his soup with a swift gulp and added, "Remember, my dear, it is not your job to save everyone. All things die in God's time, even vampires."

Lee drank down her half of the soup, a thick potato concoction that must have been homemade. Shredded leeks wedged into her teeth and she did not care.

She handed him back the thermos lid and thanked him again. "Sorry, what was your name?"

"Martin Seward. I am sort of a receptionist and historian for St. Mary's." His expression softened further. "Any time you need to talk or just want a little lunch, you can come find me. I'm usually here" She opened her mouth to ask. He cut her off. "Yes, Seward like the character in Dracula. I shall see you later, Lee."

"Bye." She wobbled on her hurt ankle, yet the mix of comforting words and warm food practically cured her. She set Val's tools under her arm. She would have to think of a different approach.

Chapter 14: "Filthy Leech"

Friday evening was an average night for the local kids of Whitby. They hung around the pier and pubs. For Lee, the night buzzed with electricity. She excitedly paced the bus stop. Her fingers wound around the ends of her hair keeping all thoughts of vampires at bay. At last, eleven minutes later than it was scheduled to be, the bus from Scarborough arrived.

Chelsea exited, her expression grim after the long journey from London. Her eye makeup had smeared from sleeping on public transportation and her hair, a frizzy, blonde style normally held in place by spray, rested limply on her shoulders. Still, when she saw Lee, Chelsea smiled.

"Please tell me you live close to here. Four hours on trains is too much for me. I can't take any more travel," was her greeting.

Lee took her friend's suitcase, which weighed heavier than it looked. She leaned upon her good ankle as she hefted the bag. "It's not far, but I warn you Mom and Dad have already taken the place over with their junk."

"That's supposed to surprise me," Chelsea replied as she followed Lee through the streets and along the sidewalks. She did not offer to take back her bag. Instead, she leaned awkwardly against her friend's side, forcing the suitcase to be kicked between them. "So? When do I get to meet him?"

The question sounded casual. Lee froze. She hadn't told Chelsea anything about the last week. "Him?"

"You know. Whoever the guy is that's been distracting you. I've barely received any texts from you about how bored you are, so there must be someone entertaining you," Chelsea teased.

"It's not like that," Lee instantly stated.

"There is a guy!" Chelsea's excited voice echoed on the narrow streets.

"No! I mean, sort of." She curled her fingers around the handle of the rolling suitcase. "I don't have to take your abuse. I thought you were here to cheer me up, not drag my good name through the mud with your slander!" Lee pointed to a building. "This is where I live now."

"Don't try to distract me with your fancy talk," her friend argued with a laugh. "And since when have you had a 'good name'? Remember Nelson? Remember what you and Nelson did in that cupboard."

"It was one kiss and it never would have happened if you had warned me about who was in there," Lee defended. "I thought it was Randolph."

Chelsea's laugh turned to a giggle. "Every woman needs the life experience of snogging one man they don't like. It gives a comparison to what snogging the right guy would be like."

"I would hardly call Nelson a man."

Lee held open the front door and let her friend in before her. Chelsea helped to pull her suitcase through the door and whispered, "You snogged this guy yet?"

"Knock it off, Chelsea," Lee warned, then shouted so her voice rang through the house. "Look what I found outside!"

The McDaniels family fussed over Chelsea all through

dinner. They asked about life, family, school, and even what she had been watching on television. Chelsea had a way with parents. Despite her dark clothing, thick makeup, and love of spooky topics, she was able to charm any adult. They all loved her. Even when both girls got in trouble at school, somehow Chelsea was always able to talk her way out of it.

After their guest settled in, Mr. and Mrs. McDaniels left for the evening in order to meet with one of the backers of the Whitby dig.

"You girls do me a favor and just stick around the house tonight. You can go out and paint the town red tomorrow, but your father and I won't be able to keep our phones turned on through this dinner."

Lee's dad added with a wicked wink, "And you know that if this meeting goes well, your mother is going to want to celebrate so don't expect us home early."

"You got it," Chelsea answered with a winning smile.

After her parents were gone, Lee set up a second pillow on the other side of her bed. She called from her bedroom out to the hallway as she made room for her friend's possessions. "What do you want to do tonight? We can watch something or play a game. I think we have a deck of cards around here someplace."

With a large book and a device for reading energy levels, Chelsea stood in Lee's doorway. "Get your coat. We're going ghost hunting."

Lee smiled at her friend, "Are you suggesting I go against the rules my mom set forth for us and go out after dark?" She knew she should have thought of the vampires. She should have insisted that the world of Whitby was not as safe as London. All excuses sounded ridiculous. Besides, Chelsea couldn't get her into too much trouble in one night. They could stick to areas with large groups of people. It was a weekend night. Nothing bad could happen.

Lee hopped off her bed and pulled on her boots. "My kit is in the wardrobe. Can you get it?"

The two locked up the house and set their cell phones with an alarm to remind them about being back before Lee's parents. They set off in the direction of the ocean since it would be away from where the McDaniels were having dinner.

"What kind of ghosties, ghoulies, and other beasties have you heard about in Whitby?" Chelsea asked as she tapped the electronic device against the palm of her hand. She only half looked at the readings as they passed the many boats quietly resting in the water.

"I haven't heard of any ghosts," Lee confessed. "But plenty of other beasts."

Chelsea frowned. "You were supposed to be researching this stuff. That guy you like must be something."

She desperately wanted to change the subject. "Come on. Let's go up to the cliff."

They trekked uphill to where a line of buildings overlooked the view of the abbey across the river. In a simplistic park area was a green bench. Chelsea ran up to it and slid onto the wooden seat. "Random!" she declared as she made herself at home.

Lee inspected the bench before she sat down. A brass plaque had been bolted to the backrest reading, "The view from this spot inspired Bram Stoker (1847-1912) to use Whitby as the setting of part of his world-famous novel *Dracula*. This seat was erected by Scarborough Borough Council and the Dracula Society to mark the 68th Anniversary of Stoker's death - April 20th, 1980."

"It's not random. It's for the man who wrote Dracula."

She pointed at the abbey and church sitting atop the opposite cliff, eerily shadowed in the moonlight. "That's where Mina finds Lucy in the book."

"Are you still reading that antique? You realize that's like reading a schoolbook for fun?" Chelsea opened her notebook and pretended to be reading through her own handwriting.

"You're just jealous because that cute boy at Paddington Station was more interested in me because I had read *Frankenstein*," Lee curtly answered.

"Oh, I am not, don't be a cow." Chelsea stuffed her notebook into her oversized purse as she noticed a group of guys coming toward the Bram Stoker Seat memorial. They were all between the ages of sixteen and twenty, each one cuter than the next. "Excuse me," she called to them running up to the group as if they were old friends.

"What are you doing?" Lee asked from the safety of the bench.

Chelsea gave her an impish smile. "Asking a local where we can haunt."

"Chels, don't," Lee insisted, but it was too late.

The three young men looked up. One of them, his head covered in soft golden-red locks, smiled at Chelsea, running his gaze up and down her sixteen-year-old form.

Flirtatiously, she asked, "Do any of you know of someplace good and haunted where my friend and I can explore?"

The one that smiled at Chelsea answered, "Course. There's the Hangman's Pub right down the road. They say it's haunted by an innkeeper's daughter who was murdered by a jealous lover."

"Sounds exciting," Chelsea replied in a breathy whisper, "I don't suppose any of you would like to show us the way."

Lee watched her friend's shameless flirting with an eye roll. She figured if they were going to a pub, it would be crowded enough that Chelsea would not end up in any situations she would later regret.

The bar resounded with a familiar dark and stuffy atmosphere. The scent of whiskey hit Lee in the face the minute she stepped through the door. The three young men twisted through the crowd, leading the girls to a booth in the back. The leader of the group kept twisting his neck around, checking that they were following.

Chelsea giggled as she slid into her seat. "I suppose you deal with a lot of tourists like us."

"Not during this time of the year," the leader of the group explained. "But there is the goth fest twice a year. This pub has to turn people like you away when that comes around."

"Hmm," Chelsea answered with a nod. "Do you boys have names or should I just assign you each character's names from 'East Enders'?"

The youngest of the three, sixteen years old with a dazzling smile and broad shoulders, replied first. "I'm Leo."

"I'm Mike," the second stated. His skin was a deep bronze color, most likely of Indian descent.

The leader of the three, who could not have been more than twenty, spoke up last. "Jonas. I work at the sports center two nights a week. I teach youth swimming."

"Chelsea and Lee," she answered, pointing to each of them respectively. With a flick of her frizzy hair, Chelsea leaned in closer to the three boys as they settled in across from them. "I suppose you boys have never seen anything mysterious around town?" The way she asked sounded more like she wanted to make out instead of investigating the paranormal.

Lee hated when her friend acted this way, this tired cliché of an engrossed girl wanting nothing more than someone to kiss. Usually, she had the rest of their circle of friends to help bring Chelsea back to earth, but alone she felt like the number of pheromones in the room could never overpower her logic.

Mike moved over to their side of the booth and set an arm around Lee. "Have you girls been in town long?"

She pursed her lips. "You been on planet Earth long?" she countered as she removed his arm forcibly.

"Sorry." He smiled at her with a sense of charm and ease that she could have sworn he had stepped off a movie screen. "I wasn't trying to make you feel uncomfortable. I was just being friendly."

"Be friendly on your own side of the booth." She grimaced and buttoned up the second to last button on her coat.

"Lee," Chelsea scolded, yet did not push the issue.

Drinks came and Chelsea's conduct continued in the same vein. Glass after glass of Guinness and cider was downed by her and the three boys while Lee patiently sipped a single pint. When Jonas's hands would begin to snake around Chelsea, Lee would poke his fingers with a fork and then look at him innocently with a fake, "Whoops."

Chelsea was too drunk to care if her friend interfered. As the evening wore on, she could have been hanging out with the Ghostbusters and kissing Slimer, and yet not known the difference. At last, Lee pulled at Chelsea's collar as if trying to catch a dog before it jumped on a stranger.

"We have to go, Chels. My parents will be back soon."

"You know wha yer problem is?" Chelsea slurred at

her. She then turned to their many new companions. "De yer know what my best friend's problem is?" They all shook their heads, obviously nowhere near as affected by the alcohol as she had been. "Lee lacks...what's that word? Conversation! No wait. Anyways, she always sesh she's going to rebel against stuff, then runs home before she can get in trouble. Not cool."

Lee set her palms down on the sticky table. "Yes, Chelsea, I know. I need to live a little. But you know what? If I really wanted to hang with the living, why do you think I joined a ghost-hunting club?"

Jonas snickered at her comment. "Well played."

"Don't side with her," Chelsea groaned. "Don't encourage her antisocial behave-eee-or! I am trying to help 'er!"

"I know," Lee answered condescendingly. "Right now, why not let me help you? You can lean on me while we walk home. Doesn't that sound like fun?"

Chelsea just let out a long moan and brought her head down on the tabletop. She covered her hair with her hands and waited for the world to stop spinning.

"We can help you take her home if you like," Jonas offered with a reached-out hand.

Chelsea smiled at him. "Oh, I don't live here. I live in London. And if you ever come to London, you're invited into my house any time."

"Chelsea, will you shut up." Lee's sense of self-preservation instantly took effect. "I don't need your help getting her home, but thanks."

"Yes!" Chelsea argued, her voice muffled by the table surface and her hair. "I want him to take us home!" She sat up once more and leaned her head against his shoulder. "Please, help us home." She then kissed him along his jawline, nearly missing her target twice.

Wrapping his hands around her forearms, Jonas pulled her up closer to him as if she weighed nothing. He kissed her on the mouth, a hard long kiss which made Lee realize she had just lost her argument.

Chelsea swayed a little as she crawled onto the young man's lap and pulled down his mouth for a second kiss, this time her mouth opened and engulfed his. His two friends smiled with that look guys gave each other in congratulations.

Lee tugged at Chelsea's shoulder and separated the pair. "Fine. You may walk us to our destination. However, the other two of you are going to stay here. We don't need a whole entourage just to walk us home."

The rejected two looked disappointed yet resigned to follow her wishes. With the tab paid, Lee forced Chelsea's coat back onto her shoulders. Somewhere throughout the evening, the thick garment had fallen onto the floor. Jonas stayed on the opposite side of Chelsea as Lee maneuvered her friend out of the pub. His hand wrapped around the small of her back, playfully tickling Chelsea's side. Her giggling caused her to fall directly into his arms.

"You know, you better just knock off that idiotic behavior now," Lee chided as she stared straight ahead, choosing paths with the most streetlights. "You are not, to coin a phrase, getting lucky tonight. If you want to leave us, that's fine."

Jonas did not answer. Suddenly, Lee realized that Chelsea's giggling had ceased. She turned and discovered that the two were vanishing around a corner. "By the pricking of my thumbs—" she grumbled before chasing after them. "Chelsea, we need to go home. Come back here right now." Her stomach rumbled with realization, yet her mind kept quoting literature as a means to stay calm.

She managed to keep up with them as Jonas spirited the stumbling Chelsea down one street then another. At last, he stopped near what Lee recognized as one of the fancy hotels she saw once in a brochure for Whitby. Instead of heading for the hotel entrance, he steered Chelsea to a small neighboring building which looked to Lee to be an abandoned shop of some kind. Her heart seized, remembering the similarly rundown building where she'd met Sibella's clan.

First, he pulled Chelsea against himself, kissing her with hungry vigor. Chelsea practically collapsed into his embrace. Lee rushed toward them.

"I am taking her home, now—" she started to shout as she ran at them.

Without her realizing, Jonas was still beside her, leaving the intoxicated Chelsea propped up along the wall. He grabbed at her shoulders and smiled. This time, she viewed two pointed fangs coming down from within his gums.

She let out a scream, however, he whisked her into the abandoned shop before she could finish the sound. Chelsea lay beside her on a dusty floor. Lee pulled her friend to her feet and ran back to the door, using what electric light shined through the boarded-up windows.

Jonas swept between her and exited, catching up Chelsea in his arms once again. "Calm down, sweetness," he told Lee as moved Chelsea's hair away from her neck. "Your turn will come."

Without a weapon or plan, she thrust herself upon him, pulling Chelsea out of the way. She attempted to punch him, slap him, and damage him in any way she could. Her mind raced and her heart leapt into her throat. She wished Mal and Miranda were with her, no matter how annoying or judgmental they could be. She should have started carrying weapons after the first vampire she saw. Her death would be her own fault. And then Mal would be right about her.

Chapter 15: "Save Us from Fears"

Lee heard a fierce snarl. Jonas held her still and breathed against her throat. A second growl came from the darkness of the old shop. Lee imagined a horde of creatures. Her death would not be quick. She struggled and Jonas kissed the place on her neck where he intended to sink his fangs.

"If you squirm, it'll hurt more," he whispered.

The thing in the shadows growled a third time and leapt from hiding. Jonas was thrown backward, howling a wounded animal cry. He jumped up and faced his attacker with sudden humility.

"Aubrey? What are you doing?" he demanded, a string of saliva dripping from his fangs.

Aubrey Ruthven pushed his sunglasses up the bridge of his nose and panted from his attack on his comrade. "You told me you weren't feeding this way, Jonas!" he barked as he stood between the girls and the bloodsucker.

Jonas let out a long whine, taking away from his terrifying factor. "Ooooo, come on, man. I can't help it. It's what I am."

"Not them, you got that!" Aubrey turned his back on Jonas as he picked up Chelsea in his arms as if she weighed no more than a plastic doll. Her form lay unconsciously slumped against his shoulder.

Jonas sighed heavily and grumbled. "Yes."

"What was that?" Aubrey Ruthven demanded, spinning back toward Jonas who instantly cowered.

"I said yes!"

"And what will you tell the others?"

"They are off limits," Jonas said in one breath, nearly tripping on the words.

Ruthven flung Chelsea over his shoulder. Her arms swayed back and forth behind him, smacking glasses off dusty tables. Lee followed, avoiding the shards scattering across the floor.

He started toward the back of the shop. "Where are you going? The exit is that way?" Lee demanded as he vanished into the shadows.

"Shortcut. You'll be safe with me. Just don't make eye contact with anyone." He reached back with one hand and moved her ahead of him, steering her through a door and down a set of black iron steps that spiraled into darkness. She walked where he directed her, trying her best not to stumble in the black underground. He opened a second door ahead of her, then took them both into a bar.

Without windows or proper electricity, the pub was lit by a mix of kerosene lamps and candles. A long wooden bar lined a wall, an old-fashioned piece similar to those she saw in photos of the 1920s. Men and women were seated at round tables with unlabeled bottles and cups. Some people wore high collars and long sleeves. One woman was rolling down her cuffs and Lee caught sight of blood. She realized that some of the people were more of the Nos Supporters.

The room hissed at Ruthven and the two rescued girls. Lee heard the bartender scoff and mutter something along the lines of "Huh, Aubrey Ruthven used to be fun."

"What is this place? A pub for vampires?" Lee whispered as she moved closer to him.

"More like a speakeasy, a hidden and illegal place where we can be without anyone bothering our lifestyle," Aubrey Ruthven explained. He squeezed her shoulder reassuringly. "No one here bites, not unless you ask them too. The humans who are here do so willingly."

She scanned the alert faces. "Then why don't Sibella and her friends come here? Everyone looks pretty healthy."

"Because not everyone here who agrees to be bitten is not always in their right mind, like your friend here. Sibella prefers to have her volunteers to be sober when they agree to let her feed."

A second door at the opposite end of the room took them up a shorter staircase. They exited back out into the quiet Whitby streets. Aubrey Ruthven continued walking with his hand on Lee's shoulder until the three of them had reached her home.

"Lee, I can trust you not to tell your vampire-hunting acquaintances about our hideout. I'm fairly certain they already know about that one and allow us that small sanctuary. Still, just in case—"

"Don't mention it, I understand," Lee answered. Honestly, she was more concerned about the twins giving her a smug speech if she revealed the night's events. She unlocked her door and poked her head into the entrance. "Mom? Dad?" No answer. "Thanks for that at least," she grumbled to no one in particular. She motioned for Aubrey Ruthven to follow. "Come on in. Do you mind putting Chelsea in my room?"

With a quick nod, he entered the rented house. He set Chelsea on Lee's bed, then followed the girl back to the front door. "Are we all okay?" he asked, rubbing his hands along her forearms as if she were shivering.

She looked out over the street, wishing the conversation had happened near the pier. The thought of watching the waves and the lull of the tide made her believe they would have somehow relaxed her. "Were we just nearly eaten?"

"Yes, I'm afraid so."

"Then we are not okay." She pushed away from him and checked along the road, expecting to see Jonas and an army following them.

"It's usually the shock that affects survivors the most, especially when no one will believe them."

"I don't think I have to worry about that. You were right though. They keep coming after me. And it's a good thing Chelsea is so out of it." She glanced back into the house. "What about her? Is she going to be okay?"

Aubrey Ruthven wrinkled his forehead. "One of Jonas's fangs scratched her. It didn't look deep so she won't be infected or suffering from any loss of blood. She'll have to sleep it off. Let her rest as long as you can tomorrow. If you have to, tell your parents that she's ill." He then reached out a hand, pressing his fingers lightly against her cheek.

Lee attempted to talk away the warm feeling on her face and her sudden nervousness. "I really don't know what I'm going to tell Chelsea though. I suppose I can convince her that she got really, really pissed. She does drink a lot when she's ghost hunting." She cleared her throat, knowing she should be grateful to him, yet wanting nothing more than for him to leave and the flips in her stomach to stop. "You saved her life, you know. Thank you. I don't know what I would've done—"

Aubrey Ruthven removed his sunglasses, keeping his

eyes shut as he leaned his face to her. Lee was trapped between his touch and his nose. The next instant, his lips pressed into hers.

Chapter 16: "Unlucky Prick of the Safety-Pin"

Ruthven stayed only long enough for her to kiss him back, then vanished before her brain could register the event. She still hovered by the doorway when her parents got home.

"Lee, is everything okay? Why do you have your coat on?" her mom asked as they came near her.

Her dad wrapped an arm around her shoulder. She was sure he could smell smoke and booze on her. She just prayed he could not also smell the blood.

"Did you and Chelsea go out?"

"She's sick," was her only answer.

Mr. McDaniels rolled his eyes. "That's what I thought. You two went out, didn't you? Well, I'll have the hangover eggs ready for her in the morning—" He moved into the house and pulled his daughter with him.

Mrs. McDaniels set her hands on her hips and sighed. "I specifically told you not to go out tonight. Really, Lee. Your little acts of rebellion are going to get you or your friends hurt."

Her father briefly came to her rescue. "Honey, we know Chelsea can be a little bit of a partier. I'm sure Lee didn't give her any of that alcohol. And they obviously didn't stay out late." He then glared at his daughter, turning his tone stern. "Still, your mom told you to stay in the house tonight."

"I know, I'm sorry."

The words completely floored her parents. Their jaws dropped and they gaped at Lee. "Quick, call a doctor," Mrs. McDaniels laughed after she recovered. "We must have a whole home full of sick people."

Lee left her parents baffled. She checked on her friend who feverishly stirred. Managing to at least pull off Chelsea's boots, coat, and stockings, she bundled the girl in an extra blanket and set a pot near her side of the bed.

She changed into her pajamas, not wanting to think about the kiss. Her feet carried her back to the bed and she curled up into a fetal position. Her brain jumped back and forth between ideas - the thrill of a kiss from someone she was truly attracted to versus the feel of Jonas's breath on her throat. At last, she hopped from bed, gathered Eddie into her arms, and tried to will her toy to fight the nightmares and confusion away. So what if she was too old for comfort from a doll? Anyone who judged her could never say they had faced against a live vampire.

Chelsea slept almost the full next day. Lee and Eddie stayed in bed with her, keeping careful watch upon the windows at night. Occasionally, the vigil paused when Lee's mother brought sustenance and hangover cures. By Sunday morning, she awoke with a short scream. "I need to stop drinking," she decided as she sat up to take a long drink of water. "I don't remember anything."

"Not much to remember," Lee lied as she helped herself to the breakfast her dad had left on a tray. "You made out with that Jonas guy. He tried to follow us home, so we had to give him the slip."

Her friend groaned, both of embarrassment and pain. "At least nothing too bad happened right?"

Lee wished she could tell. She understood now why

Aubrey Ruthven had been concerned. What she had been through was different than keeping the secret of the twins. She felt safe with them. The ghoulies in the streets were comical, something for her to poke fun at while Mal so valiantly fought it. With Ruthven, they weren't ghoulies, they were misguided lost souls, terrifying and desperate. And she wanted nothing more than to vent about everything she had just been through to her best friend.

Instead, she leaned against her wall where a bed frame should have been. They moved too much for her to ever have a proper bed. "What do you want to do today? Just stay in bed until your bus comes?"

"What? No!" I've come all of this way. We can at least have a look around the town."

"When sober," Lee chimed in. "We can do that. I have mom's card so we can get into most museums and historical places with it if they're open today."

Chelsea clapped her hands together, then winced at the sound. "Just let me shower."

"Take your time." Lee untangled Eddie from the bedclothes and returned him to the desk. "Thanks for protecting us," she whispered to the doll.

As the two friends prepared to face the day, Miranda Tepes was being followed by her brother as he ranted. "Mira, are you even hearing me? Aubrey Ruthven is dangerous."

"I know that," she grumbled, pulling on her coat and gathering her handbag.

"We have to weed him out somehow," Mal continued as he chased after her, just barely taking a moment to grab his jacket before the two of them left the house. "I think we should kill him this time, not just change the locks on the town after he leaves."

"You expect us to kill him? Mal, our ancestor couldn't kill him and he was a million times more skilled of a hunter than you and I put together." They crossed through the shop, waving to their mom on their way out. "Don't you think we should talk to Dad about this?"

Mal shuffled his feet a little as they exited onto the cobblestone street. "In case you haven't noticed, I'm trying not to talk to Dad right now."

"Why? Not talking to him isn't going to fix anything." She slowed a little so they were walking side by side.

"Talking isn't going to either." He kicked a rock which spiraled away from them toward the street leading to the steps at the base of the cliff. "Besides, we know what Aubrey Ruthven did to our ancestors. I think it's making Dad crazier than usual."

"Hence why I am waiting to worry about it until the bastard is standing in front of me ready to suck out my life's essence. Until then, I am going to buy a coffee, flirt with that guy who runs that lame walking tour through town, and maybe kill a couple of Nos after the sun goes down."

Mal was only half listening. "Uh huh. Should we go to the churchyard and finally dig it up?"

"Dig what up?" Miranda asked with an annoyed grunt.

"The artifact. The thing Aubrey Ruthven wants." Mal motioned to the hill. "If we move it or keep it with us, he can't find it as easily, right?"

"Unless he kills us, tortures us, or starts a random vengeance spree like in the good ole days," Miranda answered with a grimace. "I think it's best where it is, Mal. It'll be fine."

The two crossed the bridge and entered the closest

café. A line of lazy Sunday customers practically went out of the door, waiting on a woman who had already changed her order twice. A few aspiring writers and businessmen took over the tables with their laptops and stacks of papers. Despite the air of productivity they attempted to convey, most were truly checking their social network pages and playing free online versions of old games.

In line just ahead of the twins, they could hear Lee groan, "Chelsea, you can't have a latte and whatever that thing is that I can never pronounce. You've barely had anything to eat in two days."

"I don't care. I want a latte and my stomach can handle it. It's tough." Chelsea winked at her friend and turned to the young man at the register.

After both had said their order, they found an empty table and shared a large muffin between them. Mira pushed some money at her brother. "Get me a coffee." She started for the table, but Mal grabbed her by the arm and pulled her back.

"You can wait for me. If you're going to bother Lee, I might as well come with you."

"Uh huh," Mira answered with a teasing voice. "Right. Because you want to 'bug' Lee. Am I right?"

"Sod off, Mira."

"I love you too."

They got their hot drink and worked their way to the place where most of the muffins had vanished within the stomachs of the two teenage girls.

"Lee! Is this your friend Chelsea?"

Lee almost choked on her tea. "Mal, Mira. You come here?"

Mal simply shrugged, like he did not know the answer to such a simple question. Meanwhile, Mira stuck out her hand to Chelsea and introduced herself.

Chelsea tilted her head at Mira and Mal, studying them with her critical eye. Despite her momentary sizing up of her best friend's new friends, she smiled broadly and greeted them as if they had known one another for years. "Mal! Mira! Of course. Have a seat."

The vampire-hunting twins inspected Chelsea with a strange sense of foreboding. Mal said nothing, but Mira forced a smile and told her, "Good to meet you. What are you two up to?"

"Just exploring," Chelsea put in with a twinge of jealousy. "You know, Lee has been complaining about being bored this whole week."

Lee turned a deep beat red. "I didn't say that exactly. Chelsea likes to exaggerate—"

Mal was unconcerned with Chelsea's words. He noticed a place just below her frizzy hair where a red scratch marred the perfect skin. His eyes moved from the shallow wound to Lee who glared, silently warning him not to ask. He did anyway.

"What happened to your neck?"

Chelsea's hand clapped against the scratch as she shook her hair away from her shoulder. "Just a hickey gone wrong. Isn't that what you called it, Lee? I had a little too much fun on Friday night."

Casually, as if they were talking of any other wild teen experience, Mira asked, "A guy did that to you? Gross. Are you alright?"

Chelsea sat up a little taller, enjoying the attention and deciding she would choose to like Mira based on the girl's new awe of her. "I'm fine. I had a nasty hangover and poor Lee had to drag me home, but other than that I'm okay."

Mal narrowed his eyes at Lee. "Are you okay?" The

question was pointed and she squirmed under it.

"Fine. No problem."

Mira went on, acting as if Chelsea were her new best friend. "You know, I have the best hangover cure. Lee, bring her by the shop and I'll have some ready. Really, it's like magic."

Chelsea's stomach churned and she nodded. "Not a bad idea."

Lee could see the insistence in Mal's eyes and the eagerness in Mira's. This was no hangover cure. "We can meet you there in half an hour. I want to show Chelsea the abbey."

"See you then."

The twins left them there and Lee could not help but glare at them as they exited. She did not want them near her friend. It was bad enough Chelsea had already been exposed to the vampires. She didn't want her friend mingling with vampire hunters as well.

Chelsea complained up the entire one hundred and ninety-nine steps. She was unimpressed with the ruin and church stating, "When you find a ghost up here, let me know. Then and only then will I climb those stairs again."

They arrived at the shop below the Tepes's home. The store was empty save the twins who had a steaming mug ready for Chelsea. "What smells like garlic?" she asked as she accepted the cup from Miranda.

"Our mum. She's making spaghetti upstairs. Now this looks sick, I know, but trust me when I say it will clear up even the worst hangover symptoms as long as we catch them early enough."

Chelsea made a face at Mira's comment. Still, she downed the thick brown substance, stating that it tasted like maple.

Mal pulled Lee aside as the other two girls started a long chat about some superficial and perfectly normal topic. "What exactly happened to you two?"

"What did she just drink?" Lee demanded in a harsh whisper as she watched Chelsea tip the mug all the way up to drain the liquid into her mouth.

"It's a mix of a few things. It's to keep any Nos infections from spreading. As long as she doesn't get bitten anymore, she'll be fine. Now—"

"Fine? First of all, she wasn't bit, just scratched by a tooth. A little scratch. Barely even bled. Second, mix of what things?"

Mal slapped his hands against his sides in defeat. "Ground-up garlic flowers, two-hundred-year-old holy water, a pinch of dirt from Transylvania, and brandy."

"That's disgusting!"

"We covered up the taste with some diluted molasses. Look, it works! Now answer my question."

Lee faced Mal, removing her eyes from Chelsea for the first time as if something might carry her friend away. "I screwed up. Happy? We went out and I let her get piss drunk. These guys started hitting on her. One tried to bite her."

"And?"

"What and? We got away." Lee was not about to explain that they were rescued by Aubrey Ruthven.

Mal muttered more to himself than to Lee. "Makes sense. The way you two dress, they probably figured you'd be willing to be fed on. They don't like it when you say no."

Tugging at the edge of her black cargo skirt, Lee gritted her teeth. "If you reference the way I dress one more time—"

"Lee, let's roll. My bus leaves in three hours. I need to

go have some fun, now that I'm hangover cured and all." Chelsea waved at Lee to join her and pointed to the shop door. "You want to come?" she asked Mira.

The girl shook her head. "Nah. I've got stuff to do around here. I'll see you the next time you're in town."

"Yeesh. Hopefully, Lee won't have to live here long enough for me to have to make a second trip." Chelsea handed Mira back the mug and added a flippant, "No offense."

"None taken."

After the two left, Mal asked, "Should we tell Dad?"

"No. I don't want him speculating that they got away because Lee did something bad. And you know that's the first place his mind will go." Mira handed her brother the empty mug. "You better wash that out before he gets home. Have fun."

Log of Captain Abel Tepes 1812

My sister and her husband have upheld the family tradition in my absence and kept our home safe. He has taken on our surname, rejecting his own so that the Tepes title will continue for another generation. This, naturally, has shocked the neighbors and left them quite the talk amongst all of the "good society" my sister detests so. They have recently added to our family with the birth of my nephew, Danby, which I do believe is the only company she truly needs outside of her husband. I am anxious to return to sea, to be away from this life of shadows and secrets. An ache forms somewhere just under my left breast as I pack my gear for another voyage as far from this port as I can manage. I know the ache well. I believe it is the ache of whatever was hidden upon the hill two centuries ago calling to me. The mysterious object cries out to me, no matter where I roam, begging me to find its resting place. I shall not be the one to disturb our more guarded family responsibility. It is better to be away and miss an object I shall never see than to risk the lives of all by quenching my thirst to solve the riddle. What has been buried must stay buried.

Chapter 17: "Our Favorite Seat"

Chelsea left early Sunday evening on the bus. Lee flopped into her bed almost immediately after. A part of her wished to wake up and find Aubrey Ruthven standing outside of her window. The thought quickly turned into a shudder. Even if she had made out with him, did she want him stalking her? The thoughts melded into her subconscious. She dreamt of Aubrey Ruthven fighting Mal and Mira. She stood nearby, helplessly watching and begging everyone to stop. The entire scene appeared aggravatingly self-explanatory save for the clothing. Long skirts. High-waisted trousers. Greatcoats on the men. Ribbons flapping in her hair.

When she awoke, her mobile phone read three o'clock in the morning. Lee rolled out of bed, pulling on her jumper and coat over her pajamas. She collected the items of her ghost hunting kit, checking that nothing had been lost the night of Chelsea's near attack. She also gathered Val's dig kit, keeping it tucked under her coat. If anything, the sharp objects within could double as protection.

With boots in hand, she crept through the house and locked the door behind her. She pulled on her shoes once she was outside, giving little glances at the front door and listening for either parent. Despite her backpack pounding against her spine or the cold air smacking her in the face, Lee did not stop running until she reached the one hundred and ninety-nine steps. Swallowing a deep breath, a rush of cold air filling her lungs, Lee climbed the steps as swiftly as she could until she collapsed in the churchyard. A small beacon to ward off the thin layer of mist in the air hung on the church roof.

"Nothing can hurt me here," she panted as she settled on the bench. "Unless someone calls the police. Then again, better arrested than dead, right." She glanced to the left, then to the right, scouting the empty graveyard and the still building.

She lifted herself back up and shrugged off her ghost-hunting kit. First, she lit an electric torch, keeping the light between her teeth as she spread out her many objects for disproving paranormal activity. She switched on her electric magnetic field reader. She justified it in her mind that if the crest drew both vampires and hunters to the town, then it must have been giving off some kind of energy signature. She waved the device around her as she shifted the torch into her other hand and started to scour the graveyard. She watched the dial pass over the numbers as she pointed the old object around. Not as fancy as Chelsea's digital EMF reader, yet hers was always surprisingly more accurate.

While she stepped lightly between the graves, she watched the dial carefully, afraid to blink. Normally whenever she had a spike in the readings, it meant she'd stumbled over a power line or passed a working microwave. She wandered closer to the cliff's edge, losing any light she may have gained from the single bulb atop the roof provided.

The needle hopped. Lee stepped away, watching it fall back into place. She returned to where she had been and watched the needle jump rapidly once more.

"Is it really going to be that easy?" she whispered to herself as she removed the tools from beneath her jacket. She waved the EMF reader closer to the ground, nearly ramming her head on a tombstone.

The reading remained strongest along an aboveground tomb. Four carved columns led to an oversized lid. Nature and time smooth any carvings that once adorned the stone sides. She ran her hand over the top. No words or numbers remained.

Lee breathed a sigh of relief, thankful that she would not have to dig. Using a few sharp objects from Val's kit, she slowly made her way around the outside of the tomb, prying off the lid which had been grown over with hundreds of years of moss and decay. Each time she worried about movement from within the church, she would fall face-first into the dirt, willing herself to be one with the tall weeds. She worked for nearly an hour, her fingers freezing against the stone and her eyes straining in the dim light.

When at last she moved the lid, she slid the heavy piece carefully to the ground, tilting one side against the edge of the tomb. Her beam of light explored the inside. Empty. No crest. No bones. Not even an urn or an "in memoriam" plaque. The bottom of the tomb instead of more stone was soft dirt, protected from the harsh winter weather by its housing. She waved the EMF tester over the spot again. The numbers jumped even higher as she pointed it down into the tomb.

"Figures," she grumbled as she climbed into the stone tomb, trowel in hand. She started first furiously, using both her hands and the spade. Spiders and insects crawled over her hands. She'd shake them off in the darkness and go back to work.

Once she laughed to herself, making a realization she

wished she could share with her parents. She was Annabel Lee in a tomb in a kingdom by the sea. Mr. and Mrs. McDaniels would have been so proud.

After thirty minutes of shoveling thin layers of dirt and projecting it against the inner edge of the tomb, she struck something hard and rectangular. Her frozen, blackened fingers started to scrape along the edges of the mystery object, feeling dirt wedging beneath her nails and grinding into her palms. The thing was heavy, about the size of a jewelry box yet the weight of a brick. She had to slowly pry it from the hole, studying the gilded edges and the worn corners.

When at last she had fully pulled the box from the earth, she held it under her flashlight with a confused humph. Instead of a crest, some medieval relic of a bloodthirsty order, she found a lock box secured without any hope of her opening the thing. She didn't want to wreck the beautiful container and she didn't know how to pick a lock.

She at least tried to replace the lid, leaving her mess hidden beneath it. The sky faded to hazy blue and she raced against the sunrise. After one final shove, she left the lid partially in place and escaped.

With the box under her arm, she tried to run discretely through the town. As she crossed the bridge, she felt the presence of followers. She tried redirecting her route slightly, hoping to shake the paranoid feeling. Instead, the feeling grew more intense.

At last, stuffing the box into her ghost-hunting kit, she stopped in the middle of an intersection, the traffic light overhead blinking dimly. "Who's out there?" she asked with as much annoyance and bravery as she could muster.

Jonas and his two pals slunk from the shadows. He

walked up close to her, setting a single finger against her cheek. She shook him off and took a step backward as he cooed, "Oh, it's Aubrey's new pet. What would she be doing out so late at night?"

"You better stay away from me," she warned. "You remember his threats, don't you? Touch me again and he'll bring down his wrath upon you."

Jonas laughed heartily. "Wrath? Did you hear that, boys? Wrath." He moved in close, pushing Lee against the side of a building and pinning her there by the shoulder. "No one says wrath anymore, darling. Get with the times."

She pushed him away and spat in his face. "What do you even want with me?"

He tilted his head back and forth like a cat inspecting a bird. "You are nervous about something, but it isn't death. What are you hiding?"

Instead of answering, Lee kicked Jonas in the shin and walked away in a huff. "That's for trying to bite my best friend, you asshole!"

She continued her walk home without looking back. She heard scurrying and sometimes splashes in puddles. More vampires telling her of their existence? She pulled her backpack to her front and hugged it as she approached her home. They must have been drawn to the box without even realizing it. She couldn't keep it at home for long.

Three other sets of eyes noticed her in the early morning light. The three vampire hunters watched Lee run into her front door from their perch atop a multi-floored building. Abelard Tepes cleaned his broadsword against a crimson rag as he whispered, "Your new friend is acting suspicious."

Miranda giggled. "She's just out for a jog. Really, Dad,

you're so paranoid."

A rough shake of his duster provided a squeak of the stiff leather that spoke his suspicions. He turned to his son, silently awaiting further excuses.

Mal rolled his eyes. "Shouldn't we be focusing on how quiet it's been? The last two nights have been slow. We've barely seen any Nos at all."

"It's been slow ever since *she* got here—"

"We told you that we have this under control!" Mal blurted out.

His sister moved away from the edge of the roof. "We better get home. I want to get a couple of hours of sleep if I'm considering going to school today."

Abelard's shoulders squared as he fully faced his son. Mira laid her forehead against one hand and groaned. "And here we go."

The man pointed his blade at Mal. "A hunter should have control of his emotions. That does not sound like control, son. Now, do you want to try that again in a more respectful tone?"

One swipe of Malachi's hand and the sword was flung to the side. His brain screamed words that would not pass his lips. "What kind of control do you have? You jump to conclusions. You judge everyone. You have no friends and can't blend in worth shit. We have to do your job half the time as it is! You take Miranda's fighting skills for granted! The world is changing and doesn't need us as much as it used to, but you can't handle that because you're just a sad old man!" Each word pushed at his gritted teeth but did not escape.

Instead of his angry rant, Mal grumbled, "No, sir. I just wish you'd lay off." He rolled his eyes as his dad made an impatient motion with his free hand. "I'm just saying . . . respectfully."

"We do totally have it all handled, Dad," Miranda piped in as she attempted to lead the men off of the building. "I mean, we just helped out Lee with her friend who'd been attacked—" The girl's head fell to her shoulder. "Oh, shit."

Their father had run out of words. Hiding his sword within his coat along with his wide arrangement of weapons, he stormed over to the edge of the roof where they had climbed up using various windowsills. The twins followed from a safe distance. Mira put the fake fur of her hood tightly around her face. Mal continued to rant in his head.

They crossed the river as the sun lit up the sea spray and light rain left by the night. The sunrise had affected little of the old-fashioned, tourist-friendly lane, casting amusing shadows that played between the shops. When the small family neared the steps leading to the church and abbey, Malachi's knees buckled. Miranda caught him and pulled him back up before their father noticed.

"You feel strange? Like dizzy or anything?" he whispered.

"A little. Maybe we're getting sick."

"Maybe."

Their father went to the shop entrance at the front of their home while the twins escaped to the back stairs. "Vampire hunters," a voice called to them as they started to wearily ascend.

Mal produced a stake from his coat and held it high while Mira felt for a packet of seedlings within her pocket.

Aubrey Ruthven stepped out to where they could see him properly, dressed in a button-up shirt covered with a peacoat. His sunglasses reflected the blue of the morning light and he approached with an air of complete confidence.

"Come now. We are family, after all. Why not put down the pointy objects and let's have a civilized conversation." He held up his hands in surrender, an action which caused both twins to hold their weapons higher.

"What do you want?" Mira demanded to know, at last letting her hand relax just enough to focus on steadying her breathing.

"To talk. That is all. No fighting and no weapons. Just listen to me. That is all I ask," he explained, keeping a distance from Mal's raised stake.

"Why would we want to hear anything you have to say?" Mal wanted to know with a growl.

"How about because I don't want to fight?"

"Yeah right," Mira answered with a snort.

He hung his head and stuffed his hands into his pockets. "I know you two grew up on the stories of my crimes. I wouldn't be surprised if your family turned me into the Nos hunter bogyman to keep children in line." He frowned. The weight of his tone headed for them, threatening to knock them over with remorse. "What I did then was terrible, even for my kind. I wanted to cause suffering without thinking through the consequences. What I thought I was doing back then and what the results were—"

"Bollox!" Mal snapped. "You want us to believe that you have regret. You're a soul sucker. Your kind have always been the worst of the worst."

Aubrey waved his hands, desperation creeping into his voice. "I want an alliance. Help me find the crest, the artifact. Whatever your family calls it. Together, we can use its power to stop all of this." He motioned between the twins and himself.

Mal scoffed. "You honestly think that thing hidden on the hill could stop almost a thousand years of fighting?"

"If you had been doing the research I've been doing, you'd think so too." Aubrey Ruthven paced a little. "I've been halfway around the world. I found out more about the crest's origin."

"That's what's up there?" Mira asked in spite of herself.

Her bright eyes made the vampire smirk. "One of the last crests depicting the Order of the Dracul, passed through the hand of your ancestor, Vlad the Impaler, down to his followers. Now, this history is all verbal. I couldn't find any written proof. But my research has given me more hope than I've ever had before."

"You're saying you trusted the word of old storytellers and ancient legends and you expect us to believe you." Mal and Mira exchanged glances, silently snickering at one another in the way only twins can.

"I trust their word more than I do the writing of biased scholars. Now, will you hear me out or are you two just going to keep looking at me like you're going to eat me whole?"

They both kept their alert stances. Yet, to the shock of all three, they stayed quiet and waited to hear his words.

"The crest was endowed with magic that Vlad had collected at the same time he built up his army of Nos. The stories say that the crest was a failsafe, a way to keep his vampire followers from ever turning on him. This item is supposed to, and this is a direct quote, 'end the bloodshed between vampires and their enemies'."

Mal laughed. "Right? You want us to help you because some storyteller assured you that this crest will just magically fix everything?"

Aubrey Ruthven put out his hands and turned slightly to his left, then his right, showing off his well-built frame. "I am a walking, talking dead man who feeds on energy and you can't believe in a little magic to counteract that?"

Mal pursed his lips. He shook his fist for a moment, wondering if he could punch the vampire and run before any consequences befall him. Instead, he dropped his fist and in a low tone he almost didn't recognize he said, "I will never trust you. Whatever this is, you're doing it to give yourself power. You can lie all you want, but you can't make us believe you." He pulled on his sister's sleeve. "Come on, Mira."

Before the twins could walk away, Aubrey Ruthven shouted, "What about Lee?"

"What about her?" Mira sneered. "She isn't interested in a monster like you."

"I may be a monster, but did you ever think that maybe she doesn't see me that way? I care about her. I want to be a part of her life. You are already a part of her life. Why not consider peace for her sake?" Aubrey Ruthven wrung his hands a little, the confession burning his mouth like hot coffee.

Mira continued to glare at him. "You stay away from our friend. You're only going to confuse her—"

"I've told her everything about my history with your family," he cut in. "You can ask her if you want." Mira gaped at him while Mal stayed stoic. "I don't want secrets, not with her. I just want all of this to be over. Isn't that what you two want? I can't imagine that hunter of mythological creatures was your first choice when they started handing out careers. Think of it. You could be whatever you wanted without having to worry about constantly saving this thankless town."

Mal's ears perked up. He daydreamed for a long

minute, thinking of being normal and not having to lie. He considered Aubrey Ruthven's offer. What if the object could really change their lives for the better? Wouldn't it be worth it to try if that were true?

Aubrey Ruthven continued his speech pleadingly. "I don't know exactly what will happen if we use the crest, but if we use it together then maybe we can both have what we want. I'm not saying that I think it's going to cure the Nos or turn us human again. I don't expect I'll ever be able to marry Lee and settle in a house in the country or anything—"

Suddenly, Mal was upon him, the point of the stake aimed at Aubrey Ruthven's heart. "You aren't going near her! You got that! You're the whole reason why she's involved in any of this."

"Mal, don't!" Mira gasped, reaching for a hatchet hanging from her belt.

"Look, I didn't come here to harm anyone. If you will simply listen—"

Mal set his finger on the point of his stake, wishing had brought a crossbow instead. "Then why are you even here? You go to the trouble of tricking a girl into letting you in and then claim not to have a full plan beyond bothering us? Why come back at all then?"

"I did not trick Lee–"

"Bullshit! You put her life in danger. The Nos probably only started coming after her because they smelled you on her." In the back of Mal's mind, he added, *Probably thinking she was a Nos supporter just like I did.*

"I know, I'm sorry. It's just—" Aubrey Ruthven did not struggle or push Mal away, simply breathed heavily as if struggling to control himself. "I just thought how little I have in my life to make it better. She makes it better."

"You took away her chance at having a normal life just so you can feel better about your undead pathetic one." He pressed the point against the soft wool of Aubrey Ruthven's coat, feeling the end puncture the fabric.

Ruthven snorted like a wild animal. "And what have you two been doing? Calling her your friend. Telling her everything about us. You're just as guilty as I am in taking away her chance to be normal."

Mal snarled back at Aubrey Ruthven and pushed him away.

As Ruthven watched Mal put away his stake, he brushed at his coat and worried the pierced wool, "Admit it, you want her around as much as I do. Instead of denying what she saw and giving her the usual lies you pour out to your gullible friends, you kept her."

Mira dropped her eyes in shame. Mal stared down their opponent darkly, challenging the words with ideas of a second attack.

Aubrey Ruthven once again sighed an exhausted sound that shook his entire body. He rubbed the back of his neck and rotated his shoulders wearily. "Please yourselves. Just think about what I've suggested for her sake, if not for all of ours."

Mal and Mira started up the steps without waiting for the vampire to leave. The air around them was tense. As they entered their home Mira pointed out, "He hasn't been attacking very many people since he got here."

"That we know of," Mal countered.

According to all the journals, usually when he shows up and feeds, it always looks like an epidemic of some kind. Then, within a couple of days, the town is usually crawling with brand new bloodsuckers." Mira paused, checking to see if her mother was nearby. "Dad's been checking the hospital. No mass symptoms or any other signs that he's been feeding."

"That doesn't mean anything," Mal replied.

They approached the kitchen where they could hear their mother chatting with a friend on her mobile phone. "Oh, that's just awful." Pause. "Just too bad. Well, the kids are up. I can talk later. Bye." She pressed the off button before cheerfully asking, "So? Who had the higher body count last night?"

"What's going on?" Mira asked sweetly while rubbing at her tired eyes.

Mrs. Tepes started to prepare bowls of cereal for each of them. "Just some vandalism at St. Mary's Churchyard. You kids haven't heard anything about it, have you?"

Mal and Mira shrugged and shook their heads, despite the terror gripping their hearts. Their mother went on, "They discovered an open tomb; the lid was falling off and there was dirt everywhere. Someone had been digging. Just such a shame. They finally got all of those disrespectful tourists to stop making a spectacle of the place and then something like this happens." She poured some cereal into a third bowl and left to find their father.

Mira sunk to the table. "It doesn't mean . . . Mal, it could just be vandalism. The crest could still be there someplace."

Her brother felt another rush of dizziness and a desire to be elsewhere. "I don't think so. I think Aubrey Ruthven wasn't begging us for help. It was a trick. He already has the artifact."

Chapter 18: "Oh No, They Wouldn't Like Me"

Lee slept late into the afternoon, leaving a muddy mess of clothes in a heap on her floor. Luckily, her dad had gone out and her mum was already at work when she rose. She did laundry in peace and hid all evidence of her late-night adventures. Even her sheets and pillowcase needed to be washed and hung to dry.

Long streams of silt and gravel rolled out of her hair when she showered. A chocolate-colored river ran into the drain. Lee stayed beneath a steady rush of warm water until the floor beneath her flowed clear. She'd nearly forgotten about the bruises upon her shoulder, tattooing her skin.

The locked box stayed within her backpack buried at the back of her wardrobe. Lee came back to her room and eyed the wardrobe like an arched snake. She then propped her Edgar Allan Poe doll upon her bed, facing the wardrobe as a guard.

Rolling on her gray tights and black skirt were a strain, her muscles aching from crouching in the tomb all night. She pulled on a black jumper which hung just over her waist. The sweater had never been her favorite; she thought it made her look flat-chested and stick-like. That day she didn't care. The soft weave comforted her skin after what already felt like a long day.

She was in the process of tying her boots when the

door resounded with a tentative series of knocks. Opening without checking, she found Aubrey Ruthven standing to one edge of her stoop.

He appeared smaller. His open peacoat hung off him at an awkward angle. The sunglasses attempted to slip down the regal slope of his nose, but he caught it with a swift wave of his hand. Offering a nervous smirk, he gestured to the street. "Up for a walk?"

She wondered if he knew she had the crest. Pulling on her coat as she stepped out the door, Lee kept him in her peripheral while locking the door. "What's up?"

Ruthven waited until they had walked far enough that her home was no longer visible before replying. "I wanted to give you a little time before we talked again. How's your friend, by the way?"

"Fine, as far as I know. Made it home safe. What do you want to talk about?" Lee wanted to stare up at the hill and see if, even from across the bank, the damage of what she had done could be seen. Her eyes stared too intently on the street, the voice in her head pointing out that she was acting like a crazy person.

Her question caught him off guard. "I — we—" Realizing he was stammering, Ruthven quickly behaved as his old self, the suave ease of his words no longer betraying his feelings. "If you want to pretend it never happened, I can respect that."

The cogs within her brain lurched to a screeching halt and she grabbed his arm. "This is about the kiss!"

"Of course. What did you think it was about?"

"I—" Pink made her cheeks feel swollen. "I don't want to pretend about that."

Ruthven's face lit up. Even with his sunglasses, she could tell his eyes were grinning at her. "Excellent! Come with me!" His cool hand gripped hers and did not let go until they had reached a dock where dozens of small boats were tied up.

Ruthven rushed to one of the smaller fishing vessels and leapt within. He waved his hand over the boat. "Your chariot!"

"Where did you get this?"

"It belongs to a friend of mine. He doesn't use it very much during the day." He held out his palm to her. "You coming aboard?"

Lee's gaze went from his hand to the open sea and back to his expecting fingers. "Can you even cross water?"

"I keep home soil in my shoes. Allows me go wherever I want when there isn't a curse keeping me out." His grin never faltered. "Last chance. Time and tide and all that."

With a deep breath, Lee climbed onto the slick step. Her legs instantly took a wide stance to counteract the rocking motion of the deck. The craft seemed able to withstand the unforgiving sea, but the paint was weathered and a layer of barnacles decorated the hull. Lee set herself at the edge of the hut which housed the wheel.

"You haven't said where we're going." Unease clung to the words while she stood awkwardly, realizing only after climbing onboard how risky traversing the sea with a vampire could be.

"Trust me. You'll like this." His answer did not help, however, he smiled and she found herself sitting in the driest of the benches on the deck.

Ruthven behaved comfortably in his role as captain, turning over the engine and maneuvering away from the dock with ease. Little was said between the two as the craft carried them across the water which calmed the further, they were from shore. The spray of the sea sprinkled across their faces and clung to purple tresses. Lee shut her eyes once, playing over the idea of the soft rocking of the sea relaxed her more as Whitby moved away from them.

They never lost sight of the land, keeping the vessel in the safety of the world. Lee glanced at her phone once, realizing that it had been nearly thirty minutes of quiet contemplation - of the spray on her cheeks and the salt in her hair. She did not even mind the icy breeze looking for chinks in her coat.

The boat slowed to a stop and the engine staggered as the rhyme of pistons and cylinders halted. Lee gave him an instantly accusing look and jumped out of her seat. Whitby stayed far in the distance, a mirage at the edge of the sea.

Without a word, he pointed out to the water. Bottlenose dolphins skimmed along the top of the waves. Brief glimpses of playful faces and black eyes moved alongside the boat, showing off for the teenage girl.

Ruthven came out of the boat house and stood behind her, checking his sunglasses once before moving closer.

Noses and fins leapt from the water and dove back under the waves. As each member of the pod rose and fell with the rhythm of the water, Lee found herself caught up in the sight.

"So, you thought to yourself, 'I'll take that chick to see dolphins. Chicks love dolphins.'"

"I did not call you a chick in my mind, but yes. That was essentially the idea. Is it working?"

Lee gave him a sly glance. "I'll tell you later."

He took the opportunity to set his hands on her hips. He did not lean in or hold her too tightly. She did not shake him off or encourage him. Instead, her mind wandered to her original mission and what was hidden in her wardrobe.

"Why did Jonas attack us like that? Did he really think that Chelsea and I were supporters?"

"Jonas is an asshole. That's why he also usually goes for the neck. He thinks he's more powerful than he is. I told you not all of us are trying to exist alongside humans. They can't all be like Sibella."

"Why don't all of the vampire supporters have scars on their necks?"

"Too close to major arteries. Only the oldest and most experienced Nos can hit the veins in the neck without accidentally hitting the carotid artery. They only go for arteries if they want to kill you, not if they want to turn you or keep you around. Plus, hitting an artery is messy."

Lee wrinkled her nose in disgust. "Where do they bite them then?"

"Shoulder. Upper arm. Outer thigh or butt cheek if it's a kinky thing—"

"Gross! Fine. I'm sorry I asked." She allowed herself to lean back and he accepted this as permission to wrap his arms around her. The dolphins faded into deeper sea yet they both stared at the spot where the waves continued to ripple. Lee sighed and slipped from his grasp in order to face him. "Would the artifact stop vampires like Jonas? Or is it only going to be of use to ones like you and Sibella?"

"I honestly do not know. My sire was never very clear on details." His expression went from serious to concerned. "I should have packed a lunch or something. You must be starving."

"I'm alright. What about you? Are you . . . When do you eat?"

"I eat regular food. I only drain energy when I need to

use my powers for something or if I'm injured. Sometimes when I don't feed on energy for a long time, I have trouble controlling how much I take." His fingers waved over her head, chasing loose strands of her hair. "Do you really like this color?"

She ignored the question, tilting her head back to have a better look at him. "You know I like you," she stated bluntly. All shyness was gone and all games ended. His face beamed, but she cut him off before he could reply. "But this isn't exactly a normal situation. We should really take this slow and be careful and remember that we—"

His smile wavered only for a millisecond. "I absolutely agree. And I'm sorry that I'm putting you into an even more confusing situation. First, I wrecked your life and now I'm trying to insert myself into it. Know that I never want to influence you or upset you or—"

"Oh, shut up." And Lee pulled his face down and she kissed him. She could feel the glass lenses making marks in her cheeks. His cold hands were tracing her neck and shoulders, committing her memory.

The comfortable silence returned afterward; the quiet pensive moments were replaced with exchanges of excited smiles. The boat returned to Whitby sooner than Lee wanted.

The day did not end with the securing of the vessel at the dock. Ruthven walked her around town, telling her little details, things which were different or the same as when he had last been there centuries earlier.

"My mom would love picking your brain for historical information."

"I thought she was an expert at medieval history. How old do you think I am?"

At times, he would catch himself about to tell her a

detail and a shadow would pass over his face. The unfinished story would catch in his throat and he would change the topic. Lee wondered if he was rehashing the events leading to the murders he committed.

They even stopped to see Sibella again as Ruthven had business with her. The vampiress was less paranoid of Lee's presence this time as she saw her enter with Ruthven's arm around her waist. The other bloodsuckers and supporters in the room followed their leader's example and gave Lee a warmer welcome.

As Ruthven reported to Sibella about Jonas's actions and worries about increased hunter raids, Lee glanced around the room at the moth-eaten blankets and worn furniture.

She watched the supporters, who looked at the vampires with worried eyes and stroked their heads as they fed. She had thought of them as junkies, but now they looked more like soup kitchen workers, desperate to keep their visitors alive. Lee said nothing to them, but one gave her a weak smile as she and Ruthven left.

"Do any of the supporters work?" she asked as they neared her house.

"Are you wondering why Sibella hides in such horrible conditions? She considers it her penance for past wrongs. And she will not allow the supporters to spend money on her comfort. The others just follow her example." His voice dropped to a hush. "I want you to be careful. Sibella said that all day she had felt a stirring. Something is making her and the other blood vampires restless."

Lee thought of the box thrown into her backpack like a forgotten piece of homework. She wondered if it was the right time to reveal what she had done.

"Lee! Hi, sweetie! I didn't realize you'd gone out."

Spinning around, Lee saw her father only a short distance ahead, library books piled under his arm. Ruthven jogged forward, offering to carry the load.

"Thank you." Mr. McDaniels gratefully divided the stack between the two men. "We met the other night, didn't we?"

"Yes, sir. I'm Aubrey Ruthven. I'm a friend of Lee's."

For a moment, Lee's dad went into his own head, trying to pinpoint something that bothered him. When he returned to reality, he cheerfully motioned to the door. "Yes. Ah, well. I'm happy Lee is making so many friends so quickly."

Lee unlocked the door. Her father and Ruthven each stepped inside the house and set the books on the table.

"Are you staying for tea? I think we're ordering Chinese?"

Lee gave Ruthven a panicked stare, but the vampire coolly answered, "Thank you, but not this time. Perhaps sometime soon we can all go out and get dinner together."

The idea caught Mr. McDaniels off guard. Still, he smiled and answered, "Maybe." Ruthven let himself out. "He seems . . . nice. Is that the one you fancy?"

"You've been listening to Chelsea," was the only answer Lee gave. She escaped to her room feeling like a bubble in her chest could lift her off the floor. Her elation was only briefly interrupted by a text. It was Miranda, asking how she was and if she wanted to do anything tomorrow. Guilt threatened her happiness. Lee ignored the text and put her phone on silent.

Chapter 19: "A Friend, and That's Rarer Than a Lover"

The daylight hours waned as Lee delivered a late supper to her mother and the many dig workers. She debated on reburying the crest in a new location yet did not want to risk moving it. Already, Aubrey Ruthven had mentioned Sibella feeling strange. Still, she'd thrown on her backpack with the box inside before leaving home.

She stopped at St. Mary's on her way. The church receptionist, Seward, paced inside the building, doing a count of prayer books.

"May I come in?" she asked as respectfully as she could manage, suddenly self-aware of her spike-studded armbands and the silver skulls printed across her backpack. The insulated bags of Chow Mein and wontons hung awkwardly from her arms. Her mom's team could wait five more minutes.

"Of course." He held up a prayer book in each hand. "I think the good Christian parishioners have been taking the Lord's word home with them," he stated then added a tsk.

Lee walked up the aisle slowly, eyeing the red fabric draped over the altar and podium. She sat down in a pew just behind where the old man was counting. "I came to talk to you about desecration in the graveyard."

"I had a feeling you might know something about

that." He opened one of the books, checking that the binding was holding up.

"Right. About that." She looked down at her hands, then back up at the man, her upper teeth nearly wearing a hole in her bottom lip. "I . . . You see, I–"

"You found *it*," he finished simply as he set the books back into the pews where they belonged.

"Yes."

"And what are you going to do with it now that you have it?"

"I don't know. Hide it?" She stood up, feeling her old yens for rebellion and angst. "I'm not sorry, you know. I mean, I am sorry I destroyed that grave. But I'm not sorry that I took it. I can't let them kill each other over it."

"Who?"

"Well, there's this one vampire who— I can't believe I'm saying this. It sounds like such a cliché." She rounded the pew and faced Mr. Seward with renewed determination. "He isn't like the others. But I still don't know what he wants this crest for exactly, but he's trying to end the fighting between his kind and the Tepes family. And I don't want Malachi and Miranda to have the crest either. I don't want them to hurt him—"

He sat down and patted the wooden bench beside him. "Take a deep breath, then exhale. Do this a couple of times."

"Why?" she asked as she took her place beside him, leaving the bag of take-out on the previous pew.

"You seemed worked up. Deep breathing helps with stress. Ask anyone." She couldn't help the laugh that escaped her at his comment. She took three serious inhales and exhales before he asked her, "And do you feel like everyone will be safe now?"

Her shoulders slumped a little. "That's the trouble. I

don't. I wish I could find comfort in something, something that could give me more confidence that everything is going to be all right." She cocked her head at him with a frown beginning at the corners of her mouth. "I suppose you'll tell me to turn to the Good Book."

"Yes. Books are always the best source of comfort. I suppose if these books—" He paused to wave his hand to the Bibles in front of him. "Give you no end to your worries then I would suggest you pick a book you believe in. For example, when I have doubts and I need a voice other than the Lord's to give advice, I turn to Winnie the Pooh."

"A.A. Milne," Lee replied to show him she knew the books from her childhood.

"Right."

"My dad usually turns to Hawthorne or Longfellow. He loves Longfellow. He has a crush on the guy." She eyed her surroundings.

"And who do you turn to? Whose words comfort you?"

"I like non-fiction usually. I read a lot of science books for fun. My dad usually assigns me fiction to read. But literature-wise, I guess Edgar Allan Poe." Seward raised his eyebrows at her. "Oh, like you're really surprised."

"He isn't exactly what I would call comforting reading material."

"Not in a normal way, no. But his words are beautiful. He had this horrible, depressing life, but he could say things in a way that made it almost lovely." Lee realized how she sounded and blushed a little. "And I'm starting to sound like my dad. I better go. Thanks for the talk."

"Any time." She stood up, however, the church man forced her to pause. "And can I trust there will be no more digging?"

"I promise."

He gave her hand a squeeze and told her, "Good. 'Promise me you'll always remember: You're braver than you believe, and stronger than you seem, and smarter than you think.'"

As she pulled from his warm grip, she asked, "Milne?"

"Milne."

Lee carried the quote with her as she crossed the cemetery, the plastic sacks cutting into her cold fingers.

The words faded a bit as she entered the visitor center. She waved at the ticket agent with an annoyed grumble, "It's me again. I know where I'm going."

Striding across the field as if she belonged amongst the university students and historians, instead of being the dowdy, unimpressed daughter of one of their superiors, Lee made a choice. She needed to know what was in the box. She set the food under a plastic canopy meant to keep certain equipment safe from the wind and rain. Archaeologists flocked to the take-out like ravenous hyenas.

The table of artifacts her mother and Val had shown her the previous week had been cataloged and boxed away in clear Tupperware, which was brought out when the many interns wanted to study the ins and outs of the ancient world.

Lee found Val carefully taking inventory of the many boxes and approached him with a swagger she knew he would pick up on as fake. "Val. Val, my comrade in arms. My ally in this desolate life of reality shows and Nickelback songs. My brother from another mother. My—"

"Stop there, please. What do you want, Lee?" He set down his clipboard and crossed his arms over his chest.

"To see that key again."

"Really?" He jutted out his lips thoughtfully. "You actually want to look at an artifact? Voluntarily? Is your dad making you do homework outside of school again?"

"No, I'm just curious. It's an interesting piece. I'm allowed to be curious, aren't I?"

"You realize I don't trust a word you are saying right now," Val answered.

"Oh, come on, Val. What am I going to do? Use it to unlock an ancient power that attracts vampires?" Lee changed her pleasant demeanor to her usual cynicism and sarcasm.

"All right, all right," he answered with a laugh. "You can look at it, but you need gloves." He handed her a pair of white cotton gloves. She thought of the thin fabric as academic gloves since she also saw them worn by book antiquaries and newspaper binders. He removed the box containing the key and opened the lid cautiously. "Let me know when you're done." He set a hand on her shoulder and went to check on two students who were spending more time flirting than surveying the site.

Lee waited until he moved far enough away before she snatched up the key. Opening her bag, she fumbled with the box against the cotton gloves. She kept it hidden in the bag as she placed the key within the rusty lock. The designs on the two objects matched, giving her hope. A loud squeal and a great resistance made her almost give up, afraid of breaking the key off in the lock.

After a wiggle and a final turn, she heard the click of the old spring, and the clasp freed. The box came open. The inside must have once been lined with fabric which had nearly all deteriorated. Wisps of red thread still clung to the edges. At the center of the box was a round disk with a metal loop in the top, most likely for a sash or chain. The center of the medallion was etched deeply with the image of a medieval goat-like unicorn on a shied beneath a second unicorn leaping from within a hollow crown. This was not what Lee had expected. She had thought to find images of dragons and gargoyles.

At first, she studied the thing, running her thumb across one unicorn and wondering about how something so small could cause so much trouble.

"Lee, you need anything over there? One of the interns is going for coffee?"

The sound of Val's voice made Lee jump. She swiftly set the key back into the Tupperware, then pulled one of her cotton gloves over the top of the crest. Tossing it into the backpack, she answered, "Nope. I'm good. Thanks for letting me look."

Closing her bag and returning the lid to the Tupperware, she ran off from the dig site, waving goodbye to Val. Her mom passed by as she tried to make her exit. "Lee?"

"Hi Mom, bye Mom! Got to go. Meeting some friends." And she ran. The metal box in her bag beat against her side as she went down the stairs. Her head whipped backward every few steps, convinced someone knew the full extent of her secret.

She collided with a body. Strong hands kept her upright. "Whoa, you're running like the devil is after you? What's the matter?"

Lee looked up at Aubrey Ruthven, wishing she had raked a comb through her hair. "Oh, exercise."

"Exercise?" He seemed surprised by the answer, taking her by the arm and escorting her down the remainder of the steps.

The crest still weighed upon Lee's mind and she thought of excuses to leave. Then, his smile hit her. She suddenly forgot her mission and her nervousness. They sat on the bench at the bottom of the steps.

Lee pitched back her head in awe. "You think I can keep up with a friend like Chelsea and fit into my black skirts without working out a little? Oh, to have such fantasies. It's like you're immortal and don't have to worry about your metabolism or something."

With a smile, he leaned down to kiss her. Lee could see herself in his sunglasses and felt a twinge of regret as he pressed his lips to hers. For a brief second she remembered. He didn't know what she had done, but she decided it was for his own good.

When he came up from the kiss, he brushed his fingers through her hair, smoothing down the back. "I get to see you twice in one day. I am lucky." He nuzzled against the scarf on her neck.

"Hey, cut that out," she requested with a laugh. She sat back just a little and gave a deep sigh. A warm feeling invaded her anxious mind again. For a brief second, a voice reminded her of the importance of what rested in her backpack. The warm feeling enveloped the little voice, drowning it out with the eagerness to flirt.

"How many humans have you— Would dated be the right word? Not that such a topic is really the stuff of significance at an hour such as this."

He took both hands and set them on either side of her face. He smiled and told her, "Calm down. Do you want an honest answer?"

"I'm a realist. I'll always want an honest answer."

He rubbed his thumb along her cheekbone as he started to recite.

"Much have I travell'd in the realms of gold,
And many goodly states and kingdoms seen;
Round many western islands have I been,

Which bards in fealty to Apollo hold."

She frowned causing his finger to rest at the corner of her mouth. "You're really into poetry, aren't you?"

"Poetry is the language of the soul. Plus, why say it in my boring modern way, when Keats can say it for me so much better."

"Yeah. I'm not a big Keats fan, so I'm not entirely sure what you were saying there. I interpreted it as in the last few hundred years you've gotten around."

He removed his hands. "That isn't what it means."

"Hey, having a few past girlfriends is understandable after a few centuries."

He kissed the top of her head. "Dear sweet, Lee, are you jealous?"

"No." She was honest. "I know I'm not the first girl you've cared about and I just want to know where I stand. I am betraying the only people to befriend me in this whole place in order to snog you, after all."

Aubrey Ruthven sighed heavily. "I am your friend too, did you think of that?" She gave him a sharp look and he caved. "Very well, if you must ask. There was someone a long time ago, but she and I did not end well," he confessed. "Luckily, immortality has been helping me to forget her."

"Maybe you didn't really love her," Lee pointed out, feeling bitterness on behalf of the forgotten girl of so long ago, "If you loved her, you would have made space in your brain to hold onto her."

He crossed his arms over his chest, at first irritated with her accusation. Then, his expression lightened. "What is your natural hair color?" the man asked with legitimate interest.

Lee turned the question over in her mind, trying to think back to a time before all the dyes and angst. "Dirty blonde? Don't make me describe the exact shade."

"Imagine trying to remember something like that over centuries."

"Hair color and relationships are two entirely different circumstances, sir."

He released her face from his grip, but not before delivering a small kiss to her forehead. "I forgot how young you are. Someday, you'll see what I mean."

"I don't know if I want to," Lee stated. "I mean, I'm not particularly a fan of sentimentality, but if I lived hundreds of years, I'd want to remember my parents and my friends."

"Trust me. It's better not to."

"My mom always tells me that we should hold onto the past, even if it's painful. But I guess she would say that. Without the past, she'd be out of a job," Lee reasoned.

"And it isn't her own past she's usually holding onto," he explained.

Lee slid a little away from him and shrugged. "When I'm dead and gone—"

Waving his hand to command silence, Aubrey Ruthven noticed Miranda coming up the sidewalk. "We have company. We'll have to talk about that when the time comes," he responded secretively. The pair of them rose from the bench.

There was an almost embrace and last looks. He turned to walk away, calling over his shoulder, "I'd love to see your natural hair color someday."

Miranda leaned up against the wall, wishing she could blend into it. She couldn't be certain, but she thought she saw something more between the vampire and her new friend. If she studied them, focused on their body language she could see it clearly. The way he leaned; the way she folded her arms behind her back shyly; the way they watched each other with a mixture of excitement and fear. There was something there.

He was gone by the time she approached Lee. "What was that about?" Miranda asked as she caught the last glimpse of the Nos escaping around the corner like a rodent.

Lee turned stoic, determined to reveal nothing. "I'm not sure. He talked in circles."

Miranda stared at the sidewalk, pausing to wonder about the consequences of pursuing the topic. Instead, she skirted the issue with a simple, "I got new shoes."

Glancing down at the flat suede boots on Miranda's feet, Lee muttered, "Nice" in an attempt to be polite.

"Thanks," Miranda replied flatly. She wanted to smile and laugh and tell Lee that she was excited to hang out with her again. Instead, she stated in the same monosyllabic tone, "I wanted to talk to you."

As the pair wound through the town, Miranda was haunted by the sight of Lee and the vampire. "They were flirting," she thought to herself and the horrific realization dawned on her that maybe Mal and her father were right about Lee. Maybe she was a sympathizer. Maybe hidden on her body were the puncture wounds of allowing herself to be bitten, the track marks she'd been trained to look for. Miranda found herself watching Lee's sleeves as they moved up and down her wrists each time she moved her arm. She wanted to pull at Lee's scarf and check the pale neck and shoulders. She wanted the thoughts in her mind to shut up.

"Look. Is this going to take long? I told my dad I'd listen to some awful radio program with him and it starts in a little while." Lee moved her hands to the straps of her backpack, keeping it protectively in place.

Mira worried the thin skin of her lips between her teeth. "You know what, it can wait till tomorrow."

"Are you sure?"

"Yes. Mal wanted to talk to you too and I should really wait until he's around." Lee gave a cautious thank you and a half-hearted farewell before vanishing across the river to the other side of the town. Miranda took out her phone before Lee was even out of sight. "I'm worried that there might be a problem," she text to her brother and proceeded to describe what she had seen.

Lee almost waited for a few minutes near the edge of the steps to see if Ruthven re-appeared. She thought better of it as the contraband within her bag shifted. Instead, she went home and warmed up her laptop.

With her parents both out, her mom cleaning up the dig and her dad at a pub with another academic, and her phone on silent, Lee focused on her search engine. A full thirty minutes was dedicated to Bram Stoker and the creation of Dracula. The facts were a rehash of what the notes at the beginning of her dog-eared copy of the book had already told her.

Bram Stoker worked for an actor in a strange master-minion capacity. He wrote part of the novel while staying in Whitby and he'd taken the name for the main character from Prince Vlad III of Romania, who was part of the Order of the Dragon, also known as the Dracul.

One poorly produced documentary caught her attention. The crew had interviewed several natives of Budapest who declared Vlad the Impaler to be a national hero. They praised his actions against the Turkish invaders from centuries earlier. They scoffed at the thoughts of his missing tomb being evidence of him being a creature of the night. However, the documentary made certain to point out the amount of vampire-related merchandise shops sold to idiot tourists.

Lee started to delve into an internet spiral of Romanian royal history, discovering it included quite a few men named Radu. Vlad had been married twice, once to an unnamed Romanian who'd allegedly committed suicide and then to a Hungarian princess whose cousin had once been his ally. She started to go cross-eyed as medieval coats of arms filled her screen. The Order of the Dragon's symbol was nothing more than a cross with yellow flames. The family emblem of his Hungarian wife was more interesting, featuring goat-like unicorns against a shield, a crown, and leafy patterns.

Her fingers shaking, she removed the crest from her bag and held it to the screen. The etching of the stone relic matched the coat of arms of Ilona Szilágyi, the second wife of Dracula. Setting the object carefully back into its makeshift coffin, the girl turned to her Poe doll, which lay in a huddle near her pillow.

"Eddie, what the hell is going on?"

Snatching her phone, she debated briefly before typing in, "Do you and Mal still want to see me?"

A full five minutes left her life before the phone lit up with Mira's reply. "I'm meeting Mal at the pub. I'll send you the address."

Lee wrote down the name of Dracula's wife, knowing she would forget it. And back out into the streets of Whitby she ventured, wishing she had a plan. The crest remained in her room, guarded by the plush Edgar Allan Poe on her desk.

Chapter 20: "A Man's Brain"

Evening overcame the afternoon, feeding the pub a steady stream of early customers. Mal sat at a booth alone with a few of the family journals open around him. His sister's text had disturbed him, still, he did not want his father to see him frantically search for more information about Aubrey Ruthven.

His football team entered with much celebration as if they needed to announce to the entire establishment that they had just finished an informal practice. It was unusually early in the season for football, but the boys were determined to keep themselves in shape.

Mal watched the members of his team, longing to follow them. He wished he was walking alongside as he overheard their laughter at one another's expense. Even as they slung teasing insults back and forth, he wanted to join in. It was amazing, but he even missed the way they called him Scarecrow or Beanpole. He went from having an entire team to go to the pub with to sitting alone, waiting for his sister.

"Path-etic," Mal groaned to himself as he slunk into a booth. He hoped they hadn't seen him, but he knew he couldn't hide from the team forever.

Mira and Lee entered within minutes. His sister smiled and waved at his old teammates. If he hadn't been so busy hiding, he would've thrown a pint glass at her to make her stop. She moved through the pub, stopping occasionally to give another hello to someone she knew.

Lee followed looking like her usual disdainful self. The room bored her and the people did not interest her. And yet when she spotted him at the table, he thought he saw her smile just for a second.

The girls slid into the booth across from him. She set her elbows on the table and raised an eyebrow at his research. "You always do your homework in a pub?"

"I'm looking for information about the artifact," he answered with tight lips.

"Mal thinks we've missed something in the fifty times our parents have made us read those old diaries." Mira hopped up. "This place has rubbish service. I'm going to the bar. Lee, want anything?"

"I'm good."

Mal returned to his reading and Lee stared on, awkwardly awaiting more words from him. "What do you know about Vlad the Impaler?" she blurted.

His nose wrinkled. "What don't I know? He's my ancestor, remember."

"There's some information about it in the back of my Dracula book. It said he was married twice and that he had several kids."

Grunting, Mal closed the book. As he searched for a different volume from the stack he'd brought with him, he distractedly replied, "We are descended from the Romanian side of the family tree, Vlad III's first wife."

"What was her name?"

"Ekaterina." His eyes shot her a dark stare. "That's a family secret, by the way. Her name was lost to history, and we like to keep it that way."

"Why?"

"According to legend, it was to save her soul. She

215

committed suicide when the Turks attacked. A clan of Roma came to the castle and worried that because she took her own life, she would become a vampire. It was an old superstition in that part of the world."

"Roma? That's a kind of gypsy, right?"

"Yes. Ekaterina's grandson had a daughter with a Roma woman. Ask Mira about it sometime. It's one of her favorite stories." He added with annoyance, "And one of the only ones she can retell correctly."

"A daughter? But you have the surname Tepes?"

"That's more a title than a surname. We aren't the only members of the family. We have cousins scattered all over the world. Some are only distantly related, but we all use Tepes as our surname."

"Is everyone just assigned a corner of the globe?"

"Yes. And this is where our branch of the family wound up ever since the artifact was brought here." Remembering his purpose, Mal reopened one of the journals.

Several minutes passed silently. Lee glanced once to search for Mira in the crowded room. Her head buzzed with conversation starters. *Did you happen to see my desecration of the churchyard? I am just terrible. How would you feel about a vampire welfare system? But Vlad's second wife? I bet she was a bitch, am I right? Why not tell me more about her?*

In the end, she muttered. "That must be a good read." He did not reply. "You still haven't told me your favorite Poe poem."

Mal buried himself further into his work, not willing to give up the information.

"Oh, come on," she groaned, "You wanted to talk. Let's talk."

His expression did not change and he continued to

ignore her as she ground her teeth.

"Fine," Lee concluded, "I didn't really want to know. I was just trying to make conversation." She rested her head in her hands as Mira came back with a pint of something amber-colored. "Your brother is being more intense and angst-ridden than usual," Lee complained, her cheek resting on the sticky surface.

Mira took a sip before replying. "We both have a lot on our minds." She then reached across and slammed one of the old leather-bound tomes closed. "However, he shouldn't be quite so rude."

Mal and Mira exchanged a glance, more silent twin discussion, debating who should lead the conversation. Finally, Mal spoke with a scary amount of conviction. "It's about Aubrey Ruthven."

"What about him?" Lee's shoulders pushed backward and her nose rose into the air.

"We worry that he might be lying to you. That you might be . . . tricked by him," Mira said slowly, worried about offending the purple-haired girl. "Has he said anything to you about his past?"

"Yes." Lee wanted to lie, to get up and run with her head held high. They waited for her to elaborate and she continued. "He told me about how he murdered children to get to the crest, but regrets it. And then he was banished." A voice in the back of her mind reminded her that he'd also mentioned a woman he used to love.

"He told you that it was a crest?" Mal asked as he tapped his finger nervously against the journal on the table. "Anything else?"

"Just that he was tired of fighting and wanted peace," Lee stated with a shrug. "Why? What were you hoping he told me?" The idea of his maker demanding the object niggled at her tongue yet she kept it to herself.

Mal leaned back with a heavy sigh. "I don't know, exactly. Where the crest is, I guess. Are you sure you've told us everything?"

"You wanted me to talk to him. I've done that. And you don't tell me everything either. You wanted my help and then you don't want my help. You want to create a plan and then you plan without me. Are you using me to help banish him or do you think I'm bait?" She looked sickened, ready to reach across the table and slap Mal as hard as she could.

"No, Lee. It's not that—" Mira tried to explain, her voice sloppy with apology.

"Why don't we just tell her." Mal pointed at Lee and kept his voice at a steady deadpan. "He came and talked to us. He wanted an alliance and he tried to use you, the idea of keeping you safe and happy, as a bargaining chip."

Lee blinked at them for a minute, her head bobbing back and forth between the brother and sister. "He spoke to you?" Mira nodded. "Then why are you bothering to ask me these things?"

Mal shoved a book away from him and grumbled, "Rubbish."

Lee leaned forward, snatching up the journal he had rejected. "What was that?"

"Nothing."

"Oh no, by all means, say what you were going to say. Pontificate your ass off because maybe if you talked a little more, you wouldn't bottle up so much of that frustration. And then you would not be making a face like a constipated baboon right now." The volume of her voice rose with each sentence. Mal's frown deepened, yet his lips stayed tightly shut.

Mira calmly butted in. "Look, Lee, we just are trying to look out for you."

Lee set a finger against the binding of the journal closest to her, her skin turning pale from the force with which she pressed. "Without even looking at both sides of the story. You're going off the word of people who have been dead for hundreds of years. What about hearing him out? Maybe he really just wanted to keep me safe."

"Technically Aubrey Ruthven has been dead for hundreds of years too," Mira pointed out wincing at the thought of the tender moment she'd walked in on earlier.

Mal half stood, reaching for the journal. "Listen, you want to be a Nos supporter, that's your business, but know if you are then we can't protect you anymore."

"I'm not saying I want to be a Nos supporter or that I want to be anyone's pet or food supply. I am just saying that perhaps if you gave the matter a proper amount of cerebral function, maybe you would see that there might be something more going on here beyond monsters and slayers."

"Lee, we have something important to tell you, if you would just shut up for two seconds. We think Ruthven already has the cr—" Mal suddenly sunk back into his seat, pulling all of the journals with him. He stashed them on the bench beside him and draped his coat over the top.

The whole of the football team sauntered over. "Tepes," the captain greeted, his voice full of the ache to taunt and be cruel. "Didn't expect you to be out. Thought you'd be at home, dealing with your 'family stuff'."

Mira smiled sweetly at the team captain. "No, Baz. We do actually let him out on good behavior."

"Miranda! How have you been?" Baz leaned closer against the table. "Still going out with that wanker from Cottington?"

"Bleh, no! That was just a summer thing. What about

you? You still going to attend the fishing industry school come the autumn?"

The pair of them continued to talk leisurely, making the young man almost forget that he had come to demand answers from Mal or that the rest of the team was standing on hand. Ian was the only one who would not meet Mal's eyes. He stood at the back of the group of boys, keeping his attention fixed on a television hung over the bar.

Lee nudged Mira. "This is all super interesting, but I've got to use the loo." The girl let her out as she continued to talk, pausing only a second to give her a suspicious glance. The footballers parted to allow her by, and Mal lost sight of her once she rounded the bar.

One of the other young men, a stout lad of eighteen with a square head, clapped Mal on the back and asked, "When are you coming back?"

"I told you, Stuart. I can't," Mal said in a low warning tone. He willed them to leave him alone. He needed a power that could repel his peers and make him invisible.

"Oh, come on, mate. You're one of our best guys. You could at least help us out every now and again especially when the chavs from Scarborough come round. I need men like you behind me if I'm ever going to play for the Blues."

The other teammates, save Ian, all started to give their opinion and more reference's to the town's official team as if their school-boy group existed in the same league. The row they created alerted one of the barmen. He came over, a towel raised over his head. "If you boys are going to cause trouble, you can leave now."

Mal, gathering up his coat and books, took his opportunity to leave as well. He used the path created by the barman to hop from the table. Giving a grumble of an excuse to his former teammates and attempting to give Ian a pat on the shoulder, Mal escaped to the front of the pub. His eyes stayed forward, not wanting to view Ian's reaction.

Through the window he noticed Lee. She stood just around the corner, her reflection visible in the window of another shop. She was talking to herself, her arms crossed over her chest.

He exited, juggling the heavy tomes between his hands as he pulled his coat over his lanky figure. He'd left his bookbag at the booth and refused to go back for it. As he came around the building, he heard Lee followed by a male voice. Aubrey Ruthven stood a foot from her, his hands on his hips.

"I'm sorry," he was saying. "I wasn't trying to put you in a worse situation."

Mal stayed against the wall, continuing to watch Lee's reflection while listening to her and the Nos argue. "You spoke with them," she insisted. "Why didn't you just tell me that? And why did you talk to them? What are you on about?"

"Lee, Lee. Calm down." He laughed lightly. "You're already so much in the middle. I just wanted to try talking to them. It didn't turn out how I planned."

"I don't want them to think that I br—" Lee stopped short and hung her head. Mal could not see in the reflection what her expression had turned to.

"That's why I didn't tell you. Look, if I can get my hands on that crest, maybe stupid kids won't throw away their lives on letting men like Jonas feast on them daily and force others like Sibella to hide underground—"

"I don't know if I really want to talk about this right now," she added with an overdramatic tilt up of her chin. At that moment, she seemed more like a confused envoy, a noble diplomat attempting to remember her purpose and place.

As the pair grew quiet for a full minute, Mal dared to peep around the corner. He was unnoticeable, keeping close to the wall and stepping lightly. They would not see him unless they fully turned in his direction. Still, he held his breath, keeping a silent chant in his head that Aubrey Ruthven would not notice his presence.

Aubrey Ruthven reached out, wrapping a short lock of purple around his finger until the back of his hand rested against Lee's cheek. "Do you dye it to upset your parents? They don't seem like the type to care. I saw your mother at her dig site the other day. She had so much patience with the interns."

She slowly pulled away, annoyed by the physical content, yet wanting more. "You were watching my mother?"

"I was curious," he answered apologetically. "I wanted to know what sort of person raised you."

"You could have just asked to meet her like a normal person."

"Oh yes. Because this is so very normal." His hand passed between them as he laughed.

Lee laughed in return. She seemed comfortable, the banter working its way into her new daily routine.

Mal dug his nails into the bricks of the wall shielding him. Ruthven leaned down, about to kiss Lee when he sensed something. His face hovered over hers and he whispered, "And again, we are not alone."

Lee turned around to see Miranda. Her lips twisted in disgust at the relationship forming between her friend and her enemy. Mal ducked again behind his corner, wondering when it was that his sister had come out. She must have walked the football team out to the other end of the street, then rounded back around to find Ruthven and Lee.

"You don't have to hide over there. I can see you," Lee called out with regret.

The young woman approached slowly, her steps cautious and her hand hovering over her coat pocket where a stake lay. "Lee, what's going on?" she asked, even though she knew.

"Mira, this isn't as bad as you think it is—"

Lee was cut off by Mira's accusing rants at Ruthven. "What have you done to her? My father was right. You've been controlling her. Manipulating her."

"He's not controlling me!" Lee screamed the words, every ounce of exhaustion and frustration from within her echoing across the narrow street.

Ruthven nearly lost his balance, shocked by the outburst.

The female vampire hunter swallowed a comeback. "Okay. Then what exactly is going on?"

No longer caring how she looked or whether she hurt Mira's feelings, Lee rambled with venom. "I'm bridging the gap between human and monster. Sort of a psychological study. He is being a perfect gentleman in helping me. He's been explaining to me what it is like to be a vampire who rarely feeds on humans."

"I admit to being a guinea pig," he answered nervously.

"Yeah, right," the vampire hunter's daughter mumbled. Miranda reached for Lee's arm. "We have to go find Mal. Will you come with me?"

Lee's anger wavered as she saw tears at the edge of Mira's eyes. Giving Ruthven's hand a squeeze, she nodded. "I will, but only to explain to both of you what's going on."

Mira sent Lee ahead of her like she was protecting a child, then turned to look back at Aubrey Ruthven with a dark glare. "You better watch yourself," she told him darkly.

"I know you're just waiting for me to act, but I keep telling you. I didn't come here for a fight, Tepes girl," he replied. "I mean no harm."

She continued her deep stare as she steered herself and Lee away. Her lips remained tightly pursed together as they walked. Lee could sense the anger and worry coming from Miranda, yet she didn't care. She still thought of Aubrey Ruthven's face hovering over hers and she felt the excited flutter in her chest as she thought of seeing him again. "I'm such a sap," she thought to herself almost laughing out loud.

Suddenly, she felt Mira's hand snatch up hers. Like a five-year-old leads a friend from a dangerous stranger or through a carnival maze, Miranda walked Lee swiftly away from Ruthven, who followed.

Meanwhile, Mal returned to the door of the pub, leaning his head against the frame of the entrance. His mind ached. Lee trusted Aubrey Ruthven. More than that, she liked him. She was flirting and smiling and looking happier than she ever was when hanging around him and Miranda. He saw his sister whip around the corner, her knuckle white as it gripped Lee's hand.

She set their new friend in front of Mal as if presenting her for inspection and hurriedly whispered something in his ear. There were still tears in her eyes when she faced Lee as she moved to the opposite side of the door frame. Her arms wrapped around her chest and her skin was tinged with green.

"Mira—"

Miranda shook her head and violently rubbed away a

tear. Without another word, she ran through the pub door and into the bathroom at the back as if her life depended on it.

"I didn't mean to upset her," Lee commented to Mal who stared down at his trainers.

"We need to talk," he growled, glancing around the crowded bar and noticing Ian still inside with a couple of other members of his football team all crowding the bar. "Not here."

"I'd rather not."

"I wasn't asking you," Mal told her, then roughly grabbed her arm. He wound her through the road, away from where Aubrey Ruthven had just come around the corner, and at last stopped on the pavement at the edge of a closed and boarded clothing store, far away from the eyes and ears of drunken pub patrons.

"That hurt," Lee protested as she pulled away from him. "Was that really necessary?"

"You said we keep things from you! What do you call what you and Ruthven were doing?" Mal barked out, not concerned for her arm or her pain.

"I didn't know how to tell you."

"Have you been working with him all this time?" Mal stated, his voice dark and accusing. He knew he should tell that he too had been eavesdropping, yet his tongue felt heavy each time he attempted to admit to his crime. At last, he admitted, "No. I know you haven't. But why him, Lee? Didn't I make it clear that he's bad news?"

"I should have told you before. Aubrey Ruthven saved my best friend's life," Lee argued. "He's proven himself to me over and over again. I have no reason not to trust him. If you just listen to me—"

"Listen to you!" Mal practically shouted. "That dopey look on your face! You keep talking like you know him, but you don't know him, Lee."

"And you keep talking like you know me, but you don't!" Lee did scream. She wailed. Her finger pointed at him like a nun shaking a ruler at an undisciplined student. "You and your sister talk about me like you already know what I'm about to do or say. I'm not your friend and, I repeat, you do not know me. I didn't want to hurt either of you; I wish you'd made all of this easier on me."

"You think this is difficult. You don't know what it's like to live with monsters every single day." Mal held his hand against his forehead dramatically. "Oh, my prophetic soul. I am in such anguish. The world is an unfair cesspool of ignorance and I am the lone voice of intelligence. Poor tragic, Anabel Lee."

Lee let out a high-pitched squeal. "I do not sound like that! I would never steal quotes from 'Hamlet' to express my annoyance at the world. 'Macbeth', maybe, but never 'Hamlet'!" Then, she poked a finger at Mal's chest. "And who are you to talk? I may be realistic but compared to your angst I'm freaking Pollyanna!"

Mal grappled her hand away from him, but his shoulders shook. He was laughing. Lee's mouth twisted in confusion. She watched as Mal tried to suppress his chuckles. He scratched his chin in an attempt to cover his mouth.

"Shit. I wish I could talk to my dad like this." She quickly realized that his laughter was a desperate grasp to control his normally calm emotions.

Surprised at his surrender, Lee nodded in agreement. "No more yelling and no more talks about how bad my decisions are. I can take care of myself."

"Lee, I'm serious."

"Oh, there's a change for you."

Mal's voice returned to hushed and dark. "You don't get it. This isn't a story. He's not the sensitive vampire and you're not the girl who can save him from himself. He may be intrigued by you, he might even have feelings for you, but when it comes down to it, he is still the monster and you are still his victim. One way or another, he will hurt you in the end."

She took a step away as if to physically distance herself from Mal's words. "All you know is what you read in those dusty old books your father forces upon you."

Mal's calm exterior broke again. "I know enough of his kind! And I know what was written about him! He. Is. The. Villain. And don't expect me or my sister to save you when he shows you what he really is."

"When he has the crest, maybe he can—"

"He already has the crest!"

Lee physically stumbled at Mal's accusation.

He continued, waving his hands, his fingers creating air alongside her cheeks. "I don't know what he's up to or what he's waiting for, but Mira and I know the crest has been moved."

"That doesn't mean it was him—"

Mal grew so angry, he spat when he spoke his first word. "Who else would it have been, Lee? He has the power! He could have found a way around going into the churchyard. Hell, he could have sent a Nos supporter in there. All he would have to do is tell them where to dig."

"It wasn't him, Malachi! You're just too prejudiced to see it! Why would he want your help if he already had the crest?"

"To fool us! To give us false hope! To get close to us, like he's trying to get close to you! He's just using you, Lee, and once he uses that crest, we will all be in real danger."

She slapped him. The motion was swift and cut through the air with a slight whish. Her hand hit his cheek which was rough from not shaving that morning. He did not seem hurt by her touch. He stared with his mouth hanging open and his hand pressed against the place where she had struck.

"Aubrey Ruthven did not take the crest. I did." She panted heavily between the words, yet had come too far to stop her rant. "I didn't give it to him if that's what you're worried about. But I won't give it to you either. I've hidden it and until I know what it does or until you and Miranda, and he start to get along, it's staying hidden."

"Lee, you idiot." His hand fell slowly. His expression melted into a forlorn loss. "You just put yourself in more danger. We can't protect you from this."

She held her chin high and balled her fists at her sides. "I don't need protection; I need you to listen and try to see something beyond the hate you were raised with."

His tone went back to the normal mumble. "It's not hate. It's common sense."

Lee was speechless and shocked by his sheer partiality. She turned her back on him and walked away quickly. She glanced back once to see Mal, his tense shoulders slumping in defeat as he sat down on the curb. He held his head in one hand as if exhausted. In that second, Lee felt sorry for him. She suddenly wished she hadn't squabbled.

Different emotions twisted within her and never before did her mind feel so completely out of control. Was it her feelings for Ruthven doing this? Was it some weird side-effect her first intense want for another person? She wondered if maybe the crest affected her.

Maybe her connection with the ancient artifact clouded her mind and took away her self-control.

Lee remembered the handsome face of Aubrey Ruthven awaiting her down the street. All other concerns pushed their way to the bottom of her stomach and excitement was all she allowed to the surface.

Constance Tepes 1789

Today I return from what may be my only journey away from Whitby. I left by carriage a fortnight ago to stand witness for Maria's wedding. I was so desperate to go, that I traveled unchaperoned. On my trip back from her new home in Liverpool, I held company with mostly crude, older people who complained the entire way of how the bumps in the road affected their aching bones. Save for one man.

The carriage picked him up on the road from Blackpool and he rode with us all the way back to Yorkshire County. He made me laugh and kept the journey's tedium to a minimum. He even rescued me from the inappropriate advances of a traveling merchant, who was then thrown from the coach.

As we neared the borders of Whitby, the horses grew anxious, as if spooked. And then the carriage stopped. The vehicle halted right at the edge of town and would not be moved. There were no rocks beneath the wheels or livestock in the road; no visible reason why the carriage would not move. The man seemed unnerved by this. I climbed out to inform the driver I would simply walk home and to please retrieve my baggage for me.

The driver asked my friend, the man, if he would escort me a little way, then he would meet up with us further down the road as soon as he discovered the cause of the delay. And then, I saw my new acquaintance in the light of day. I saw his handsome features just as they had been described to me by my forebears in their diaries. Gold glowed within his eyes, and I was mesmerized.

Aubrey Ruthven, the enemy of my family who was banished from Whitby so long ago, shrugged his shoulders in my direction.

"I thought perhaps I would try and see if the curse still holds," he told me as if we were still the friendly party from within the carriage.

I nearly reached for my weaponry from within my cloak, worried about the carriage driver standing witness to my destruction of the demon.

He sensed my defensive pose and held up his hands in protest. "You have nothing to fear from me, Tepes daughter. I did not come here to start up the old quarrel. I simply came with a hope that perhaps my unspeakable deeds were, if not forgiven, at least forgotten. I will come again sometime later. Perhaps I will finally be able to make amends and your descendants will be willing to listen." And he bowed to me.

Truth be told, I yearned to believe him, to allow him access to my home and undo all of the good my ancestor did in locking him out. I managed to proclaim that such a day would never find him. He knew of his own evils and his remorse had to be false.

And so, I return home, ready to keep my family history safe and secret. Oh, sweet God in Heaven, protect me from ever again having to face such a charming monster.

Chapter 21: "Absorbing Lives"

Nearly a week went by without a word spoken or text between the twins and Lee. As Mal walked home after a long perimeter around the shadowy outskirts of the town, he took stock of his life. He took note of the bulge in Miranda's jacket where she hid a wooden stake. The Star of David around her neck glittered in the streetlights. His own face and neck were speckled with blood and mud. His feet dragged as they crossed the river toward home.

Miranda leaned on the railing of the bridge overlooking the place where the river met the sea. Mal walked up to her and slapped his own hands against the rail. His sister had been unusually quiet for days.

"Thinking about Lee?"

"She's not a bad person, Mal," Miranda insisted.

His face stoic and his voice flat, he responded, "But she's helping him all the same. Even if she doesn't mean to."

"I think that if she'd given him the artifact we'd know by now."

"Just because she hasn't yet, doesn't mean that she won't soon. You know what we have to do."

The edge of Mira's jacket muffled her answer as she pressed her chin to her chest. "We've waited this long. Wait a little longer."

Each night, both watched their father with guilty knots in their stomachs. Yet neither could bring themselves to tell the truth. As long as Abelard Tepes thought the ancient relic was still safe in St. Mary's Churchyard, the twins could make their own decision about what was to be done about Annabel Lee McDaniels.

"If we wait too long, it could be too late to stop whatever Ruthven has planned. Lee is going to get people killed." He spoke clinically, keeping his chin lifted high.

Miranda gripped the top of the railing tightly. "Bullshit. You like her too, Mal. I know you do!" Her brother's face fell as she continued, "I know she's a pain and long-winded and needs to incorporate some color into her wardrobe, but you know what, she's my friend. I'm not going to let you or Dad make her disappear."

"And when the world ends because you wanted to save your 'friend', what will you do?" Mal growled with conviction, obviously convinced that such a catastrophe would take place.

"Then we better just make sure that doesn't happen," Miranda simply stated. "You know what? Lee is right. You are more dramatic than she is."

Malachi and Miranda finished their way home as the sun started to rise. Mira poked at a hole in her jacket while her brother stretched out his aching joints. Crimson splattered the shoes of both teenagers, and their weapons supply was lighter than usual.

"This week has been like a bad children's book," Mal complained.

Mira lit up. "You're right! We mashed two Nos on Monday, trampled three Nos on Tuesday, whaled on a gaggle on Wednesday–"

"Thank you, Dr. Seuss. That's enough."

"I wasn't done," she whined.

"Yes, you were." Mal rotated his shoulders and groaned. "Ever since—" Mal glanced around the dimly lit room for his parents. "Lately the Bloodsuckers have all been acting like it's St. Patrick's Day and the beer is free."

Mira stopped fussing at her jacket and sighed loudly. "Do you think Dad has noticed?"

"He's been trying to convince every member of the family to come here and give us back up. Yes. I think he's noticed. If he has his way, then he's going to have a dozen vampire hunters at Lee's door, whether she is guilty of helping Aubrey Ruthven or not." Mal took a stake from his pocket, inspecting the point that had splintered in an attempt to save himself from an attack earlier that night.

"Then why do you want to tell him?"

"She's still with Ruthven, Mira. And she has the crest. We haven't seen her in a week, and we have no way of knowing what she's going to do with that thing in the end." He tapped the stake against his leg. "We don't even know what it does."

Miranda skipped around her brother joyfully. "You know what, Mal?"

"What?" he grumbled, obviously annoyed by her rather loud expressions of happiness.

"I'm quite glad we met Lee," his sister declared.

"Hmm, even if she ends up helping one of the most feared Nos in Britain take over Whitby and use what our ancestors buried on the hill against us?" Mal stared down Miranda with a grave expression, but his shoulders were slumped with a mixture of exhaustion and depression.

"She won't," Miranda told him with complete confidence. "Wait and see. She'll see right through him. Give her time."

Mal dropped his attention down to the floor and grumbled, "Like I said, she likes him. What makes you think she'll listen to us over the guy who's sweeping her off her feet?"

"Give her a little more time," Mira repeated, peeking out the window. "Dad's leaving." She pointed to a man with a heavy coat on his back and a small suitcase at his side waking through the street.

"He must've gone down through the shop." Mal ran downstairs and toward the man, his sister close at his heels. "Dad, where are you going?" he demanded as he approached, the wind catching his breath in little clouds.

Abelard Tepes was unconcerned with his children's surprised expressions. "How was the hunt tonight, you two?" he asked as simply as if asking how their day at school had been.

"Fine. But where are you going?" Mal repeated.

"Manchester. Your cousin, Bathilda . . . you remember her?"

Mira answered first. "The one with all of the parrots she trained to chant, 'Death to all blood suckers.'"

"That's correct." Abelard looked a little uneasy. His lack of fondness for birds hung on his expression. 'Loud, feathered, shit machines' he called them. Mal and Mira knew only something serious would take him there.

"Well, Bathilda has agreed to come and help us, but only if I and the other cousins come to see her first. She wants a family council."

"In Manchester? Why not just have it here?" Mal insisted.

"Manchester is more centrally located than here. They want to decide whether the threat of Aubrey Ruthven is enough to take them all from their own cities for what could be a long time." Abelard rubbed his neck. "I trust you two will handle things until I get back."

"Right. But seriously, why don't you all just have an

internet family chat or something? Why do you have to leave?" Mira pulled a little on her father's arm as if physically willing him to stay.

"The real danger is if Aubrey Ruthven gets his hands on the artifact buried in St. Mary's Churchyard. It's going to take more than just the three of us to battle if he acts as brutally as he did the last time he was in Whitby." Abelard set his hand on Mal's shoulder. "Son, can I trust you to do your duty while I am gone?"

Mal stared at his father. He thought of a thousand answers, of explanations, of a cry of understanding. His stared hardened as the bitter words passed his tongue. "Yes sir."

Mira stepped between the two, saying encouragingly, "You know, Dad, I can handle things if Mal wants to work on anything else?"

Mal attempted to poke his sister in the side, but she moved out of reach and blinked innocently at their father as he said, "I don't see why you'd need to. Besides, he has a better head for the family research. It's important to remember what Ruthven is capable of in order to keep your guard up. Work together and it will all go smoothly."

Mira shook her head with an impish smile. "No, I was thinking about if Mal wanted to go to a football practice here or there. I was talking to Baz, the team captain, and he said they'd still want to have Mal in the rotation, even if he could only play a couple of games this season—"

"Mira, we've been over this. Our job as a part of this family is to be within the shadows of town, to live as much on the outskirts as the Nos do. And Mal, as the only son, must follow this rule more than you, because he has to pass on the family name. Your brother understands this. Don't you?"

Mal grumbled, "Yes, sir." He turned his back to his

dad, adding, "Have a good trip."

"But Dad, I could always carry the family name—" Mira tried to insist.

Abelard shushed her, setting an arm around her shoulders. "Miranda, I know. You're as good as your brother and I'm not trying to downplay your abilities. But it's better that a son must always stay here in Whitby and pass on the family business. Now, can I count on you to help protect the town while I'm away?"

"Yes, sir." This time her voice was the small mumble of the defeated.

"Good girl. I love you both. Now, get home to your mum before she worries." He stared down at his suitcase and Mira realized how she would miss her stubborn, pig-headed Dad. She hugged him and told him to call when he got to Manchester.

"You shouldn't have pushed," Mal said as they walked away.

"At least I tried," she countered. "And if you are playing football and going to the pub, then I can handle Lee in my own way."

"You really want to give her infinite chances, don't you, baby sister."

She frowned at him. "I thought I was older."

"It's possible. But I'm taller."

He paused outside of the shop door as they arrived home. Mira unlocked the entrance and turned to him. "What's the matter?"

"Weird feeling." He looked out at the street behind him and then back to his sister. "You go on up. I'm just going to double-check something."

"What if you run into trouble?"

"Keep your mobile switched on and don't take off your shoes. I'll give you a ring if something big comes up."

He started to walk away as she shook her head at him.

"You and your feelings," she called out with an annoyed "humph". She disappeared into the shop as Mal rounded the corner.

He started up the hill, the sun struggling to rise and follow him. He paused outside of St. Mary's Churchyard, debating on which direction his instinct was pointing him to.

"You feel it as well," a voice stated.

Mal spun around, seeing Aubrey Ruthven hovering on the road, his long stylish coat clean of the morning dew. The Nos offered a halfway, coming as close as he dared to the entrance to the cemetery.

"Feel what?"

"That the crest has been disturbed. Everyone down there, all of my kind, can sense it even though they don't know that's what it is." He pointed to the quiet homes as the streetlights blinked off. "I bet they've been keeping you pretty busy."

"If you really want an alliance with us so badly, why don't you tell the blood suckers to knock it off so my sister and I don't have to keep killing them? You're a Soul Stealer. You should have some sway." Mal edged a little closer to the cemetery, ready to fight with the powerful old Nos if he had to.

Aubrey Ruthven rotated his head as if weary. "You really do not understand us as well as you like to think. I may be considered an ancient and hold, shall we say status, but that does not make me a monarch. I can convince the others not to attack certain people or not to hunt in specific areas. That does not give me the power to stop them from doing what is in their nature or what they must to survive." He crossed his arms over his chest, heaving a sigh that produced no breath. "Jonas is the one you really need to look out for. You know who Jonas is, yes?"

"Yes. He's one of the oldest blood suckers in town. He usually preys on willing goth kids and I've never heard of him killing or turning anyone. Most of the time, he lets his supporters go after a month or so. Then he just replaces them with a fresh and even more willing one." Mal and Mira never had actually hunted Jonas, yet his handy work remained evident all over Whitby.

"He's planning something. He left the town for several days earlier this week and refuses to tell me why."

Mal stuffed his hands into his pockets, giving him even more the look of a beanpole. "Why tell me any of this? What are you playing at?"

"I told you before; I want us to help each other." Aubrey Ruthven pointed to the cemetery. "We should use the crest together before Jonas makes it too late for both of us. You could have taken it from that churchyard at any time you chose."

Aubrey Ruthven's words about the artifact caught Mal's ears, forcing his brain to churn. Lee McDaniels really had not told her new Nos 'friend' that she had moved it. Perhaps his sister was right about the strange girl. "What about Lee? Why do you want her involved in all of this?"

"Is it so difficult to believe that I simply want the pleasure of her company?" Aubrey Ruthven's bright golden eyes peeked over the top of his sunglasses. They slid down the bridge of his nose. "Or are you stuck to the medieval idea that my kind are nothing more than demons inhabiting walking corpses, incapable of our old human emotions?" When Mal did not reply, the Nos pushed his glasses back over his supernatural gaze and added teasingly, "Or is this the Green-Eyed Monster working on overtime thanks to all of those teenage hormones?"

Mal replied with a sharp, "What?" before he could stop himself.

Aubrey Ruthven's perfect mouth turned from its clever smirk into something sad and sympathetic. "I understand. She is, in an almost inexplicable way, rather fascinating. I cannot blame you for having a crush."

"I don't have a—" Mal cut off his sentence, feeling stupid for having an argument about girls with one of his family's enemies. "Look, if you really want to prove that you want us to work together, find out what Jonas is up to. Give us a reason to trust you."

"Lee trusts me. Can't you put your trust in her in me?"

Mal turned away. "There's the problem, I'm not sure if I trust her either."

"Aubrey Ruthven still wants an alliance?" Miranda sat across from her brother in the coffee shop with a muffin and a half-drunk latte sitting in front of her.

Mal kept glancing out of the window at the people passing on the street. "Maybe he wants to give us one half of a 'best friend' necklace." He eyed a pair of women in their early twenties wearing onyx corsets as tops and velvet chokers about their throats. "Is it just me or are there more tourists milling around than usual for March?" Mal questioned as he pointed to a group of teenagers clad in black.

Mira brushed the crumbs from her hands and told him, "I'll get to the bottom of this." She dashed outside, stopping a group of goth kids who were too busy comparing three different maps to notice the preppy girl in front of them.

She directed them to where they needed to go and received a paper from them. She returned to her seat with a grim expression.

"Did you see this?" Mira asked with a frown. She pushed the flyer in front of her brother.

The paper was black with white lettering. Images of thorns, roses, skulls, wings, and cross-shaped tombstones bordered the words reading "Whitby Goth Ball: come one, come all in your darkest evening wear. Certain to be a memorable event." The date and time were listed at the bottom with no location specified.

"So what? Whitby hosts half a dozen goth events every year." His sister scrolled through her phone as he folded up the flyer.

"It's not a city event, I just checked," Mira explained.

Mal smoothed out the paper. "It looks like something *they'd* come up with. Calling all food sources. They're building up their strength for something."

"Do you think they're trying to recruit supporters, or do you think they mean to kill?"

"I think we have our work cut out for us." He sipped his coffee and grumbled, "I thought caffeine would help."

"Help with what?" Mira asked as she took back the flyer and stuffed it into her pocket.

"Thinking."

"You're wasting that coffee then, brother dear."

"Very funny." He pressed the paper cup between his hands, letting the warmth settle into his bones. "I can't decide what to do about Lee."

"Do? Why does something have to be done?" Mira blinked at Mal as if he had described a foreign crime she could not comprehend.

"Don't look at me like that. You know that if a war breaks out and Lee sides with them, we will have to. . ."

241

He leaned back, rubbing the stubble on his chin. His voice turned clinical. "We will have to kill her if she tries to stop us."

"Mal, don't say things like that. It isn't going to happen."

"He's got her believing him, Mira. That's all it takes."

"She's smarter than that!" His sister frowned at him and grumbled, "Maybe if you talked to her, she would believe you instead."

Mal got up from his seat, slamming his hand against the back of the chair as he moved to push it in. "First of all, why me? Second, I have talked to her and she didn't listen."

"No. You lectured her and yelled at her and made her not want to be around us." Mira lost some of her anger as she stared down into her coffee, focusing on the steam rising toward her nose. "Did you ever think that maybe there's something special about her? Some reason why she's here?"

Mal straightened his posture while he let out a laugh. "Are you trying to convince me that fate wanted us to know angsty, delusional, can't decide if she wants to brood or be theatrical, Annabel Lee McDaniels? You must think that fate has a great sense of humor."

"She found the artifact on her own. Aubrey Ruthven used her, and I can't imagine he had not tried to use girls to invite him back to Whitby before. He used her, then wanted to keep her alive. Why would he do that?" Mal shrugged at her and she added, keeping her gaze on the coffee. "Plus, I think it's interesting that you and Aubrey Ruthven have the same taste in girls."

With an angry grunt, Mal excused himself from the table.

"You have a bad habit of walking away from a

disagreement," his sister called smugly as she dipped her finger into the foam of her latte.

As soon as Mal stepped outside, he was caught off guard by an anxious shout of his name. He sped up, attempting to lose his follower down an alley on the next street over. Still, the other persisted. Ducking into a darker passage, he hoped he'd escaped.

Instead, he heard, "Mal, you know I can outrun you, right."

Mal came back out into the alley to face his friend Ian with a firm frown. "What do you want?"

His best friend stood before him, using his football bag to help block the exit. "Just to talk, mate. Just because you aren't on the team anymore doesn't mean we can't still get a pint or talk." Ian's expression was resolute. Mal would not be able to escape him with a sour glare this time.

"I told you, I've got—"

"Family stuff. I know. But does that mean we just can't be friends anymore?"

Ian was ready to say more; ready to pour out the weeks of frustration and abandonment he'd felt. However, being a teenage boy, the words would not come easily.

A figure emerged from the shadows where Mal had previously hidden. It was a man, short and thin, dressed in a shabby jacket from the 1980s over a Hawaiian shirt and Khaki pants. He stayed in the dimly lit end of the alley, walking backward as he studied the two boys.

Ian addressed the stranger quickly as he realized he'd just lost Mal's attention. "Oy, we're trying to have a conversation here."

The man responded with a hiss, baring his fangs like a threatened dog. The Nos ran at the pair of boys. Mal dodged to the left, pushing the Nos out of Ian's path. "Shit! Ian, get out of here!"

The vampire charged again at Malachi, hands outstretched. Mal held up his arms to block the attack. Then, the vampire did something he did not expect. Instead of grabbing at Mal's neck or head, he maneuvered his hand beneath the swinging arms of the hunter and took ahold of Mal's waist. He picked him up and flung him in the direction of the shadowy alcove. The boy landed in a heap, feeling his arm dislocate as it bashed against the doorjamb.

Ian ran up to the scene, his hands digging through his football bag. Removing his spiked cleat, Ian discarded his bag onto the ground. "Hey ugly!" he shouted as he slapped the cleat into the vampire's face, leaving gashes across the monster's nose and cheek.

Mal managed to get back onto his feet. He snatched up Ian's bag, wishing football included stakes and knives. "Run!" he ordered to Ian as the Nos clawed at his own bleeding face.

The two boys escaped down an alley and into one of the twenty-four-hour corner stores. Ian leaned against the newspaper stand just inside the entrance of the shop. "Is that guy following us?"

Glancing once outside of the shop, Mal pointed to the empty street. "No. No, he's not following us." He tried to hide the pain in his arm as it moved slightly.

"Good. Let's get Magnums," Ian suggested as he noticed the ice cream case.

Mal watched as Ian began scrounging through the large freezer like a squirrel distracted by something shiny. He laughed. "Ian?"

Ian looked up from the freezer with a chocolate ice cream bar hanging out if his mouth. "Yeh?" His voice was muffled by the desert.

The man behind the counter started to shout at them in Hindi, to which Ian muttered between bites, "I'm going to pay for it."

Mal set money on the counter for Ian's ice cream and some extra so he could get something, but mostly to quiet the shop keeper. Leaning over the freezer, he faced Ian's chocolate-covered expression. "What do you think just happened?"

The question caught Ian by surprise. He removed the ice cream from his mouth long enough to say, "I just saved you from a druggy. Why? Was something else going on?"

Pausing to process Ian's reasoning, Mal, at last, responded after a minute, "Yep. That's exactly what it was. Thanks, mate."

With his tongue once again blocked by the treat, Ian told Mal, "Helyaeyehickedass" which Mal assumed translated to, "Hell yeah, I kicked ass."

"I owe you one."

The pair were enveloped in the awkward stillness. Mal shifted his weight; the rubber soles of his trainers provided the only break in the silence. Deep down, he knew Ian must've been aware that the fanged man couldn't have been a drug addict. But that was Whitby. Everyone was raised to deny and live their lives with blissful ignorance. Scooping out his ice cream, Mal slammed the freezer closed with his good arm.

The boys left the shop in continued silence, Mal's injured arm tucked against his side while he kept pace with Ian. They weren't going to have the talk that Ian struggled with. The talk was no longer needed.

"What's up with you and the creepy girl?" Ian wanted to know when they were almost back at the café. "I saw you fighting with her outside of the pub."

"Oh." Mal responded, "Mira's friend. She just has this boyfriend who's dangerous. I was trying to make her see that. Mira isn't going to be hanging around her anymore."

"She has a boyfriend? Seriously? I thought you were dating her."

"What? Why?" Mal did not like the way his voice cracked like he was still going through puberty.

"I don't know. That's just what I thought." Ian kicked at the ground. "You should break her up from that dangerous boyfriend and date her. I'm just looking out for your best interests, mate. It's about time you got some."

Chapter 22: "Blood Transfusion"

Lee dug into one of the cardboard boxes, lifting stacks of books from their musty prison, and set them on the floor. At last, she found a leather-bound volume with the words, "The Complete Works of Edgar Allan Poe" in gold lettering printed across the front. With eyes shut tight, she flipped open the cover and landed her index finger on a random page in the center of the book.

At the top of the margin, she noticed that she had opened to one of Poe's short stories, "The Black Cat". Her nail rested over a specific passage which she read aloud, despite being alone in the room.

"I am above the weakness of seeking to establish a sequence of cause and effect, between the disaster and the atrocity."

"Lee, your father wants to watch *The Raven*. Come spend some time with your lame parents."

At the sound of her mother's voice, Lee set the book down and took a deep breath. A normal night with her parents. She could be normal for a night. She could pretend that nothing strange was going on.

She lounged on the couch with her mom while her dad skipped through the DVD menus from his chair. He pointed the remote with determination, ready to slay each and every copyright law reminder.

"I'm sorry we've been working so much," her mom

said more to the television than to Lee.

"You haven't been working any more than normal." Lee adjusted the pillow leaning against the arm of the couch.

"It feels like it. It feels like we've barely seen you since we got to Whitby."

"Yes, stranger. What have you been up to?" her dad added jokingly.

Lee focused on the image of Vincent Prince standing amongst the gaudy, cheaply furnished set. "I've been hanging around vampires."

Both of her parents chuckled and her dad added, "I knew you'd like that book. I hope you haven't been spending all your time reading." Her dad gave her a long look. "I haven't seen your new friends around lately. The brother and sister?"

"They aren't my f—" Lee glanced guiltily at her father. "I've been busy."

"Busy having fun, I hope. 'Youth comes by once in a lifetime', remember."

"Longfellow," she muttered with a small smile. "Dad, why do you love Longfellow so much?"

"Because his poems have an element of the heroic to them." He watched his daughter, realizing how hard she was analyzing his words. "Lee, what's wrong?"

"Nothing."

Vincent Price stared up at a portrait of a woman made up of oranges and browns in a style that betrayed the film's medieval look. The actor moaned to the 1960s painting with a purposeful, over-the-top flare. "Come back to me, Lenore. Come back."

Lee stretched out on the sofa, forcing her feet into her mom's lap. "Why did you name me after something so sad?"

"I don't look at it as sad. We named you after a poem about love."

Lee rolled her eyes. "A tragic love doomed by the heavens themselves. Great job, that."

"No. A first love of the young. When you are young, it is always forever love. You never fully get over that first person you fall for." Mrs. McDaniels laid a hand on her daughter's foot. "I remember my first love. It was junior high and he was a whole eight months older than me. We were together until my sophomore year of high school. When it ended, I was devastated."

"Why did it end?"

"Nothing bad. We were sixteen. We both wanted to date other people and we were growing up. We were becoming separated by our wants and goals."

Lee's dad frowned. "I didn't date when I was your age."

"That I believe," Lee giggled. A cushion was lightly tossed at her head. Sensing that her parents were about to ask her about her own love life, Lee pointed at the screen. Vincent Price parted a curtain to see a large black bird tapping upon his window. "Here comes the raven."

Just then her phone buzzed. Lee sat up slowly and reached for the lit-up device sitting on the book-covered coffee table. The mobile vibrated again as she read the screen. Chelsea was calling.

"Do you want us to pause the film?" Lee's dad wanted to know.

She gave him a shake of her head as she escaped to her room for privacy.

"Hey! Where have you been? I've been texting you for almost a week—"

"Lee, love. It's Chelsea's mom." The worn, familiar voice instantly made Lee's heart plummet to her feet. "I just wanted you to know . . . to be aware. Chelsea's is . . . We've taken her the . . ." The woman paused to hide the choke holding back her words. "She's going to be in the hospital for a couple of days. It's just for observation. I don't want you to worry. I just wanted you to be aware—"

"What exactly is the matter with her?" Lee knew how harsh the question seemed.

The woman could better control her tone as this question, suddenly becoming a medical professional in her own right. "She's tired all of the time. No energy at all. Her skin has gotten so pale, and her heartbeat is very unsteady. Today she fainted. The doctor says it looks like anemia, but it came on so suddenly that she's worried there could be a more serious underlining cause."

Anemia. A loss of blood could cause those symptoms.

Lee did not fully remember what she said to Chelsea's mom before going back to her parents. "I have to check on something. I'll be right back." She pulled on a pair of boots before either of them could ask her a question.

Barreling outside, Lee stopped dead in the middle of the sidewalk. She did not know where to find Ruthven. She had made out with the guy, and she had no way of contacting him if she needed to. She ran instead to the abandoned house where Sibella's followers allowed her in without their usual paranoias. The glare of the neon and the scent of decay barely resgistered within her mind this time.

It took the teen several painful gasps of air before she could speak. The vampire lady waited patiently, offering Lee a lumpy cushion to rest upon.

"I can't stay but thank you. I need to talk to Ruthven. It's very important. Do you know where he is?"

"No, but I can have the message relayed. Is there

anything we can do?" She motioned a graceful hand around the dimly lit room and Lee saw the droplets of blood scattered along her fingertips.

"What about Jonas? Do you know where he is?"

"What would you want with him?" Sibella's voice turned dark. "If you are interested in helping us, then do yourself a favor and stay away from him. He manipulates and twists his intentions until you find yourself asking him to drain you dry for reasons you can't even understand."

"I don't want to talk to him. I just want to know where he is."

Sibella looked to her followers, most of them looking livelier than they had the first few times Lee had come. She waved her finger to an eager young woman. The spritely girl ran to her mistress and offered her wrist. Sibella gently pushed her arm down and said, "Fan, you spy on Jonas for me every now and again. Where has he been lurking as of late?"

Fan did not seem disappointed or happy that it was not time to be fed upon. She simply lowered her wrist and shrugged. "He isn't here, the last I checked. He went south."

Lee anxiously sought the girl's shoulder, giving it a slight shake. "South? Like London south?"

"I don't know exactly, but I guess. London could be an option."

Pushing away from Fan, Lee started sprinting out of the room, calling her thanks over her shoulder.

"Just a moment!" Sibella's cry stopped Lee as the atmosphere of the room changed. Perhaps coming alone had been foolish. The other vampires and supporters slunk into the darkness, giving their lady privacy. Sibella rose unsteadily, her thin frame creating a statue of worship at the center of the dingy room. She moved to Lee and put both hands on her face.

"Lee," she said softly, running her sharp fingernails lightly along the teen's skin, "I like Aubrey Ruthven and I know how much—" Her tender strokes stopped, and her gaze met Lee's with nothing but pity. "I worry for you. You are very human and he is very much not. And I have seen this story end tragically many times."

"We know what we're doing, I think," Lee replied with a blush.

Sibella's hands moved down, taking both of Lee's. The cold skin tried it's best to keep a loose grip. "I will tell you something, Lee. I am actually older than him. I was born in the times right before the Romans left Britain. I even once met St. Hild herself. But I'm weak. I've always been weak. I have made my own mistakes. So many mistakes. But I have all of eternity to make up for them. You do not. Be careful with this life, my dear."

With a confused nod, Lee pulled herself away and back out of the room. "I will," she answered awkwardly, not sure of what else to say.

She sprinted home but took a different route hoping that she would collide with Ruthven along the way. When she neared the chip shop, she caught the echo of a familiar voice insistently ranting. Lee hung on the corner as she saw Mal pass her without notice, a mobile phone pressed angrily to his ear.

"Dad, I get that but—" He paused to pull the phone down and give it a frustrated scowl. Returning the electronic device to his ear, Mal continued in an exasperated tone. "I can stay friends with Ian. You said I couldn't play football. You never said I couldn't have any friends." Another pause. Lee could almost hear Abelard Tepes's worried rant on the line. "No Dad, I know what's at—" Pause. "I know this is seri—" Apparently, he was being cut off every sentence. At last, he shouted, "I already know Ruthven doesn't have the artifact! He told me!"

Realizing his mistake, Mal shut his eyes tight and held his breath, praying that static had muffled his words at that exact moment. No such luck.

This time, Lee could make out certain words from the phone. Words like "You let him" and "Kill him" and "chance". Mal stumbled over an excuse, saying how Ruthven was too quick for him and that the conversation was so swift. He was careful not to mention Lee's part in any of the story.

Mal's frown deepened as his father ranted some more. The conversation at last came to an end with him confirming that they would talk more when Abelard returned in a day or two. Mal also reassured him that he was on his way home to review the family journals about the "night Ruthven became their enemy".

He left with the phone squeezed angrily between his fingers. When he was gone, Lee's mobile started to ring. Her feet angrily drove into the ground, carrying her away. She did not even check to see who the caller was until she was back in her own home. The missed call had been from Mal.

"What's wrong, Lee?" her mom asked.

The girl faced both of her parents as they sat, blissfully ignorant upon the furniture, surrounded by the books and objects she'd known most of her life. She thought of the crest, buried at the back of her closet.

She wanted to tell them that she was in over her head. She desperately wanted advice, but what advice could they give? Don't get mixed up with vampires and vampire hunters?

"I couldn't get good reception. I had to go outside," she lied.

"Who was on the phone?" her father asked, then pointed to the telly. He had paused the film for her anyway.

"Chelsea's mom. Chelsea is sick."

Mrs. McDaniels sat up a little straighter. "Nothing serious I hope."

"I hope," was all Lee could manage to reply. Her best friend was the victim of a vampire and there was nothing she could do to stop it.

Chapter 23: "Go Safely, and Leave Something of the Happiness You Bring"

Lee entered St. Mary's church quietly, keeping her footfalls light. That morning had been one of long contemplation. She'd sprawled across her bed with Eddie tucked under one arm and the crest held out in front of her. She and the doll had a long talk about what she should do with it. At last, as the morning waned into afternoon, she put the crest into her backpack and left the house without a word to anyone.

Seward greeted her with a quiet smile. "What brings you to see me?"

She held out her backpack to him like an offering of surrender. "My best friend is sick, possibly dying, and it's basically my fault. I invited her to see me when I was already caught up in this vampire-hunting artifact madness! Why was I able to find it?"

His smile waned and he motioned for her to follow him. They wandered out into the churchyard and to the large stone cross. "There are many powers this town has been blessed and cursed with. I don't know why something has blessed or cursed you to be a part of it all. But maybe some reflection can help you find an answer for yourself."

"You mean pray. You want me to pray to this Caedmon guy for answers?"

He turned her shoulders so she faced the cross head-on. "I mean, do whatever you need to do to find the answers for yourself. This place has been under the protection of many strong women since its earliest known history. I'm sure St. Hild herself questioned how to handle responsibility." Seward pointed at the sky. "I'll give you a little time. Do you want me to bring you a cup of tea?"

Lee positioned herself in the grass in front of the cross, her legs tucked under her until her feet went numb. The plastic cup of builder's tea went cold between her palms as she stared down the engravings. She tried closing her eyes, silently speaking to some force greater than herself to give her a sign. Lee's parents had never been religious beyond how religion shapes a culture or literature. Lee's own mind had always leaned toward facts, what she knew to be true beyond any doubt. But science had not given her an answer to the blood suckers and soul stealers.

The sun went down, but Seward allowed her to stay a little after dark. At last, he helped her to her feet and escorted her out of the churchyard. Before she left, she held out the backpack one last time. "What if I leave it here? Bury it again? No one would ever know, and everything could go back to the way it was."

"I think it's too late for that," a woman's voice called from the dark path leading to the hill stairs.

Sibella's pale features shined in the dim light. She nodded once at the church employee.

Seward set a fatherly arm over Lee's shoulders, but she told him she would be fine. She handed him the cup and walked at a slow pace before stopping directly in front of the lady vampire. Seward hung at the gate of the churchyard.

"It's weird to see you outside," Lee told her with caution. "Are you here because of Jonas?"

"I'm here because of you. One of my followers said they saw you sitting out here for hours and he thought maybe you had some insight into why all of my kind has been feeling in the best of health of late."

"You have? That's good, though, right?"

"Good for my kind. Not as good for the people of this town." She started to stroll in the direction of the steps. Her footfalls were more like floating, delicately carrying her without a sound. Pointing to the lights of the many homes and shops, Sibella wrinkled her nose. "There has to be balance. Yes, my kind must live and I know what we must do to survive. But it should not be like this. A blood bath is coming. Number of deaths rose almost overnight from young idiots who think their new strength gives them the right to turn Whitby into their banquet. This is my home. This is where I feel safe. I won't have the world discover us because of a group of blood-sucking morons."

"People are dying?" Lee studied the thin features of the woman as wisps of hair danced around her deep-set eyes. "Do you know why? Why they are acting like this?" Her breath held within her throat like a jagged pill while she awaited Sibella's answer.

"You have the artifact; the object Ruthven came here for."

Lee tensed, waiting. "And you want it for yourself?"

Sibella tilted her head at the teenager with confusion. "Do you trust me enough to allow me to show you something?" She held out a cold hand. "I swear I mean you no harm, Lee. I just want you to understand what my intentions are in all this."

Reluctantly, Lee allowed the ice-cold digits to encase hers. Suddenly, they moved like wind, Sibella pulling her in two swift maneuvers. The first took them to the fencing which kept tourists from Whitby Abbey and the second took them over the fence to the muddy dig site on the other side.

Lee rotated her shoulder, the leap having nearly pulled her arm out of the socket. Sibella said nothing as she let go of the girl's hand and started the trek toward the shadowy ruins. Lights had been set up within the old abbey, making it a beacon on the hill for the town to be proud of. In the yellow lanterns, the main wall gave the windows the look of eyes glaring at Lee.

The vampiress did not stop until she brought Lee to the few pathetic graves half buried in the dirt. "I told you I met St. Hild once, long ago. She understood the importance of compromise. Even then, forces that her church deemed as heathenistic, the remnants of pagan beliefs were drawn to this place. She wanted to keep her followers safe. She prayed for a blessing, a gift that could be bestowed upon people who could keep her beloved home safe. And for that, I respected her. But it wasn't until that object you possess came to our shores that I saw the true power of her gift."

"Are you trying to tell me that I was blessed by St. Hild and that's why I was able to find this thing? I'm not even from here!"

"Most of the young women chosen rarely are. I suspected it of you, but I wasn't certain until I started to feel so strong . . . until I figured that you had Ruthven's stupid toy."

"Do you know what it's for? He says it'll create peace and will help your kind, but I don't what exactly that means."

Sibella leaned down and gave her a cold kiss on the forehead. "You want so much to trust him, but you can't bring yourself to fully do so. That's good. You shouldn't listen to me or him or anyone else. You have St. Hild's gift. Trust that to be your guide."

"Do I get like superpowers now or something?"

The woman laughed, her fangs glimmering in the moonlight. "Only the power of intuition. Come. I will take you safely home." She gently took her hand once again and sped her back over the fence.

With her feet back on solid ground, Lee asked, "Can we walk the rest of the way? No more flying and leaping. My arm can't take it."

One of Sibella's followers, one of the healthier-looking of the young men, had been waiting for them at the bottom of the stairs. He pointed to the end of the old street where Lee could faintly make out shadows. A figure straddled something in the road, breaking and tearing sounds echoing against the cobble stones.

A pair of bloodshot eyes turned upon them. Red stained the figure's mouth and hands as it stood, still grasping the thing it had been couched over within a strong grip. It took Lee a long time to realize that the something was a woman, petite and broken, no longer able to fight back. A pool of blood dripped from her ripped-open shirt and onto the street. Her killer flung her down and wiped the back of his hand with a loud slobber.

Sibella stood her ground against the vampire looming at the end of the lane, her long dress flapping as she widened her stance. "Roger," she said to the follower calmly, "Kindly take Lee the rest of the way home."

"My lady, are you strong enough—"

"I gave you an order and I assure you that I am quite well. Now go!" At that, she snarled and her back arched. Both of her hands tensed, ready to rip at the other vampire with her sharp nails.

Lee was pulled away from the scene as the pair ran at one another. Roger, as the follower was called, had to struggle to keep her at his pace as he ran. "Shouldn't we help her?" Lee screamed. She kept looking back at the battle. The attacking vampire spat blood at Sibella, blinding her for only a moment before she flipped him over her shoulder. With the other vampire on the street, she straddled him. Her fiercesome fangs descended upon him in defense, ripping at his neck. She dribbled his flesh from her mouth onto his face, revenge for his spitting at her. The vampire kicked back up onto his feet as Lee lost sight of them.

"What can we do? We're humans."

Roger left her on her street, panting and checking his pulse constantly. "I need to get back. My lady will need to feed after a fight like that."

"Do you think she's okay?"

"I'm certain of it. If you are truly concerned, you can come back with me. I'm sure she'll need some fresh blood besides mine—"

With disgust, Lee turned away from him. "Gross. Good night!"

As she came closer to her front stoop, she saw a male figure in the shadows. For a moment, her heart soared, thinking Ruthven had come with an update about Jonas. Then she noticed the second figure and realized it was the Tepes twins.

"Just what I need," she grumbled as she shifted the backpack on her shoulders.

They met her halfway in the street, Mira holding out one of the heavy family tomes in front of her.

"Can't whatever this is wait until tomorrow?" Lee begged.

Mal looked at her solemnly. He kept one arm close to

his side, barely moving it. "I don't think anything can wait. Our father is coming back home with a small army of vampire hunters. Before a small war breaks out, we wanted you to see what we found."

"It's about Ruthven. Mal's been going back through the journals and he found this one in our grandma's old cedar chest. I don't think either of us had ever read it before."

"Is this another story about times your family tried to keep him out or about how he . . . did what he did? I know all about that." Lee glared at the leather binding being offered to her.

"Just read it. If it changes anything for you then you can come with us. If it doesn't then we'll leave you alone," Mira explained.

Mal would not meet Lee's eyes as she accepted the book. "It's the first passage," he told her almost guiltily. "I—" He gave Mira one of their secret expressions before adding, "We don't know fully what it means, but we promise we're going to find out."

Lee sat on the bottom of her stoop and adjusted the book to better see the handwritten words.

Journal of Phillipa Tepes, 1683

Today I attended the wedding of a Cholmley, the only member of that family I could dare to call a friend. I know this is now solely based upon the secret which ties us. I work hard to keep that secret as does she. Watching her upon the arm of her new husband, a man I know her to be indifferent to, made the importance of our deception all the more relevant. She seems to think this is her penance. I believe she still loves the monster.

From this day onward, I shall no more address her when we pass or acknowledge her beyond minor acquaintance. The perils she faced alongside me will be the only adventures I will not even convey within these pages. I have not even revealed the details to Giles, dear as he is to me.

All that which I can reveal is that the monster, Aubrey Ruthven, is banished. His banishment will never return my brothers to me and their loss has driven my mother mad with grief. May God keep them, and may he forgive what I must do next.

Whitby shall be guarded for so long as St. Hild's Gift holds true. And more importantly, that which my family brought to these shores over a century ago is safe. Even my father and brother agree that the final resting place will not be shared through the ages. Let it be forgotten. Let it not be the trial of our children and their children.

My heart has already broken five times over and yet, it does not seem to cease feeling pain. I came to the realization that Mary and my brothers will not attend my wedding, that she will not sit and talk with me in the old ways, or that she will continue to carry the burden of St. Hild's Gift without my aid. Within a mere fortnight, I have lost almost all that I love and my only companion.

May God protect her, as I no longer can.

Chapter 24: "I Gave Her My Nights and Days"

Lee's eyes studied the words "monster", "Ruthven", and "banished", all three of which had an angry slant to the handwriting. The pressure of the ink against the paper left a deeper imprint than the sad words telling of a friendship forced to end. Lee wanted desperately to thrust the journal away from Miranda.

Mira watched her with concern. "Are you worried about what it says?"

"No. No, it was a long time ago. People change." Emotion escaped her voice.

Mal added in a low growl, "People change. Monsters don't."

"He isn't a monster. I mean, yes, he feeds off human energy in order to sustain his immortal lifeforce, which I will admit sounds a little monstrous." Lee stopped, taking a deep breath. "That sounded bad. Forget that part. All I mean is that being a vampire does not define who he is as a person. Many good men throughout history had to do terrible things to survive."

"And many monsters convinced the world they were great men in order to gain power." Mal pointed an irritated finger at the journal. "Hundreds of years of writing saying he is not good. Why can't you believe it?"

"Because it's all your family! You are prejudiced against him because hundreds of years of testimony told you to be. If you were true heroes, you could see beyond that."

With both hands in front of him, fingers outstretched as if he wanted to strangle Lee, Mal snapped, "Why do you talk like that? This isn't a Jane Austen novel! Talk like a normal person!"

"Oh, so it's me you just don't like? Is that why you won't listen to me? Fine. Let me put it in normal speech for you." She sneered at the word normal and her sneer stayed put as she continued. "Stop trying to convince me that he's a monster!"

Mira gently set the book into a messenger bag hanging from her shoulder. "What about Mary Cholmley? She loved Ruthven too. And it sounds like she helped Phillipa banish him. Don't you wonder about that?"

The other girl he'd cared about. "Of course, I'm curious, but all of these people are long dead. How are we supposed to find out more?"

Mal raised his hand as if to answer her question more politely. "I can try to see it. I told you that sometimes I can see the past. Looking that far back won't be easy, but if it tells us how to either kill or banish Ruthven, I'm willing to try." He studied Lee, estimating her reaction. "Has he ever mentioned Mary Cholmley before?"

Lee shook her head.

"I know he's your boyfriend, but wouldn't you feel better knowing? Why not come with us."

Lee thought about Sibella and the idea of instinct. Every fiber of her being screamed out to know more. "Where are we going?"

"To the shore. It's easier for me to do this closer to the water."

They walked to the beach, Mira offering comforting smiles to break the tension created by Lee's blank stare and Mal's silent insistence on walking ahead of the other two. There were people sitting on benches, smoking or just enjoying the salt-laced air.

None of the bystanders showed interest as the three teens removed their shoes and waded into the water. The artic waves hit their ankles and soaked the hems of trousers. Lee disguised a shiver as an attempt to keep her coat from catching on the wind.

"It's easier for Mal to do if he had a mental tether." Mal gripped Mira's shoulder and she offered a hand to Lee. "Put your hand in his."

As Mal's free hand reached for her, Lee frowned. "Why would touching give you a mental tether? That makes no sense."

He snatched her hand and squeezed her fingers fiercely. As she protested painfully, he replied, "Like that. Pain is a good way to wake someone up. If I'm in a trance for longer than a few minutes, pull me out." He relaxed his grip and the warmth of his palm against hers counteracted the chill of the lapping water.

Mira used her free hand to carefully balance Phillipa Tepes's journal in front of Mal. He focused on it, let his vision go cross-eyed. His mind tried to feel the pain that had gone into the paragraphs they had shown to Lee, the loss of a friend, and the loss of family. All his anger, fear, and frustration over Aubrey Ruthven also stirred within him. The water drowned out his breathing and that of the two girls. The water stopped its sting against his calves. The journal blurred against his vision, and he turned his head to see where he'd been taken.

Mal stood at the River Esk at night. Only a foot in front of him stood Ruthven with his arms around a sixteen-year-old girl. The wind picked at her soft brown tresses and golden shawl, trying to pull her from the vampire's grasp. He rested his chin upon her forehead as she leaned into his chest. She stared in Mal's direction, her eyes full of worry and sorrow.

His vision lost focus again and when he could see once more, he saw Ruthven leaving a house on his home street. Crimson droplets fell from his hands and soaked his fine clothes. He'd left the door wide open where a bloody form of a teenage boy slumped. The boy's eyes, similar to Mal's own, stared blankly into the dark. Gold orbs glowed from within the vampire's face. He radiated light. Only once did Ruthven look back upon his gruesome message. The unnecessary carnage drew a smirk upon the plump lips.

The world spun and another dark scene unfolded. The same girl sat along the beach with another girl, her same age. The social difference between the two was clear. Ruthven's brunette wore a satin gown with a long bodice and loose, paneled sleeves. He recognized the high fashion of the Restoration period from the history books his father had made him study. The second girl wore a red jacket-bodice with a brown skirt, the style of the working class. A white cap covered her jet hair and off-set her Eastern European completion.

The work-weary orbs at the center of her face, black in the moonlight, accused the first girl. Mal could not hear them, but he saw the anger of the poorer girl and the shame of the richer. They yelled at one another, their words coming through to him as if through a pane of glass.

Finally, the wealthy girl leapt to her feet and ran to the edge of the water. The tide came in over the tops of her fine shoes and soaked the hem of her gown. The second girl ran after her, tears in her eyes. The anger changed to despair. They hugged with all the affection of sisters. Both cried as the freezing water came up around their ankles.

Mal turned from the touching moment, finding the rich girl behind him standing on the west bank with the ruins of the abbey behind her. The same yellow shawl as before had been draped over her nightgown. Mud caked her clothes and hands. Her brown curls, free of all pins and ribbons, wildly hindered her vision as she moved away from a mound in the ground.

Then, a sharp stab into his wrist. Lee was digging her nails into his skin.

The vision released Mal as he gasped for air. "You've been out for almost five minutes."

Mira pulled all of them back to the shore as she cried out, "Your eyes actually rolled back into your head. It was really gross."

"She was the one who buried the artifact in the churchyard," he managed to say between coughs. They pulled him up on the beach as he regained his usual glum composure.

"Who did?" Lee asked first. She stamped her feet in the sand to warm them and flapped her arms around her arms.

"I think Mary Cholmley. I saw our ancestor, Philippa, too." He explained the scene to them in as much detail as he could manage before the image faded from his mind. Mal panted and squinted in pain as he spoke.

"You couldn't hear anything?" Mira wanted to know.

"Too far back. It's like an old recording. Too much damage over time wears it down. I only heard whispers. I think Philippa mentioned her brothers' deaths and something about St. Hild. And a gift."

Lee tensed. "St. Hild's Gift."

"Some old legend. I read about it in one of the earliest

journals. It's this idea that women are blessed to keep Whitby protected. Mal held his fingers to the edge of his nose. Pink seeped through.

"You're bleeding," Lee stated as she watched Miranda hand him a tissue.

"You're so observant. You clearly are the daughter of university professors." Mal's voice was muffled by the pinching of his nose. He carefully kept his head level upon his neck.

Miranda gave her brother a less than sympathetic pat on the back. "This is why he doesn't use that power very often. It can actually lead to permanent brain damage. We had a second cousin who died from trying to see visions all the time."

As they pulled back on their shoes, their teeth chattering to fill the silence, Lee decided she couldn't stop there. "We need to do more research. Let's go back to my house."

Lee's parents were more concerned with why three teenagers stomped into their kitchen shivering with sand-covered feet than they were with the late hour. Mrs. McDaniels made tea and Mr. McDaniels hung everyone's dirty, damp socks to the furnace. Then, they left the three of them to their own devices.

Lee did most of the typing, her fingers flying through each search engine with ease. She logged into genealogy websites using her parent's e-mail and accessed several online journals.

As Lee dug into the internet, Mira rearranged her closet and Mal held Eddie over Lee's shoulder as if the doll were observing her. Swatting his hand away, she growled, "Don't you have any other family journals or something you can look through?"

Mal backed away until he sat on her bed. "Everything

else in the family journals about Ruthven is just more boogeyman tales. Nothing concrete."

An hour went by before she found anything she thought could possibly be related. Lee turned her computer screen to the twins showing a portrait from the seventeenth century.

The lady wore a loose-fitting blue gown with one billowing sleeve having escaped from her brown shawl. Brunette tresses were swept away from her face yet left to rest soft at the nape of her neck. The long bridge of her nose separated two dark, intelligent eyes.

"Who is she?" Mira wanted to know as she set aside two black skirts in order to come stare at the screen.

"Mary Cholmley," Mal stated. "That's who I saw in the vision."

Lee read aloud from the website. "She was a lady, daughter of a baronet. I think she got married. Twice actually. You want to see a portrait of her first husband?"

Without waiting for them to respond, Lee typed a few keys and clicked the mouse several times. A swelled melon of a man wearing a long, highlighted wig and an embroidered dressing gown filled the screen. He held a paper in one hand and pointed at it with the other. His multiple chins were held in place with a simplistic white cravat.

Mira wrinkled her nose at the unattractive man.

Lee laughed. "I know right! She married him when she was just sixteen. And they were cousins! Let's hope her second husband was better looking."

Mira offered a half shrug. "Maybe he was a nice guy."

"Are you kidding? This was the 1600s. Rich women didn't get to marry the nice guy. They married the guy who could make their parents more money."

"Which means that dating a vampire bad boy would

have been the ultimate rebellion, except maybe dating a Catholic," Mira joked.

The idea sunk in with Lee for the first time. This girl, now long dead, may have once loved Ruthven and he possibly loved her back. Or were they using each other? In the vision, Mary did have the crest after all. She had been the one to hide it from all vampires and future generations of vampire hunters. Did Mary do this to protect one side or was it to save herself? Was it to forget a lost love or prove she was done with him? Lee didn't know which turned her stomach more.

Mal set Eddie down carefully on the bed. "Okay, so we know for sure who she is, but we don't know how she's connected to getting rid of Ruthven. We know he seduced her and that she was friends with our ancestor—"

"Which put her right in the middle of everything," Lee stated unflinchingly.

"Maybe she was using his attraction to her to trick him," Mira offered. "She might've lured him out of Whitby before someone cast the spell that locked him out."

Mal balled his fist. "A spell we still don't have."

Lee's father poked his head in. "I'm all for academic discovery or online gaming or whatever it is you three are up to in here on that laptop, but it's past midnight. Are you two okay to get home, are you staying here tonight, or are we calling you a cab?"

Mira thanked Lee's parents a few times as she placed her mug of tea in the sink and pulled on her dry socks. Mal had little to say but gave both parents a grateful nod of his head.

As Lee walked them to the door, her face must have betrayed the questions swirling in her head. Mal paused, leaning in to whisper to her. "Sorry."

"For dragging me into this? Everyone keeps saying

that," she grumbled.

"No. You seem really upset. I'm sorry that you found out like this your Nos boyfriend—"

"Had other girlfriends. He's hundreds of years old. I can't have been the first. I already knew that."

"Not that. You're really questioning him now. I can see it in your face. You really are wondering if he's the bad guy."

"Isn't that what you wanted me to do?"

"It's still a rubbish way to have to deal with it. Sorry, I didn't see more in the vision."

She recalled how he'd claimed to see Ruthven smile after he'd killed Phillipa's brother in the vision, but she did not want it to be true. He couldn't be the villain. But she'd needed him the last couple of days. She needed to know what to do about Chelsea and the crest. And Ruthven had not come to help her.

Looking at Mal, she made her worried confession. "I think Jonas followed my friend to London and has been attacking her. Her mom called me last night from the hospital."

"And Jonas hasn't been seen in a while," Mal confirmed. He did not seem to want to worry her, and he handled the news better than she thought he would. She'd expected a lecture, a speech on how she'd put her friend in danger. Instead, he answered, "If you can, talk to her directly. Find out exactly where she's been bitten, how many times, and whether Jonas has given her anything to drink back. I'm sure she's fine, but the more details we have the better we can handle it."

"You mean if you need to kill her?"

"Or reverse the process of turning before it gets too far if he is trying to turn her. But I doubt it. Jonas doesn't really create new vampires. He looks at it as competition for food." Mal quickly repeated, "I'm sure she's fine."

"Come inside before you freeze to death," Lee's mother called from within the house.

Mal gave a short awkward wave as she turned back to her front door.

After the door was bolted behind her, her dad announced, "Lee, something came for you in the post. I completely forgot."

A brown rectangle rested atop the kitchen table. Retrieving scissors, she cut through the tape and freed the book within. A laugh gurgled within her while tears filled her eyes. Within her hands now rested *The Vampyre and Other Macabre Tales*.

A note bookmarked the titular short story for her. "As I promised that day in the train station, I finished reading and I'm passing this book onto you. I hope you enjoy it. Deena."

Lee called out, "It's the book Deena was reading."

"That was nice of her to remember. You should send her a book back," her dad replied as he steered her down the hallway toward her bedroom. "Which book was it?" Holding it up, Lee's father released a mighty chortle. "That was it! Oh, it's been bothering me like crazy."

"What has?" She watched her father snatch the book from her and thumb through the pages.

"Why your new friend's name was so familiar? Aubrey and Lord Ruthven are the two main characters of this story. He has the same name as the hero and the villain." He handed her back the tome. "That's such a funny coincidence. No wonder you like him. You both have literary names. You should tell Deena. Well, good night."

"Yeah. Night." Lee gave a weak laugh. She was not entirely sure if her father had disappeared into his own room before she cracked open the book a second time. The final words of the story ate at the worried hole in her stomach.

"... but when they arrived, it was too late. Lord Ruthven had disappeared, and Aubrey's sister had glutted the thirst of a VAMPYRE!"

Chapter 25: "Such a Look of Hate"

That night, Lee dreamt of the girl in the painting. She lay diagonally across a gilt bed, her dark curls formed wild rivers across the blanket. A low-cut night dress gave a perfect view of her neck, bloodied and tattered. Her whole head stiffly turned to lock her dead eyes upon Lee and whispered, "Take care."

When she awoke, she tried to seek out the logic of her mind. She wanted that little voice to tell her that nothing could possibly be outside of her control. She continued to research on her laptop while reading through parts of the book she'd just received. It was dusk before her mom poked her head in.

"Lee, why are you still in your pajamas? You sick?"

Lee glanced down at the oversized Black Sabbath tee-shirt and flannel trousers she'd slept in. "Just being lazy," she answered finally.

She showered and dressed with her mind still entirely on what she'd learned the night before. She washed her hair multiple times and tried to put her shoes on the wrong feet.

Just as she got herself organized, the doorbell rang. Her dad answered and announced that her friend wanted to see her.

Ruthven hovered just within the doorway, keeping a respectable distance from her father while they chatted.

"There she is!" the vampire announced as she approached. "Want to go for a walk? It's a little warmer out tonight."

Silently, she nodded and grabbed her coat. Ruthven sensed the change yet said nothing. He simply shook her father's hand and away they went.

They strolled about a block before Lee asked, "Is it a good idea to be out? I heard that the attacks have gone up."

"You're with me. No one will hurt you," he assured her, draping an arm across her shoulders.

She allowed the physical contact, the coldness of his skin radiating near the back of her neck. She blurted, "I looked up the name Ruthven. They started as a Scottish Clan in the eleventh century. Any relation?"

His expression turned guilty. "That was the name my family adopted. We started as a proud Norse-Scots heritage, but one of my ancestors swore allegiance to England. A few years before I was born, my father's cousin was even given a seat in Parliament, but my father preferred a life that was considered a little less civilized. He encouraged his sons to fight the English. I thought I would die in the Anglo-Scottish wars."

"What happened?"

"I didn't realize that I had already died. Years earlier I traveled. I studied. I wanted to prove to my father that I could be both – a contemporary warrior and a scholar. I met many people on my travels, including the one who sired me. I accepted my fate but did not fully understand it until that day on the battlefield."

"What year did you die?"

"1503, I think. I would have been nineteen. Everything was such a game to me, I didn't even think of how my world had changed."

"And your sire wanted you to come to Whitby?"

"Yes, but you already knew that. Are we playing this is your life?"

Lee raised her fingers up to awkwardly entwine with this cold pale hand draped over her shoulder. They steered near a row of houses, protected from the wind by the tall walls. She shut her eyes tightly as she asked the next question. "And is that when you met Mary Cholmley?"

His arm loosened from her and his steps stopped. "How could you possibly have heard of her? No one knew—" He shifted his sunglasses upon his nose as the realization hit him. "The Tepes daughter. Mary must have told her."

Lee did not confirm his suspicion, simply stared at him intensely. She wished she could face his eyes and read his expression. "Who was she?"

He frowned and his arms dropped to his sides. "I wanted to be with her. She was the first love of my immortal life, the first woman I ever considered breaking my vow for. I was ready to leave Whitby without the crest and take her with me instead."

"You wanted to turn her?"

"I wanted to be with her," he repeated.

"What happened?"

"She was wealthy, and her family had plans for her to marry a cousin. I even tried to present them with a fortune that I had accumulated over my first century to persuade them to let her marry me instead. Her family said no. They said no when they didn't even know what I truly was. I couldn't benefit their position any better."

Lee's throat dried. She swallowed desperately before speaking again to prevent a crack int he words. "Did she know what you are?"

"Yes, and she didn't care. We were going to leave together. Beggars Bridge." His mouth quirked with a perfect balance of sorrow and hope. "Mary was to meet me there. But she never came."

"What's Beggars Bridge?"

"You follow the River Esk many miles from here to the Village of Glaisdale. A farmer named Ferris was in love with a rich squire's daughter. I think her name was Agnes. The river separated them and whenever it was swelled, he could never reach her. He left and made a fortune. Then came back and married the girl. He built the bridge so the river could never separate anyone again."

"And Mary agreed to meet you there? What did you do when she didn't come?"

"I tried to come back to Whitby only to discover that my way was barred. I could no longer come into the town. The Tepes family had found a way to lock me out. And I never saw her again." He reached out for Lee's shoulder with a sudden desperation. "I swear that I will not allow that to happen again. They won't separate us and they won't—"

"Why is everyone always grabbing me?" Lee grumbled as she took a step back. "And no one is trying to separate us."

"Oh no?" His tone turned from frantic to dark anger. "Why do you think they told you about Mary? And don't try to tell me it wasn't them because how else would you have known?"

"It doesn't matter. I'm still here, aren't I!" Lee snapped, surprised at her own defensiveness. Recovering herself, she tried to seem sympathetic. "Why do you think Mary didn't show up that night?"

He growled, his head looking to the west. "Isn't it

obvious? The Tepes girl told her what I did to her brothers. I've told you before that it was my greatest mistake and when I say it cost me everything, I am not saying it lightly."

"Then why did you do it? You murdered children—"

"You're asking me this now? After what I have already told you, after what those hunters already told you? You knew I was a monster and made it seem like you didn't care! That you trusted me!"

"Then why didn't you tell me about Mary in the first place?"

"I am entitled to secrets! To pains that are too deep to live through again." He pounded his fist against a wall, the brick crumbling and caving to his strength. "This is not about the crimes of my past! This is about them! Those hunters are turning you against me. Instead of believing in me, you went running back to them."

Lee wondered if the display was meant to frighten her or anger her. She crossed her arms over her chest. "I was trying to help! It isn't like this is a normal situation. You can't expect me to be cool all of the time. Besides, I have been trying to find you for days and you haven't even been around! Did you know that Jonas has not been seen and now my friend Chelsea is in a hospital? For what? Oh yeah, blood loss!"

The words struck the man rather roughly, taking away his anger with a drop of his jaw. "Why do you suspect Jonas?"

"Because Chelsea is just stupid enough to invite Jonas to follow her to London."

"He has plenty of people to feed on here. It would be strange for him to go all the way to London." Ruthven pulled her into him and in a soothing tone added, "I'm sorry. I shouldn't contradict. Maybe you're right. I'll ask around, but I wouldn't be too worried. I'm sure your friend is just a little under the weather for perfectly human reasons."

For the first time, Lee felt uncomfortable in his arms. Her breath was caught in the centimeters between her mouth and his shirt. The embrace stifled her and made her desperate to look beyond the side of his cheek and up to the sky overhead. Yet, she allowed the hug. The awkward moment gave her time to re-evaluate without him defensively screaming at her.

She stood with him like that until he gave her a deep kiss and offered to take her back home. Again, she kissed him back and gave him a smile when he promised to come tomorrow with news of Jonas. Still, an emptiness consumed her. She no longer marveled at his dazzling teeth when he blew her a kiss and grinned before leaving her on her front stoop. And she did not wish him to turn back and stay longer. Lee revealed in the realization that she felt lighter watching him go.

Chapter 26: "Light of All Lights"

"Dad will be back tonight," Miranda explained. She sat in the kitchen with her mobile phone clasped tightly between her fingers. "He called while you were with Ian. Don't worry, I didn't tell him where you were."

Mal nodded gratefully as he grabbed the pitcher of juice from the refrigerator. "Is he bringing anyone back with him?"

"Four or five family members who are all talking about bringing another four or five other family members. I suggest we start patrol early tonight before Mum gets into too much of a cleaning frenzy." Miranda glanced continually at her phone. "Still haven't heard from Lee. I was hoping she'd text or ring or send up a flair or something."

"To tell us what? She's still dating Ruthven and we have a whole bunch of relatives coming to attack Ruthven. There's not much we can do at this point." He tapped his hand on his sister's mobile as a sign for her to stow it. "I actually have a feeling. We need to go check something."

At a different kitchen table in a different part of town, Lee's head lay flat, her purple hair fanned out around her like rays of light.

"That looks productive, whatever you call that," her mother commented as she set a sandwich down in front of Lee's nose. "How was your walk last night with, what is his name again?"

"Aubrey Ruthven," Lee said, but half of the name vanished into the table's surface. Lifting her head and resting it in her left palm, she asked in a tired voice, "Mom, how do you do something sort of . . . mean without making someone think you're purposely trying to be mean?"

"You need to break up with him?" Mrs. McDaniels responded.

Lee's eyes widened. "How did you know?"

"I'm still your mother and I'm not an idiot. What's up, besides the fact that I think he's too old for you."

At that confession, her daughter wanted to laugh. "I . . . I think I just need a break from him to decide if . . . if I actually want to date him, I guess."

"Chelsea wasn't here long enough to have a good opinion. What do Mira and Mal say about this?"

"They hate his guts, so I'm not asking them. And I can't get ahold of Chelsea. I called yesterday and her mom says she's always asleep."

Pushing the sandwich plate, a little closer to Lee's hand, her mom shrugged. "No matter what you say, he's going to take it personally. If you want, you can use your father and me as an excuse."

"I can?"

"Sure! You know, your grandma used to do that for your Aunt Jill and me. If there was a guy, we didn't want to hurt by rejecting, she would tell us to tell him that she didn't want us dating steadily yet. But if you're going to use that excuse, you have to do it now. Somehow it doesn't hold the same weight when you're twenty-two and no longer living with your parents." She nudged the sandwich plate a little more insistently. "Besides, if you decide you want to try dating him again, he can't be as bitter. After all, you were just respecting your parents' wishes."

Biting into the sandwich and allowing the cream cheese to dribble onto the corner of her mouth, Lee felt better. She had an out, at least until she could get the crest out of Whitby. That night, she'd formed a new plan. She would take it to London and leave it with one of her other friends until she could get Ruthven and the Tepes kids to talk things out. With the crest out of Whitby, perhaps the violence would slow enough for peace to be made. But she couldn't do any of this if Ruthven insisted on being her protector and boyfriend.

Mira and Mal left to patrol a little earlier than usual. The sun had barely ducked behind the horizon when they set down a back alley to avoid the parade of relatives being led by their father across the bridge. They traveled up the backside of the hill to the church. By the time they reached the metal fence protecting the abbey from vandals, the sky was a thin line of oranges.

"What weird feeling were you having about here exactly?" Mira wanted to know as they jumped the blockade.

Mal grunted as he landed. "I don't know. It's an instinct not a forthright text message. Just keep your eyes open."

"My shoes are going to get muddy," his sister pouted. "Your instincts need to start kicking in before I decide what I'm going to wear."

With a roll of his eyes, Mal scanned the field. Their natural night vision made the blurred lines of the ruin come into perfect view. Behind them, the glow from St. Mary's Church as it turned on its lights for the evening backlit their path in an eerie yellow. He briefly glanced in the direction of Lee's home.

Meanwhile, Lee practiced the words in her head the entire time she changed her clothes, tied the laces of her boots, and zipped up her coat. She wore her worry and reservations plainly on her face, hoping it would come across as regret for what she needed to do.

There was no plan to meet with Ruthven that night, but she was hoping that after their previous conversation, he would be anxious to stay close. She wished he carried a mobile phone. She found it hard to believe that anyone wouldn't have one, even the undead.

If Ruthven had been on her street, he did not come when she called out to him. She wandered to their usual haunts for about an hour. She debated on crossing the bridge to check the bench at the bottom of the hill, but worried about meeting up with the Tepes twins. Instead, she turned her feet in the direction of the shore. It was still early in the evening so the streets were full of people wandering home with shopping sacks or wandering into pubs with worn expressions. No one thought anything of the teenager walking alone with her eyes trained upon the darkest nooks and crannies.

Taking a sharp detour through a narrow passage, Lee separated herself from the other citizens of Whitby. The roar of the water drew her closer, allowing her to smell the sea air before she saw it. Her thoughts wandered to the date aboard the boat. She tried to feel heartbroken. To be sad that something that started with a wonderful day could be over. Slowing her pace slightly, Lee ran her hand along the building on one side of her. The texture did not register nor did the sounds around her. She realized all she felt was pity. Some part of her liked having Ruthven around, liked the attention he gave. Beyond that, she simply regretted how upset he might be.

"Maybe he won't be upset at all," she rationalized. *"It's not like I'm the first girl he ever dated. He'll forget me in a few centuries anyway. Oh shit. A few centuries. He really is too old for me."*

Her conscious mind brought her back to her surroundings. Her boots stood still on the pavement, yet she heard footsteps. Her first instinct was to call out, yet she assumed if it was someone she knew, they'd have addressed her already.

She bolted down the alleyway and out onto the beach. Her boots instantly sunk into the white sand, making her feet heavy as she ran. There was no use in trying to outthink her pursuer; they would easily find her tracks in the sand. For the first time in her life, Lee thought of screaming, long and shrill, and with all of the terror of a damsel in an old horror movie.

Then she heard a deep chuckle and a cheerful voice ask, "I love all of this playfulness, but aren't we both a little old for tag?"

Ruthven was beside Lee in seconds, his face lit up from the run. She panted as she stared. This was not how she wanted the conversation to begin. Her eyes must have betrayed her thoughts, but the vampire's smile waned.

"What's the matter?"

Mira and Mal trudged back near the fence surrounding the abbey. "Nothing out here. This was a waste."

Mal wasn't listening. He was focused on the direction of the church. He leapt over the fence at a run, leaving his sister to follow. Just beyond the churchyard, barely visible in the light from the building, was a pack of vampires. There must have been seven or eight of them, snarling, kicking, and gnashing their teeth at the hidden victim.

Pulling a stake from within his coat, Mal rushed into the crowd stabbing one Nos directly in the neck, then pulling the wooden object back out. He directed the point into the monster's heart before the rest of the group could comprehend what was happening. Falling to his knees as they turned their grasping hands toward him, Mal ducked to the center of the circle where a balding man lay bruised and bloodied.

Getting back to his feet, Mal took a short blade from the back of his belt. On the other hand, he uncapped a vile of holy water which was splashed into the eyes of two Nos. They withered to the ground in pain and Mal took the opportunity to hack at their shins so they could not rise again right away.

Mira appeared behind one, a female vampire, gasping her by the neck and wrapping both legs around her torso. She wrestled the vampire to the ground and hacked off her head. The remaining four vampires split into pairs and each went for the throat of a twin. Mira unwound a coil of rope from her belt and tossed the other end to her brother. Like a maypole, they rounded the vampires, tying up two of them while the other leapt out of the way.

Mal secured the knots while Mira attacked the remaining Nos. She leapt upon one of them, driving a stake from within her coat into his back until she felt him go limp. The final vampire escaped, flying away down the hill before she could catch up. Instead, she ran to check on the unconscious victim. He lay in a fetal position with his hands covering his face.

The captured Nos howled. "Why does this burn?" one of them screamed.

"Hawthorne rope," Mal explained. "Now tell me, why

were so many of you trying to feed on one man?"

The silent Nos bit his fangs into this bottom lip until it bled, but the other seemed all too ready to confess. "We weren't trying to feed. We were told to get information."

"Information? From a human? I don't understand."

"Take this rope off!" the vampire wailed.

"Tell me why you were torturing that man," Mal barked back.

The second vampire released a painful gasp. "Don't you know? Can't you abominations feel it? The artifact has been moved. And he knows."

Going to his sister's side, Mal gently removed the victim's hands and turned him toward the light. He vaguely recognized him.

"Who is that?" Mira asked as she pulled out her phone to dial the emergency number.

"I think he works at the church as a historian or something. Mr. Stewart?"

Lee finished her practiced speech, surprised that she had tears in her eyes. She hoped her words sounded truthful. Words of parents and youth and waiting and hoping. She was done. She no longer wanted Ruthven in her life, even if she did not say it. But guilt and pity clung to her.

The news left Ruthven looking bewildered. "I could talk to your parents. We could talk to them together. We could show them—"

"They just want us to take a break. They're parents. They worry. Besides, didn't you even say that you wanted me away from everything that's been happening? Maybe we can try again when everything calms down."

"Calms down." He laughed as he repeated the words. "You haven't been paying attention to what's happening in Whitby. I don't know if things will ever calm down again."

Those words struck Lee with a harsh blow. She needed calm. She needed everything she had caused to go wrong to be alright again. Still, she kept her lips tight about the crest. Instead, she kissed him, wanted it to be goodbye still hoping he could not sense it. The tense muscles in his face gave her a sense of added unease. Something shifted, in his manners, in his breathing, even in his kiss. Lee turned from him.

Before she walked away, she thought she heard him say between heavy sighs, "I'm going to fix this."

Chapter 27: "Remorseless Wars"

Lee's phone lit up, waking her from her nap. Her schedule of late had been sleeping through her days and staying up late at night.

"Hello," she muttered groggily.

"Hey, skank," a voice happily told her.

"Chelsea, what's up?"

"Nothing. Just called to talk. How's your new boy toy doing?"

"Fine. Not my boy toy anymore." Her chest lightened as she remembered how she had not told Chelsea much about Aubrey Ruthven. "How are feeling? Your mom said you were in the hospital. I've been trying to ring you for forever."

She grew quiet for a long minute then replied, "They sent me home. I'm supposed to go back if I get worse again, but they couldn't figure out what was wrong with me."

Lee felt herself sitting up anxiously. "What do you mean?"

"Oh, last week I just kept having all these weird nightmares and I've felt really weak. They're making me stay indoors and take all these vitamins. I hate it. I'm really okay, now."

"What kind of dreams were you having?"

"You remember that guy I almost hooked up with at

the pub when I was visiting you? What was his name?"

"Jonas," Lee answered, her voice wavering as bile churned in her stomach.

"Yeah him. I kept having these dreams for like three nights in a row where he was in my room and kept telling me to just lay still. Then, in the dream, he'd start kissing my neck. I'd feel his lips there like he was giving me a hickey or something, then a sharp pain."

Lee suddenly remembered the night Jonas attacked them. Chelsea had told him that if he ever came to London, he was welcome in her house. "And did you have any marks on your neck when you woke up?"

"Just that same scratch from that night when we went out. What a weird question! Jonas wasn't a vampire or anything, Lee. Stop trying to freak me out."

"But you haven't had the dream lately? Now that you are feeling better?"

"Nope. No dreams. Why do you ask?"

"Chelsea, I've got to go. Do me a favor, sleep with garlic tonight and I'll call you tomorrow."

Chelsea laughed. "What? Lee, don't tell me you actually think he was a vampire!"

"Just humor me. I'll talk to you tomorrow." She hung up the phone and pushed off her blanket. Her boots lay in a corner. She pulled a pair of socks on over her black tights then tied her boots securely to her feet. Flinging open her door, she suddenly realized just how quiet her house was. It was Sunday. Normally at this time her parents would be up, organizing papers while they watched their favorite programs. Beyond the hallway, the house was dark and nearly silent. Chelsea's words of attack hung in Lee's ears and a sense of dread came over her.

Lee came out slowly. "Mom?" she called out, "Dad, are

you there?"

As she neared the family room, the television provided the low sound of commercial jingles and news reports, like ghostly voices echoing through the flat. Lee checked her father's study first. The stacks of papers were all in place and the computer slept. Out in the kitchen, the refrigerator door sat open. Cool air wafted through the house and an open carton of milk lay on the kitchen floor amongst a white puddle.

As panic filled her, Lee repeated, "Mom? Dad? Where are you?" She jumped over the puddle and began to yell, "Dad! Mom!"

One of the couch cushions was sliced open, the cotton stuffing disemboweled. The front door was closed, but the deadbolt hung in pieces. As she opened it and gazed out into the street, Lee found a red handprint staining the wall next to the door frame. She held up her hand near the crimson shape.

She had slept through their attack. She stumbled with her cell phone searching for Miranda's number. Her hand shook as she listened to the rings after clicking the correct name.

The chimes stopped at four and a confused voice asked, "Lee?"

She had to swallow down the vomit rising into her throat before answering. "Mira? My parents are missing. The house has been turned upside down and there's blood—"

"Lee, what are you talking about? What do you mean your parents are missing?"

"I mean they're gone. I think it was—" The thought of vampires entering her home and taking her mom and dad seemed so far-fetched. What would they want them for? "It's just—Have you heard anything? Do you know if *they* would kidnap people?" She didn't mean to say "they" the word vampire was suddenly forbidden like calling forth Bloody Mary.

"Lee, Nos don't kidnap." Miranda did not need to say the next part, but she could interpret easily what she meant. Nos fed or killed or had people willingly follow. "Describe the scene for me. Do you want Mal and I to come over or—"

A knock on the door distracted Lee from the phone call. She answered the knock within seconds, finding Aubrey Ruthven looking concerned. "I have to call you back." She clicked end on her mobile before fully opening the door. Instead of inviting him inside, she ran out onto the street.

On the other end of the line, Mira rushed into her brother's room. "That was Lee. Her parents are gone."

"What do you mean gone?" he asked from where he sat whittling a new stake.

"I don't know. She hung up on me. We need to find her before she shows up here with the house full of Nos hunters."

He nodded with understanding. "How are we supposed to sneak out with half of the British Tepes clan in our living room?"

Mira went to his window and stepped out, her feet wobbling along the side of the building. Mal watched her carefully walk down the side of their house and rolled his eyes. "You do this a lot, don't you?"

"Shut up and come on."

He awkwardly moved out onto his window ledge, dangling his legs near her. She moved a little further down and helped him swing from one ledge to another until both feet could touch the ground.

As the twins left their house, Lee approached

Ruthven slowly. He caught her up in an embrace. "How are you? I just heard of what happened?"

"Where are my parents?" Lee demanded, speaking so quickly that she spat into Aubrey Ruthven's shoulder. She pulled from his grip.

"Jonas took them. I think I know where. Don't worry, I can talk to him. I won't let anything happen to them. They're safe where they are," he swore to her. "Please, don't be worried."

"You could let them go. Then you wouldn't have to protect them and I wouldn't have to worry," she insisted angrily, then added a pleading. "Please. They listen to you."

He wrapped his arms around her again and rocked the two of them for a moment. "Nothing bad is going to happen. Everything is going to be alright."

"Oh yeah? My parents are in the clutches of blood suckers, the vampire hunter twins are against me, and, according to you, the world is going to end," Lee ranted, annoyed by the gentle sway of his attempted comforting. "How do you know everything is going to be okay?"

"Because I love you. That's all I need to know."

"What?" At first, Lee's heart fluttered. It was the first time someone she liked or dated had ever uttered such a phrase at her. Then her logic kicked in. "How? We barely know each other."

"It doesn't always take long a time. Sometimes love happens after a day."

Lee wished he'd stop throwing the "L word" around like he was just telling her hello. "Just like you loved Mary Cholmley?"

"No. Nothing like that." He released her to stand face to face, his eyes gazing into hers. "I know I've put your life in danger and for that I'm sorry. But I will never be sorry that I met you."

Lee stumbled backward a little. Her brain kept screaming at her, *"What a cheesy line! He needs to do better than that."* Yet her mouth answered with, "What are we going to do? Why would Jonas take them?"

Aubrey rubbed her back thinking his sentences through before speaking. "The crest. A rumor has been running around town that you have it."

Lee dropped her eyes. "Why would he think that I have it?" she asked quickly.

"It's all any of us want. Look, I only have so much clout with Jonas, but if he thinks he could have the crest and overpower me then I doubt what I say will be much good."

Her stomach tilted back and forth as she felt the next words escape. "I know where it is." She met his stunned eyes. "I didn't want to tell you, not until I knew what it does. I was just trying to keep you safe. You and Mal and Mira. I wasn't trying to create more trouble."

"I know, I know," he whispered, again sounding like a person desperate to comfort a child.

"What are we going to do? I don't want him to get the crest, but he has my parents! Maybe we can trick him somehow."

"Whatever we do, we'll do it together."

Lee, for a moment, forgot about her parents, the crest, or the vampire hunters. She thought of the life she dreamt of. She'd never fantasized about romance or grand plans. She just wanted her life to be more interesting and independent. Somehow such dreams escaped her thoughts when Ruthven came near.

He forever remained the most handsome man she'd ever known, and he looked upon her through his dark glasses with intensity and passion. "Together?"

"You and I are going to be together. I promise you that," he swore to her, grasping him tightly to her.

For the first time, she realized he had no real scent. When other people came close, an odor caught in Lee's nose to build a memory. Not even the salty grit of the Whitby streets clung to him. "You mean to turn me into one of you?" Lee emitted like poison, "I don't want to be like you." Her eyes closed, grasping at thoughts that could only be her own. Her own mind needed to win. Even in Dracula, Mina fought back.

He held her tighter and professed with an impassioned breath, "I love you."

Her hands moved between them, giving her leverage to push off. Her fingers stubbed on buttons and seams frantically. "Jonas can't come into my house," Lee pointed out. "He's never been invited. None of them have."

"They could have sent a Nos supporter for your mother and father."

"I've seen those people, the supporters. Most of them were too weak to stand. I can't imagine any of them being able to carry my parents out of here." Realization swept upon her, stifling her breath. "You have been in my house before," she remembered.

"What? No, I haven't. You invited me in once and I refused. Remember?"

"Not then. Before. When you helped me with Chelsea. You brought her inside and put her in my room." Lee's knees wanted to give way. She tried to build up her anger, to allow her rage to overtake any sorrow that would steal her strength. "You lied to me," Lee whispered, at last pulling out of his embrace. "I'm so stupid."

"Never say that," Aubrey Ruthven insisted, reaching out his arms to hold her again.

Lee flinched away from him. "No. I should have known better. Mal was right about you."

"Don't say that!"

"Stop telling me what to do!" Lee screamed the words like a child throwing a tantrum. "You just got what you wanted and you used me to get it! I fell prey to a cliché. I wanted you to be—"

"I am. I can be your Heathcliff, your Romeo, your—"

A humorless laugh emerged from Lee's anger. "Stop. Please, stop right there! Look at how all of those stories ended." She had no tears in her eyes, but her voice was mournful. "I will not die for you."

He took a stumbling step away from her. "You don't mean that. You'll see. . . I know you will see. You love me and you'll want to be with me. After I use the crest—"

"My parents, you said Jonas took them."

"Yes. He has them now."

"But you obviously had a hand in it. So, what do you want from me? You want me to tell you where the crest is in exchange for their lives?"

"No! Your parents are not in danger of death. I won't let the others kill them. But I had to do something. They found out that I was after the crest. Lee, just tell me where it is, and I will put an end to all of this."

He was pleading. His face wrinkled in desperation. She thought of believing him or trusting him and each time she thought of giving him the location of the crest, her parents' faces outshone any hope.

"I can't tell you where it is." She leaned against her house and swallowed down her fears. "But I can bring it to you. And when I do, I want you to give me back my parents and then get the hell out of my life."

Ruthven removed his glasses angrily, his yellow eyes flashing. His hands grasped her shoulders. "I lost you once. You can't ask me to go through that again, Mary."

"That wasn't me." She twisted her body and her arms struggled to break his grip.

Clutching her with renewed intensity, he responded, "But it was! You are so like her! I feel like when I kiss you, Mary's soul has returned to me!"

Lee wedged her forearms between them and pushed herself a few inches away from him. "It wasn't me! Besides, I lied. My parents weren't trying to keep us apart."

His grip tightened. "What are you saying?"

"I just needed a little time away from you—"

"To sell me out to the hunters." Aubrey's voice had turned flat. His gold eyes shimmered, the closest he could come to tears.

"No! I needed a break from them too. I wanted time to think." He released her. She set a careful hand against his back. "I wasn't trying to hurt you. But you must see that my parents didn't do anything wrong."

Aubrey Ruthven backed away. At first, his face revealed all the pain and heartbreak of a human being. Then, his features cooled. He pursed his lips and stood on the street, suddenly appearing taller and nobler. After a low bow from his waist, he turned away from her. She expected him to walk away into the night. Instead, he started to disappear, his body wafting away a little at a time until he turned into a green fog that crept away into the Whitby streets.

Chapter 28: "I will not let you go into the unknown alone."

Mal and Mira did not make it far from the house before their father crossed their path. "Where are you two going? You already missed the family meeting. I am proud that you went out last night without being reminded, but we have a bigger issue to deal with."

"We just needed some fresh air," Mira lied. "It's so stuffy in there with all the relatives. Everything smells like garlic and hawthorn."

Mal clenched his teeth and met his father's eyes. "We're going to help Lee."

"Lee. The girl who got involved with the Nos? Right now she is not your priority."

"Her parents went missing," Mira explained with desperation in her voice. "She just wants them back."

"This is what happens when you get involved with a Nos."

Mal sighed heavily. "That's stupid."

"Pardon me?" His father blinked, swaying slightly as if Mal's words pushed him.

"The word Nos. It's stupid. They're vampires, Dad. Just call them vampires. We are vampire hunters and they are vampires. Some of them might be holding Lee's parents hostage. And you won't help."

"We can't interfere between Nos and their followers.

You know the rules."

Mal felt himself crack. He felt the years of words he didn't say come flowing out of him in an anxious rush to help the goth girl. "Lee was not a supporter! She didn't know what to do. We all put her in a mucked-up situation and now you're refusing to help her. We caused this mess as much as the vampires."

Abelard's knuckles whitened into fists. "Why is this girl so important?"

Mal did not back down. He faced his father with complete confidence. "She's Mira's friend. Our friend. She's the only friend we have who knows us. And that's our job, right? To protect people. She's a kid, Dad. Just like us. And she needs our help."

Abelard calmed down just enough to release his palms flat at his side and his voice steady. "Our job is protecting all the people and until we know where the artifact is and what Ruthven wants with it, no one is safe. I'm sorry about your friend, but we need to think about the town as a whole."

Mal shook his head. "You think about the town as a whole. We're going to check on Lee. Come on, Mira."

His sister stood petrified in the road for half a second, turning her gaze back and forth from her father to Mal. At last, she shrugged apologetically at her father and ran after Mal.

"That was pretty cool."

"Don't get too excited," Mal responded. "We still have to deal with Lee. After what we found out last night, I'm not giving her a chance to talk her way out of this."

They found Lee pacing her front steps. Her fingers wove worriedly over her hair and interlocked in front of her in almost a prayer motion. She stayed her distance as she saw them approach. She didn't cry, but her entire face read defeat.

The twins silently followed her through her front door and surveyed the scene. As they investigated, they heard her whisper, "It was Ruthven."

"What?" Mal moved closer to her yet kept himself at arm's length.

With a look of shame and disgust, Lee explained, "I broke up with him last night. He came in here and took them because he wants the crest." Her eyes stared directly into Mal's with the same shame. "And me."

Mal said nothing, but Mira burst out, "You invited him into your house! You said you wouldn't. You said you'd seen *Lost Boys*!"

"Yes, like nine times, and really all that movie taught me was to be afraid of Kiefer Sutherland and the grandpa from 'Gilmore Girls'."

"Well, I guess that's understandable," Mira offered, then dropped her eyes realizing she was not helping.

"I should've known the vampires would have figured it out," Lee grumbled. She sat on the only intact couch cushion and stared at her clasped hands. "I wasn't exactly subtle when I took the crest."

"Actually, they didn't know until last night," Mal told her. "Someone else knew, though. Do you know that man who works as the church historian?"

"Mr. Seward? He's been helping me. Is he okay?"

"He's in the hospital now. We saved him from a group of vampires last night. He wanted us to tell you he was sorry. He wouldn't have told them about the crest, but they hypnotized him and then beat him when he tried to fight it."

"I don't blame him. I just hope they didn't— I'm just glad they didn't—" Lee couldn't finish the sentence, instead choosing to move her gaze from her hands to her shoes.

"He told us something else he'd figured out." Mira moved next to Lee, setting an arm on her shoulders by crouching down. "He said that you have St. Hild's gift. It's why the artifact called to you in the first place."

Lee thought of Sibella's words to her but pretended to be surprised. She wasn't ready to reveal her talk with yet another vampire. "Wait. That supernatural prophecy thing Mary Cholmley had?"

"It explains a lot," Mal added.

"You're saying this ancient gift picked me?"

"Yes."

"Why?"

"I don't know!" Mal kicked at a rug with his heel. "Maybe it's because of your name. You're named after a girl who died in a kingdom by the sea, right?"

Lee lifted her head slowly. "You know the poem of Anabel Lee?"

"I told you that The Raven wasn't my favorite."

She blinked at him with a color rising on her cheeks. An instant later, the blush was gone. "Wait, are you saying that I'm going to die?"

"No!" the twins insisted in unison.

Lee felt Mira's grip on her tighten and she couldn't help laughing a little. "You're both terrible liars. What do we do now?"

"You still have the artifact?" Mal asked.

Lee nodded. "It's not what everyone thinks. It's not the Crest of Dracul. The family crest of the Szilágyi. I looked it up online."

"Who?" Mira wondered out loud.

Mal sighed at her. "You really need to reread the family history. That was the Hungarian family of Vlad III's second wife."

"Why would I need to know that? We're descended from his first wife so—" And Mira stuck out her tongue at him.

Lee rose from the couch. "I'll go get it—"

"No."

The girls stared at Mal in surprise.

"We have half of the English side of the family ready for a fight tonight and I think it's safer if you and the crest hid out."

"But my parents!" Lee moved across the room in two determined steps. "I caused this. I should fix it." She stood only inches from his face, ready for a yelling match.

For a second, Mal faltered, looking at her with perplexity. "Let us worry about them. You keep the crest safe. Is that a deal?"

"No. No deal. You don't get to tell me what to do!"

Despite the raised volume of her voice, Mal stayed quiet. He reached out once as if he wanted to touch her hand then retracted the movement. "I'm not trying to. But according to what I understand about St. Hild's gift and what Mr. Seward told us last night, you are supposed to keep the town safe, same as we are. And right now, the best thing you can do is keep Ruthven from getting the crest."

A shrill sound from Lee's mobile phone caused Mal to retract his hand and break eye contact. She retrieved the phone from her pocket. "It's Chelsea. Hold on."

She answered the call with annoyance. "Hey, it's not a good time—"

Ruthven's voice, bitter and harsh, came through the line. "If you want to save them, you better hurry."

"Where's Chelsea?" Lee screamed into the end of the electronic device.

"Be at the abbey tonight. Bring the crest." The call

ended abruptly, nearly cutting off his final word.

Lee let out another frustrated scream and thought of throwing her phone at a wall. After a moment, she calmed down and told the twins, "He has my friend too."

Mira twisted her face in confusion. "Do you think Jonas snatched her?"

"Probably."

Mal stated confidently, "We'll rescue her too. You just keep the crest hidden. Lock the doors, and put up objects that you have faith in around the windows and doors, in case they send anyone to attack the house. We can do the rest."

Without another word, he went outside. Mira wrapped her arms around Lee. "He's right. He's a pain in the ass, but he's right. We'll get your parents and your friend. And then we'll figure out what to do with the crest."

Lee nodded reluctantly. She followed outside and watched them until they vanished down the street, feeling momentarily useless. Physically shaking her head like shaking away a bad dream, Lee pushed despair aside. She knew what she should do.

Chapter 29: "Dreadful Thrall of Night and Gloom and Fear"

The teenage girl ran back into the house, pulling on her coat and grabbing her ghost-hunting kit from the wardrobe. As she took a last look around her room, wishing she had some kind of weaponry, she noticed her Edgar Allen Poe doll sitting on her desk, looking a little neglected. He was tucked into her belt.

"Eddie, I know you're not much for adventure, but I'm going to need your help tonight."

Lee dug through her backpack and flung open the Tupperware. The crest shined up at her as if it had been waiting for her to return. She pulled a necklace out a tangle of jewelry on her desk, a cameo of a skeleton on a silver chain, and replaced her ornament with the crest. The large symbol weighed painfully against her skin and caused her to shiver as she tucked it into her shirt.

The Tepes household was a din of swearing and battle tactics. The family ranged in skin tones, hair color, and height. Still, certain aspects showed the genetic link, most notably the sharp, dark eyes. Those almond-shaped portals to their souls showed fear and annoyance.

Most of them dressed in average clothing, hiding their abilities like speed and strength under a "mild-mannered" façade. A few went the opposite route, choosing to invest in leather trousers and designer sunglasses.

The floor was littered with splintering stakes, vials of clear liquid, crossbows, arrows, mallets, swords, and even portable sunlamps. Some of the items were ancient, well cared for heirlooms that had hunted down the undead for centuries. Most were new, state-of-the-art weaponry which had been adapted for their purposes.

Karen Tepes hung at the edge of the crowd of vampire hunters, perched on the arm of a chair, looking just as annoyed as they did. She tapped her fingers against her arm, the black ring moving rapidly up and down. When her children entered, they stopped short at the sight of so much family crowding the cramped space.

Mira went to her mother's side. "What going on?"

"They've been fighting like this for hours. Where have you been? I'm sure your father wants you to take his side in this madness."

Mal retrieved a chair from the kitchen and dragged it into the room. Perching atop it, he shouted a resounding, "Oy" over the top of the din. As the conversations about blood suckers and soul stealers quieted, he addressed his relatives with the same expression as his mom. "Listen up. Aubrey Ruthven is here. A friend of ours . . . she screwed up because she didn't know any better. Ruthven has her parents and is trying to use them to get the artifact from her."

"Where is the artifact?" Abelard interrupted.

"Safe."

"Malachi!"

Without looking in the direction of the scolding sound of his name, Mal continued. "It's safe, Dad. Just trust me for once. If we want to kill Ruthven or at least drive him out again before he does manage to get his hands on it, we have to strike tonight. It'll also mean saving our friend's parents."

"Saving them," an aunt called out. "Strigoi don't take prisoners."

Mal rolled his eyes at yet another old word for vampire. "Ruthven is using them as a bargaining chip. There's a chance he left them alive and unharmed."

A cousin, only twenty years of age with stringy blonde hair looked ready to spit. "And what about your friend? Does she understand what this will mean for her or her parents? We can't have them knowing—"

Karen Tepes interrupted at that moment. "How about the pure and simple fact that she is a frightened girl running out of options? You want to keep her on our side, then help her. Be the saviors you all keep feckin' insisting that you are."

Mira and Mal exchanged impressed glances. Their mom then added, "I'm serious. If you are not all packed up with your gear and out of this house within the next two minutes, I will feed you all to the Nos myself." The room wasted another four seconds gaping at the thin human before the yelled, "Move!" The vampire hunters scattered.

Only the twins hung back. "Mum," Mira gratefully wrapped her arms around Karen's neck, "You are my hero."

Within one minute and forty-seven seconds, the family had packed their various pointed objects of destruction within their long coats and the pockets of jeans.

At first, Lee felt only anger. Rage pushed her feet forward and kept her moving through the streets as if she were being chased. She thought of Aubrey Ruthven for the first time as her enemy, someone who had used her and betrayed her. Somehow, the feeling of his arms around her and his breath on her cheek crept into her thoughts and stole her anger. Lee stumbled as she slowed. She cared about him in some way, even if it was only a small, growing love. She felt that ache in her chest that she always thought was nothing more than a metaphor. Trying to sort things out, Lee found she couldn't pinpoint a reason. Why had she liked him? He'd been condescending and overbearing. His transparent charm should have never won her over.

She wandered up the steps toward the abbey. Clouds rolled in overhead, casting ominous shadows across St. Mary's Church. The wall surrounding the ruin was unattainable, with no footholds or any overturned rubbish bins to stand on. She went to the tourist center, crossing through the courtyard with stealth she did not know she had. She willed her feet to be light and her breathing to be quiet. She expected to find the place locked up. The lights were out and from what she could see through the window not even a security guard remained. She gave the door a tug, just to test it. It swung easily, allowing her entrance. Ruthven was expecting her, after all.

"It's a trap you know."

The thin woman came out from the shadows. A crowd hovered behind her, a mix of vampire eyes glowing beside human faces.

Lee pressed the crest within her jacket close to her chest. "Hey Sibella, I was just looking for Ruthven. He left me a message that he'd be here. Are you looking for him too?"

Sibella nodded to a pair of vampires, a burly man and a spritely woman. At her silent command they moved to either side of Lee, arms at their sides and shoulders squared.

Panic set in. Lee held out her hands as if she could hold back an attack with sheer willpower. "Sibella, please—"

"You brought it, didn't you," the woman coldly wanted to know.

"No. I wouldn't be that stu—"

"Stop, Lee. We aren't here to hurt you. I heard about your parents."

"Wow. Your spies are good" Lee dropped her arms, trying to seem casual. "Fine. Why are you here?"

"To help you drive Ruthven out again. You need to understand that this is my home. This is all of our home. Even though he has been my ally in the past, I suspected what he had planned and can't allow it. We will protect you."

Lee studied Sibella and felt momentary comfort. Something about the vampire made her feel more at ease than with anyone else caught up in the mess she was in. Something beyond Sibella herself told Lee to trust in what this ancient woman told her.

"What about the Tepes family? Mal and Mira made it sound like they were going on a family vampire hunt. Won't they kill you all?"

"You can convince them not to," Sibella stated with confidence.

Lee scoffed. "My track record has not been the greatest at building that bridge, in case you haven't noticed."

"You kept Ruthven from being hunted up until now, didn't you?"

"No. They just couldn't find him."

One of her personal guards, the burly man, coughed

lightly before cutting into the conversation. "Some of our supporters have been watching Ruthven. He visited with Tepes's kids. They could have attacked him then, but they didn't."

"They don't think they can beat him on their own." Casting her gaze once again to Sibella, Lee changed the subject back to her original point. "I don't understand. Why aren't you siding with Ruthven? Isn't he trying to make vampire life better or something like that?"

"What he wants to do is unnatural and put us under the sway of a dark power." She used a single hand to gracefully push her hair behind her with a sniff. "Plus, he had his goons threaten a dear friend of mine."

"A friend?"

"Yes. You know him. Seward."

A dry laugh moved quietly through Lee's gaping mouth. "Of course. Why not? This is great. Let's go get ourselves killed."

The Tepes family traveled up the hill with no plans. They swiftly passed a group of tourists having a smoke outside of a nearby hostel, not giving the foreigners a chance to even register the strange troupe racing up the hill. They jumped the fence surrounding the acres of protected land and the abbey in waves.

The first group to leap over were the most experienced, the fathers and mothers who had fought the creatures of the night for decades. Some could scale the wall in a single stride while others used grappling tools.

Two vampire sentries raced at them, ready for the fight. Abelard removed a leather sack from his coat and dumped the contents at the feet of the enemy. Uncooked grain scattered upon the grass.

At first, the pair snarled and continued their attack.

Their bodies convulsed and their arms twitched. The taller of the two fell to the ground first, picking at each grain and muttering under his breath. Occasionally, he would pause and attempt to fall upon the Tepes family with fangs flashing. His partner also fell to his knees to join in the count. Two of the Tepes' uncles took the opportunity to swiftly remove the heads of both vampires, one with an axe and one with a heavy broadsword. The heads rolled upon the grain, the pellets sticking to the blood and hair.

From where the younger Tepes relatives stood the sounds of carnage did not carry. Still, droplets of blood and ash caught in the air.

A cousin who stared in confusion turned to Mal. He explained, "Nos who are less powerful are compelled to count small items. It works best on their graves right before they rise for the first time. You can keep them there until sunrise counting and they can't stop."

The cousin's eyes stayed upon one of the dismembered torsos through the fence. "How did Uncle Abelard know they were not going to be powerful Nos?"

Mira helped boost her cousin over the fence while she added, "They never give the powerful ones the job of guarding. The real fight is going to be wherever Ruthven is."

"I haven't been in a big fight before." The cousin, a girl a couple of years older than the twins, paused partway through her climb. "My dad says to die in the fight is the only good way to go."

Mal started to climb the fence and nudged his cousin with his elbow. "How about not dying? I think that's a better plan."

The family moved in a pack, keeping their pace even. Soft steps tread across the grass as Whitby Abbey loomed in the distance. Thick clouds shadowed the structure. The once windows sneered at the approaching hunters as twisted, human-like figures slinked along the ruins. Catching the scent of the humans, the silhouettes turned in their direction. A pack of half a dozen vampires lunged forward, some leaping before running at their attackers. Others moved stealthily along the outskirts, attempting to circle around the Tepes family.

Abelard loaded his crossbow, aiming it at one of the vampires moving along the edge of the fence. "Kids! Fall back! Come be our backup when it's needed!"

"But—"

"Mal, do I as I say!"

Mal and Mira moved toward the fence as the rain clouds moved further. The pressure stung their heads as they watched their parent poised with medieval weaponry.

The coming storm deadened the air, giving everything a heavy feeling of dread.

"Maybe you all better hang back here for a minute," Lee suggested to the entourage. "Let me try talking to the hunters first."

Her bodyguards waited for a silent signal from Sibella, then left the girl's side. With a deep sigh, Lee checked again for the crest despite the significant weight and trudged toward the troop of vampire hunter children watching the battle.

At the back of the group, she spotted a tall, lanky boy wearing a long jacket. She called out his name softly, nervous about the others hearing her. He turned and his dark eyebrows shot up.

Mal ran up to Lee, grasping her by the shoulders. "What are you doing here?" His stomach churned like a taffy puller as he tried to drag her away before his father spied her.

Lee turned her arms, hooking them over his grip to free herself. "That hurts," she groaned as his fingers dug in. "Let go of me, Mal."

"I can't. They'll think that you're going to him, Lee. I'm sorry." He stared at her confused expression. She had blue eyes. Mal had never looked before, but he could see himself, the cold, disciplined version of himself that his father wanted him to be reflected in her eyes. Instantly, he released her and blinked away the memory of his own dark stare. "Run."

"What?"

"Run away, Lee. Just get out of here!" Mal spat out the words with a fierceness, betraying the emotions he suppressed. "Mira and I will do what we can to save your parents."

Lee rotated her shoulders, still feeling where he'd squeezed her. She glared a little and ranted, "I came to help you. Look, I brought the calvary—"

Several of the Tepes family members ran over, blood splattered across the back of their hands. Abelard proclaimed between huffs, "We need a plan. They know all our moves."

Lee suggested with a smile. "Hey there, Mr. Tepes. I know you probably aren't thrilled to see me, but I need you to put down the crossbow."

The man's weapon had gone up on instinct. He held within his sight the group coming out of the shadows. Lee stepped between the vampire hunters and Sibella's clan.

"I know this looks bad," she pleaded. "They're here to help. Just believe me for this one night. Tomorrow you can go back to killing each other."

"Move aside, girl!" one of the Mal's aunts spat at Lee.

"Just listen to her," Mira attempted to scream. "She wouldn't do this if she thought it would put her parents in danger!"

Sibella stepped forward, only glancing once away from her would-be attacker to see the other Tepes adults still sparing with Ruthven's followers. Before Abelard could come closer, striking the weapon into the ancient lady's flesh, Sibella whipped a strand of hair from her deep-set eyes. The motion also prompted the vampire hunter's free hand to clap over his mouth without his will. He struggled, wiggling as best he could from her control as she held him in place.

"You will listen for the sake of your own life and that of your family, Abelard Tepes. We have never quarreled with one another. What this young woman says is the truth. We have come to guard our town." With another sweep of her fingers, his hand fell from his mouth. "Ruthven was once the servant of someone I fear. I hoped he was no longer working for her. Clearly, I was wrong. I don't know his full plans, but I do know that we are all in danger."

The leader of the Tepes clan gritted his teeth. His relatives clamored from behind him, anxious to kill the pack of abominations facing them down.

Then, Mal and Mira stepped out from the group. Mira took Lee's hand in hers and Mal stood on her opposite side, taking the place of her vampire guards.

Miranda Tepes looked upon Sibella, offering a tiny smile. "I can't speak for the rest of my family, but I can assure you that as long as you're fighting alongside us, my brother and I will not try to kill you."

"Thank you." The short speech seemed to amuse Sibella who suppressed her lips turning upward.

Malachi Tepes held out his hand to the ancient

woman, allowing her cold fingers to grip his own. "A truce," he stated in his usual deadpan.

Lee studied him, trying to determine if he was angry or relieved about the situation.

The aunts, uncles, and cousins present started to object, but Abelard held up his fist to silence them. Lee wasn't sure why he was the head of the family. So many other members seemed older and wiser. Yet, the motion left them still as the distant sounds of battle still formed on the hill.

"If Malachi has made a truce, then we must honor it. Tell the others and let's go back into that fight before we lose." Before turning away, Abelard glared at the goth girl. She did not shrink from his gaze but kept a safe distance from him.

The family ran back into the fight with Sibella's clan waiting for the right moment to join. The vampires following Ruthven slashed and hacked, a wild fighting style where bare hands tore chunks from their enemy's skin. Sibella's clan moved with grace and speed, dancing around opponents before killing with a slice of an arm or a break of a bone. The hunters employed a mix of different fighting techniques throughout time. Some hacked while others used weapons and skill.

Lee kept both Mal and Mira back by her. "I brought the crest. I thought maybe if it affects you both, you could find a way to use it." She unclasped it from her neck and held it out.

Mal looked at the offensive object. "We don't even know what it does."

Mira pushed Lee's hand and the object at her brother. "Then find out."

He glanced at the battles taking place within the shadows of the ruins. Silhouettes of claws against skin and stakes being pried from human hands were visible as a light rain cast a veil across the scene.

Mal saw one man, tall and confident, with his hands clasped behind his back surveying the fight. Ruthven perched himself atop a stump that had at one time been a column. From there, he remained both in command and safe from harm.

"I see him too," Lee grumbled after she followed his gaze. "I don't see my parents though. Or Chelsea."

The young man pushed the crest back at her. "You better hold onto this in case you do have to make a trade."

"Wouldn't a trade be a bad thing?" Lee countered.

Her hand brushed the crest and suddenly they were both swept up in a gust of wind. Not far from them, sounds of struggle carried across the hilltop. The sick crack of breaking bones and wood against flesh drowned away for her only.

Lee moved closer to Mal, both clutching the crest tightly. Before them stood a woman in a long, medieval robe. Her hair flung wildly around her, and she held something over her head. They saw her crying out, but her words would not reach their ears. As the scene focused, they realized she stood in a tomb with a small boy limp in her arms.

She wailed over the child, then heaved him over her head as if to offer him to an unseen power. Then she collapsed upon the floor and gathered him into her arms. Her face was a mixture of despair and hatred. She blamed someone for the little boy's closed eyes and still lips. She held his unbreathing face to her chest and sobbed. The words came freely, spit flying from her drenched face. Although Lee and Mal could not hear her, they could see she accused someone of something. When no one seemed to hear her, she laid the child on the ground amongst the stone alters and coffins. A dagger was taken from within her cloak.

She sliced into her hand and pressed it against a stone etching on the wall. Lee recognized it as the crest they held in their hands. She cried out something. A promise. A bargain. She screamed until there seemed to be no air left in her body. The stone cracked under her grip and when she had finished her lament, she slid to the floor. The crest had broken free from the wall and lay within her crimson hand.

She whispered a final plea. This time her tears were gone and all that remained was the resolve of a powerful woman. This was a woman who was used to control and for the first time, she had none.

A moment later, the toddler opened his eyes, which glowed with the same gold as Ruthven's and other soul-seeking vampires. Both arms stretched out to the woman, and she gathered his cold form against her breast once again. She held out her wounded hand to him and he drank greedily from her palm with fangs prepared. And the woman was grateful. The relief embraced her now that a monster replaced her child. Anything to keep him.

The crest lay upon the ground, nearly forgotten. When her son had drunk his fill, she carried him in one arm and the crest in the other. She stood with all the dignity and grace of a queen. The tear streaks had vanished, replaced by triumph. She curtseyed to the unseen force which had listened to her prayers and turned from the dark place.

They followed her to a hall where a monk waited. He seemed shocked at the sight of the child, but before he could express his true horror, the woman pressed the crest to his forehead.

Fangs instantly protruded from his upper and lower gums. They poked over the top of his lips, exposed to the world. His body twisted up and shriveled away. The monk transformed into something different, not a soul taker and not a bloodsucker. He was something truly monstrous. His body contorted to one side as the skin on his face melted against his skull, giving him a gaunt look. His finger grew long and sharp, knife-like nails flexed. He did not speak to his attacker. Instead, he bowed.

The single creature shuffled ahead of his new mistress. Despite a haunch and slow movements, the monster had a steady purpose. A soldier in a turban and loose-fitting clothing entered the stone room. He reacted to the new breed of vampire with instant defense. He did not allow shock to waver his hand as he drew his sword. He ran at the monster who stood calmly between the woman and the Ottoman warrior. When the soldier neared, his blade moving through the air with skill, the monster reached out one long nail. The claw scratched the soldier on the back of the hand.

At first, the Ottoman was unaffected by the scratch as it turned bright scarlet. His sword attempted to hack at the monster, then fell from his grip. He clutched at the wounded hand as it had been severed. Within a minute, he changed. He twisted and mutated into the same creature as his assailant.

With the pair of monsters following, the woman marched ahead, ready to conquer the world.

The scene faded and the pair returned to reality. The battle continued almost exactly where it had left off. A line of red dribbled from Mal's nose.

As he rubbed his face on the back of his sleeve, Mal rambled. "What was that? I've never seen Nos like that. Is that what the crest does? Create those? But then why aren't there more—"

Lee cut him off. "That was hundreds maybe even a thousand years ago. Maybe those monsters were killed off a long time ago and then the crest was lost. I think that woman was Ruthven's sire."

Giving Ruthven another glance, the boy released the artifact and allowed Lee to stuff it back into her coat. "He wants it for her, right." Mal gave her a smile. "Up for a little payback?"

Raising her head, the corners of her mouth turned upward slightly. "Sounds therapeutic. Let's go vampire hunting."

They jogged to catch up with Miranda who led their cousins into the fray. She fell back just enough to offer Lee a crossbow similar to their father's. "Hang back on the edges and be our backup."

"What about some extra protection?" Mal suggested as he readied his weapons.

Lee pulled aside the edge of her coat to show the Edgar Allan Poe doll hanging at her waist. "Why did you bring your doll?" Mal asked when he noticed the handmade plush toy tucked into her metal studded belt.

Lee pulled Eddie out and held him in front of her. "An experiment."

Mal rolled his eyes. "Fine. Here's the plan. You stick close to Mira and me. We'll clear a path and get close to Ruthven."

"What happens after we get close to Ruthven?" Mira questioned. A vampire, a male with sideburns, came at her. She held up an axe, cleaving it into the creature's neck. "Do you mind? We're on a time-out."

The vampire held his throat and blindly reached out his hands at her. She hacked again, jumping over him as she did. When she landed behind him, she finished the chopping at his neck. The head rolled to the ground across the feet of one of their uncles. He gave Mira a critical look, as if her kill had been sloppy. She stuck her tongue and went back to her conversation.

"That's it? We run toward Ruthven and demand he gives back Lee's parents?"

"That plan sucks," Lee responded. "Pun intended." She scanned the battlefield. The rain became a steady curtain, further hindering her vision. Still, she found what she wanted. "There. Jonas. He has my friend Chelsea. Let's deal with him first."

"Do you think really Chelsea is here too?"

"Yes. She never goes anywhere without her mobile. And I'm going to kill him."

"We'll help you," Mira cheerfully replied.

"Am I going to have to drive a stake through his heart, stuff his mouth full of garlic, and chop off his head?" Lee asked with pure interest.

"That's overkill," Mal explained.

"This guy tried to turn my best friend into one of his undead brides. I think overkill is in order," Lee countered as she loaded the first arrow into the crossbow. "Plus, maybe he knows more about Ruthven's endgame."

Mira shook her shoulders. The faux fur of her lined hood had been flattened by the rain and her coat was blotched with dark spots. She glared up at the droplets, then turned her gaze upon her friend and brother. "Oh well. Let's get this over with."

"Maybe you'll be struck by a moment of brilliance in the nick of time," Lee joked.

The twins started to jog toward the patch where Jonas was tossing their least favorite second cousin over his shoulder and across the field. Lee followed with the crossbow clutched against her chest. The wooden handle was a smooth, varnished wood. A crank and pulley made the loading of arrows much simpler than the older models her mother studied. Her finger grazed the metal trigger, and she heard a squeak from the tense bowstring.

The squeak brought her mind back into focus, running through the field as blood and fangs flew through the air. Sibella's team attempted to round upon a group of Nos guarding the edges of the abbey ruin. They made sure to stay clear of the Tepes family while their supporters shouted helpful warnings.

As she dodged a punch from one of Mal and Mira's relatives, the monster turned on her. He reached out a hand to grab her, his skin brushing the soft cloth doll hanging from her side. His hand then recoiled, and he hissed at the burn marks scaring his fingers.

"That's pretty cool," Mal confessed.

She tucked Eddie back into her belt. "Someone told me that I needed something to have faith in to keep me safe."

Mal leapt at the vampire as it rushed Lee a second time, angrier than before. He stabbed it swiftly, then sliced off the head with little effort. He gave Lee a crooked smile as though nothing had interrupted their conversation. "In Poe we trust."

"You two can flirt later. Come on!" Mira waved her axe at the pair, panting at the effort of speaking over the grunts and howls of two different species at war.

Jonas had just finished his thrashing of their second cousin. His fangs inched near the tan flesh ready to rip out a major artery when Mira tossed her axe. She'd intended to pierce his shoulder, but instead, the spinning blade grazed Jonas's tee-shirt.

"Shit!" Mira rounded to retrieve it. "Keep him busy."

Jonas threw down the Tepes cousin and inspected the

damage to the cotton garment. Brushing at the sleeve with little additional concern, he smiled sweetly at Lee. "Look at you! Chelsea's best mate got a new toy." His mocking tone darkened. "She told me all about you. You don't frighten me, girl."

"Where is she?" Lee demanded. Earthquakes fought her fingers as she attempted to lift the crossbow.

When Jonas didn't answer, Mal called out, "Why bother with this? My family didn't consider you much of a threat. You're giving up a comfortable life to be Ruthven's Renfield?"

"Comfortable! I live in an alley. Ruthven is going to give me back the life I used to have when I was rich. He's going to turn us into an army. He will make us truly immortal. Humans will be under our control, bred for food and amusement only."

"He is going to turn you into monsters. Mindless, grotesque puppets." Lee raised the crossbow higher, squinting her right eye along the shaft of the arrow until she was focused on his eyeball. "Now. Where is Chelsea?"

He laughed and held up a mobile device, shaking it mockingly. "Chelsea isn't here."

At first Lee felt relieved, but then realized what that meant. First, Jonas tried to make her his meal ticket, then he stole her phone. Chelsea couldn't deal without her phone. Lee aimed the crossbow directly at his heart and fired before he could protest.

The dead vampire lay across the grass, rain pouring against his face. Lee swooped down and retrieved the mobile. "No one takes away a teenage girl's phone!" Turning in the direction of the abbey, she shook the rain from her cropped hair.

Mira held her arm. "I thought we were going to come up with a plan."

Staring at the ruins of the once great building, Lee felt the dizzy spell she'd had before. Only this time, it filled her with a sense of purpose and confidence. "I think I know what I'm supposed to do. The question is, do you both trust me?"

Mal shrugged. "It would be stupid to say no at this point."

Mal and Mira cleared the path for Lee as they ran in the direction of Whitby Abbey. The rain pounded against their cheeks and backs. Their toes gripped within their shoes, silently willing themselves not to slip in the mud. As each villain ran at them, the twins beat them back. They threw vials of holy water which mixed with the rain and blinded their opponents temporarily. Mira's axe hacked away at arms and legs, anything to slow up their attackers. Mal stabbed at the chest of three vampires, leaving the stakes within their still-breathing chests. As the Nos scrambled to remove the weapon, the three teens continued their run.

Suddenly, a large crowd descended upon them, jaws gnashing. "I'm out of stakes," Mal announced as his sister tried to create an opening within the mob with her hatchet.

"Lee, give him the crossbow and run as soon as there's a chance," Mira shouted over her grunts.

Obeying, Lee then held out Eddie like a shield, not caring how silly she looked.

Mal scrambled with an arrow, attempted to turn the crank, and load the projectile as quickly as possible. The rain made his fingers slick and the shaft of the arrow kept sliding away from him. It landed in the mud, stepped on by a female vampire's foot. Lee gave him another arrow from the supply they'd provided her with while still holding Eddie out in front of her.

Mira's arms were aching as she alone fought back the mob. Her movements slowed and her vision was marred by the downpour. She could sense the monsters folding in upon them and knew she didn't have the energy to stop them.

A loud growl echoed through the night, followed by a scream. Sibella and her troop had fallen upon the crowd, tossing them backward with single swift motions. Sibella herself moved through the battle, her delicate legs wavering only slightly through the grass. She motioned for the trio to come with her. Lee was the first to follow, with the twins close behind. The noble vampire lady led them away from the scene as her people fought against each other.

The vampire took them around the side of the ruins where Ruthven could not see. "You two had better hang back or he might attack you first." The twins exchanged one of their silent conversations to which Sibella added, "Lee has all the leverage. Let her try to end this first." She wrapped her frail, chilled fingers around Lee's, holding their clasped hands between them. "Be brave. Know that we are here and will protect you if it comes to that."

As the girl fixed her purple hair and moved confidently toward the leader of all the madness, Mal watched her carefully. And yet, when he spoke, he directed the words at Sibella. "You really don't want Ruthven to win, do you?"

"I've spent the last few centuries letting Ruthven believe I was his friend. I'm older than that bitch who sired him, even if she is more powerful. I cannot let her win."

Lee glanced back once to see that the vampire and the twins were talking civilly as the rain pounded down around them. When her head swiveled back around to see her target, she saw a pair of shadows in her path. They carried themselves in a way that was comforting and familiar, despite how they shivered in the rain.

At first, Lee's heart leapt, and her steps quickened. "Mom! Dad!" Then a thought occurred to her. Every film and book she'd ever experienced had made her wise to this situation. Her parents were unguarded, moving to meet her with shock, tensing their legs and bruises polka dotted across their outstretched arms.

"Dad? Mom? Stay there." Stopping in her tracks, Lee wanted to turn and yell for the twins but was scared to take her gaze from the pair who moved closer to her. As they moved nearer, she could see the red tears smearing their faces and the evidence of a struggle in the rips of their clothes.

"Lee, what is going on?"

As her crying mother came closer, Lee screamed. Her parents both had long nails and golden eyes. She backed away with a second yell. Mal and Mira rushed forward, calling for their relatives for help. Mal created a barrier between the girl and her parents while Mira set her arm around Lee's shoulders.

"He's controlling them," Mira explained.

Lee gulped heavily, forcing down a lump of bile. "Are they turned? Are they vampires?"

"I don't know."

Abelard and an aunt repositioned themselves, the man having reacted instantly to the requests of his children. The aunt drew a circle in the mud around the possessed parents with the toe of her boot while Abelard rounded them in the opposite direction with a lasso. He attempted to keep them tied in place while the aunt drew symbols in the mud with her figure and chanted. Lee's parents snarled and struggled.

They called out her name in long, sickening moans.

"The circle will hold them for now. They can't cross the barrier," Mira explained as she gently released her friend. "They won't be able to hurt anyone or get h— Lee! Come back!"

The teenage girl did not listen. She broke away from the group and the sight of her parents clawing like animals at an invisible shield. She jogged through the broken walls and arches. With her jaw squared, she ended her journey behind Ruthven.

He turned at the sound of her heavy boots splashing against the ground. He wore no sunglasses, his golden eyes shining at her with hurt, fear, anger, and so many other emotions that seemed to cycle through him within seconds.

Hopping down from the broken column, Ruthven went to her, ready to speak first. Instead, Lee motioned for him to follow her. They walked away from the battle and through the half-buried cemetery along the side of the abbey. Lee stayed silent until they stood at the edge of the cliff where only the wind and rain could interrupt them. No unexpected attacks or saviors to cut into the conversation.

"You want this." Lee held up the crest with an innocent tilt of her head.

"I wanted to believe that if you had it, you have given it to me freely." His head leaned down against her. He breathed inward against her scalp. "I meant it, you know. I love you. If I bring that to my sire, I'll be free of her control. We can have whatever life you want."

Wiping some of the rain from her eyes, Lee studied the sea as it violently crashed along the rocks below. "She wants to put all of the vampires under her control. Do you even know what this even does?"

"I do," Ruthven confessed. "She swore to me that my chosen will be safe. You will be safe."

"Was Mary going to be safe?" The question forced Ruthven to take a step backward. Giving him a stony expression, she added, "She was the one who banished you. She had St. Hild's gift."

"That isn't true. She loved me."

"She couldn't love you any longer. You killed her friend's family and betrayed her trust. You made her think that you are a good man—"

"I am a good man!" he growled.

"Look around you! Look at all this! Your own kind is fighting against each other. Your own kind is fighting against you! You're selfish. You're just a selfish child."

Ruthven set his hand along her cheek. "I love you." He said the words slowly that time, carefully, giving them time to hang in the air between them.

Narrowing her eyes at him, Lee smirked. "I don't think so." Pulling away from him, her legs sprinted over the mud to the edge of the cliff. She shot her arm back until she heard her shoulder pop and felt her muscles ache. The crest flew from her fingers, tossing end over end through the air. He gave her a withered look, a realization he'd lost any power over her. Leaping over the fence, Ruthven let out a wail as it descended into the sea. He changed, his body melting into a green mist that collided with the water and was lost beneath the foam.

Mal and Mira rushed to Lee's side, pulling her away from the edge as the ground started to give way. "Why would he do that? Mira cried.

"It's his purpose given to him from whoever sired him. He has to get the crest then he'll be free." Lee explained as she pulled at the sleeves of both twins, ready to go back.

Mal held her back for a moment. He surveyed the field and ruins. "It's going to be daylight soon. Sibella and her clan already left. We have some of Ruthven's followers captured, but a lot of them got away. Lee, your parents—"

Without waiting for him to finish, Lee ran back to the scene of the battle, nearly sliding into the mud. Her heart was seized up against her ribs, but still she ran.

Chapter 30: "The old centuries had, and have, powers of their own"

The sun climbed over the edge of the sea, slowly bathing everyone in a soft glow. Abelard and his family huddled nearby, their voices turning low. Lee watched her parents anxiously, expecting the warmth of the light to somehow free them. Both her mother and father continued to fight at an invisible barrier, bruising their hands and arms until they fell to the ground and tried to dig.

"They can't leave the circle," Mal explained as he and Mira stood beside her, watching her shiver in the morning air.

Lee glanced nervously back at the group of vampire hunters, arguing and gesturing in her parent's direction. "What are they going to do?"

Mira shook her head in disgust. "I heard my aunts talking. They aren't Nos. They've become like minions. The only way to break a spell like this is to kill the Nos who cast it."

"Or break it with a stronger spell," Mal added. "Which none of us know, because none of us have ever dealt with this kind of control before."

Her eyes turned wild, and Lee started for the circle. "They're going to kill them, aren't they!"

With a quick tug, Mal pulled her back. "Lee, don't!

They'll kill you too!"

"They're my parents!" She twisted her arm, ready to defend the snarling creatures seated in the mud. The rope which Abelard had used to keep them in place lay tangled at their feet.

"After what you saw, how can you still think they can overcome this spell on their own?" Mal let go of her to shake his hands at her in frustration. "How can someone so smart be so stupid, huh? Come on! Tell me, Annabel Lee!"

He had said her name in mocking, yet in that second the growling and squish of fingers against mud paused. The McDaniels couple, for only the briefest of moments, stared at Lee with soft expressions. Then, their brows lowered and their teeth gnashed once again.

Exhaling with triumph, Mal ordered his sister to keep the family distracted for a few minutes. She didn't bother asking what his plan was as he drew himself to the ground, crouched as close to the circle as he dared.

He cleared his throat and recited in a strong, calm voice. "It was many and many a year ago in a kingdom by the sea, that a maiden there lived whom you may know by the name of Annabel Lee—"

"What are doing?" Lee demanded, taking a place on the slick ground beside him.

"Like you said, they're your parents. Maybe we don't need a full spell. Just something to remind them." Turning to stare down the pair, he went on, "And this maiden she lived with no other thought than to love and be loved by me. I was a child and she was a child in this kingdom by the sea—" Her parents showed no change save for a lean of their heads in his direction.

Lee scooped up a handful of mud, ready to fling it at him. "Are you trying to use the power of love? This is so stupid. And lame. You. Are. Lame."

Mal ignored her and continued, trying to remember what he could of the Poe poem. "But we loved with a love that was more than love— I and my Annabel Lee— With a love that the winged angels of Heaven—"

"Nephilim," Lee interrupted. "The winged Nephilim of Heaven coveted her and me."

"What?" Mal tore his gaze from her parents. "Who uses Nephilim in a poem? The line is winged angels."

"I think I know the words to the poem I'm named after, and I know it's not angels. Poe names a specific type of angel. I think it's Nephilim."

"You think?"

"I know it's not angels! The word angels comes up later in the poem when it explains how she dies."

"Seraphs," a weary voice interrupted. "Winged seraphs of Heaven."

Lee and Mal whipped their heads to see Mr. McDaniels rubbing sleep from his eyes. Mrs. McDaniels was studying the brown stains running across the backs of her fingers.

"Lee, why are we at my dig site and covered in mud?" She eyeballed her daughter suspiciously, "Or do I not want to know?"

Mal helped both parents to their feet, then Lee. He leaned in and whispered, "Let my dad field this one. He has some good explanations they might believe."

After he was done talking to them, Abelard went to Lee. "They should be alright. Just keep telling them it was a dream. If they ask beyond that, tell them there was a cult under the influence of a new drug who tried to rob your home."

"Fair enough." Lee gave Mira and Mal her own secretive look meant to say, "That's the best your dad could come up with?"

Abelard harrumphed before speaking. "I hypnotized them pretty well so they should think it's a dream. My sister is taking them down the hill and when they are home, we'll help put everything in order. They will wake up again feeling sore and confused, but it's the best we can do." The man crossed his duster-clad arms across his chest, causing residual raindrops to scatter. "Now, I know it must be very trying and confusing for you to have your first love betray you and try to kill your parents. If you need to talk—"

"He wasn't my first love," Lee stated calmly.

"What?"

"He wasn't my first love. We dated for less than a month. He was hot and charming, and we got along, but I'd hardly call him my first love. You really need to stop taking everything so seriously, Mr. Tepes."

"Oh." He gave his children a bewildered expression as the teenage girl used the moment to escape from the awkward conversation. They both grinned and ran to catch up with her.

Lee walked with them as she watched some Tepes relatives escort her parents down the hill. They passed the spot where Lee had killed her first vampire, the sunlight turned him to dust. "What about Chelsea? Is she going to be okay now that Jonas is dead?"

Mira scooped up a handful of Jonas's ashes. With her other hand, she retrieved a glass vile from within her coat. After sprinkling the ashes into the container and closing it, she explained, "If you really want to make sure she's free, mix this with water and make her drink it."

"You're kidding, right?" Lee responded with disgust.

"Nope. It'll restore her health and keep her from craving being bitten."

"Is there any advice you can ever give me that isn't disgusting?"

"Welcome to vampire hunting." Mira jogged away and called back, "I'm going home to shower and nap. Come over later. We'll watch films and paint our nails. You know - relaxing things."

Lee couldn't help laughing at how casual Mira was. She turned to Mal and asked, "What about you? You going to go help make my parents think it was all a dream or are you going to prep for painting nails with us later?"

"I'll do whatever my dad says I should do." He shrugged.

"After all this, that is still your attitude? What the hell? I mean, what the actual hell?"

Mal snapped back. "I hate this! I hate that we have to protect this town and have no choice in what we do! A member of our family always has to stay in Whitby. I can never leave here! Did you know that, Lee? I am supposed to stay here, marry, add more vampire hunters to the family, then die, all in the same little house. You wear your black clothing and dye your hair like you're rebelling against something, but really what do you have to rebel against? Your parents like you the way you are. They let you be who you are. My dad won't even let me play sports on weekends."

Lee wrinkled her nose at him. "Stop whining." She spoke harshly, yet without any sense that he had insulted her. "You have a choice. Is there a spell keeping you here? Are your parents locking you in at night? No. You can leave if you want to." She took his hand. "But you stay. And every night you keep a lookout for danger and rescue people who don't even know they nearly died. Did you ever think about that part of it? You choose to stay."

"No. No, you don't understand the sense of duty my

dad had lectured me with all of my life—" Mal started to argue.

Lee leaned over and kissed him lightly on the cheek. "Mal, I didn't mean that as a bad thing. You choose to stay because, under all your grousing and annoyed expressions, you are a good person. It's in your nature to save people. So, do what comes naturally. Just don't forget to do it in a way that makes you happy."

He stared at her; his mouth pressed together in a tight line. His hand had begun to squeeze hers without him realizing, the feel of her friendly kiss soothing the anger from his face. "You think I'm a hero?" he asked at last, his words stiff and awkward.

"You're no Zorro, but you have my vote for town savior." She pulled out of his grip. "Do you think your relatives can handle my parents? I have to do something before I go home."

"Um... sure?"

"Great!" And she spirited away without another word.

The young woman slowed her steps when she entered the hospital. She straightened her skirt and rubbed at her face, hoping no blood or grime remained along her cheeks or brow. She waited patiently at the desk, making sure to be exceedingly polite while asking about who she wished to see. The sterile smell of the building cut against her nostrils and eyes, a sharp contrast to the smell of dirt and copper clinging to her hair. The nurse behind the desk eyed her suspiciously but gave her clear instructions of where to go.

Taking the lift to the second floor, Lee kept her eyes down. She wondered if every person she passed in the hallway could see the changes she'd experienced. When she reached her destination, she found a room with two beds, one empty and one containing Seward, and a nurse reading charts.

"The girl in the graveyard," the man croaked from the bed.

"Hey there," Lee greeted, taking in the purple and red of his face. Casts had been set upon one leg and his left wrist. A heart monitor kept in time with a clock on the wall.

"Have you come for spiritual guidance?" he wanted to know with a grin. He sized up her appearance and added, "No. No, I doubt it. Silly question. Have you come to trade quotes?"

The nurse continued her check of Mr. Seward, ignoring Lee. He was a thin man in blue scrubs who must have been at the end of his shift based on the way he dashed around the room.

Hanging in the doorway, Lee waited for the nurse to leave before she held up a brown paper bag for the man in the bed to see. "Brought you breakfast. Sausage rolls."

"Aren't you the clever lady," Seward responded, adjusting himself into a better upright position against the pillows.

Lee created a makeshift table setting on a tray, tearing the bag to make a greasy plate and moving a cup of water closer to his reach. "I just came by to tell you that you don't have to worry about the crest anymore. It's all taken care of." She brushed her hair out of her face and smiled before settling in a poorly cushioned chair near his bedside.

"Hmm, I wonder what that will do to the number of vampires usually attracted to Whitby? More importantly, I wonder what it will do to our tourism?" the man mused. He shook Lee's hand in a friendly, congratulatory way.

"Did you do what you set out to do?"

"Not entirely. But I saved what was important."

He crossed his arms over his chest, holding onto his elbows. "And what will you do now?"

She glanced behind her at the open door, wondering if they should be talking so freely. Seward broke a sausage roll in half and told her, "Don't worry. If anyone overhears us, they'll just assume I'm senile or that the pain medicines have taken effect."

"I'm going to go home and rest." She squirmed a little in her seat, tapping the heels of her heavy boots together. "I— I brought you a message too."

"A message?" Seward looked at her curiously with a mouthful of food. Crumbs clung to the corners of his lips.

"Yes. From Sibella." Lee watched him carefully, trying to gauge his reaction.

"Ah." The man continued to smile. "She gave me away, did she?"

"That's why you know so much about what goes on in Whitby, isn't it?"

"I'll have you know that I am very clever as well, but, yes, I may have been given some insight long ago when she and I knew each other. I suppose you would like to know that story?"

"You don't have to tell me if you don't want to."

"I'll make a deal with you. Tell me your story about what happened tonight and I'll tell you the story of my adventurous youth."

"Deal."

As the Tepes clan walked back from Lee's house where the mess had been cleaned as best as they could and her parents tucked into bed, Mal eyed his dad nervously.

"I think we both need a good day's sleep," Abelard declared as he stretched out his arms which cracked loudly.

Mal swallowed down a lump in his throat. His father wasn't scary and could not kill him, like the army he had faced earlier. Yet, standing up to his father took more thought and courage. "Dad, I'm staying on the football team."

There was a pause, as if his father needed to process the words. "Mal, not this again. You know you can't. You need to be in Whitby and on alert. I won't be around forever and—"

"Maybe our family won't have to stay in Whitby. The crest doesn't have power over us now. Or Mira could stay. She loves it here more than I do. And what about Sibella? We might be able to make an alliance with some of the Nos." He took a deep inhale and then allowed the rest of his sentence to flow through his mouth like a worried ramble. "I'm not saying I don't want to be a vampire hunter, but I want to have a life too. I want to play football or go to the pub or go out on dates." He paused shutting his eyes tightly and awaiting his father's protests. When no quarrel came, Mal went on. "And I want to go to Uni next fall."

"We can talk about this after we've both had some rest," his dad tried to say once again.

Mal cut his dad off. "No. No, we're talking about this now and then we're not talking about it again. I am going to Uni and I'm going to be a vampire hunter. I can do both and I am going to. Am I clear, sir?"

His father exhaled loudly. He was quiet for such a long time, Mal wondered if he'd started to sleepwalk. At last, he heard his father concede with a simple, "I suppose...You and I can look into some of the universities close by."

Mal nodded and realized that he was smiling. Then, he saw Lee walking in the direction of her home. Giving his dad a grateful and questioning expression, Abelard waved a hand in the direction of the young woman.

"You just saw her an hour ago! But go talk to her if you want. I can't stop you, from anything it would seem." The older man grumbled to himself with hands stuffed in pockets as his son and daughter left his side.

Her whole self moved with calm, her head hanging in an attempt to catch her reflection in the largest puddle collected on the pavement. A lock of her purple crop cut fell over her eyes. A shadow moved into her light just as she moved a hand to swipe away the offensive hair.

"Why do you dye it?" the shadow asked.

Turning to face him, she scowled. "Mal, why should I explain it to you?"

"Why not?" He shrugged. "You told him."

Lee's eyes shot up, cold blue shining in the noonday sun. "You were listening?"

"N...no," he stuttered. "Mira saw you."

"Why would she tell you? It's none of your business." Lee angrily pulled on the hair in front of her eyes. "If you must know, I'm planning on changing it."

"Because he liked it," Mal muttered the words almost ashamed to express them. His head jerked about as if fighting exhaustion, attempting to hide her questioning gaze.

Lee stared for a long time. She thought back to all the changes of topic and the times Mal barked bitterly about Ruthven. She saw him blush when the vampire rival topped his best efforts. She thought of the words of the vampire himself, calling Mal a "pup" determined to follow her. As the realization came upon her, she felt her face grow warm.

"Do you have any suggestions?" she cautiously asked.

Mal seemed distracted by something just past Lee's left shoulder. "Suggestions?"

"What color should I dye it next? I've already done black so many times and I'm utterly sickened by the color blue ever since my mother bought me a wardrobe to match."

He thought for a moment. "What about red? Like a really bright red?"

"Blood red," she excitedly replied, "in remembrance of current events."

"If you need something to remember this by, then you have problems," he gruffly stated, once again falling into his critical pattern.

Lee sighed, still a little overwhelmed. "I do believe, sir, that such a label is too far established to be said so flippantly." He eyed her with a mixture of annoyance and amusement. "Right. So, red it is. I'm going to ask your sister to assist me later. You probably have more dark forces to tangle with."

"I do; football practice." And he grinned at her. He pulled at the corner of his shirt. "I may need to clean up a bit first."

"You are a little ripe."

He faked a frown, his eyes still laughing, "So, you going to convince your parents to get out of here, go someplace safer?"

"Is there any place really safe?" she asked, returning his mischievous smirk.

"Yes. Some places aren't Whitby. Just because the crest isn't here doesn't mean this isn't still one of the best feeding spots for vampires in the country. After all, thanks to Bram Stoker we have one of the biggest annual goth gatherings around. No way all the Nos are going to scatter to the winds with all those willing victims constantly coming to visit."

He sobered a little. "You should go. Get away from Mira and me. The sooner you never see us again, the sooner you and your parents will be safe." He stared her down, his familiar serious expression and deadpan tone entrapping her to listen. "Honestly, I'd feel better about all this if I never saw you again."

At first, she thought to be insulted, jumping at the argument to show how cruel his phrase choice had been. Her brain slowed, stowing the anger away, too exhausted to fight. She considered his words, thinking of her first initial fears and her desire for her life to be normal again. Pulling out her Edgar Allen Poe doll and hugging it to her chest, she told him smugly, "I just had a Nos as my boyfriend. I can handle having you two as my friends. Nope, I think you're stuck with me for a while."

He shuffled his feet a little and muttered something. She asked him to repeat himself. He kept his eyes low, but said his words again at a volume she could barely hear. "I think we would've missed having you around." His face flushed for a split second, a moment so short Lee wondered if she had imagined it. "Could you find Sibella again if you needed to?"

"Why?" Lee's defensiveness returned and she felt her heart threaten to break.

"Just because I wasn't too willing to make an alliance with Ruthven doesn't mean I'm not willing to at least listen to other vampires. She seems like someone sensible. Do you think she'd be willing to talk to Mira and me?"

A beaming smile and hope made Lee look like an entirely different person. "I'll ask her."

"Thanks." He pointed in the direction of the bridge. "I'm going this way."

She motioned to the house he had just left. "I'm that way."

"Need me to walk you home?"

"Not this time. But maybe I'll take you up on that offer another day." Lee added an awkward, "Bye" before walking swiftly up the landing and through her front door. The entire time, a new little smile bubbled within her as an idea formed in her brain.

Mal watched her go. His eyes followed her until the door shut, taking her from his sight.

Lee's parents knew nothing of what had happened. They awoke feeling ill and sore and chose to stay in bed, just as Abelard promised. They nearly fell off their mattress when Lee offered to bring them soup on serving trays. She sat with them while they ate, bringing the telly into their room so they could watch a few game shows together. When they both dozed off, she took the time to nap as well with Eddie tucked under her arm. By late afternoon, her parents felt refreshed and ready to face the day, although they stayed in their pajamas and dressing gowns for good measure. After all, they already weren't working that day.

Lee gave them each a hug after she dressed and told them she was going out, "Unless you need me for anything else?"

Mrs. McDaniel practically tossed the remote at her daughter. "What are you up to, Anabel Lee McDaniel? Is there a concert coming up? Do you need to borrow money for something?"

"Nothing!" Lee insisted as she hovered in their bedroom doorway. "Why does something have to be up?"

"You are acting a tad odd," her father put in and pointed at his slippers which had mysteriously and conveniently been placed directly under his side of the bed. "You can't blame us for being suspicious."

Lee went to their bedside and wrapped her arms around her mother's neck. Mrs. McDaniel awkwardly patted her daughter's back while giving her husband a questioning expression. He returned her look with a baffled shrug. "I'm just glad you are both . . . you." Lee pulled away and regained her teenage composure. "I'm going to go now. My mobile is on so if you need anything just give me a ring."

Lee ran from the house as her phone rang. The number for Chelsea's mom came up on the screen.

"Hello."

"I can't find my phone! Can you believe this? It was new too!" The boisterous anger made Lee smile to herself.

"How are you feeling?"

The answer made her feel wonderful. "A lot better. I just wanted to let you know that life is unfair and you can get ahold of me through this number for a few days."

"I'm going to come see you soon, so stay healthy." Lee text back as she crossed the bridge and turned onto Old Church Street.

"Good," Chelsea responded. "You can give me an update on your love life. I can't help feeling like there's something you haven't told me."

She smiled at the text but chose not to answer. She marched up to the shop door of Tepes's tourism shop. Karen Tepes sat behind the register. "Lee, how are you doing?"

"Good. Is Mira awake?"

"Upstairs waiting for you. Something about you two

needing to do some shopping to celebrate your recent breakup," Karen explained as she sorted charge slips. Lee moved behind the counter, but the woman set a hand on her shoulder. "Are you really well, my dear?"

She nodded emphatically. "I think I had a narrow escape. I could have ended up on the wrong side of the family tree."

Karen Tepes gave her a warm, motherly expression then pointed for her to continue up the stairs and into the house.

Miranda already had her shoes on, and her coat slung over a chair beside her handbag. Around her, different relatives snored away on whatever item of furniture they had managed to make into a resting place.

She placed a finger to her lips, scooped up her belongings, and led Lee down the back steps. She made a shopping list as they walked. "I think you need a new skirt, tights, and top. Possibly a new pair of shoes—"

"Why do I need all that?"

"Trust me. The blood and yuck will never fully wash out. Better to just buy new."

A series of brochures had been stuffed into Mira's handbag and threatened to escape. "What's all that?" Lee asked pointing to papers.

"Mal's doing research on universities. He's such a nerd. I can't believe he already has all that stuff laid out. I've been helping him hide them, but now that he might actually get to go, I've had to dig them all out," Mira answered while she swung her handbag back and forth. "Let's go before all the good shops close."

Lee answered distractedly. "Is Mal still at football?"

"Yep." Mira hooked arms with Lee and added secretively, "We can stop by and bother him if you want."

"No!" Lee said a little too quickly then changed the

subject. "I need hair dye too."

They shopped for many hours, and then Lee and Miranda arrived at the Tepes's house without ceremony, the newly purchased box of hair dye lying in a paper sack. As they set newspaper and old towels out in the cramped washroom, Lee felt a realization eating away at her mind.

"Mira?" she asked from where she sat upon the toilet seat in an old tee-shirt stained with every shade, she had ever dyed her hair like a memory of colors.

Miranda barely looked up as she laid out the plastic gloves and instructions on the bathroom counter. "Hmm?"

"I think your brother might like me." The words came out at first as a question, then switched to a statement halfway through.

Miranda removed the bottle of dye from the box, inspecting the dark liquid. She smirked at her friend and replied, "Figure that all out by yourself, did you?"

The sun started to dip in the sky as the players continued to chase the ball back and forth across the long field. The goalie stood shivering with his gloved hands out waiting while the other players sweated through the chill wind.

Ian and Malachi excused themselves to a bench. Mal tightened the laces of his trainers, ignoring the scuffs and grass stains.

"Glad to be back?" Ian asked as he wiped at the beads of perspiration falling into his eyes.

"Glad to have me beating your ass out there?" Mal countered, loving the sound of his easy-going razing.

His teammates called out to him from across the field, but his attention fell upon a lone figure silhouetted on the edge of the green. Red eyes glowed and sharp teeth flashed. Mal ran out to await the start of practice. One eye watched the ball as it was kicked about, the other remained over the dark man.

"Tepes!" Baz called out as a sphere of white flew through the air toward Mal.

His foot moved with speed he forgot he had, making contact with the rubber until it was airborne. The football whizzed from the field to the sidelines. There was an echoing "pop" as the ball hit the stranger squarely between the eyes.

The vampire staggered backward and fell onto the grass, the football landing beside him. While the rest of the team rushed to check on Mal's victim, the young man smiled to himself. "Maybe I can have it all." He pulled the dazed vampire up by the arm and loudly lied, "I better take this guy for a concussion." As the weight of the monster started to hurt Mal's shoulder, they made it out of sight of the team behind a building. At that moment, a stake came out from the young man's shin guard.

Epilogue: "I Pray God Never to See Your Sweet Face Again"

"I need you to wait here." The young bloodsucker addressed his visitor with a sniff. The hair on his head was slicked back while the hair on his chest peeked through the buttons of his shirt. Every inch of him suggested wealth and power, yet he acted more like an insulted butler.

Aubrey Ruthven glanced around the courtyard. He took a deep breath of night air and chose a seat from one of the many benches nearby. He casually placed his small suitcase at his feet. "I don't mind. Beautiful Romanian nights never hurt anyone."

The vampire sniffed once again, this time following the sound with a disgusted growl at the back of his throat.

After he was sure he was alone, Ruthven removed his locket from his pocket. He was careful to move the hinges slowly as he opened the glass casing. He set a short, violet lock within, allowing it to entwine with the dark hair already occupying the heart. With a longing look, he closed the locket once more and, instead of returning it to his pocket, he buried it deep amongst the possessions of his bag.

He did not know how many minutes passed before the haughty vampire butler returned. The man sneered.

"You've caused a bad mood."

"I usually do." Ruthven smiled and the man's sneer faltered.

"Yes . . . very well. Come on. She's waiting."

The Journal of Malachi Tepes

Here I am, the latest in a long line of Whitby Nos hunters. I have read every one of the known family journals up to now, probably twice. What can I say I don't have much of a social life? Then again, what member of this family does?

In a few weeks, I start University with my twin sister, Miranda. I'm going to be living in a different city, in a room that isn't above a tourist shop and playing football with a new group of guys, getting visits from my mate, Ian, on the weekends. Maybe I will even date someone who can be part of both my normal life and my weirdo destiny.

This makes me a first in this family. And I'm going to get my degree and I'm going to still be a part of this family. I will protect humans from the Blood Suckers and the Soul Stealers. But I'm doing this because it's my choice, not because it was fate or duty or a curse.

I'm sure Miranda's journal already talks about why we can have both and why anyone else in our branch of the family will have the same opportunities. But let me tell you my version of the story. It'll probably be more accurate than Mira's anyway. It starts with a girl by the name of Annabel Lee.

Afterword: Not Another Vampire Novel

The first time I read Dracula I was a teenager annoyed by how long it took Lucy to die. Granted, at the time, I wanted to be more distracted because I was reading during a rather painful allergy scratch test on my back. By the way, my allergist office always says, "We like you" when you're covered in itchy red responses. They adore me.

Since then I've read Bram Stoker's novel six or seven times. Not so much for the horror, but because I liked Mina. Despite what Frances Ford Coppola would have you believe, she is a strong character in love with her fiancé (not the vampire) who tries to fight what happens to her. The chapter titles in this book all come from Dracula. I feel a little proud of myself that I didn't stuff the novel with random Bram Stoker facts. Why don't questions about Bram Stoker ever come up at trivia? I would kick so much ass.

Along those lines, you might be asking, "Why are there so many Poe references if this is about a Stoker book?" Because I have a sickness! That's why! When Edgar A. Poe was a child, he lived in Scotland for a year. I don't think he ever went to Whitby, but in my earliest drafts of this book I was constantly trying to make connections between British gothic horror and American gothic horror. Not sure exactly why I wanted to turn this novel into a

Megan E. Vaughn

literature essay; luckily Lee's parents became more prominent characters and gave me a place to let go of my pretentious needs.

What is difficult to relate is the research I did for other parts of the book. Don't get me wrong. I love research. I am an utter nerd. But this book went through so many rewrites, my original list of sources was lost with my previous computer. I'll do my best to give credit where credit is due.

I have been to Whitby exactly once in my life and I mostly hung out at the abbey ruins and onboard a replica of an eighteenth-century frigate. Parts of this book are the actual streets I walked down, some descriptions come from photographs I saw online, and others I confess to just making up. I did use quite a few public websites such as the English Heritage website, the Whitby tourism site "Visit Whitby", and several online articles about St. Mary's Church. I also have a copy of the Heritage Foundation booklet of Whitby Abbey, which provided information for the building now used as the ticket office. I did borrow the family name from this building, however everything else about the Cholmleys I put in this book is pure fiction. For research into St. Hild or Hilda of Whitby, I had to rely mostly on Catholic history websites and my notes from English medieval history classes I took over a decade ago.

I won't give a full bibliography, but I relied on many sociology and mythology sources for information on vampires. For the history of Vlad the III of Wallachia, I relied on the books of Radu Florescu and Raymond T. McNally. I also watched several documentaries, but several turned out to be less-than-academic. They were good for a giggle at least.

Overall, this novel over the years got beaten to a pulp, stretched on a rack, laid in the sun to bake, and finally started to cooperate with me after a putting up a mighty fight. I probably can't take credit for that as I was clearly torturing this poor book. The people who gave this book tough love and taught it to behave were Kira Shay and Matt Medders, so thank you to them. Most especially to Kira as she had to read multiple drafts and hear a great deal of my whining (yes, Matt, even more than what you had to hear). A thank you to Scott P. "Doc" Vaughn for the artwork and for also putting up with some book-related whining. Thank you to Beth Lake for being a fantastic editor. Thanks to Tom and Rachel for technical and sanity support. Lastly, thanks to my parents who were nice enough to not tell me what was playing on TCM on days I said I was working on this book. I should probably also thank them for being good parents. Afterall, I never tried to rebel and date any vampires, so they must've done something right.

Megan E. Vaughn

Megan E. Vaughn became a writer to distract from the fact that she does not know how to read. She has been locked in an epic battle with dust bunnies ever since she moved from Wisconsin to Arizona as a child. Beyond that, she has earned her degree in history, traveled to many historical ruins in various places, and forced her friends to pretend to be impressed by historically significant rocks. Currently she lives...right behind you! Ha! Made you look.

www.ingramcontent.com/pod-product-compliance
Lightning Source LLC
Chambersburg PA
CBHW021240190726
48289CB00005B/1419